A Binary Life

Kay & Ed —

 Delighted that Stan &
Kay enabled our "binary
paths" to meet on
December 28ᵗʰ, 2007.

 Willard

A Binary Life

A Novel

Willard K. Pottinger

This is a work of fiction. Names, characters, places and incidents either are the product
of the author's imagination or are used fictitiously, and any resemblance to any actual
persons, living or dead, events, or locales is entirely coincidental.

This book was printed in the United States of America.

To order additional copies of this book, contact:
Xlibris Corporation
1-888-795-4274
www.Xlibris.com
Orders@Xlibris.com
38972

READER'S PATH

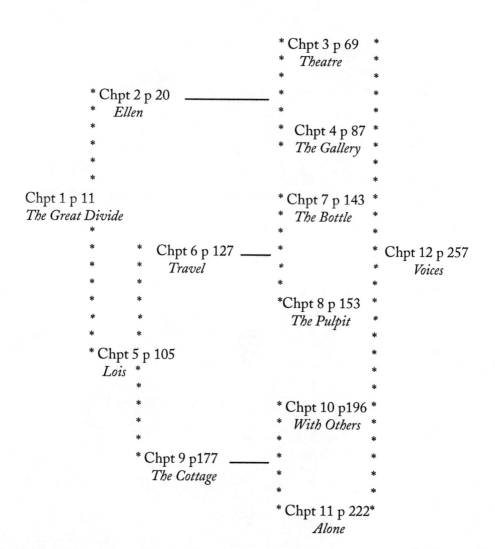

Acknowledgments

The first pre-drafts were entrusted to the computer in the office of the English department of Zhenjiang College, Zhenjiang, Jiangsu, China where my wife and I taught English and history for one year. Thanks to the Administration and secretaries for access to this most enabling of modern tools.

Then, back home in Canada, when final drafts were eventually completed, Brian Henry helped bring better order out of the chaos of early writing. William Aide, Richard Berryman, and Georgina Hewitt provided helpful comments about clarity or lack thereof, and did not seem to object to my suggestion that the chapters can be read, as the Reader's Path encourages, otherwise than in strictly numerical order.

Meanwhile, my wife, Enid, continued in her accustomed good humour despite my corralling of dictionaries and my long absences at the computer keyboard.

Preface

"Oh, if I could have had my life over again! . . . could have looked even differently. I would have been . . ."

from *Mrs. Dalloway* by Virginia Woolf

Two roads diverged in a yellow wood
And sorry I could not travel both
And be one traveller, long I stood . . .

From "The Road Not Taken" by Robert Frost

But the poor man might have had a very different life. [The testimony of Dr. Herzenstube at the trial of Ivan Karamazov.]

From *The Brothers Karamazov*
by Fyodor Dostoevsky

CHAPTER ONE

THE GREAT DIVIDE

Someone vaguely familiar bends over and whispers something that must be encouraging. But oh! the deafening pain and the relief of the dark. Silence, please. Just a little silence, a moment of quietness, a tiny oasis in this desert of boundless sound. Always, always the murmurings of innumerable voices as if this were a—what—a beehive? Ah, an aromatic scent, unlike the iodine and the disinfectants. Think back—a flower, a gardenia? Or a rose or an orchid? Yes, a rose. Day after day, a rose. Was that a kiss? The scent and the memory of a woman's face, all fading.

There is no time, just a layering of sensations that might be sorted into a here and a there, a before and an after, a this but not that. The burden of these thoughts is lifted by a laugh, an unseemly, inappropriate laugh that might have been acceptable there but not here, before, but not now.

The laugh peels away layers of my insulation. A voice penetrates my . . . my . . . penetrates me. A laugh from the past, a voice that I know, but a laugh that dissolves into a sob. A happy sorrow? Perhaps more of a sorrowing joy, a tentative rejoicing that I am still here, able to be wrapped in laughter, able to be. To be or not to be. Perhaps I can persist in being. Yes, I will. I will continue to be.

I'll hold on, like the crew on Gericault's raft of the Medusa. I feel as they must have felt, huddling on their unseaworthy craft. Like them I strain to hope for a merciful midnight ocean.

"Do you remember, Alan, the day we, the day that we walked the streets of London in the rain? We . . ." The smiling voice dwindling off again into silence, pulled into a menacing black hole, a black hole that would pull me in too. If I would let it?

But the smiling voice had said "Alan." I can taste that name, see its colors, breathe its scent. But there is no solidity, nothing to grasp, nothing but a special sound that can deliver . . . what? That can . . . yes, deliver me, "Alan."

Over me sounds twirl like a Van Gogh sky. Words spiral like his stars with energy and indirection. Footsteps patter along a hallway to the accompaniment of subdued voices. Voices swirl around, swoop near enough for breath to be felt, then dart away hurriedly, urgently on tapping feet. Words agonize to link together despite hiatuses: "Drip . . . morphine . . . more . . . careful . . . ." Every piece of the puzzle is black, and the room is dark. But why worry, why struggle? There may be an eternity in which to assemble the whole.

" . . . long as you want to stay. I'm here with you as long as you want to stay." Who's that? I remember those words, those very words. I know your voice. Are you here with me now? And how can I separate here from there, now from then? Where is here? Don't leave me as you left once before. "I'm here with you as . . ." Gone, but for how long?

In the gloaming of my blind sight it is now a man's face that hovers over me. A tear sparkles, and a smile too. I should know that face. It helps—he helps me separate the now from the then. But the burden of this present is too heavy to bear, too threatening. There are dangers to be avoided, all those whips and scorns of time. Better the sleep of death? Goodbye, friend unknown, laughing, tearful friend who knows an Alan—who knows me.

Not again, please. Sibilant sounds of hushed whisperings drag me up again. Can there be no escape, never any rest, but these semi-silences that grate on my . . . on . . . me! Must you two dispute here and now? Isn't there some "there" somewhere else where you can tear silences to shreds? Words, words, words!

" . . . assured, doctor, that we have diagnosed his injuries. Our team has decided on a proper course of treatment. No need, Dr. Liang, for you to doubt our thoroughness. And besides, you are more than well aware of the inappropriateness of any doctor treating a very close personal—"

"You're not telling me I can't visit him, surely."

I know that voice, and his name, too. Liang. Dr. Victor Liang. I'll tell him to stay and instruct the other meddling medicos to . . . what, or how? The weight of words wearies my . . . my mind, and paralyses my tongue. That's right! I do have a mind, a tongue, a mouth, teeth. But the tongue feels unfamiliar angles of teeth, and a tube, and gaps where teeth were. Oh! the dangers of being. Where is that black hole when I need it?

"Of course not. But, doctor, I must ask that you not persist in interrogating my nurses. Your friend will receive the best of care, and under my personal supervision."

"I understand. Of course, you're perfectly right. All I ask is that you call me either at home or at my office if there's any change. Here's my card."

"We will, Doctor. And you should get some rest. I understand you've been here since Saturday noon. That was quite a fuss you caused, you know. Our night nurse is usually quite unflappable. She had to call for assistance. You were terribly upset when you saw the extent—when you first saw him."

"Yes, it looked to me like he had fallen through a skylight and crashed onto broken glass. The patterns of lacerations and contusions were very strange."

"We're quite hopeful he'll come out of the coma. If he was not so traumatized to erase all memory, he'll be able . . ."

Leave me, leave me, oh, please leave me. Just let me be, let Alan be.

But wait, not yet. Don't go just yet. What was that she said? What did I hear through the cobwebs, sounds filtered through gauze? I heard her say, "When you saw the extent . . ." Extent of what?

No, don't say it. Some things better left unsaid. Words can create, but damn it all, don't you know they can destroy too, destroy even me! I am but a few words from extinction. Don't utter them. Leave me instead with the perfume of the rose, with the tear and the laugh, . . . the rose, the tear, the laugh, the . . .

Are there moments of silence? I mean absolute silence. Or am I oblivious to slow moving hours of quietness, and only pulled out of the quicksand of unconsciousness by bedside yattering or shaken by the clattering of carts like this one?

"Me again, Al. Eugene. Don't get up or you'll trip over my mop and pail. You'd skid on this newly washed floor and then you'd have to speak. Just lie there and whistle while I work."

Would that I could, Eugene. Would that . . . I . . . Would . . . that . . .

" . . . unable to get any response . . . tomorrow . . . I bring flowers? Is he able to smell anything or . . . favourite music . . . He used to like—no, I mean he likes classical . . ."

Yes, yes. Bring a bouquet of roses, highly scented roses. And the soothing texture of a 'cello—Schubert's Piano Trio in E♭ What an epiphany that was when I first heard it. That taxi ride in the rain and the horrendous booming rock music. "Driver, can you find something gentler?" And on the next station, a new kind of music for me. I didn't know what a trio was or who Schubert might be. A piano trio ought to have three pianos, but no, there were two other instruments. The poor driver thought me crazy when I told him to keep driving around the block. I couldn't tear myself away from the interweavings of the strings and the piano, the echoes, the flights. That day, that piece of music became an oasis, a landmark, an escape.

If the fragrance of the rose and the harmonies of the trio blend, oh, that could be the elixir I need. Each phrase a summons to live, to love, even to laugh, not alone but in concert with others, all wafted on the breath of a rose. And while you're bringing things, include one of my smaller seascapes. Perhaps one of my creations can recreate me with its colorful silence, its restful aquamarines and greens. So, yes, do come again, tomorrow and tomorrow and tomorrow.

But the yesterdays, what about all my yesterdays? What led to this impasse, launched me onto this sea of troubles? What decisions did I make that rendered such a calamity possible? If perhaps I had stayed single and not married, chosen a different hobby, or if I had left some event earlier instead of later, where now might I be?

Briefly, very briefly the shrouds lift and I see myself standing in the Rockies at the Continental Divide with—someone. It was autumn, yes, October. We stopped the car on seeing the highway sign, "Great Divide—Parking Ahead—Keep Right." Despite the drizzle and the fact that our rain coats were, as usual, buried in some suitcase, we hurried hand in hand over the rain drenched path to the decisive line that divides east from west. But what couple needs a raincoat when they skip under the umbrella of honeymoon excitement? Perhaps if we had not stopped but gone on . . . ?

Mist had deposited droplets of water on the glistening stones and from where we stood we watched two thin lines of water trickle and twist, one to the west towards the Pacific Ocean, and the other eastward to Hudson's Bay and the Arctic and the north Atlantic. Ellen—yes, it was Ellen! planted herself on the east, and I on the west within kissing distance. Above the Great Divide we embraced, droplets slithering down my western arm onto her eastern coat. She put her foot in the way of the east-bound trickle, making a small ridge that dammed the water. Slowly it gathered and pondered, then oozed westward. There would be no turning back. Water can't run uphill, nor can I go back to some great divide in my life and run down the opposite slope to some other fate. If I could, perhaps I would only tumble down to some other bed in some other hospital, with the smell of stale whisky instead of flowers hovering in the room.

What great divide—or divides—in my life have led me to this pain-wracked bed? The terrain, the perilous terrain even now abounds with great divides:

today's to be or not to be, tomorrow's to travel the undiscovered country or not. Maybe if I had said "yes" instead of "no" one day, or painted more still lifes and fewer models, or taken a job here instead of there, maybe then I would not be imprisoned in the gasping, grasping uncertainty of this grey hole.

Who's there? Somebody's there, I can hear you breathing. Speak, will you? No, you're too busy flipping the pages of a magazine and sighing. You're waiting too, aren't you? For me, I suspect. For me to speak or move or open my eyes.

Flip, flip, flip. At least my ears are open. We're in for a long wait, I'm afraid—me in the dark and you in a different kind of darkness I guess. A scraping of a chair on the floor as somebody else is coming in.

"Ah, you're back so soon. We met last week, remember? I'm that afternoon nurse you were questioning about your father."

Your father! So you're Mark or Charles! Let me hear your voice. You've found me.

"Sorry I . . . Oh, I've got it. You must have met my twin brother, Charles.

Mark! You've flown up from Chicago. What a tonic. So both of you must know where I am, and how I am. Give me some news about myself.

"Ah, twins. No wonder I thought I had seen you a few days ago. I just thought you had had a haircut. His is quite long."

"I'm Mark Thompson, with a purely business length haircut. That brother of mine is from Ottawa. Me, I'm from Chicago. I get out of my hectic office and manage to fly up here to see my dad only once a month or so."

When were you here before? I don't remember. "Once a month" you say? Have I been here so long?

"Well, Mark, as I told your brother, it's important that you speak to your father. His brain scan indicates considerable activity. We need to keep his neurons active, and, as we now know, possibly even growing. So even if you run out of things to say, read to him. I've got your address and phone number. If there's any change . . .

Wait. Don't black out on me. Mark! I need to hear about you and the family . . . . Gone. That confounded silence, that eternal—no, not eternal . . .

I turn around amid the rebounding clatter of broken metal, dodge the shrapnel of splintering glass and strain forward to feel—nothing, nothing but a blood warm darkness. And then a fearful silence that could be death's vacuum—a silence that has to be heard to be believed. It makes me wonder, is this what it's like? Non-being? Barely perceptible sounds breathe a kind of life and reach for me, snatching me from the hole, the spin, the nothingness. I whirl around and up into Van Gogh's skies.

" . . . looks a little better this afternoon, doesn't he? More color in his cheeks. We've been able to reduce the morphine considerably doctor. I'll leave you two with him. If you need me, I'm at the nurses' station down the hall to the left. You'll be sitting up soon, Alan, just you wait and see."

Weight and sea. No, weight and see. Ah yes, wait and see. Of course. But "just" wait, she said. That little word makes it sound so simple: "Just" do this. What an intimidating word that belittles the person who doesn't for the life of him know how to "just" do anything. Do they also serve who just wait and see?

I'll try to be the perfectly patient patient. But what would I see if I dared open my eyes. Nursey sounds as if she has a double chin and green eyes and short hair—auburn. I'll paint with words, draw perspectives and meanings. What colors do vowels have? Yes, my words can create no less effectively than theirs; let me try. Let's "see": her nurse's skirt will be too short, or is that possible? What's possible and what isn't? Must I be limited by the possible? Maybe I'll do the impossible. Let them be the ones to "just wait and see." Weight and . . .

" . . . active in amateur theatre, you say? Well, that doesn't surprise me. What, made a name for himself as an actor, I imagine. I saw him at Hart House Theatre years ago. He played a wonderful Macbeth, and a year later, was to have played Hamlet before an illness knocked him out."

"So I heard. Imagine, having to cancel out on such short notice. That must have put a real dent in their program. Wasn't there a . . . what do you call it, a replacement actor?"

A fishmonger perchance? Or is he not like a weasel, ready to weasel in on my role? Understudy, you fools, an understudy! Can't you hear me? My thoughts fly up, my words remain below.

"I knew he spent a lot of time at his cottage, but—"

"Really? You say he owned a cottage? That's news to me."

"Yes, most weekends he would be up there building and repairing things. There wasn't anything he couldn't fix or rebuild—shingles, pumps, an old dock, chimneys, you know. That cottage was an absolute wreck when they bought it. But Lois and the boys loved it up there. I had no idea he was into amateur theatre. But that just goes to show you."

"Lois, you say? I thought it would be Ellen."

"That relationship ended in a very sad way. Don't you find it amazing that he'd have time for his job, his painting, the theatre, and for such a time-consuming thing as a cottage?"

"Maybe we shouldn't be talking here, right beside his bed. I've heard that dying people can hear—"

Dying! That's not . . . no! Not at all! I am choosing "to be" not "not to be." When you've learned how to resurrect a derelict cottage, you know how to make "this old house" come alive again. Just you wait and see.

Disembodied voices whispering about a disembodied me. And why this succession of ominous past tenses? Into what outcast state would you fling me? Surely all losses will be restored and these sorrow . . .

Glass rains all around me. Shards slit my hands, lacerate my face and pierce my clothes. Now, the silence of death, until shoes scrunch over broken glass. Hands paw at my collar, fingers press my neck. There's a tightness in a voice, a tightness but no grieving. "He's done it, Louis, Red's done it. God! so much blood. He's . . ." Ah, the bearable lightness of being, the unbearable lightness of non-being, the . . . the . . .

That confounded abyss again. And they said that nature abhors a vacuum. Ha! I'm inhabiting one.

"Alan . . . Al. My pal Al. You can open your eyes. It's all O.K. Al, you're safe now. It's Roger."

I know that. I may be blind, but I can see. And I'm not deaf. Now Roger, don't you dare fade out on me like the rest of them. You've flown over to help lift me out of the dark, so stick with me. Do you remember my surprise trip to your digs in London? You thought I was . . . what was her name? Oh, help me out of this prison, this—this solitary confinement. I know that's why—

"This time, it's my turn to cross the pond. If you can hear me—"

Of course I can.

"—we can reminisce about the old days at U. of T., and that time you woke me long before dawn, and I thought you were Bertie—"

Yes! that's her name. Did you hear my thought about her just a moment ago? Did you? Could you? Roger? If you can, what I need from you, old pal, before I come back, is to know where I made the wrong turn, when I took the path that led to other paths that led here. How can I be, as you so cavalierly say "safe" as long as I am on the wrong road? You remember Mrs. Dalloway. We crammed for that lit. exam at U. of T. together, remember? What was it she said? I can barely make it out—"Oh, if I could have had my life over again! . . . could have looked even differently. I could have been . . ." Been what? like whom? Am I on the wrong road? Let me run uphill, back to some crucial divide, and meet you on the other slope. You'd be there, wouldn't you? Roger? Wouldn't you be? Old pal?

Gone. My God, have I travelled up and then down the other side? What divides in my life would I have to locate to change things? Perhaps it was our decision to buy that, as she said, "absolute wreck" of a cottage when I—we—might have travelled instead. Or married that girl instead of this? What if I'd said "yes" to—to whom?—to Lois, instead of—why these tears?—instead of . . . oh, the weight of being, the wait of non-being—instead of saying "yes" to Ellen. Ellen and Lois. Lois or Ellen? Lois or . . . or . . .

CHAPTER TWO

EITHER ELLEN OR LOIS:

Ellen

It was all Roger's idea that Alan should have gone to that U. of T. Christmas dance many years ago where he met Ellen. "Vivacious Ellen," they both called her. Roger felt he could take some credit for their marriage, or blame. What astonished him was the unprecedented speed with which Al made up his mind and declared, "Roger, this is the girl. Ellen is the one." And who could blame him? She was a dazzler, energetic, witty, bright eyes, long red hair—at least it was when they met.

Roger had to use some considerable persuasion to pry Al out of his cave where he had retreated after breaking off with Lois. That was three weeks before the fateful Christmas dance.

"I'm finished with women, old pal. Forever!" he had declared over his third or fifth gin and tonic. "Goodbye Lois, a good goodbye to all women, for good!"

"Come on, Al, even if you've been once bitten, you aren't obliged to be twice shy."

There was a long smouldering pause and no response, not the warmth of a smile, not even the chill of a sneer. His pinched lips and squinting eyes proclaimed his determination to be celibate until his dying day, which, judging by his alcoholic induced catatonic state, appeared imminent. One could never have imagined that life was about to begin again for him. His thin taut face was absolutely grey. Greyer than when he had that debilitating bout of the flu that robbed him of his role as Hamlet. After he abandoned Lois and before he met Ellen, Roger was sure he'd be the perfect lead in *The Misogynist* if it ever came around.

Al lifted his newly refilled glass and studied the bubbles as they let go, floated to the surface and vanished, forever. Seeing the bubbles disappear inspired him to exclaim, "Finished with all women for all time, just like that." He confirmed his declaration by guzzling the entire glassful and punctuated the act with a resonant and unrepentant burp.

In later years, Roger often wondered if his friend ever recalled that drunken vow. Perhaps he should have stuck with it.

"To coin a cliché, Al, don't cross your bridges before they're hatched." Still no response. He was in no mood for jollity. Nor was he in any frame of mind to concentrate on their Christmas exams after that final goodbye that left Lois's face frozen, stunned and tearless. What an ill-timed Christmas gift that was for her! Both of them would find it difficult to concentrate on their year-end studies.

Somehow, he managed to squeak through his English Lit and his Fine Arts exams. As his parents always said, he's a survivor. His old pal knew he could also survive his Loislessness. Besides, as years passed, it became more and more evident that his first love, his enduring passion was painting. He loved his women lavishly, luxuriantly, but only on canvas. And if you ever saw him in a leading role in theatre you'd know his second love was for women on stage. "I ache to find my Ophelia," he would say, even after he was married.

Roger's immediate self-imposed task was to assist his friend to rejoin the human race following his lamentable separation from Lois. He began his campaign of rehabilitation by inviting some classmates to a post-non-football party. Students like Al who hated the game and were tired of feigning interest in it also loathed the after-game bash that left a legacy of headaches, jeans stained with alcohol and ash, and not a few unwelcome pregnancies. So he rounded up a dozen friends who promised at his party never to utter the words touchdown, quarterback, coach, pigskin, tackle, or especially "Lois." There was a $1 fine for each infringement, and lesser amounts to be determined by everyone present for other words even distantly related to the game.

Early in the party, Cynthia, little, submissive, serious Cynthia was overheard to say the "f" word: Football!

"That deserves a fine in excess of one dollar," roared Zander, shaking with mock indignation, "far in excess for such egregious disregard of etiquette!"

"Such a person deserves to be banned from this party," one of the girls insisted. "Who would dare to be so . . . so . . . Words fail me," she said in false exasperation.

And then began a game of thesaurus, each word resulting in Cynthia's eyes growing larger and more serious, even frightened as she understood how heinous had been her crime.

"Inconsiderate!" shouted one, eliciting nods of agreement. "Unconscionable" cried another—a burst of applause. "Contumacious"—a prolonged roar of approval. "Antiesthonic!"—a brief pause, followed by a rhythmic chanting of the nonsense word of which no one dared confess ignorance.

The shouting died down as everyone began to realize the target of this rage was tiny, meek Cynthia whose eyes were registering anxiety verging on tears. Then Zander reversed gears and proclaimed, "Cynthia, our UNfootball Queen," a refrain that led to her being hoisted onto shoulders and hailed as their mascot.

Roger found himself wishing that Al would arrive to enjoy the fun. As the minutes ticked by he recalled Al's response to the invitation, "Oh, I don't know,

Roger. I'm not sure that I feel up to a party just yet. I'll decide tomorrow. You're liable to try fixing me up with some chick. Don't rush me."

He did not come to this, Roger's first attempt at his rehabilitation. As long as Roger knew him, he was a Hamlet—never could make up his mind. It had taken him a full two years at U. of T. to respond to the fact that Lois was in orbit around him. She was no comet flashing past. She wanted to be closer than a moon circling his earth, more like a satellite responsive to his NASA. The unmitigated anguish he experienced, wondering whether or not to call her back down to earth beside him, was pathetic. Her self-effacing personality seemed to feed his reluctance. She was one of those people who never want to intrude, who are content simply to observe either nearby or from afar.

"Oh, let's not rush him," Lois would say as each season passed, moving her knuckles against her mouth as if suppressing a thought that would release tears. A long pause, then, "Don't you try to push him. I'd rather he took his time and made up his mind all by himself. He's got other things on his plate beside me—his studies, his painting, his roles with Hart House theatre. If it's to be it will happen."

He could not make up his mind whether she was playing hard to get, or was not really interested in "life with Al," or was genuinely shy and retiring. In the end, the step was too steep for him to take. Lois was devastated when Alan proposed—of all things—that she not waste her time waiting for him.

There was only one final term left in their university careers, and that would not be enough time for all the scattered parts of his personality to reach a consensus about a future that could include her. Repeatedly he enumerated many factors, countless variables: How eager was she to be Mrs. Alan Thompson? Would he be able to support the two of them as an artist, his career preference, or should he switch to law as his parents often suggested? Should he, could, or would he pursue a post-grad degree after only three years of study? What if Lois found work in a community which would take him away from his roots? What if either of them failed to graduate this term?

Ye gods! Alan was a master of the "what-if?"

Although you could call it interfering, Roger at first hinted, then subsequently suggested, and finally insisted that since Lois had been so close to him for so long, he ought not terminate their friendship, especially before Christmas. "For heaven's sake, Al, what kind of Christmas gift is that!"

She would have been more than willing, eager even, to remain in orbit for one more term during which time he might have wanted to decide differently. Or perhaps, he was subconsciously searching for the kind of vivacity and exuberance that someone more Ellen-like would possess.

"How often have you and Lois enjoyed dancing, you two? How often have you shared deep concerns about the future?"

It seemed odd that they never discussed their own future, rather the course of their affluent, narcissistic society, a highly materialistic future they both deplored. Each of them peered so far into an abstract utopia that they missed the concrete present. If he had opted for Lois, his life would have taken a very different turn, and, as Roger eventually discovered, he would have been much happier.

"Don't you try to push him, Roger," she used to say. "Let him make up his mind by himself."

All too often, time would expire before he acted, in this instance to retract his goodbye to Lois. The clock or the calendar would frequently decide for him, as indeed it did once more. After their parting, Lois buried herself in her studies to kill what she told Roger was the "lethal" pain of rejection. "What is not to be, Roger, won't happen." He felt powerless to argue with that kind or irrational circular thinking.

Among the three of them, Al suffered least. He was relieved. Roger was disappointed, and Lois, crushed. His friend had thought they were destined to grow close to each other as the years, even the decades passed and they entered those theoretical futures they had so passionately been discussing.

"What's not to be won't happen. Hogwash!" Roger muttered. He held to his equally irrational belief that if there is a danger that something desirable is not to be, you have to take action to make it happen. It was just such an attitude that would cause him to drop everything at his office years later, fly back from London to visit his comatose friend in the Toronto General Hospital.

Neither Al nor Lois was impulsive. It was Roger's hope that since each was deliberate, willing to consider all options, eventually they would arrive at congenial, mutually beneficial stages. But no, after their separation, it gradually dawned on Roger that his continuing friendship with Lois seemed only to remind her of lost opportunities, unachievable dreams, and impossible joys; consequently he, too, abandoned her to her studies. It was no surprise that immediately upon graduation, she planned to move as far away geographically from Alan as he had removed her emotionally. That would mean never seeing her again.

For Al, every decision was a kind of birthing experience, and the labour pains often looked excruciating. Again, as had so often happened, his pal had to play the role of catalyst, and the upcoming Christmas dance provided that opportunity. Grace, Roger's girl, was going back home to New Mexico to be with her family or else simply to escape the frozen slush of Toronto's streets. He had been counting on going to that dance with her. Over the last two years at university dances, whenever bands broke into Spanish rhythms, Grace flashed and sparked with energy, her long shiny black hair flinging this way and that with every switch of direction. As they glided across the floor, she twirling, people stood back and admired their proud erect posture and her beautiful legs. What a disappointment to wave goodbye at the airport.

"Come on, Al, I'll be going to the dance alone too. You won't be the only single at it. They've advertised that it's a singles' as well as a couples' dance. Surely you've got to blow off some steam after those exams. You've done more than retreat into this cave of a room here. You're positively spelunking. There's fresh air out there and sunlight and, mercifully, half the population will be women."

He finally came, he quickly saw, and sparkling Ellen immediately conquered. It was also her final term that lay ahead. They hadn't even noticed each other before an automatic exchange of partners on the dance floor propelled them into each other's arms.

Their meeting had not been planned, nor foreseen; neither was their introduction smoothly executed. What do you say after you say "Hi"? Besides, the raucous music was so deafening that any serious attempt at communication was impossible unless you shouted. And shout they all did. To his classmates and to anyone who would listen, he gleefully reported the near disaster of their first meeting.

"Alan!" he shouted. Roger and his new partner were right beside him when he bawled his introduction into the air that was ricocheting with drum beats, cymbal crashes and guitar thrashings. They observed her look of utter astonishment. All three of them, Alan, Roger, and his dancing partner could barely make out her initial response under the flickering, colored lights. "Yes, but how'd you know my name?" she was calling in reply.

"I didn't. I don't"

He told Roger later, still recollecting her amazement, that she thought he had hollered "Ellen."

"No, I'm Alan."

"And I'm Ellen."

"Yes, Alan."

"No ..."

They at least attempted to catch each other's name. Roger, on the other hand, never did discover his new partner's name. She fled after that dance. They both predicted that this yelling would terminate either in body bending hilarity or in impatient dismissal. Happily, the laughter won out. Alan desperately needed a good laugh, needed a whole tsunami of levity to flush out the backlog of excessive exam cramming, to say nothing of the debris left behind by the break-up with Lois.

"No, Alan!" he was trying again. Then the two of them exploded in guffaws that rendered them positively hazardous to the nearby dancers who were gyrating in what in those years were considered socially acceptable ways. Off they ran out the main door into the marble floored lobby, she hauling him and he deliriously happy. They disappeared, leaving Roger smiling but his partner frowning. She believed strongly in the "safety in numbers" theory; so when the thrashing and bashing died down, she flung a "thanks" at him, added a promise to "see ya," and disappeared across the floor.

Roger punished himself for not having attempted to catch her name. What ever became of her? he wondered. What might have become of us if we had connected?

Ellen heartily approved of Alan, his painting, his theatre work, in fact, approved of everything he said and did. She had, however, no opportunity at the beginning to observe his inability to reach decisions, partly because she tended to reach them for him, rendering them both happy, for a while. In the meantime, what excited her was his painting. And her excitement became his inspiration, even to the point of her suggesting that her father help him put on a one-man show at the university or in some Toronto gallery or in her hometown, North Bay.

Late one Saturday night, really late, around two in the morning, he came banging on Roger's apartment door. Fortunately the two other U. of T. students who co-rented were still out partying. The university term had hardly begun, so nobody was burning any midnight oil studying. Al had been at Ellen's apartment, touching up her painting, or more likely, just touching up Ellen.

He opened the door cautiously and saw one agitated Alan in the hallway. "To what do I owe the dubious pleasure of being raised from the dead by the late Alan Thompson?"

"Roger, you gotta help me. She wants me to move in with her."

"Tonight!" he bawled. "Now? You want me to help you move in with her before sunrise? Can't she wait till tomorrow?"

"Yeah, I know it's late. But no, not to move. I just need you to help me decide."

"Come in before you wake all the neighbours. You know it's late." Alan nodded guiltily. "Good. But do you know approximately how late it is? Is she Cinderella and you're going to turn into a pumpkin?"

He threw himself onto the couch, snow-covered windbreaker and all. "It'll mean leaving home. What are Mom and Dad going to say? She says there's a vacant room down the hall from her that would be perfect for painting in."

The unwelcoming host knew it was cruel to put it so bluntly, but he lowered his voice, preparing for a crescendo and asked accusingly, "You want me to decide for you? I should make up your minds—your many minds?" With voice rising in pitch and volume, "At two-fifteen? A.M.?" His eyes were blazing, Al's clenched tightly shut.

After a minute of weighty silence, Roger said, "You know whatever you decide will open certain doors and close others. Maybe for good."

His shoulders dropped, "I know. That's exactly what scares me." And he remained scared for two weeks until he finally took the plunge and moved in. She had decided for him.

In the remaining final term and for months after, Alan did fewer still lifes and much to Ellen's delight, focused on the human body, hers, to be precise. There were pencil sketches, pastels, gouaches, acrylics, chalks, oils, all of Ellen, draped, nude, sitting, supine, over-the-shoulder. Well, she was, after all, a very pretty girl—long red hair, long slim legs, in fact everything about her was long: her fingernails, her laugh, her memory for rebuffs and snubs. The only thing that was short about her was her patience.

"Oh, god! Unrut yourself!" was her favourite admonition when she encountered slow drivers or people who were reluctant to strike out into new and challenging paths. Oddly, though, she enjoyed the *nouveau riche* rut in which she had been brought up.

Roger often dropped in to watch him paint yet another of her portraits. He noticed how much she enjoyed observing the artist drink in her every contour, shadow, line, all the tints of her lovely body. Something powerful, ineffable even, occurs in the silent language of looking, a kind of coalescing of all the pauses in conversation where one is searching for just the right nuance. Roger's eventual progress into journalism made him conscious of the difficulty in finding the *mot juste* especially when you know the elusive word may strike your readers as obscure. But in conversation between two people who are in total agreement, or to use that beautiful Amish phrase, enjoying "intercourse," those pauses are eloquent. The silences are the rests in music that enable us to distinguish the notes and appreciate the harmonies. Al and Ellen delighted in such pauses, he painting, she modeling.

Following a session of eager painting, he would join her on the couch. He loved it when she untied his painter's apron, slid him out of sweater, trousers and underclothes. He had loved the feel of his brush on the canvas as it stroked the shadows of her breasts. But painting her with his tongue was equally thrilling. During one visit, Roger saw a bunch of condoms on the end table beside the couch. Al told him their favourite joke, "It isn't far to go from painting to panting." His pal wasn't sure how distant is the love of art from the art of love. Al perfected the former, Ellen, the latter.

After a binge of Ellen-painting, he would hold aloft his latest sketches or oils of her and proclaim repeatedly, "Roger, *this* is the girl!" with each repetition stressing the next word. "Roger this is *the* girl . . ."

"But your vow? After you cut out on Lois, I thought you said goodbye to all women."

"Yeah, but I was drunk. Remember?"

Her enthusiasm for him was equally extravagant and much more public. Grace and Roger could hear her at the cast parties amid the laughter and drinking following a successful run, "Wasn't he just terrific! The way he lifted the vial, gazed at the poison, then said, 'Come . . . Sweet . . . Death.' Wasn't that the greatest?"

Grace was interested to hear that Ellen was in teachers' college, studying to be an elementary school teacher. On a spring afternoon as puffs of clouds played tag in the sunshine, Grace, Roger and Ellen sat munching pita sandwiches on a bench beside Philosophers' Walk. Grace asked her some penetrating questions, not so much to get answers as to know her better, her values, goals, priorities.

"Do you think it will be difficult to find a job in an acceptable community? Would you prefer a rural school or one in a large city? Doesn't it sometimes scare you to think of how, as a teacher, you can influence a child?"

"My dad has contacts in North Bay," Ellen said with a little shrug and a giggle. "It would be great if I could teach there." Then with palms pressed together between her thighs, and her knees swaying, her tone suddenly turned solemn. "Yes, it does sometimes frighten me when I think of it, how you can help or hinder a child's attitude to, well, to just about everything, music, books, science. Life, even."

The listeners felt Ellen practised her pert little pout and her tilt of the head just a little too winningly. It certainly worked on her Romeo.

Within months after graduation they were married. Roger was to have been best man, but a scholarship to the prestigious London School of Journalism meant he had to be in England three weeks before the happy event. Grace would still be at the university taking a post-grad degree; so she was, as she insisted on being called, "Best Woman"—none of this "Bride's Maid" stuff. All Roger got to know about the event was by Al's email and Grace's perfumed snail mail.

Ellen's parents, Mr. and Mrs. Orgle, seemed to be torn between disappointment and pride concerning the location of the wedding. Puffing on his endless supply of expensive cigars, Mr. Orgle told Alan that his wife had been fantasizing ever since Ellen reached puberty of a nuptial in the largest church, preferably the pro-cathedral, of which North Bay, their home town boasted.

When Mrs. Orgle overheard that conversation, she fanned away the cloud of blue smoke and took Al aside to set the record straight. "My husband thinks I'm unhappy about celebrating the wedding in Toronto instead of North Bay. It's not that way at all. Not at all. Several of our closest North Bay friends will be in Toronto for the event in the university chapel. Won't they have some grand stories to circulate to the gossip hungry folks back home? We're delighted with the site, simply delighted. No hotel ball room or anything like that for our ceremony. A university chapel. We're thrilled. Just thrilled." With upturned head, meditative smile and closed eyes, she inhaled the ecstasy of her vision—a social triumph. She would wear a periwinkle blue dress highlighted with white ruffles at the neck and wrists.

Mr. Orgle had insisted on inviting the local member of provincial legislature. It appeared to Al that the invitation was designed to impress the upper echelons of the chemical plant where Ellen's father was the personnel manager. In fact, there were rumours that the plant would soon be needing a new vice-president. Board members are always impressed to see their company officials hobnobbing with provincial legislators, although the presence of a federal parliamentarian would have scored higher.

At the rehearsal, while Mrs. Orgle was preening, she felt she had to flaunt the status they enjoyed in their home town. "Oh yes, of course my husband knows the Provincial Member of Legislature. He has even played golf with him. We're not certain about whether he can attend. He's an awfully busy man. Awfully busy. But after all, it's just a two minute walk from his offices to the university chapel." She leaned forward, pursed her lips in a knowing way, and in a conspiratorial tone whispered, "With the coming election, he'll need every vote he can get."

Al complained in his email that mainly because of the visiting political dignitary, things took a more formal turn than either he or Ellen really wanted. "But thank God Orgle is paying for the monkey suits."

Although things looked formal, they didn't sound it. Ellen's parents didn't hire an organist, using instead taped music for the processional and recessional. Fran, a classmate of Ellen's was good with karaoke and to the accompaniment of a full symphony orchestra belted out "I'll Never Walk Alone." It turned out to be a real tour de force, though when the tape jammed, she paused, frowned, then smiled and broke into an impassioned rendition of the last verse *a cappella*. The applause, although well deserved, surprised everyone, and most of all, the blushing soloist who grinned and curtsied theatrically. The bride gave a little leap of joy, several quick claps and looked over her shoulder at the guests as if to say, "Isn't Fan just terrific?" Even the minister tucked the script under her arm, applauded, and called out, "Brava! Encore!" But they couldn't unjam the tape, and Fran eventually took her seat, beaming.

Keeping her overseas beau informed, Grace wrote, "Despite Al's apparent cheerfulness, his occasional sombre and reflective pauses revealed that something was amiss. Was it that Ellen's parents were overbearingly present or that his were unbearably absent? His father, a district chief in the Toronto Fire Department had got himself badly injured in a waterfront industrial fire. Al has probably emailed you the details about how Mr. Thompson insisted that the wedding had to go on.

"Pat, his wife, was torn between staying at his bedside and being mother of the groom. At the rehearsal she said that if her husband took a turn for the better, she'd be at the wedding. Unfortunately, just hours before the marriage ceremony he lapsed into a coma. She kept the news from Alan and his bride-to-be because up to the last moment, Mr. Thompson rasped that the wedding must go on."

Ellen's parents managed to put their disapproval of Alan on hold. They had been wishing for a young man of some financial means. It was true that he did sell some of his water colors, but it looked like it was going to be Ellen, the teacher, who would keep them afloat.

Rather than expose themselves to the gossip of their social peers in North Bay, the Orgles footed the bill for a honeymoon flight to the Rockies. Their conversation was sprinkled with offhand comments: "Our daughter and new son-in-law honeymooned in Banff. He's an up-and-coming painter, you know." Then a few weeks after their return, "Ellen and her new husband just can't stop talking about their magnificent trip to the Rockies last month," and neither could her parents. With studied casualness the Orgles made their friends aware that there was money in that marriage, but whose money was never made clear.

Both Grace and Roger knew whose it was, and so did Fran, but few others were in on it. A rented car enabled the couple to experience the breath-taking scenery of the Rockies. They brought back dozens of photos. Her parents saw to it that they mailed copies to friends and relatives. Those magnificent peaks and forests were a tonic to Roger in the flatland that is the lower Thames where he was immersed in studies. Some of those panoramas, Al wrote, were inspiring him to try some mountain landscapes. "Roger, old buddy, I could use a little inspiration for my painting—for my life," he confessed in a mid-winter email.

In addition to his touristy pictures there were some more personal, more memorable and revealing photos: Al cavorting by the mist-cloaked natural hot springs; both of them at their cooking fire beside their tent at the base of Kakabeka Falls; Ellen standing by a trickle of water at the Great Divide. It would seem that all Divides (especially with a capital D) are great—as what divides "yes" from "no," or life from death. Anyway, in photographs, that trickle at the "Great Divide" could have been any incipient stream anywhere.

To Al's great relief, his wife managed to find a teaching job in Toronto. He couldn't imagine reaching much of a market for his painting in North Bay. Mr. Orgle did arrange a one-man show there, but according to the newspaper report, the vernissage did not arouse much excitement. Two of the three paintings that did sell were purchased by a chemical plant for their lobby.

Because of the high cost of housing in Toronto, they had to make do with a tiny apartment. "But just till we get on our feet," they told their parents. "With him having two left ones," Mrs. Orgle huffed "that will take some time. Quite some time."

When she discovered it was a basement "hole," she informed Alan she would visit them only when they moved to the kind of accommodation her daughter "deserved," and not a minute before. "Not one minute." It was only to Alan that she gave that news, not to her daughter, for "the husband is totally responsible for providing for his wife." Ellen wept at hearing her mother refused to visit them; Alan managed to conceal his delight.

He reported this to his pal and closed off his email with a cryptic remark, "Ellen, Ophelia isn't." A reply came back instantly asking if he would settle for a Juliet.

"No, Juliet is passionate, daring, confidant, determined. Too strong."

"To say nothing of loving, lovable, beautiful, romantic. But Ophelia?" was Roger's next move in this epistolary chess game.

Al's retort was immediate, "But me no buts. My Ophelia will be sheltered, vulnerable, shy, sensitive."

As months progressed, correspondence became as brief as it was infrequent. Perhaps the blame rested with Roger since his assignments and studies in London occupied and preoccupied him an increasing amount of time.

Even Grace began to wonder if he was too busy to give a thought to her and in her letter pleaded, "Are you convinced that a visit to Toronto this summer is impossible? Even a couple of weeks together would be wonderful. Are you as lonely as I am? Besides, your friend Alan also needs some encouragement. He seems to be drying up. 'Artist's block,' he calls it. Ellen tells me he seems to be relieved to cook the meals and do the laundry and all the housework. It gives him a feeling of accomplishing something, although there is not much to do in a one-bedroom apartment. Still, she's grateful that he cooks, does the dishes and the laundry, because since she has some grade six classes, she comes home from teaching quite exhausted with stacks of papers to mark.

"As for me, I'll be starting on my thesis this summer, but would be thrilled to share my time and bed with you. How about it?

"Tons of love—miss you, Grrrrace."

So she wanted to know if he was as lonely as she. Bad guess, thanks to an American girl, or more accurately, another American girl, Bertie. She was a career oriented woman who was glad for a coffee, a chat, and an hour of frantic sex, but nothing personal. "This isn't to go anywhere," she instructed.

Roger would get a phone call at unpredictable hours of the day or night, "I'll be over in half an hour." Never, "Would it be convenient if . . ." or "Have you got a class this afternoon?"

She demanded no money or favours, so she was not a prostitute. Nor did he; so he wasn't one either, unless they both were, paying each other in kind perhaps? At least it kept the wolf in the door and filled an emptiness with a more tolerable kind of emptiness. Grace had to survive without her lover that summer.

One fog-shrouded winter day—one of a two week stretch of grey flannel skies—the phone rang at 5:50 a.m. Before Roger knew he was up, he stumbled over his one and only chair, managed to pick himself up and wade through piles of books and papers scattered over the floor. It was dark. In his confusion he couldn't determine whether it was a nightmare or reality. By about the tenth ring, he found the telephone and hollered, "For God's sake, Bertie, are you so sex starved that you can't wait even one day!"

Well, how was he to know it wasn't Bertie? She was famous for her careless attitude to time and to the feelings of others. He had told her not to call before seven o'clock, eight preferably, unless it was an emergency. "This had better be a certifiably valid emergency, a death at least," he shouted.

"Roger! I'm in town," a man's voice announced.

The sleepwalker recognized the voice instantly. "Al, that you? Not in England surely."

"Yep. The plane just got in. I found a quick discount flight; so you're stuck with me for ten days. And who is that Bertie woman? I presume it's a woman."

"Hey, man! It's great to hear your voice. And it'll be even greater to see you in person. How'd you get away? What hotel are you staying in? Is Ellen with you? What on earth brings you over—"

"Whoa, there. Slow down. Only two questions at a time. I'm here just to see you and staying at the 'Chez Roger'."

Foolishly he asked if that was some small no-star hotel in the centre of London.

"No, it certainly is not. Or rather, yes—yes, it is. I think it's near the university."

"Never heard of it. What's the address? I'll meet you there."

"You're living in it, Clutz. The Chez Roger, a very, very small no-star hotel, where the entertainer is the incomparable sex-famished star of stage, screen and bed . . ."

He held the telephone in front of him and frowned at it, then said, "Well hell! Of course, all right. Welcome to the Chez Roger, all eight square meters of it, two of them being the bed, three more, table and books. But we can squeeze you into the remaining three square meters, Al."

"We?" he asked, imagining bunk beds for a male roommate who had to vacate the premises every time Bertie arrived.

"No. You're in England now, where the royal use of 'we' is still honored. I rise, bow, and declare to you with all regal dignity, 'We are pleased to have you stay with us' as long as you don't spill Guinness on my papers or throw up on the reports that tile the floor in 'our' room. But hold it a minute! Is Ellen with you?

"Fret not, sir Roger. We are alone, just ourselves and I'"

"Very funny." He told him how to get from the airport by train and taxi and expected his surprise visitor to arrive in about an hour and a half, at the Chez Roger.

In his mini-roomette there was a sink but no toilet. After reassembling piles of books and papers, he washed, dressed, and sat on the bed to reflect on the Al he had first met over five years ago as freshmen at U. of T. He wondered how a year and a half of marriage alters a man. He was slender when they first met, quick to smile, with dark and very mobile eyebrows, a real asset for an actor. In fact, the Alan he would greet would be heavier, given more to frowning than to smiling.

The alarm clock, set for his normal hour of waking, interrupted his reveries and almost coincided with the clatter of the front doorbell. And there he was! "Welcome to my castle. Terrific to see you. You look exhausted" he said as he dragged Al's one suitcase into a room that had no space for even it. "How's Ellen?"

"How's Grace? I mean, she's still Best Woman for Ellen and me, and we know that she misses you very, very much. So let's talk about Bertie."

Roger tried valiantly to explain that it was only a dalliance that, in her words, was not to go anywhere. "I keep in touch with Grace as much as I can. But these studies are more than a full time job."

"But you do find time to keep in touch with Bertie too, as much as you can. Don't worry, I won't squeal on you."

His overwhelmed host took a rain-drenched coat and hung it on one of the overburdened hooks on the back of the door. With a sigh he said, "I have a feeling that your silence about her is going to cost me ten days' free accommodation."

It's a deal," Al said with an accusing smile, "provided—provided that chef Al provides the meals."

Roger was eager to shake on that before his guest could realize that there was no kitchen. They would eat out at one of the college cafeterias or in a greasy spoon down the street at chef Al's expense.

Roger noticed how the fun-loving bachelor had changed. The formerly high spirited artist-actor appeared resigned, listless even. Forlorn, he sat on the bed and told Roger he was tired, and tired of being tired. Grace was right in her reference to his artist's block. The failure of his one-man show in North Bay was a shock to his self-confidence, and no one in Toronto seemed interested in showing—much less buying—any of his countless portraits of Ellen.

After a meal of classic pub food, topped off with spotted dick, the two men relaxed over their bitters and eyed each other guardedly. It was patently clear that Alan had travelled across the ocean, with or without Ellen's approval, to see his classmate and pick his brains. Roger would soon discover that the trip was made despite Ellen's objections. "Where's the money to come from for this excursion of yours? Have you no friend to talk to who is within bussing distance? How can you possibly leave now when I may need you here more than ever?" It would take several weeks before he could have any idea about what she meant about needing him "now more than ever."

Roger could only speculate about this visit. Was it to announce that Ellen wanted a divorce, or that they both were considering a separation? Judging by his friend's morose demeanour there was certainly the possibility of suicide. But surely, London was hardly renowned for that. Niagara Falls could have saved him the expense, or even the Toronto subway system. Maybe he made the trip to say goodbye.

Roger knew he had to begin somewhere, somehow, and opted for a light-hearted gambit. "So, according to your last epistle, you are not wed to Ophelia?"

"And not to Juliet either. Probably because I'm no Romeo, at least off stage."

"Ah, but a Hamlet, you are."

On and on they jousted, Al soberly, and Roger with increasing frustration. He realized it might take most of Al's ten day visit to get to the heart of the matter.

During the stay, whenever Roger had to meet with his tutor or sit writing unavoidable papers at the college library, Al toured London, and returned suffering from visual indigestion from the National Gallery's superabundance of marvellous paintings. "I didn't know which way to turn, which galleries to skip," he said. "And I haven't even located the Tate where I want to bask in all the Turners."

He had difficulty converting his appreciation of the art he admired into a desire to create any himself. In fact, he seemed overawed by skills, techniques, and subtleties that he feared he could never emulate. "No wonder nobody wants the crap I've been putting on canvas. Who in his right mind ever would? Roger, it's understandable why Ellen is losing patience with me. If I have to hear her 'Unrut yourself' once more, I'll . . . I'll . . . In fact that's why I'm here. I'm not sure you'd spend any time with Bertie if she talked like that, day after day."

Roger, of course, clown that he was, couldn't resist pointing out that, "*au contraire*, she urges me to 'rut on!'"

That smouldering pause again. "We are not amused," he replied dolefully. "What should I do, Roge? You've pulled me out of a dark cave before, and now I'm spelunking again."

His host considered himself an experienced motivator, but no counsellor. With only two days remaining before Al's return to Canada, he decided to call in sick to his profs and tutor to spend as much time as possible with his wistful pal, hoping that he would not throw himself off a bridge and get run over by the heavy Thames boat traffic.

Bertie was as angry as hell that he had postponed the "coffee hour" for a week. That didn't stop her from phoning though. She suspected he was taking up with some alluring classmate and was glad to hear him commiserate about suffering from lascivious withdrawal as much as she. To put her mind at rest, he arranged for the three of them to meet for lunch. Fiasco.

Both Al and Bertie were too preoccupied with their own private predicaments to engage in interesting conversation. Once the preliminaries were over—(He: Where are you from? She: How long will you be in London? He: What are you studying?—the talk lapsed into desultory analyses of the meal—Roger: How's you chilli con carne? Bertie: I always used to wonder what I'd get if I ordered spotted dick. Al: So that's what Bubble and Squeak is! Roger: Do they always dump mint sauce on top of lamb chops in this country?)

She didn't stay for conversation over coffee. She wished Al a happy flight home, gave her coffee mate an unusually peremptory buss on the cheek and left. The rattle and clatter of dishes and the close positioning of overcrowded tables didn't encourage lingering; so the two men walked out into the lane, hoisted their umbrellas, strolled for hours, and trolled for a brighter future for Al.

"So what awaits you back in Toronto?"

No answer. Whether he wouldn't or couldn't, Roger was not sure. A sigh, a downturning of the mouth, an upraising of his dark expressive eyebrows and a shrug, but no answer. They walked on in silence. Al wasn't attracted by the clip-clopping of two mounted police constables and soon after, Roger had to restrain him from walking across a street against the traffic light. Nor did he notice that the gentle rain had gradually increased to a downpour. Roger wondered if he was even aware he was in London, England. During the last year back at home in Toronto while Ellen was at school, teaching, Alan had been walking the streets of Toronto day in and day out, unseeing and unthinking.

Friends are supposed to listen, and Roger didn't like what he was hearing: sounds of defeat, dejection, disappointment. "Let's go into the next pub we find."

Journalists are taught to observe, to interview, record data, and to communicate. So that became his modus operandi. They sat near a fireplace and ordered their pints. He gently queried Al about his relationship with Ellen, his thoughts about not providing much income for their family, what he would like to do if this were a perfect world, (no response), what he thought about taking courses in computers, or law, or teaching, or a trade, until Al finally broke out of his passivity and angrily said, "Quit it! You're beginning to sound like her. And her mother and her father. That's all she does—nag, nag, nag. Let's change the subject."

In silence they downed a couple more Guinneses each, watched the flames dance blue and yellow in the fireplace, and listened to its hiss and whisper. "A gas fireplace," he muttered with contempt.

"At least it can dry us," Roger offered. "Maybe it'll warm us a little."

"Yah, maybe, but not our souls. Mine is stone cold right now. It will take a lot more than a phoney fireplace to defrost it."

That did it. Roger decided that the time to communicate was at hand. He paid for the ales and led him back to the Chez Roger. He unrolled the futon for Al to flop on, then as this Toronto version of Hamlet dozed, he wrote his report for him to heed or reject. If he could make up his mind. Roger planned to give it to him as they parted at the train station. He wrote:

> Decision time is now. Not next week or next year. Life is not going to get any easier with each passing hour. I've noticed how hard it is for you to make decisions, partly because there are so many Alans inside you. There's Alan the frustrated artist, skilled, competent, imaginative, creative and unappreciated. There's Alan the husband, guilt-ridden because of his inability to make the kind of living that Ellen and her parents consider adequate and acceptable. Beside that man stands Alan, the son of a deceased, successful, accomplished, influential father who, with his wife, has always wanted you to be happy. And you're not.

Here is a term I want you to learn: "emergent behaviour." This is behaviour that surprises us in the middle of complex interrelationships and networks, just when we think we've figured which end is up and everything goes swimmingly 99% of the time. But in certain combinations of contexts, something becomes the last straw, the tipping point. Then, kaboom! The unforeseen occurs.

I know this is an analogy from biology, especially as revealed by computer simulations, but it throws light on a lot of otherwise inexplicable human behaviour.

The scary part is that, as our lives pursue their normal path, reflecting and established values, morals, predilections, habits and preferences, certain factors can gang up on us and push us off track. We become disoriented, confused, lost, depressed. Maybe, just maybe, even suicidal. An unwanted behaviour emerges.

The good news is that this pattern is normal. Alan, old boy, you may be standing at the intersection of many vectors: your emergence out of the comfortable worlds of the university and of bachelorhood, the grief at your father's coma at the time of your wedding, and later his death, relating to a beautiful girl who was your model and is now your wife—and maybe not a model wife, the departure of a best friend to London, etc, etc, ad nauseum.

My emergent behaviour, encouraged by your unexpected arrival *chez moi* is that of counsellor. Take heart, though, for emergent behaviours don't always have to be negative or destructive. They may be serendipitous.

What proves that I am not a reliable counsellor, however, is that I am going to tell you what to do: (1) Instead of walking the streets from morning till night, go see a professional counsellor, a medical doctor, or a psychiatrist. (2) List your options which, to me, appear: (a) take a break from your art work and revisit your skills as an actor. If it's an artist's block, something my happen to crack that block wide open and enable you to take up the brush once again. (b) find a job that can temporarily provide some small financial satisfaction, that can break the daily walk trap and can diminish Ellen's complaint about her being the sole bread-winner.

Keep me posted.

Your friend, and emergent Counsellor [!]

Roger

After their farewells at the train station, Roger didn't hear from him for three weeks. Bertie complained that he was acting as if Alan were still staying with him, he talked about him so often. He was developing a habit of introducing another of Al's foibles just as she was turning on her sexuality.

"You just may have to choose," she said impetuously, "between him and me!"

As for Alan, the train ride to the airport was harrowing, overcrowded and stuffy. The ten-day diet of greasy food and ale took its toll as panting, he lugged his bulging suitcase to the ticket desk. He agonized over what to buy Ellen at the duty-free shop, and finally decided on perfume that was still far too expensive.

He found his aisle seat on the Air Bus, tucked his hand luggage and the costly perfume into the overhead compartment, collapsed into his seat, and waited for take-off. As the plane's engines indicated imminent departure, he extracted Roger's missive from his jacket pocket and examined the warning on the envelope, "Do not open before 35,000 feet."

That would be about seven miles, he calculated. Surely he was a lot more than 35,000 feet from the Chez Roger; so he tore open the sealed envelope. He hoped the message included some advice about what to tell Grace. She would be eager to hear about how lonely Roger was and how desperately he missed a woman's tenderness.

His seat mate was dividing her attention between the runway markers that flashed by with increasing speed to her left, and the grunts and expletives that the letter reader emitted to her right.

"Yes, you've got that right," he mumbled, unaware that he had spoken aloud. He was reading about the many Alans that inhabited his body. He was stunned at how seriously Roger regarded his friend's situation. "Suicidal!" he gasped. He turned to his seat mate, and without seeing her, exclaimed, "a psychiatrist?" She edged away as if the escalating outbursts could involve her.

Stories of flight rage had recently been front page stories. If she had glanced at the bottom of the letter, she might have misread—as indeed Alan had—the signature as "Emergency Counsellor." Perhaps she had, judging by her trembling.

His unkempt clothing and unshaven face destroyed all hopes of an attractive, congenial seat mate, one who might have said with a suave tone, "Toronto? Yes, that's my destination too. I know the city intimately. Your first visit? Well, may I show you around some of the interesting sights?" Fantasies abound on intercontinental flights.

As soon as the seatbelt lights were extinguished, he rang for service and ordered a double scotch. It took an unconscionably long time to arrive as he indicated in an overloud voice to the steward and to his cringing seat mate, and an unconscionably brief moment to be consumed. "Psychiatrist," he spluttered and rang for another double.

His emotional and physical fatigue, augmented by his several drinks resulted, much to his neighbour's relief, in a profound if sonorous, sleep.

There would be no one to greet him at the airport. Ellen would still be in class. Everyone he know would be working. He alone was unemployed. His only attempt at civility towards his mate came to an abrupt end when she asked, "And what do you do?" His curt reply, "Nothing. Not a damned thing" further demolished her fantasy.

He stood in the jostling crowd, alone, at the luggage carousel and watched the anxiety in the eyes of people new to this land. Some of them, like him, were alone, some unable to formulate the questions that troubled them: "Is this where luggages from Calcutta arrives?" "I wait one hour for my boxes from Istanbul. I am in right place, no?" There were no family members to greet or reassure them either. How they must have envied the screams of delight, the ecstasy of recognition, the thrill of reunion of those who were welcomed. The loneliness of the long distance traveler, he thought.

As he waited for his suitcase to tumble down the chute, he withdrew Roger's crumpled letter from his pocket, tapped it impatiently on his fingers, then turned to locate a garbage bin. Seeing one near the gate, he strode over to it and addressed the envelope, "How's this for emergent behaviour?" With an exaggerated flourish he let his friend's counsel flutter onto the pile of old newspapers and banana peels.

A twenty minute taxi ride took him to their basement apartment, "the hole" as Mrs. Orgle still insisted on calling it. The clouds frowned and threatened to deliver the identical downpours he had endured in London. His suitcase thudded on each of the six steps that led down to his apartment. He unlocked the door and was greeted in the dim hall by two hampers of unwashed clothing and bedding. In the kitchen, stacks of dirty dishes awaited him in the sink and on the counter.

"Thanks for the warm welcome," he said to Ellen's portrait that hung askew beside the clothes closet. "It's nice to know that I was missed." The small rooms reeked of unidentifiable odours. He knew that Ellen was obsessed with air fresheners and deodorants. She did not smoke, nor did she grant smoking privileges to visitors. For him the sheer unlikelihood—indeed impossibility—of human perspiration, cigarettes, pizzas and spilled beer veiled those very smells from his consciousness. But they lurked in his subconscious, teasing and tweaking his thought.

It was three p.m. Toronto time, eight p.m. London time. Ellen would not be home for two hours. Something about "enumerating choices" Roger had said.

Those that faced him intimidated him. He made a mental list: unpack, or start on the laundry (if the apartment washers and driers were available and operable,) or wash, dry and put away the dishes, or begin supper preparations (if there was food in the refrigerator and in the cupboard—which there wasn't,) or lie down for a much needed snooze. All the Alans sat down on the sofa to weigh the prose and cons, to prioritize.

It took less than ten minutes to reach a consensus, a period interrupted by desultory whiffs of the unidentifiable odours. With immoderate determination, an attitude he seldom exhibited, he donned a coat and went for a walk, always an alternative option.

He climbed the six steps to the ground level, crossed the lobby, pushed open the door and confronted an unremitting decision: to turn left and follow the quiet residential streets, or right towards the busy shopping street and beyond it, the path southward into a forested ravine or northward into a cemetery. He stood pondering.

An elderly woman, weighed down with plastic bags, shuffled towards the main door of the apartment. "You're back, Mr. Thompson," she said. "How was the Queen?" It was Gladys Boadman, their upstairs neighbour. "Your lovely wife was telling me about your trip."

He opened the door and relieved the woman of several weighty bags. "Here, let me give you a hand." The choice of left or right could wait. It always did.

"That was some welcome party you came home to last night," Mrs. Boadman said with a chastening smile. "Kept me awake till three. Can't say I agree with your selection of music." She unlocked her door and ushered Alan in. "Just put the bags on the kitchen table. Will you have a cup of tea with me? Won't take a minute."

Alan was assessing his chances of ferreting out some details about yesterday's so-called homecoming party. Who attended and why? Was Ellen alone with the last to leave? He stood motionless, blocking the doorway to the kitchen, clutching the heavy bags and frowning. Ah, he thought, the odours. Yes, that explains it.

"Go right on in. Tea? Or would you rather have a coffee? Instant is all I've got I'm afraid."

Alan placed the bags on the table, careful not to crack the several bottles of sherry. "Sorry about last night's orgy," he said. He turned to Mrs. Boadman, dipped his head and flashed a roguish grin, inviting some kind of response, hopefully a full description of who and what and when. He'd get to the why of the party himself, later, when he encountered his wife.

"I didn't want to complain," the elderly woman said. "I was young once too, although you'd never know it to look at me." She paused, guessing at reasons for his hesitation to choose a beverage. "Or will you have a sip of sherry instead?"

"Thanks, no, Mrs. Boadman. I really should get some food and start supper." He backed away towards the door.

"Bet they ate you out of house and home. Not even a few slices of that stack of pizzas you ordered left over? Next time be sure to invite me to your celebration. It gets mighty lonely up here, especially when everybody's have a whale of a time just ten feet below me. And quit that Mrs. Boadman stuff. I keep telling you it's Gladys. Or just plain Glad."

"We'll be sure to invite you next time, Just Plain Glad."

"And thanks for carrying up the bags. My legs don't like climbing even without a heavy load. I wouldn't have lasted long dancing last night even if you had thought to invite me."

In an attempt to prolong the rare socializing, she asked, "What time did you arrive from overseas yesterday?"

"I didn't. I arrived just fifteen minutes ago."

"But the party last night . . . Oh dear me."

"No, Glad. Not 'Oh dear you.' It's 'Oh dear her!'" as shaking his index finger he pointed either down to his apartment or to hell.

He backed towards the door, gave her a glance with quizzically upraised eyebrows and a slow nod. Gladys pressed the tips of her fingers against her open lips. After a dramatic pause, he slowly closed the door and marched down the steps to the lobby of the building where he reflected on the party and the suddenly recognizable smells: pizza, beer, cigarettes, and sweat. As expected, the choice of right or left still waited for him.

The choice transmuted from a matter of direction to a question of scrutiny, concentration, introspection even. He knew he couldn't face the jostling of the crowded main street, the noise of car doors slamming, the shouted reminders to "put some money in the parking meter," and the inevitable replies, "I don't have any quarters! Have you got any change?" Then there's the arrogant, aggressive, intimidating cyclists, in-line skaters and skate-boarders who would rather maim pedestrians on sidewalks than be crippled by automobiles on the roadway.

No, it couldn't be to the right with all its screaming advertisements, traffic and noise. He needed to be alone with his thoughts that kept evolving into suspicions. He was suddenly grateful that there wasn't a third choice, a street that mercifully did not abut the road immediately in front of the apartment.

With collar pulled up, his thoughts raced ahead while his feet took him slowly through the drizzle. There was an unwelcome number of pieces of a puzzle to assemble: homecoming, pizzas, cigarettes, sweat, party, beer, music, dancing? a phoney homecoming, stacks of pizzas, foul cigarettes. Cigarettes even!

A car horn blared and tires skidded up to the crosswalk. Without a sideways look, Alan continued across the street but scowled at the interruption in his train of thought: foul cigarettes, the sweat of passionate dancers, a wild party, spilled beer, loud music, intimate late night dancing, who?

On less vexing walks, he would observe the gradual and inevitable transformation of the neighbourhood—old mansions, some being subdivided into multi-unit rental dwellings, some for sale with the threat that once two or three adjacent homes became available, a tall, overshadowing apartment building would be erected. The neighbourhood had become a united nations with saris, turbans, dreadlocks, qipaos, kaftans—as Alan would have observed at the bus transfer stop ahead if he had been able to focus on anything beyond his own personal and increasing ire.

Totally preoccupied with the party and its pizzas and its foul cigarettes, and all its beer, he failed to notice the impatient cluster of commuters that blocked the sidewalk around the bus stop head. When the cat's away, he thought, the mice—mice? "Not mice," he muttered to the sidewalk. "Rats," he exclaimed, "That's who. Rats!" and looked up into the faces around him which registered emotions that varied from indignation to fear. As if to convince them of his righteous indignation, he shouted, "That's who. Rats!" All backed away, opening a path, except for one burly, silver studded, leather jacketed, glowering youth. Alan added insult to injury by stepping into the group and walking around his potential attacker who shouted derisively after him, "You're the one who's a rat!"

Alan thought he heard someone shouting behind him and made a note that this once quiet neighbourhood was becoming populated by thoughtless rowdies. Everything is changing, even his twenty month old marriage. A bus passed him, and behind him, squealed to a halt and swallowed up the pool of annoyance and fear, to disperse it along its route.

If Alan had looked back, he would have seen the youth toss a wallet into the bushes, surreptitiously count a bunch of bills and, laughing, thrust them into his jacket pocket. Crowded bus transfer points were his location of preference. He was wily enough not to pickpocket at the same place twice within a month. He jogged and skipped towards his next rendezvous with fortune.

Alan, unknown to all but one of his selves, was following the quiet, tree-lined route that led eventually to his favourite pub. When he finally emerged from his ruminations and realized he was approaching the Mug and Jug, he resolved not to enter for many reasons, the chief being that he did not want to erase the memory of delicious British ales. Anyway, in the last ten days he had consumed enough pints, had OD'd on scotch during his flight, and needed to be in full command of his wits when he confronted Ellen about last night's orgy. He was unanimous about heading home immediately when a familiar voice shouted at him from the window of the Mug and Jug Pub. "Al. Alan Thompson! Welcome back. We missed you."

It was Russ, the Character-in-Residence who, because he so frequently presided from his perch at the window table, people thought was the owner of the pub. A short, stout, white haired man, he had been formerly identifiable by his splendid mane of red hair. Hence they called him "Rusty." But now in his early seventies, his Einsteinian crop required a change of nickname.

Russ never forgot a name. His antenna alerted him to conversations at nearby tables, especially when people were introduced to others or rebuked by name: "Butch, I'd like you to meet a friend of mine, Cedric. And this is Laura," Russ would overhear. Or "Oh, for heaven's sake, Monty, get your facts straight before you sound off."

Then, weeks later, Russ would spot the person passing by and shout something outrageous through the open window: "Cedric, there's a phone call for you at the bar." Once the passer-by entered, mystified and hesitant, Russ would eventually apologize about misunderstanding the bartender's call, and offer to buy the baffled man or woman a drink, much to the amusement of the regulars who enjoyed Russ's creative invitations.

Today it was, "Al! C'mon in, drinks on the house. Get in on it." And who in his or her right mind could turn down such an opportunity? Only when he entered and sat down did he realize that the pub was empty except for Russ. He accepted a pint nonetheless.

"You look sort of put off," Russ said. "Have a bad time of it over 'ome?"

"No, not till I got back. What do I find, but Ellen threw a party. Booze, dancing, pizzas and cigarettes. Music till three in the morning yet."

"Just cigarette smoke?" Russ asked. "You don't have to worry until you smell cigars. Then you can be sure there's a sugar-daddy lurking in the wings."

"Oh, thanks for the consolation."

The offended husband, failed artist, unemployed actor and returned house keeper was enumerating all the infuriating sights and smells that had assailed him, when Russ suddenly leapt to the window and called to a sauntering pedestrian. "Monty! We need your advice. C'mon in. Drinks on the house."

Monty entered guardedly. "Sorry, do I know you?" he asked.

"We were in here about ten days ago. Yours was Kilkenny, if I remember correctly. This is Al, Alan Thompson. The Mug and Jugsters call me Russ. Anyway, Al here needs a second opinion."

"I do?" he asked, extending a hand to the nonplussed conscript who was climbing onto the third barstool at their elevated table.

Russ explained. "He's been married almost two years, looks after all the cooking, all the cleaning and all the scrubbing while his wife goes off to teach some little school children. Earlier today, he came back from ten days in England to find that while he was away—on business probably—she threw a wild party—dancing, boxes of pizzas, booze all over the place. She doesn't know yet that he has found about the festivities. All the greeting he gets is a pile of used bed linen and stacks of unwashed dishes and glasses. A classic case of "when the cat's away, the mice—"

"Rats, I tell you. Rats!" Al said in a stentorian voice that caused the barkeeper to throw an anxious glance towards the floorboards beneath their window table.

Both Monty and Russ nodded with sympathetic understanding. The Character-in-Residence continued, "So what Al needs from you, Monty, is some advice. Should he go back to England, stay here till closing time, divorce his wife, return home, clean up her mess and cook supper, or all of the above? Murder is not an option. Yet."

"Gee, I'm not sure," Monty said. That's never happened to me. In fact, it's never happened to anybody I know." He paused to assimilate the data, and looked unseeingly beyond the window into the late afternoon gloom. Alan followed his glance and was surprised to see no longer the street but their reflection, a triumvirate, high and lifted up, sitting in judgment on an unrepentant woman. Her father, Arne Ogle, Q.C., smoking an impressive cigar, stood defiantly beside her.

Alan's artistic expertise enabled him to compose a vivid picture, and his experience on stage was about to construct a dramatic scene.

"To begin with . . ." Monty said, causing Alan to snap out of the courtroom back into the pub, "to begin with, I wouldn't wash the dishes or cook today's meal." Russ nodded solemnly, pursing his lips. "And since you are not supposed to know what they ate and drank, you could arrive with several boxes of pizzas and a six-pack of beer, and . . ."

Alan jumped to his feet. "That's it! There's a beer store down the street and a pizzeria on the way home." He shook Monty's hand, tossed a "thanks" to Russ, and hurried out into the drizzle.

Though the street was now dark, his plan gained clarity and brilliance with his every resolute step. On the screen of his imagination he projected the entire scene: she would have sprayed air freshener, finished washing the tell-tale glasses, and would nervously be slipping into something seductive as he entered the apartment. To ward off any hugs or kisses, he would thrust two boxes of pizzas into her inviting arms and plant the six-pack on top. "Let's have another one," he would declare.

"Another what?" she would ask. Her lower lip would tremble.

"A-Nother Par-Ty, that's what," he would articulate with icy deliberation. "And let's invite all the rats."

She would grasp his meaning instantly.

In his preoccupation, he nearly passed the beer store. He made his purchase, crossed the street and walked several blocks to buy two pizzas. Two very large pizzas.

Because he was busy cueing his mental DVD, he once again failed to notice the crowd of passengers jostling to climb onto the bus at a transfer stop. Nor, as the bus drove away, did he grasp the significance of a young man in a black leather jacket left behind, arms akimbo, shaking his head in obvious disappointment. It wasn't raining, a serious challenge for a pickpocket. Tonight's light drizzle didn't drive the people together like cattle shouldering their panicky way onto boxcars. The heavier the rain, the more likely he could lean into the people he had been studying. He had watched a young man repeatedly pat his back pocket where his wallet bulged, causing the dark blue jean material to fade. He had looked for prim, middle aged women who would touch up their lips but fail to snap the purse shut after replacing the tube of lipstick. He did observe an elderly man remove a roll of bills from his raincoat, then dig out some coins and briefly return the roll to his inviting pocket, but then extracted it and shoved it deep into a secure inner pocket. "Damn!" Like fishers, pickpockets work more successfully in the rain. But in this light drizzle, his luck was down—until he saw a man across the street carrying two large boxes of pizza and a six-pack of beer. To the youth's delight, the man was turning off the main drag to head up a quiet residential street. Alan was four blocks from home.

This was one of his favourite routes for walking and meditating, especially after rain or during a fog. The leaves glistened and as a breeze stirred, raindrops pattered through the foliage making concentric circles in street puddles. They performed for him alone to see. Except for the rare car that would swish and splash past, the street was usually his alone. But not tonight.

Tonight, close behind him, heavy footfalls were about to overtake him. He glanced back and saw silvery studs flashing on a dark leather jacket and long yellow hair that glowed surreally under the sodium streetlight. Alan stepped aside to allow the youth to pass. Instead, he stopped, grinned at Alan, and exclaimed, "Yah! The rat man. I seen you today. Hey, you can't drink all them six by yourself. I ain't had a drink for days. How about a bottle? Just one."

Alan felt alone, trapped, defenceless. There were no cars or pedestrians, nothing but the gentle tap of raindrops on the dark pavement.

"I got no money on me, but I'll pay you back, I promise," he said with a pathetic plea that sounded as if this were a matter of life or death.

His life, Alan read, or my death. "Sure." He stopped and placed the two boxes on the lawn beside him, extracted a bottle from the case and handed it over.

The well dressed thug snatched it, deftly unscrewed the cap and guzzled half the contents in one gulp. Alan picked up the boxes and without waiting for an expression of gratitude, walked away. As soon as he stepped out, he regretted continuing in his original direction, for now three blocks separated him from his apartment, and only one to the busier main street behind him.

Seconds later, the stillness was shattered by the sound of a bottle smashed on the sidewalk. Alan lengthened his stride and glanced right and left, hoping to find people entering or leaving their home. How could it possibly happen that in a city of almost three million, there could be not one person in sight? He increased his pace, taking comfort that he was now only two streets from home.

"Hey! Wait up," came the plea behind him. "You can't eat both of them pizzas all by yourself. Lemme give you a hand."

Anyone pulling aside a window drape or peering into the dark would see a man taking short, quick steps, apparently in a hip-swivelling walking race, except that he was bearing two boxes on his outstretched arms and a case that swung beneath. Another competitor close behind was cheating, for, between his rapid steps, he appeared to jog.

Alan released the six-pack. It slapped the sidewalk. One bottle exploded. He hoped his pursuer would stop, but when the footfall of boots sounded even closer, he threw down the pizza containers and darted ahead.

A forceful push on his upper spine drove him faster than his feet could run. He stumbled headlong forward, unable to avoid a fire hydrant. He didn't hear the crack of his skull on the metal, nor feel the hand that extracted the wallet from his pocket. In response to a kick, his body gave an involuntary twitch. Without stopping to collect the food and drink, the youth dashed into a driveway beside a deserted house, leaving a body lifeless and bloody like a badly mangled rat.

The driver of the first car that eventually sped by commented to his wife that today wasn't garbage day, and "look at the boxes and the clothing that have been dumped in front of that house."

"No civic pride at all! Disgraceful," the passenger replied.

Minutes later, a second car slowed down long enough for the driver to lower her window, note the address of the house, and use her cell phone to call 911.

She was already late for supper and decided that she couldn't do anything that paramedics couldn't do better. And besides, the whole scene might be a scam.

Alan regained consciousness as he felt himself being rolled over and lifted onto a gurney. When the ambulance door slammed shut, he drifted back into a place of blackness and silence, where no siren could penetrate.

He was in shock, not simply because of the concussion, the wrenched back and the ribs broken by the kick of a heavy boot. He was in shock because he was in a different world, one where a quiet street could spawn brutality. Its loveliness was nothing but a beguiling mask that concealed indifference. The trauma was the awful discovery that as familiar as words like violence, tragedy and terror are in the news, they are most violent, most tragic and terror-filled when they happen to you. The hurtle from spectator to victim sapped all his energy as his lowered temperature and almost non-existent heartbeat indicated.

The police found a boarding pass in his pocket, were able to identify him and telephone his wife. She waited beside him in the hospital, stroking his hand. In his brief span of consciousness, he was torn between an oasis of nothingness and a world of pain. Gently, soothingly Ellen was calling him away from a serene darkness into a discomforting light. "I need you more than ever, Al. We need you."

His groan testified that he felt broken and useless, broken as a man, useless and unprofitable as a husband.

It was as if he verbalized his denial with eloquent clarity, for Ellen repeated her plea. "No, Al, I do need you now, and in less than eight months, our baby will need you."

"Baby?" he gasped. He turned his head towards her too quickly, and his wide-eyed gaze was replaced by eyes clenched in pain. "Our baby?"

"Yes. I suspected I was pregnant before you left for London. That was why I didn't want you to go overseas. Last week, a pregnancy test and a visit to the doctor confirmed my hopes. When I told the women teachers at work, they threw a surprise party for me at the apartment last night. So you see, we need you."

Another groan, a compound of self-recrimination and of release. He sank once again into unconsciousness, this time, a deeply restorative sleep. When he awoke half an hour later he raised her hand to his lips and despite his broken ribs and half-closed eyes, said, "Great good news. I'm happy for you. Happy for us. And here I was thinking only of me. Yes, I need you too."

Many people live lives of unquiet commotion, scurrying to meet deadlines, scrambling to minimize debts, skimming headlines to keep up with the news, eating fast food on the run, cursing the backlog of unanswered emails. For such, a stay in a hospital offers stagnant pools of inactivity, breeding restlessness, boredom, and ill-tempter.

But after he abandoned his painting, Alan became accustomed to slow comfortable hours in the apartment with its limited tasks. He had come to enjoy walking along the ravine, chatting with Russ and his court at the pub, reading in a park, and contemplating the miracles of nature that flourish even in the city: the halo that surrounded his shadow on dew covered lawns at sunrise, the parade of ants hastening to a discarded piece of bread and jam, the slant and bounce of hail, the gurgle and splash of rain hurrying out of downspouts. Infinitely varied were the unanticipated sounds, sights and smells he experienced on his walks. And what astonished him most was the uniqueness, the unrepeatableness of each event. No one else would see that leaf fall. This diamond flash of a snowflake reflected only to him, only for him.

The three days in the Toronto General Hospital afforded him hours of unhurried reflection. He mulled over each event since his return from London—the discovery of piles of dirty laundry and dishes, the evidence of a wild party, the encouragement of the pubsters to confront Ellen, the frightening flight up the deserted street, the attack and theft, the interview by police, the unexpected news that Ellen was expecting their baby. All were like smooth stones that he fingered and polished over and over again.

He deliberated long into the sleepless nights, replaying each scene and imagining alternatives. What if he had stayed longer in the pub or if he had turned back to the main road instead of continuing along the dark street, if he had run instead of walking the final block and a half, if—and to this he returned repeatedly—if he had chosen to walk to the right on leaving the apartment, then everything would have been different.

But, he repeatedly concluded, water under the bridge, spilt milk, the horse has bolted, the cat's out of the bag and among the pigeons, the feces have hit the fan. And here I am trying to force the water back upstream, to uncrumble the cookie, to close the barn door retroactively, to shoo away the pigeons and bag the cat.

The thought of activating his original vengeful plan against Ellen with all its angry accusations and rampant suspicions now caused him to shudder. How bizarre that the dark cloud of the attack, the theft, and the hospital stay had such a bright silver lining: the avoidance of a furious shouting match with his pregnant wife. But that cloud, even with its lining, now loomed over a world that was suddenly unfamiliar to him, a world whose tranquil parks and blossoming shrubs and dewy haloes could conceal villainy. Into such a threatening world their baby would be born.

Three days after his admission to the hospital. Ellen took the morning off work to drive Alan home to the apartment. In her telephone call confirming the time of his discharge, she delivered what she thought would be welcome news, "Grace will have lunch with us today. She's eager to hear how Roger is making out in London."

"Well, he's doing lots of that," he answered. "I can hardly wait to hear what I have to say to her."

Somewhere between her ascent to his room and their descent in the elevator, the rains came. He grumbled about a quite unnecessary wheelchair.

"Drat! I didn't think to bring rain coats," she said as she fumbled for her car keys, then forgot to engage the brakes on the chair, and wrestled to get him into the car.

The arrival was less of a hassle, but as he stepped out of the car, he noticed the rivulet of water flowing along the gutter towards the distant ravine. If they had parked a few meters higher, he would have seen the trickle moving in the opposite direction. He stopped and shuddered in an attempt to bring some past experience to mind—the wetness shining off leaves and stone; holding hands astride insignificant runnels running east and west, fleeing from the Great Divide. Ellen pulled him out of his frozen position.

Poor Grace. When she arrived, she didn't know how to kiss a man whose head was partially swathed in bandages and whose rib-protecting gesture fended off an eager hug. And he didn't know how to describe the extra-curricular activities of Roger.

"He was so busy that I didn't see much of him," he cautiously explained. "In fact few people do. I toured art galleries and museums on my own while he wrestled with assignments. He lamented the loss of one who brought him such happiness."

"Meaning Grace," Ellen suggested.

"Who else?" he said, and nodding toward Grace, added, "His American beauty." Grace blushed happily. What nibbles of truth he could offer, she devoured with relish. His travels about London, however, his experience at the hand of the leather-jacketed thug, and Ellen's pregnancy provided enough material to divert the conversation away from sexually overactive Bertie.

It took Ellen only a few weeks to string together certain observations of her husband's behaviour. Even then she wondered if it was only her pregnancy that made her hypersensitive to a few of his little inexplicable gestures, hesitations and comments.

For example, in addition to the brief episode at the curb, when asked if he preferred tea or coffee, he would not answer. Or as she chose to think, he simply did not answer. She would decide for him. On several weekends when she was marking papers at home, he left to go for a walk, but returned in less than ten minutes. Gladys Boadman upstairs reported that she often saw him standing motionless in front of the apartment as if perplexed.

A few days later, instead of going for a walk, he began to sit at the kitchen table and repeatedly, almost obsessively play solitaire. One evening, Ellen, who had volunteered to be the accountant for her local branch of the teachers' union, was working at her financial reports. As she heard the snap of the cards, she wondered at his reluctance to go out. He must want to be near me as my pregnancy progresses, she thought. Trying to concentrate on her figures, she was distracted by his mutterings, "Red seven on a black eight," click, click, click, "black three on a red four. Ace up. King over," flick, flick, flick, "Jack on a ten, two up . . ." then a prolonged silence followed by sounds of rapid breathing that verged on sobs. She put down her pencil, gathered her papers and observed his distress. He seemed oblivious to her stare. She walked around the table, caressed him and looked at the cards. What she then heard was "two black fives, two of them. Which should I move to the six? This one or that?"

She tried to calm him by saying, "It's only a game. It doesn't really matter which one you move. Here, let's try this."

Her resoluteness consoled him, if one can be annoyed and consoled at the same time. His blockages mystified her. And as so often happens between husbands and wives, they didn't discuss the problem. What began as a curiosity, eliciting raised eyebrows, smiles and shrugs, progressed to perplexity, inviting a variety of explanations. Was his concussion more serious than they thought? Was it his anguish over the death of his father or his failure as an artist and bread-winner or an unreadiness to be a father himself?

An unusual effort was required to drive him out of the apartment, even to make the necessary food purchases. Mrs. Boadman saw him twice a week take tentative steps out the front door, pause, then impulsively walk in double quick time towards the grocery story. Had she followed him inside, she would have observed his bewilderment before the myriad of sizes and flavours and prices available for each item. He began to feel like a refugee who, having fled from a land of deprivation and starvation, is dumbfounded by the riot of choices. Whereas it used to be a question of bread or no bread, now there are varieties of pita, bagels, whole wheat, gluten free, rusks, multi-grain, chapatti, garlic bread, pumpernickel—each more appealing than the other. Eventually, Ellen had to take over food shopping.

"If you're unwilling to see a doctor, how about joining the 'Y' or trying your hand at painting again," she suggested. "Go visit your friends at the pub. You can't just sit there, unwilling even to pick a T.V. channel."

How could he make her understand what he saw: paths that bifurcated and forked into the dark, always into the dark. Whatever happened to the straight and narrow way, he wondered. He admired the trees that branched out fearlessly. He envied the brook down in the ravine that cascaded over rock ledges, separating into rivulets all of which, thank God, managed to reunite.

Exerting an extraordinary resolve, he determined one rainy morning to follow both of the courses that the water took at the little divide in front of the apartment. He had not far to pursue the rivulet to the left. Just before it reached the corner, it pooled about a sewer, swirling fragments of leaves, then disappearing. He stood stock still under his umbrella following the flow of water in his imagination, down between the metal bars of the drain, down into its dark, subterranean channel, fed by innumerable vile smelling tributaries, flushing dead leaves, dying insects—flushing death as far as possible from human consciousness and social conscience.

"Drop something?" The stranger's question startled him. He too was carrying an umbrella and mercifully was not wearing a leather jacket with silver studs. "I once dropped my car keys, and wouldn't you know it, they managed to fall precisely between the bars of the grill."

"No, nothing," Alan stammered. "Well, not keys exactly. Just some change. Not much, really."

"That's good. I wouldn't want you to have to poke around in that slime and muck to find a diamond ring. Have a good day despite the rain," he said, turning to hop over some puddles.

Alan walked back towards the watershed, and where the rivulet was strong enough, he picked up a twig, dropped it into the flow, and followed it along the curb. The first drain was clogged with leaves. The water swirled and spread in a wide, thin flood across the sloping street, sweeping nature's detritus before it. It joined empty plastic bottles and scraps of paper that circled briefly in low spots before tumbling towards the ravine. Speeding cars on the main street flung sheets of water in bursts at the empty sidewalks. Alone, Alan pursued the gathering flow as it headed towards the valley.

The path leading to the brook below was paved. He balanced over some stepping stones that looked as if they were fighting their way upstream. He reached a rock in the middle of the current that was bounding and leaping against the flow. Leaves pirouetted in swift eddies before they slid over a variety of rills that cascaded over the worn granite ledge. This was what he had come to see—one stream diverging, dividing and subdividing. But look! Downstream, the strands and threads of water all rejoined. The brook regained its identity. Maybe Ellen is right, he thought. It's only a game. It doesn't matter which path they follow.

He recrossed the stepping stones and climbed the walkway homeward, happier than he had been in days. Much to her surprise, Ellen observed how he began to move and act more decisively almost as if he were driven.

One afternoon when she was at work, teaching, a telephone call interrupted Alan's lone noon meal. "Al! It's Russ, over at the Mug and Jug. A few of us having lunch were sharing rumours about you. Clark and Joe heard you were beat up and spent some time in hospital. Is that true?"

"Too true, Russ. Yes it happened on my way back from the pub about a month ago. But I'm back up on my hind legs again."

"Great," he said. Alan heard Russ pass the news along to his courtiers, "He says he's survived the attack. What's that? . . . OK, I'll ask him. Al, the boys want proof that you're alive. Can you make it over to the pub before three?"

Across from the pub stood a large silver maple tree, providing shade for whoever paused and sat on the corner park bench. As Alan walked along the busy street, he noticed, perhaps for the first time, this stately tree. He stopped and stood transfixed. Russ, Clark and Joe, sitting at the window stools, wondered if he was suffering from a seizure, frozen, looking skyward. After a minute of motionlessness, his body seemed suddenly to unlock, and he hurried across the street to be reunited with his now anxious buddies.

"I'm alive," he said on entering, "and I got scars to prove it."

"So we noticed," Clark said, thinking about Alan's apparent bout of catalepsy. "Well, welcome back anyway," and they all joined in to greet him. The bartender brought over a pint of Alan's usual, "This one's on the house, Al."

He recounted the story of how the attack spared him the error of mistakenly charging his wife with any number of indiscretions: unfaithfulness, debauchery, adultery. "It was a surprise party some women teachers threw when they found my wife was expecting."

After expressing congratulations and setting him another pint, they lapsed into silence, wondering how to put their concern into words. Finally Russ spoke for them all, "So what's with that tree across the street? Did you see a great auk or a passenger pigeon or something on it?"

"No, I just saw the tree. I finally saw it, after all these months." His eyes brightened at the prospect of sharing something that excited him, something important to him that he wanted to be sure was significant for them too. "I mean, have you seen it?" he asked enthusiastically.

"Every day," Russ sighed, "five days a week. And it's probably there all seven."

"No, I mean really . . . seen it?" He turned his gaze from face to face, eager to detect hints of body language that might declare, "Yes, Al, I know exactly what you mean. You've seen it too, then!" but there was a certain grimness of expression, a look of puzzlement, embarrassment almost, as if he were taking off his trousers right there beside their window seats.

He began to feel that he was trying to light a fire using damp wood. He would have to fan the dying embers, vigorously.

"Well, maybe I should say that as I stood over there and looked up, I saw them, not all of them, mind you, but most of them." He paused to allow the three to take in the full meaning of his clarification.

"Them," Joe said. "You saw them." It was not a question, simply a confirmation that he heard what Alan had said.

"That's right! I saw the branches, and other branches coming from branches, right from the trunk to the tips of, to the tips of . . ."

Joe filled in the blank, "of the branches."

There was a glimmer of hope that Joe caught the profound implication. Alan encouraged this flame, "Yes. So when the sap reaches each fork, it doesn't matter how it diverges. Just like in us, blood flows from an artery into one of many arterioles, then branches into one of hundreds, maybe thousands of capillaries. It's like what happens when you get, say, two black fives in solitaire. Do you see? It doesn't matter which one you pick."

Since all three were tilting their pints, no one responded to his question. Clark and Joe concentrated on trying to replace their glasses in the precise centre of their circular coasters. Russ broke the silence, "I hear the Maple Leafs have signed on a new coach. Do you think he'll do any better than the last one?"

His look of consternation gave way to dismay as he gazed from averted face to down turned glances. The fire went out, and Alan excused himself. He, too, went out.

Over the ensuing seven months, his new preoccupation began to infect Ellen. He tried to replay for her what he had failed to explain to the pubsters, "All the branching in trees and circulatory systems is natural. It's organic. It's the product of genetic algorithms and environment. Do you see what I'm getting at Elle?"

She stopped chomping an apple. "Not really," she said with a mouthful. She gulped. "In fact, not at all."

He continued, his enthusiasm unabated, "But the whole point is that making choices—"

"Which you're not good at—"

"—which I'm not good at, is not preprogrammed like the growth of a tree. It is something beyond the natural. And that's why the results can diverge and lead who knows where!"

"Al," she said, and swallowed her next mouthful, "Al, you think too much."

He clenched his teeth, grimaced, and thought she doesn't think too much. In fact, she doesn't think. Period. She dog-paddles over the surface of the lake unaware of the awe-inspiring depths below. "Yeah, maybe I do," he appeared to concede.

What a time for an expectant father to behave so strangely, she mused. Just when I need to fight off my own demons—night time fears of birthing complication being only one. It takes all the strength I can muster to banish the statistics one hears about infant abnormalities and diseases.

She resisted thoughts of his having an emotional breakdown. "Whatever trauma he experienced will pass," she told her mother over the phone. The silence at the other end of the line betokened disbelief. "Arne" sighed her mother with shoulder drooping exasperation, "she refuses to consider any possibility he will commit suicide, absolutely refuses. And, no doubt she adamantly ignores all those newspaper accounts of murder and suicide that regularly hit North American headlines. What are we going to do?" Arne flicked ash from his stogie and nodded solemnly as if he had been listening.

The birth of Ronnie mercifully changed all that. The seven pound, four ounce baby was not afraid to slither eagerly into this world of worlds. His arrival struck Alan as a vote of confidence in all the possible tomorrows. Ronnie's birth led to his father's rebirth.

Because Mr. Orgle was too busy at his North Bay chemical plant, his wife flew alone to Toronto, booked a fashionable hotel and visited them for a few days to make sure the baby was being cared for properly. She made it clear that this "hole" in which Ronnie was going to be brought up would damage him in some way. "Everybody knows that basement apartments spawn mould. Get our grandchild baptised just in case."

"In case of what?" asked Al, frowning. "Well, you never know, that's all. You never know." On leaving, she made them promise to drive north so that Arne could see the baby as soon as possible. They promised to drive up for the long week-end a month later.

Ellen's mother wasted no time in arranging a surprise baptismal event for her grandchild. Only after much shopping around did she find a congregation suitable to their station where the cleric was willing to perform the sacrament despite the Thompsons' lack of prior connection with the church. The deciding factor was the significant profile grandpa Orgle had in North Bay's industrial world.

Instead of being a happy, harmonious celebration, the event turned sour when Alan refused to participate. "Sorry, I don't want to be a part of that rigmarole. But go ahead if you must. You can do it without me." Ellen and her parents were furious. "Good God! What will people think?" she demanded. "Everyone will suspect you weren't the father, or that we've already separated or that you don't respect tradition, or that a Torontonian is too good to stoop to a North Bay—"

"Or," interrupted Alan, "or that I dislike hypocrisy. The church expects us to make vows and promises We don't even know what they are yet!"

His mother-in-law tried a different tack. "How is it, Alan, that you hesitated to choose between turning right or left and between drinking tea or coffee, yet you can make up your mind instantly about participating or not participating in the baptism of your own son? Your only son! How is that?"

Arne, practising new skills he was learning in anticipation of becoming a vice-president of the chemical company, attempted to mollify the mounting hostility. "Consider this simply a social event that has no cosmic significance whatsoever, an opportunity to see and be seen by the town's limited supply of socialites."

Alan was not persuaded. The ceremony proceeded without him.

The visit to North Bay terminated early following the reception in the church hall. For much of the five hour drive back to Toronto, they argued about Mrs. Orgle's public explanations, "Alan did so much want to attend the baptism," she had gushed. "He really did. But an attack of migraine simply made it impossible. We were happy he recovered in time for the party after." She would have been happier still if he were "gainfully employed instead of loafing around the house day and night," she muttered to her daughter. "What kind of a role model will he be for Ronald when he grows up—when they both grow up?"

Back in their Toronto apartment, Alan seemed to find his bearings once again. He even looked forward to endless walks with Ronnie—on busier streets though—at first with the carriage, then, a few months later, with a stroller. As months blossomed into years, he briefly guided Ron on his tricycle. It would not be—it was not—long until his son would proudly ride away alone on his brand new bicycle to play at the school playground.

Al could hardly believe how little he missed his former loves, painting and acting. The slender chores in their small apartment left him time to read and walk the streets of his beloved neighbourhood. He enjoyed giving a helping hand to his aging neighbour upstairs, Gladys, and she delighted in sharing a few sips of sherry with someone—anyone as the months and years slipped by. The penultimate stage in Ron's growth was to drive his sports-minded son to soccer, hockey or basketball practices and games according to the appropriate seasons. Neither Al nor Ellen was eager to experience the eventual ultimate stage, when Ron would, predictably, ask for the car, "just for a few hours," or worse, "just for the weekend."

Much changed during that sixteen year procession of time. Ellen was now a vice-principal. The family was able to afford a small house in the Beaches area of Toronto, due mostly to the inheritance Ellen received after the death of her father. Ronald, his mother and father flew to England for the long-delayed wedding of Roger and Bertie—no, "Roberta," as she now called herself.

Back in Toronto, while walking to the bank to pay credit card bills, a chance encounter in a shoe store was a significant turning point in Alan's life. It wasn't so much the shoes on display in the window that attracted him. He had been walking past dozens of shoe stores without remembering that his good pair had worn out weeks ago. What stopped him this time was the bouquet of red roses, looking lost, misplaced even, in the collection of boots, sandals, slippers, loafers, spikes and running shoes.

As an artist, he found the display arresting. The juxtaposition of nature-made roses and man-made shoes was provocative. As an actor and student of theatre, he considered the staging dramatic. He went into the store and stood looking out at the window display.

"May I help you?" a clerk asked. She was a little on the plump side, short brown hair, business length, and wore a no-nonsense navy skirt and white blouse. It made sense that her silver brooch should represent a stylized rose.

"Yes," he said, still contemplating the flowers. "But I was wondering, is this a florist's shop or a shoe store?"

Her gentle laughter indicated that this was somewhat of a familiar joke. "That's what my boss wondered when I put them there. We do sell shoes, but I love roses."

He leaned over to admire the full width of the window. "All the shoes are standing around, open-mouthed in astonishment," he said. "And so was I, out there on the street. But I do need a good pair of loafers, like those in the corner." He turned towards her to be sure she saw where he was pointing. "Do you have those in brown?" he asked.

As she headed into the stock room, she glanced back at him and seemed on the point of commenting on something. She obligingly found dark and medium brown models and intently watched him decide on a selection.

"Pardon me for asking," she said, "but didn't you use to act at Hart House Theatre?"

Startled at so long buried a memory, he smiled and slowly lifted a shoe towards the ceiling and intoned, "Is this a loafer which I see before me, the heel toward my hand?"

They laughed and she exclaimed, "I was there. I saw those performances. You wouldn't have noticed me, though. I was the prop manager. Marianne. Marianne Loiselle." She thrust forward an eager open hand. "And you're . . ."

"Alan. Alan Thompson. What a memory for faces you have!"

"No, not faces," she said, "I just never forget a voice, especially one like yours. I bet you're a radio or TV announcer by now."

"All I announce is 'Dinner is served.'"

"So you're a maitre d'."

"No—well, yes—for my wife and son. I used to do a lot of painting—not houses. People, landscapes, cityscapes. But now I'm a house husband. I haven't acted since Hart House."

"Nineteen, twenty years? What a loss. Would you believe it, Mr. Thompson, I'm still connected with the theatre, a community theatre now. I went back after my two sons started high school. My husband, Gord, says I spend too much time at it. But it's so much fun. Better than watching him lounge in front of the idiot box night after night with a bottle of beer in both hands."

"So Marianne has been bitten by the stage bug."

"And the rose bug," she was quick to add. "Is there any chance that the stage bug could re-bite you, not so much as an actor, but as a scenery painter. The community newspaper praised our choice of plays, lauded several of our actors, but scoffed at the amateurish settings and scenes for our last two plays. We could use you. We desperately need your artistic skills."

He was struck by her enthusiasm, the way she clasped her hands, her index fingers making a steeple pressed against her lips, her wide open sparkling eyes, the way she leaned forward and appeared to hold her breath, eagerly anticipating his answer.

"That's a possibility," he said. "Yes, a definite possibility." He was touched by her sigh of relief. "But I should talk it over with my wife."

Ellen was delighted that he finally found something to do. And Ron was amazed to see what his father could paint. They all worked to transform the spare bedroom into a painting den, for Alan so enjoyed designing and painting the flats at the theatre that he filled his spare time at home creating landscapes. The willows, waves, sunrises, sunsets, and storms along the shore of Lake Ontario not far from their house came alive on his canvases.

The Beaches Community Theatre had only one paid employee, the manager, who also looked after accounts, purchasing, advertising, and recruiting of volunteers. Now, following the success of their latest production, the board decided to hire a second employee to act as carpenter, set designer and painter. Reliable volunteers still looked after lighting, sound and ushering. Marianne was more delighted than ever to manage the props. She was the one to propose Alan for the new paid position, and was commissioned by the board to transmit to him their offer of employment.

"It's barely above minimum wage," she said apologetically. "It's all the board can afford, at least for now. But I wish you'd accept the position."

Ellen was prompt to point out, "At least it's a job, Alan. Finally a paying job."

Ron made a different proposal. "Dad, you're a terrific painter. What are you going to do with all those shore scenes and landscapes and still lifes you've got stacked in the den? And everybody is saying that if you can paint those flats so wonderfully, you could sell your work. I think you should open an art store. I could help out, and Mom could be the accountant. You sure would make a lot more money running an art store."

"So," Ellen said, "you have three choices. To sit around here and find yourself replaced by a carpenter/artist that the theatre does hire. Or you can take the job they've offered, or you can open an art gallery. My vote is for Ron's idea. But you have to—as Roger told you a long time ago—you have to make up your minds. Our son has just made a great suggestion. I'd be glad to quit my volunteer accounting job with the teachers' union. Too many bosses there. I'd look after the gallery's books."

His wife and son were relieved to observe his reaction to the choices. "Another fork in the road, another branch," he said, this time with a smile. Time to be of one mind. "Yes, either a gallery or the theatre. The theatre or a gallery . . ."

Chapter Three

Either Theatre or Gallery:

Theatre

I was surprised to hear Marianne say that we should arrive at the donut shop this evening in separate cars. "Gord is angrier than usual at how much time I spend at the theatre," she whispered as we waited in the wings to check the placement of props and furniture for the second act. "Have you any idea, Al, of how angry he can get?"

Yes indeed. I've had a glimpse of his explosive temper. A month ago they arrived by car to unload boxes of props for our next play, *Frankie and Johnny in the Clair de Lune*.

"Gord," she'd pleaded, "would you help us carry in some of these?" He shouted back that this was her play, not his, "So get the hell a move on."

There were lamps, ash trays, a telephone, TV set, radio, stool, pillows, bedding, and cartons of kitchen utensils. Even two toothbrushes. The heavier items—stove, fridge, sofa bed, would arrive next week by truck. How much easier if we had a theatre of our own and didn't have to store stuff between plays in people's garages and basements. I suppose we will continue to use the high school auditorium until we can afford to rent and renovate a small warehouse.

Ahmed, the lighting technician, Marianne and I had carried everything in while an increasingly angry Gord supervised. "Can't you find some others in there to give us a hand! I'm gonna pile the fuckin' stuff on the bloody road. My bowling starts in half an hour and it takes that long to cross town to get there in this damn traffic." He was one of those people who stop you from doing something to explain at great length and volume why you should do it faster.

A week later, I was waiting for her in the front lobby of the high school auditorium. She would probably be loaded down with props and Gord, of course, would not help her, but would chastise her for taking so long.

Feelings of nostalgia flooded over me as I gazed at the trophies in the display cabinets, especially the drama awards. I found myself kneeling with nose pressed against the glass to look for my name engraved on a shield attached to the Provincial High School Drama Festival Cup. Our school had won it twenty years ago. Or was it even the same cup? Above it were the usual framed photos of sports teams. Memories of playing soccer in the rain transported me to the change room where all the team members vied with one another to claim the dirtiest team shirt or the longest slide in the mud. Our most exhilarating questions began, "Did you see me when I . . . ?"

A car door slammed and shattered my reveries. Marianne was lugging an overstuffed box as she headed towards the front steps of the school. There would be sun glasses, a box of Band-Aids, a hairbrush, bread knife and a dozen other items essential to the play. Her husband rolled down the window and shouted after her, "My God, Yanne, you're only looking after the props, aren't you? You'd think you were making a fuckin' film about the middle ages, the amount of stuff you say you need. I'll be finished bowling by ten. If you're not in front of the building by 10:25 you can bloody well walk home." With a screech of tires, his red Chevy catapulted away.

"Doesn't that get to you?" I asked. We walked towards the large high closet where we cram the flats. She thumped the carton on the floor and stared at it. With a resigned look she turned, bit her lip, then asked, "You mean his nasty moods? No, Al, you learn to tune them out after a while."

Fortunately it was only on Wednesdays that he chauffeured her. The other three days, she drove herself and returned home after our *tete a tete* at the donut shop.

On the night of our first blocking session onstage, Marianne placed the smaller items where they belonged. Recalling her love for roses, I surreptitiously placed one red rose in a vase on the refrigerator for her and all the audience to see.

I was taping the seams of the flats when she walked onstage accompanied by the costume mistress. She silently read her props list and pointed to each item, checking the director's instruction. I watched her reaction to the unexpected flower.

"Who put that rose up there? Liz, did you? It's not on my list."

"Where would I get a rose? It must have been Sandra. My guess is she forgot to put it on your list and brought it tonight herself."

"But it's not in the play. I've read and reread it so as not to miss anything."

"Well, you know directors. Some of them think they're gods. Ask Sandra. I've got my own problems. Frankie says her bathrobe is too small."

I was beginning to wonder if I should come clean, when Sandra strode on stage. "All ready, team? Anything missing, Liz? Marianne? Hold it! That rose." She hurried over to the refrigerator and lifted down the vase, admired the flower, closed her eyes and hugged it. Then she began waltzing around. "Yes! The possibilities are wonderful. What a brilliant idea. I know it's not in the play, but let's see what stage business Frankie and Johnny can make out of it. Marianne, you're a freakin' genius." She hurried off to tell the two actors, leaving the three of us in astonished laughter.

After the rehearsals, usually I'm the last out. Marianne waited for me in her car to drive us to the donut shop. It looked like I'd have an extra task for each stage rehearsal and performance: to ensure the appearance of a rose. I carried it to the car.

"Oh ho! So it's you, Al. I should've guessed. Of course—the bouquet in the display window."

I handed her the rose in its vase. "Now, every time you smell a rose, think of me. And I promise to provide a fresh one for each rehearsal and performance. We'll put it on the table between us while we sip our coffees. A touch of class."

When I expressed uneasiness about our meetings, she explained, "I tell Gord that all the cast members and volunteer helpers go out for a coffee together. He's usually asleep in front of the boob tube when I get home. I can even climb into bed before the lout wakes up."

We got into the habit of going together in her car, but tonight she has insisted we travel separately. Tomorrow is the final show. Thanks to the theatre's improved ratings we perform each play six times, Thursday to Saturday of two successive weeks. That's a lot of roses, but she and Frankie love them. And so do I.

After the final show there is a five week lull before I begin constructing the sets for our next play which opens two months after this one closes. Those five weeks deprive me of some wonderful conversation, some much needed friendship, and some innocently intimate moments with someone who means more to me with each passing week. We did manage to meet during the odd lunch hour between productions. The shoe store gives her only thirty minutes; so we just go to an unremarkable restaurant buried on a small side street.

"Now, what's this about the sudden need for separate cars this time?" I ask as we hunch over our lattes at the donut shop. I breathe in the rich perfume of the rose. "Do you suspect he's spying on you—on us?"

"You know Liz?—the tall skinny girl who works with costumes?" she says.

Here she goes again, I think. Ask Marianne a yes-or-no question and the answer is so circuitous, so convoluted, that often she gets derailed in the details. I wonder if that drives Gord crazy. When I'm not in a hurry I enjoy her panoramic approach. It lets me into her mind, into her past, her personality. It sets the stage for the scenes of her life, scenes in which I would like to be more of an actor.

My answer comes out quite musical, a slow scooping down and then up on the first and last words, "Yes . . . I know Liz." I'm going to get Liz's pedigree; so I fix my attention on breaking and buttering my muffin and settle in for a fascinating genealogy.

"Her brother bowls with Gord," she says.

The starkness of her statement, its total lack of elaboration, startles me.

She watches me position the knife on my serviette with care, as if I'm preoccupied with precision. I turn towards the plate glass window beside us, attracted by the headlights of a car nosing towards the wall. Doors are flying open. Two women emerge and, giggling, enter the store.

I break the silence, "So he knows that the cast doesn't go out for a coffee." We digest the thought until I ask, "How long has he known, do you think?"

"The last three nights he's been awake when I got home. And last night he asked me if Liz joined everybody else for a coffee after the show. He knows, Al. He knows."

She sips her latte and looks through our reflections on the window, trying to spot a red Chevy or a lone person skulking in the parking lot. "I think he'd hang around the school to see if we sit in your car or mine, or if we leave separately."

Usually I hold her hand across the table, but tonight our gestures are more robotic and deliberate, less spontaneous, not in the least erotic.

I feel like a driver in a luxury car, speeding along a familiar four-lane highway in the dark. Then with no warning, a large sign appears that screams, "No Exit. Dead End."

There must be a way around that sign, I think. "Look. Tomorrow is closing night. That's one night when everybody really will be going to the cast party. Does Gord know where it's going to be?"

She smirked. "He says he's not the least bit interested in going to any pansy party of actors and artists. And besides, it's the hockey final. Nothing will tear him away from that. He's bought a couple of cases of beer and two or three of his friends are coming over to celebrate Toronto's victory—they think. He won't want me home early."

"Great," I say. "Then we won't go either. To the party. You know how the janitor lets us lock up the school after the show on Saturdays. He skips out early. And when everyone has left, we'll have the whole place to ourselves. Just to be safe, park your car a block away, not in the school lot."

"I'm drowning," she replies, "I'm trying to swim back to shore but there's this tremendous undertow."

Now what is she on to? The words sound vaguely familiar, and a sad smile freezes on her face.

She continues as if reciting, "My arms and legs are going a mile a minute but . . ." She pauses and glances slyly at me, "But . . ." and then she gives me several encouraging nods.

Of course! I know the speech. It's Johnny in the play, speaking to Frankie. I've heard it at a dozen rehearsals and at five performances. I backtrack on the dialogue to take a run at completing it, "My arms and legs are going a mile a minute but . . . but they aren't taking me . . . to . . ."

"Any closer to . . ." she prompts.

"They aren't taking me any closer to where I want to be." I sigh with satisfaction.

"Where's that?" Frankie and Marianne ask.

I am not certain who answers, Johnny or me. "With you," one of us says. "I want to be with you."

How astonishing that a play—why do we call it a "play"?—that a play can be so real! "Did the voices of Frankie and Johnny become ours?" We often heard and overheard them at rehearsals. "Under the subliminal influence of those two lovers, did we become like them?"

I want to tell Marianne why I think drama captivates us so entirely. It does more than *enter*-tain; it *sus*-tains. A play, when presented well, is not simply an entertainment; it's a sustainment. It surpasses even that, for it enables us to ascertain who we are and who we could be. It's a, yes, an *ascer*-tainment. I'm sure that she would agree, but tonight is not the time for such philosophizing. "Well, what do you think, Frankie?"

"I think . . . I think that I, too, want to be with you. But I'm not an unmarried Frankie. Neither are you an unhitched Johnny."

"You could be Ophelia." I begin to lift my hand to put it over hers, but she snatches it away, leans back and casts a furtive glance out the window. "Let's talk this over tomorrow," I say. We take a final sip of our coffees and gather our coats to leave, separately. As usual, she holds the vase and addresses the rose, "You smell wonderful."

At home, Ron and one of his team mates are in our living room watching a video of their latest basketball game. "Our coach wants us to see why we lost 30 to 48. Go into the kitchen, Dad, and make yourself some toast. Then come back in five minutes."

"Why?"

"Because I miss three baskets in a row at the end of this quarter," he says, pounding his fist repeatedly into his open palm.

Peter, a tall, lanky boy, leaps to his rescue, "But be sure to come back 'cause he makes two impossible shots right after that."

Ellen is in the kitchen adding columns of figures. "Hi," I say.

She frowns and mumbles the numbers she is in the process of totalling. After a pause she replies with a sigh, "Two hundred and seventy-four," and looks up. When did she begin to lose that glimmer of welcome, that flicker of recognition that used to signal her delight in seeing me? She's becoming more and more like her mother. Will I end up more and more like her father, intimidated, gruff, defensive?

"Report card time?" I ask, sympathetically because I have seen the columns of test marks that have to be calculated, all complete with averages, highs, lows, medians and means.

"Not this time. Balancing the accounts of our teachers' union. You're home early, much earlier than usual. What are you doing?"

I stiffen on hearing her question. That's the trouble with a concealed part of your life. You're never sure of how to interpret simple questions. I stall for time, "What?"

"You're making toast. You never make toast at this hour." I hope my exhalation of relief, my sudden relaxation, are not too obvious. I didn't want her to go on and enquire, like "What did you think I meant—What were you doing after the play?" She knows it's out by ten-fifteen, and here I am coming home after 11:00.

"I'm just following our son's instructions, to make toast and go back to see the basketball video in five minutes. Do we have any cake or cookies for the boys?"

"We do if you bought them," comes her sharp reply. "See you in bed. I'm dead, but T.G.I.F. Anyway, it's late. It's so often late when you come home. Tell the kids to keep it down. Peter is staying overnight to go with Ron to tomorrow's practice."

I make extra slices of toast and carry in pots of jam, marmalade, and peanut butter. "Thanks Dad. How did *Frankie and Johnny* go tonight?"

I cast an anxious glance at him, pause to swallow, and feel my face flush. Then relieved, blurt "Oh, the play. Yes, terrific. The crowd loved it. A standing ovation again. And a full house too. Looks like we'll be out of debt after this run."

I'm grateful that someone in this house shows some interest in what I so much enjoy and work so hard at. If I were acting in the plays, Ellen might relent and enquire about them. She might even attend and relive those happy Hart House Theatre days when she first ecstased about my acting. Instead, there is only the pained silence of a stage widow. I think she resents the enjoyment I experience in the theatre.

Saturday passes in slow motion despite my having to drop Ron and Peter off at an early practice and do the week's food shopping. Ellen is still asleep in bed when we drive away. I imagine a variety of scenarios for this evening. All of them branch off into possible futures, like maybe an intensification of an affair that remains hidden or a divorce upon discovery or, worst scenario, two divorces. More likely a tearful plea from Ellen that terminates the Frankie and Johnny affair.

A screech of brakes and angry shouts remind me I am driving a car.

In the play, the characters eat a meatloaf sandwich and Johnny downs a couple of glasses of milk. While I'm shopping, I'll try to find the closest thing to a meatloaf sandwich in the deli section, but buy a bottle of champagne instead for our post-play play.

On returning home, I find the house in darkness. A note is propped up against an empty plastic apple juice bottle. "Al, you got away before I could tell you. Mom phoned last night. She's flying down from North Bay this morning and will stay at the International Hotel on Bloor Street. We're having lunch there and we'll go shopping. Mom wants to see what kind of plays you're involved with. Arrange for two good seats for tonight's performance. Looks like I'll get to see it after all. See you after the show. Elle."

I rarely phone Marianne during her work hours, least of all on a Saturday when she's bound to be busy. But here goes.

"Superior Shoe Store. Marianne speaking. How may I help you?" she says in a sexless, professional voice. I've heard her say those very words to me back stage in the sultriest, the most seductive of drawls. But this time, I'm in no mood for foolery. "It's Al. We've got a problem."

Apparently there are customers nearby, judging by the *double entendres* she is forced to use. "Why yes, sir. We do indeed. We have been carrying those for several weeks now."

"Very funny, but this is serious. Ellen and her mother are coming to tonight's show. That could cancel our plans." There is a long pause. "Marianne, are you there?"

"Nevertheless, we will be pleased to satisfy you. I am willing to remain after hours despite the unfortunate occurrence. Will the two ladies be available to remain also, to assure a proper fitting?"

"Aha! I see what you're saying. Of course! Ellen and her mother will expect me to go to the cast party, but they won't want to remain for it. I'll chat with them after the show. Then they'll eventually leave with the rest of the crowd. I might even encourage Ellen to stay overnight at the hotel. You're a genius. Sorry I panicked."

"It is always a pleasure to be of service," says the formal voice.

"See you in the Clair de Lune, Frankie."

Don't ask me how many times I replay the opening scene of the play in my imagination, a scene Marianne and I have watched from back stage a dozen times. As I wash the lunch dishes, I picture it in all its masked eroticism. The stage is completely dark, and for the first two minutes, the theatre goers are treated to an aural drama, complete with moans of ecstasy and sounds of passionate kissing. When the stage lights are slowly brought up, the audience sees a couple in post coitus attitudes, lying on an opened out sofa bed.

For the last two or three performances, during those opening minutes, Marianne and I stand backstage in the dark in a tight embrace. Tonight will be different, ecstatically different, for, in addition to performing our ritual before the stage lights are fully up, we will have the stage to ourselves after everyone has left. Then the star performers will be Marianne and Alan in the Clair de Lune.

At the very moment when I lean over the sofa bed to hand Marianne her glass, not of milk, but of champagne, the phone rings. The enchanting stage vanishes, and the kitchen of our house with all its mundanities assails my consciousness. Reality is so damnably cruel and clamorous compared to reverie. And demanding, too.

"I'm coming, I'm coming," I shout toward the telephone. Why Ellen chose a red telephone I'll never know. It looks to me like a hot line to somewhere, North Bay, probably.

"But it matches the curtains and the clock," she would explain repeatedly. "It has to complement and not clash, doesn't it? Well, doesn't it?"

"Hello!" I shout into the offending 'phone."

"Sorry, Al. Did I wake you? You sound sorta grumpy."

"Yes. Well, not really. I was just washing the lunch dishes. Did your mother arrive safely?"

"She did, and she suggests you join us for supper at the International. Then we can all go together to the play. It will save the expense of a taxi out to the auditorium."

I'm having difficulty connecting her mother's plan with mine. "I guess that could be arranged," I allow. "Don't forget though that I have to check the stage and help arrange the props. So we'll have to be there early. Afterwards I'm expected to be at the cast party."

We agree on an early supper. Mrs. Orgle is wearing a long skirt, finely pleated, a stunning flowered blouse, pearl necklace and matching earrings. Ellen chose a flattering dress, a full, green skirt, a plain darker green silk velvet bolero jacket, and white blouse. I'm wearing jeans, respectable but not designer, a work shirt and a zippered jacket and running shoes.

"Well, don't you two tie for first prize," I say.

Mrs. Orgle casts a frosty glare at her daughter for sitting down without the assistance of a waiter. She remains frozen in her hauteur until a tuxedoed serf with equal hauteur glides towards her and slides back her chair. She settles into what is immediately transformed into the head of our circular table. "I am surprised they let you in here. But I guess that does count as a jacket," she reluctantly admits.

For the next half hour, the conversation repeatedly intrudes on my dreams. As they talk about their purchases and bargains, I drift off to the dimly lit stage and the empty auditorium: we are in the sofa bed, naked. Marianne is taking a bite of the ham and cheese sandwich that I am feeding her. I smile at her, recalling how I couldn't find a meatloaf sandwich. A large crumb falls onto her breast. "No, let me get it," I say, lowering my head to collect the crumb's with my tongue.

"You find our purchases amusing?" asks Mrs. Orgle.

I am snatched away from my dream. "Amusing?" I ask displaying all the guilt of a boy caught reading a girlie magazine.

"Yes. The way you were smiling about our shopping. You should have seen your wife, the shoes she tried on. I did love the gold sandals with the jewel on the instep, Ellen. They'd go beautifully with your brown outfit, you know the one that . . ."

Just about here I fade away to the stage again. I fling back the sheet and sit on the edge of the bed.

"Where are you . . . what are you doing?" asks Marianne.

"A surprise." I waltz over to the fridge to extract the bottle of champagne. I hold it aloft. "Surprise," I beam.

"Magnificent," she croons.

"What? The champagne or the frontal nudity?"

Mrs. Orgle puts down her knife and fork, tilts her head and says, "You look somewhat preoccupied. You can't be worried about the play surely. Ellen has been telling me it's quite a hit. Over the last two years she says you've been saving the theatre company. Is there something wrong? Arne and I are great contributors to the little theatre in North Bay, so we know how fragile amateur show business can be. Why, just last month, the woman who was to be lead actor in . . ."

I am in mid flight when I overhear dear mother-in-law saying, "So, are you?"

"Am I . . ." My mind stumbles back to the dining room of the International Hotel.

"Worried," Ellen says. "Are you worried, mother want to know."

I am becoming adept at being imaginative. "Yes. Yes I am. Quite anxious. The school wants the stage and storage area cleared by tomorrow noon. That's really quite unfair. They know cast parties go on till two or three. And now we'll have to start removing stove, fridge, sofa bed, scenery, costumes, props—everything—before eight a.m. I don't know how we'll be able to do it."

Once an actor, always an actor, I think, congratulating myself. "Say, why don't you two take the car. I think I can find someone to drive me to the party, and hopefully a few members of the crew will come back and get an early start on packing up."

Careful, Al. Don't look too eager. "Damn it all. That's the down side of not having our own building. They don't pay me half enough for this kind of overtime." To testify to my contrived annoyance, I charge at my fillet mignon with determined concentration.

Ellen picks up her mother's mood. "Mother has always said you should try looking for a real job, one that pays a decent salary."

This evening is a time for compliance. "Perhaps I should. Once this season is over, I think I'll look around for something, something a little more . . ."

"*Sen-sible*," Ellen's mother is prompt to say, in italics.

"Yes," I agree, "a more sensible job." Ellen has tipped her head down, and with raised and plucked eyebrows, is looking accusingly over her glasses at me. Maybe I'm not such a good impromptu actor after all.

With more than a hint of disdain, Mrs. Orgle pays the bill. After a few interminable minutes of chitchat, she casts a pained look over her shoulder at a hovering waiter. He catches her drift and obsequiously guides her chair back as she rises, offers a condescending smile, and navigates her convoy out of the luxurious dining room.

At the auditorium sales desk, when it comes to providing the tickets, I prevaricate about their being complimentary, "Here, I'll look after this bill." Ellen's eyebrows rise yet again.

As I head them to their seats, I can sense a degree of disapproval wash over Ellen and her mother, for, since there are no curtains, what do they see on stage but a bed-sitting room. "I hope your play isn't all about sex," Mrs. Orgle says with a withering look. Then she drives Ellen into the row to scan for their seats.

When the house lights dim and the aural drama begins, both Marianne and I appreciate the irony of what Ellen sees and we are doing. Ahmed, the lighting technician, had been gleefully threatening to extend the opening period of darkness, forcing Frankie and Johnny to prolong their dark, erotic act. And tonight, he makes good on his stratagem, much to the audience's amusement and our pleasure. We can hardly wait for the play to end and the auditorium to be ours.

Tonight the applause is surprisingly prolonged and the final bows more numerous than usual. The actors and director even drag me out and gesture to the audience that the sets are my creation. During the gleeful hubbub of the exiting crowd, I meet Ellen and her mother in the lobby. I know for a certainty as sure as God made large yellow lemons that they are withholding praise because it might be interpreted as approval of my work here. So I quickly focus on a different topic.

Gesturing toward the Provincial High School Drama Award on display I say, "It all began with this silver cup, all the excitement of acting and stage production. Twenty years ago our school won this trophy, and I was the lead actor."

Mrs. Orgle approaches the cabinet, peers at the glass, pats some stray strands of hair flat, then turns sideways to be sure that her reflection indicates her coat is falling correctly. "And you're still making plays, twenty years later. They should hand out trophies for doggedness."

"When will I see you both again," I ask, flashing a resigned smile.

Mrs. Orgle seems not to be in a hurry to hope for an early reunion. Ellen answers, "I'm driving mother to the airport tomorrow before lunch, so, if it's all right with you, I'll spend the night with her at the hotel."

Her mother gives her a hug. "And we'll have a lovely decadent breakfast. Sorry to hear you must be back at what you call work so early, Alan."

I am just about to reinforce my pseudo anger about the need to clear off the stage before noon when Liz, our costume mistress, dashes into our midst. "Be sure to get over to Connie's place for the cast party. Pete and I will be looking for you both."

Thank God she runs off before Ellen can explain that she won't be there. The only "both" that Liz ever sees at productions, rehearsals and performances is Marianne and I.

Reggie, the caretaker, is turning off lights to encourage the stragglers to hasten out. He told me he's hoping to catch at least the final period of the hockey game. He may even see more of it since the game is being played in a later time zone out west. Catching my eye, he strides over and offers me the key that locks the exits that have crash bars. "Don't forget to check every outside door before you go, Al. There are eight in all. And then remember, once you're out, you're out. I can't give you a key to get back in. Be sure to turn out any stage lights. Whatever other lights that will be on after I go are to remain on. OK? And thanks for closing up for me." He doesn't linger to hear my expressions of gratitude.

I join a few people on stage who are collecting their prized contributions to the stage props: a telephone, floor lamp, purse, skillet—things that otherwise get forgotten and somehow disappear. Marianne is gathering items into boxes, fearful that over the next few days some students might want to claim things like the salt and pepper shakers, the bread board, the bread knife.

One by one, or more likely, two by two, the volunteers shout, "See you guys at the party." Ahmed calls down from the lighting booth, "Pull the master switch for the stage when you're finished, will you Marianne?"

At last we are alone on stage. Distant laughter is cut short by slamming doors. I turn out all but one overhead light. Marianne adjusts the shade of the bedtable lamp and straightens the sofa bed sheets in its dim light.

"I've made a meatloaf sandwich for us," she says, and I laugh at the thought of my ham and cheese sandwich in the fridge. "Did you get the milk, Johnny?"

"Better than that. I've got champagne. We'll have to drink it out of milk glasses, though, Frankie." Despite my saying "Frankie," I'm not thinking Frankie, not even Marianne. I am thinking Ophelia.

A door at the back of the auditorium clatters open, and I whisper, "Oh, God! I haven't locked the doors."

A woman runs down the centre aisle crying, "Am I ever glad there's somebody still here!" It's Liz. "I left my purse in the corner and it's got this week's pay in it. Pete would kill me if we had to wait till Monday for it."

I switch on the overhead stage lights and watch her lunge into the corner and pull her purse out from behind a box. "Thank you, thank you, thank you," she calls out to whoever might still be here as she hugs her purse and hurries up the aisle and out.

"Let's you lock the doors. For sure," Marianne says.

"Right. And we won't admit latecomers until our version of the play is over," I say as I hurry towards the back of the auditorium.

I lock and check all doors, and when I return to the auditorium I am stunned by the transformation of the stage. She has extinguished all overhead lights. I stand at the back in one of the few pools of light and see only a dim blur on stage, the bed faintly lit by the table lamp. I feel my way along the wall and reach a recessed passageway whose well lit steps lead to one of the side exits. I freeze when I see a figure in what appears to be a long coat pass between the lamp and me.

A blast shatters the silence. I duck back into the passageway and crouch low, all too aware of how clearly the exit light exposes me to any gunfire.

Marianne shrieks out a laugh. I peer around the corner in time to see her tittering and laughing uncontrollably. The dark echo-absorbing auditorium swallows most of what she says between giggles. I hear the odd word, " . . . bottle . . . cork blew . . . scared me half . . . ."

I emerge from my hiding place and bound, now fearlessly, towards the steps onto the stage and see that it is not a long coat, but a bathrobe. "I thought you were shot."

She is pouring bubbly into milk glasses. "The cork went," she chuckles. "It just popped!"

I walk up behind her, reach around her waist, embrace her and whisper, "It ejaculated."

She shrugs me off, "Don't be silly now. I'm trying to pour."

As I lie in bed beside her, my clothes piled on the chair, waves of emotion flood over me: first night of a honeymoon, opening night of a new play, self-reproach at infidelity, yearning for intimacy, fear of being watched, conflict on stage between acting and being.

"Meatloaf and champagne," she is saying. "What a confection for affection."

The nightly rose lies beside the bedtable lamp. She picks it up and we both inhale its penetrating scent. She exchanges the rose for her champagne, lifts her glass and declaims, "A toast. To Johnny and Marianne."

I raise mine. "To Frankie and Alan." We clink, and I notice that I alone have taken a mouthful. "What's wrong? Drink up."

She lowers her glass to her lap, "I heard . . . It sounded like the thump of a theatre seat."

A loud shout filters through the darkness, "No! A toast to Yanne and me. It's curtain time for you two."

She leaps from the bed, the glass clattering to the floor, and turns off the table lamp. I grope for my clothes.

"It's him. It's Gord," she cries. "He's here."

We can follow his stumbling approach only by the direction of his hollering. I can find trousers but neither underpants nor shoes. Her clothes must be back stage for I hear her fight to locate the doorknob. Suddenly all is silence, broken only by the pounding of my heart, the overturning of a chair behind the scenery. Gord must be clambering up the front of the stage. He has only to follow Marianne's whimperings and groans. Sounds indicate she must be tripping over brace weights and prop tables.

I feel my way backstage through what the audience knows as the bathroom door and quietly slip through.

"Time to come home, Yanne," Gord shouts. "Let's not make this too god-damn hard."

He must have lit a cigarette lighter, for I see a flickering under the flats. Monstrous shadows begin to swirl and sway as he steps behind the sets. I can see her clutching her white robe around her, pressing herself against the back wall beside a cupboard. She has not been able to find her clothes.

I can't see him, but her gestures tell that she does. He trips over a brace. The sets wobble and his lighter goes out. "Damn you, you whore."

"I'll come, Gord. I'm coming," she cries.

"You're damn right you are. And never mind the clothes. If you can be on stage like that you can be like that in the car. Now get!"

"I'm coming," she whines. They lurch and trip past me, back onto the dim stage. "You're hurting. My arm. You'll break it."

Barefoot or not, naked from the waist up, I follow them up the side aisle. As he flings open the doors to the lobby, I finally get the courage to shout. "You heard her. She's going with you. No need to—"

He jerks towards me, thrusts her aside, leaps at me and grabs my neck. "You two are finished. You got that? Fuckin' finished! Understand?"

His throat grip prevents me from saying a word. Marianne struggles to separate us. He swings me backward, back against the display cabinets. I kick and punch until he smashes me into the glass and wedges my shoulder behind the window frame.

When he releases me, my heels slide on the blood-splashed fragments of glass. I feel myself lowering onto the remaining sharp broken panes.

I hear a woman shrieking. I hear a door slam.

I feel

I

Chapter Four

Either Theatre or Gallery:

The Gallery

CAST (in order of appearance):

Millicent Wray—Sales Clerk

Ron—Son of Alan and Ellen

Alan Thompson—Proprietor of a new Art Gallery

Red—the Enforcer

Louis Fondrake—Management and Security Agent

Ellen—Alan's Wife and Co-owner

ACT I

An art gallery that is barely established, few paintings, little stock on shelves. The main entrance is centre upstage. An easel displays a painting, a stepladder leans against a wall.

Millie—Could we delay the set-up of your new paintings, Mr. Thompson until after your meeting with Mr. Red?

Ron—I can give you a hand with the set-up, Miss Wray until the bus for our team leaves.

Alan—There will be no meeting with Mr. Red or with anyone, Millicent. From your remarks about him, he doesn't seem to be a buyer, and given our current cash flow problems, we can't buy from any more salesmen, not for the present time.

Millie—Sir, if you'll pardon my saying so, he was angry, quite angry when he returned that second time and you hadn't remained to meet him.

Alan—Well, if it's that urgent, remind him that I'm here six days a week from 10:00 till 2:00. His insistence on seeing me after hours is not at all convenient.

Millie—He is due any minute, Mr. Thompson, and I'd rather not have him confront me a third time. Actually, the man unnerves me.

Alan—Relax, Millicent. He's an overzealous artist who knows a new art gallery needs new stock. He'll be looking for a place to display his third rate paintings. Believe me, I found out the hard way that starving artists at times can be quite desperate.

Ron—[carrying in some stock: easels, frames, etc.] He didn't look like a starving artist to me, Dad. Dressed pretty classy, arrived in a big car.

Millie—He even had a driver. And besides, he kept saying it would be a shame to see a new art gallery close down before it really got going.

Alan—So why, Miss Wray, if the meeting is that imperative, why did you tell him to come on Wednesday night? I think you know I always pick up my wife at her aerobics class on Wednesdays.

Ron—She didn't. He just said he was coming Wednesday and for you to be here when the store closes.

Millie—It would be good for business, he said. So I found it-

Alan—Let's work out a compromise. I'll get Mrs. Thompson at 9:00 and bring her straight here by 9:20. She wanted to do the books anyway and order some supplies.

Ron—[arranging paintings on easels] I wish you'd stay, Dad, even for a few minutes.

Alan Well I can't and I won't. [turning towards Miss Wray] You handle him till I get back. It will be good experience for you.

Ron—You always say that every time you want me to do something that you don't want to do and that I don't either.

Alan—I wasn't speaking to you, Ron. As our new salesperson, Miss Wray will benefit by the experience. Look at the time! I'm getting the feeling you're both trying to [phone rings] keep me here till he comes. It's not going to work. I'm late already. You get it, Millicent. It's probably my wife. Tell her I'm on my way.

Millie—I would much rather ask [Al leaves] her if she wouldn't mind taking a taxi just this . . . Oh, damn! [angrily picks up the phone] Thompson Galleries—I mean [more gently this time] Good evening, Thompson . . . Yes. Mr. Red? No, he's stepped out for just a few minutes, but he'll . . . Well I did, but . . . Yes, I told him . . . I did repeat to him what you said about the success of the . . . No, sir, I was sure you said "success" . . . But even if I had told him "survival" he'd still have to pick up his wife who . . . He will be here, I can promise you that. However I am not his boss. I am simply . . . Hello? He hung up. He hung up on me.

Ron—I'm not surprised. He wants to talk to the boss.

Millie—So that was one experience that didn't work out very satisfactorily. Rule number 1: always let them think they're talking to the owner or at least the manager. Anyway, boss or no boss, he says he'll be right over to speak to your father. I hope you can hang around till he gets back with your mother. I don't want to face him alone.

Ron—Sure, I can stay. The bus doesn't leave the gym till 10:00. This guy is no starving artist, but I'll bet you a tube of cerulean blue that he'll be a supplier who's pushing his line. [mockingly] If you don't have my product on your shelves nobody will put a foot in your gallery. [Red enters, stops and stares at Ron's act] Word will get out and spread like water color on wet paper [he climbs onto a chair and declaims] that if you are not selling my irresistible line of paints or paper or easels or frames or—

Red—Am I butting in on a play or what?

Millie—Excuse me. Good evening Mr. Red.

Red—Forget the mister business. It's just "Red." [he looks around, assesses what he sees and finally approaches Ron, still on the chair] This better be Mr. Thompson.

Ron—I am Mr. Thompson junior. I believe you want to speak to my father.

Red—Where is he? He better be out back.

Millie—Mr. Thompson will be here momentarily. May I show you some of the gallery's latest acquisitions?

Red—I'm not buying, and by the looks of things, nobody else is either. This is my third time here and not much has moved, either in or out. Your shelves are still half empty and all those huge gawd-awful excuses for paintings in the front window are scaring away any buyers. That's my guess.

Ron—Well, guess again, Red. [stepping down from the chair and approaching Red.]

Millie—Ronald! That's no way to—

Ron—Those "gawd-awful excuses" as you call them happen to be my father's creations.

Red—Oh well, then—

Ron—It does take a mature, a sensitive eye to see their merit. Those are variations on a still life, and their colors contrast with—

Red—Look Junior, the only still life I'm interested in is your father. Now where is he? As the surgeon-general would say, his absence could be hazardous to the health of this gallery. [he leans against an easel. It falls over.]

Millie—Hey! Be careful—please. [she stoops and picks up the easel and its display]

Red—Here's a cellphone, Junior. Get your father on it. I want to talk with him. [Ron backs away. Red follows.]

Millie—He's in his car and there's no cellphone. Our business hasn't reached the level where he needs one. At least not yet, but we're growing.

Red—Are you now? That must be news for all of us.

Ron—It's not likely my father will be buying from you when he does get here. So if I may suggest—[Mr. Louis Fondrake enters. He is immaculately dressed, about 40 years old, grey hair.]

Red—Mr. Fondrake! He ain't here. Would you like me to . . . you know, at least . . .

Fond—Isn't this the third time, young lady? I had hoped the arrangements might be signed, sealed and delivered this evening [turning to Ron] Are you by any chance a joint owner of his . . . of this . . .

Red—Ha! Yah, a joint owner of this joint.

Fond—Thank you, Red. Will you walk around and take note of any hazardous areas. Perhaps the young man would show you the premises, the basement, fire exits, and so on.

Millie—Oh dear, and we haven't unpacked our fire extinguishers yet. You're Fire Prevention Officers, are you?

Red—That's rich. Fire Prevention Officers. Ha!

Fond—In a way we are exactly that Miss. You might say we are.

Ron—Sure, I'll show Red around, but only after my father returns.

Millie—In the meantime, if you'd care to set out those arrangements you wish Mr. Thompson to sign, I'm sure when he comes he'll be happy to study your proposals. Are you architects?

Fond—We've moved into a paperless world, Miss. The signing, sealing and delivering I referred to is only a manner of speaking. Red, we'll wait in our office outside. When Mr. Thompson returns, we'll be back. Dawdling under such inhospitable fluorescent lighting hurts my eyes.

Red—I'll look around the place on my own. I don't need Junior here to tell me where doors and windows and alarms are.

Fond—Come back to the limo with me now, Red.

Red—It won't take five minutes. I like to know what we're dealing with.

Ron—You better do what he says. I wouldn't want you to get lost or get in any trouble with your boss.

Red—You're the one who can get lost.

Fond—Red, Red, Red. No altercations please. Sorry Miss to have caused a scene. [looking at Ron] Entirely unnecessary. No need to inform us of Mr. Thompson's return. We'll be watching. Thank you. [to Red] Out! [they exit]

Ron—I hope Dad gets back soon.

Millie—He said he'd be here by 9:20. You'll stay won't you?

Ron—Of course. I've got thirty minutes before I have to be there. Those guys scare me too. But our overnight bus does leave at 10:00. The tournament begins at nine tomorrow. I hate to leave you and Dad alone with these guys.

Millie—You won't need to worry. Your father will be able to handle them. He's dealt with some pretty daunting challenges getting the gallery this far—fighting zoning laws, wrestling with the rental firm, starting a new business.

Ron—True, and I really admire him for taking this gamble. There's a whole lot more than I ever imagined to opening up an art store.

Millie—Gallery, Ron, gallery. Your father does not like to call it a store. I'm sure glad he took that gamble. It gave me a job. I've been anxious about what good all my fine-arts studies were going to do me since I graduated. It has been three whole years, you know.

Ron—And for twenty years he was a house husband. Now he's back to his first love.

Millie—While we're waiting, let's get started on setting up these new paintings of your father's.

Ron—Yeah, more "gawd-awful excuses." If Dad can't handle those guys, we'll turn mother loose on them. Then they'll beat a hasty retreat when they have to deal with her.

Millie—Mrs. Thompson wants those two large canvases taken out of the front widow, Ron. "People have looked at them long enough," she says. "If they're hesitant to buy a painting, they won't start with a huge one, one that's probably not within their budget." [Alan and Ellen enter a side door.]

Ron—I'll set out some of these—

Ellen—Those big paintings are still in the display window, Millicent. I thought I told you to take them out yesterday. They're still there.

Alan—So he didn't come after all.

Ron—Oh yes they did, and they weren't happy.

Alan—They?

Ellen—Ron, give me a hand with these big ones.

Millie—Yes, Red and another man—well dressed. They're waiting outside right now.

Ron—Yeah, in their mobile office, their limo.

Ellen—Do I have to move these by myself?

Alan—Just hold it a minute, will you, Ellen? You're not in that aerobics class now. Sit down till we find out about those two men.

Ellen—Well, while you two are talking—There, I've told you, a big car has just pulled up outside—

Ron—It's been parked there since 9:00 o'clock, Mother.

Ellen—and two very well dressed men are heading towards the store.

Alan—The gallery, Ellen, the gallery.

Ron—Only one well dressed man, Mother.

Ellen—You can at least count, can't you? Or do I have to do that by myself too? [Fondrake and Red enter. Ellen unctuously] Good evening, gentlemen. How may I help you?

Red—By getting' outa the way.

Ellen—I beg your pardon.

Fond—Please excuse him, ma'am. Red was born to be a boxer. He thinks the most convincing way for people to communicate is with their fists. My apologies. Ah, Mr. Thompson, at last we meet. Fondrake, Louis Fondrake.

Ellen—And I am Mrs. Thompson.

Fond—I've been wanting to meet you for some time now.

Ellen—Well thank you. [Fondrake gives her a slow burn and turns his eager gaze at Al.]

Alan—So my assistant, Miss Wray, has been telling me.

Fond—You have some interesting art creations here, very unusual, and most are your own works?

Red—Unusual? What's so unusual about garbage?

Fond—Red, will you return to our office. Leave the phone with me. If you observe anything I should be informed about, just call from the car. No need to come in yourself. I think there's wrestling on channel 17. No boxing, unfortunately.

Alan—May we show you some of our most recent works?

Ron—Excuse me, Mr. Fondrake. Dad, I was hoping you could drive me to the gym. Our overnight bus leaves in 20 minutes. [to Fondrake] We've got a basketball tournament in Albany, Mr. Fondrake. But I know you'll be busy for a few minutes.

Ellen—It's after closing time, Ron. Your father can take you.

Fond—I would prefer that he remain, Mrs. Thompson. Let's say the prosperity of the gallery rather depends on our meeting tonight.

Alan—Ellen, would you drive him? The team counts on him being on that bus.

Ellen—I've got taxi money in my purse. You'll have to call a cab.

Fond—Permit me, Ron. I have a phone in my hand and with speed dialling it's faster than you can say—see—Yes, a car to 348 Westlake Drive. No, a store, a new art gallery, one passenger. Thank you. A kind of priority line, you might say.

Ellen—Well, you certainly know how things get done. We can all take a lesson from you, can't we Alan?

Alan—Now, what is this urgent business you have, Mr. Fondrake?

Fond—Oh, call me Louis, please. I want our relationship to be long and cordial. And if this is one of the new style galleries—or a delightful old style—I suspect you serve tea or coffee to prospective . . .

Ellen—Of course. What, then, will you have Mr. Fondrake?

Fond—A herbal tea would suit me perfectly, thanks.

Alan—Perhaps you would make some herbal tea for all of us, Ellen?

Ellen—[addressing Millie] A large pot of herbal tea, Millicent for Louis, myself and Mr. Thompson.

Millie—Certainly, ma'am.

Fond—And Mrs. Thompson, you certainly know how to get things done, too, I see.

Ron—[picks up his gym bag, gives his mother a kiss] So long everybody. Wish me luck. [they wave and offer encouraging words. He exits by the front door.]

Fond—You have a fine boy there, Mr. and Mrs. Thompson. You must be very proud of him. [his cellphone rings] Excuse me, please. No, it's all right, Red. I called a car for the boy. He's on his way out now. Yes . . . just Mr.

and Mrs. Thompson and the young lady. About fifteen minutes I should think. Oh, and Red, if the results of the pizza enquiry come in, give me a call immediately. [to Alan and Ellen] Now! I've been following the progress of your gallery, Mr. and Mrs. Thompson, and I am somewhat disappointed that sales have not been brisk. As a matter of fact, they haven't even been slow.

Ellen—But how does that concern you?

Fond—All too quickly, Mrs. Thompson, all too quickly—

Ellen—Please. Call me Ellen, if you would.

Fond—Certainly. [while wandering about the gallery admiring paintings and examining articles on shelves] All too quickly, Ellen, new galleries close down for a variety of reasons, like inadequate advertising, bad management, unsuitable location, insufficient stock, faulty burglar alarms—

Ellen—Reluctance to renew window displays.

Alan—I fail to see how or why our prospects should be any of your business.

Fond—Ah, but that is my business. That is precisely my line of business. You've hit the nail right on the thumb, so to speak. Helping others increase their profit margin, by directing customers to you, by insuring the safety of your property. That is my, well, call it my vocation. But above all, I have a soft spot in my heart for good art. I've managed to accumulate some fine pieces: a Ruault, a Vincennes, several Dufys, plus some sculpture.

Alan—Are you proposing that I sell or display some of your holdings, Mr. Fondrake? Surely an art auction would bring you much more that I could. You mentioned inadequate advertisement a moment ago. Well, we simply cannot afford any advertising at all.

Fond—I know, I know that, all too well. No, I propose to offer you our managerial service.

Alan—Offer your what?

Fond—Our managerial service, Mr. Thompson. May I call you Alan?

Ellen—And what do your managerial services include?

Fond—Primarily advertising, management, accounting and security.

Alan—By management do you mean that you would select the art?

Fond—Not at all. Your tastes in art will be rigorously affirmed. We will simply look after timely displays, organize openings, artists' showings, bring in well-known citizens to be photographed in your gallery. We're not amateurs, Mr. Thompson. Some would point out that we have quite an impressive record. [He hands both Alan and Ellen his business card.]

Ellen—And how much would this cost, Louis?

Fond—Our opening price is 35% of the profits.

Ellen—Very amusing. And what is 35% of zero?

Fond—But Ellen, it wouldn't remain at zero, I can assure you of that.

Alan—And I suspect it wouldn't remain at 35% either.

Fond—That's negotiable. As your profits mount, that would be negotiable.

Alan—We would need some references, a resume of experience in the art world, some acquaintance with your accounting methods. We already have an alarm system. And my wife and I would need to talk this over. When do you want an answer?

Fond—I will make this easy for you. I am going to assume, Alan, that your answer is "yes." You will find that this is an offer you can't possibly turn down, a real win-win proposition. Gentlemen's agreement. We'll begin next week. You will be more than satisfied with the ad that will appear in this Saturday's newspaper. It has been photo ready for a week. If you're not satisfied, just let me know. I'll have Red drop by from time to time for any feedback.

Alan—This is a little too swift for us, Mr. Fondrake.

Ellen—Maybe for you, dear, but Louis does seem to know how to make things happen.

Fond—Just inform me if your answer is no. Until then, it's yes. You won't want to say no, Alan, when you both see how effectively we work. Now, I must be on my way. I don't like to stand still. Follow the profit graph upward, is my motto, Ellen. [Millicent enters carrying a tray and stands amazed to see Mr. Fondrake leaving. He shakes hands with Mr. Thompson.] Gentlemen's agreement, Alan. [then bows to Mrs. Thompson], Ellen.

Alan—But before you go . . . Mr. Fondrake!

Ellen—Louis, could we . . . [Fondrake exits.]

Millie—Did I miss something?

Alan—I think you did. I think we all did.

CURTAIN

Act II (Six months later)

[CD music, Schubert's E♭ Major Piano Trio. Paintings have been taken down. A stepladder is against a wall.]

Millie—Well, that's the last of the cleanup, Mrs. Thompson.

Ellen—The visitors' book still hasn't been examined, has it, Millicent? I want everyone who left name and address to receive an advance announcement of our next artists' showing.

Ron—Our next one? Good heavens! Our next showing? We've hardly finished this one and Dad is already talking about another?

Ellen—Not your father, Ron. Louis. Louis wants Thompson Galleries to have a higher profile. And you know as well as I do it's high time we did.

Millie—Like the last one, this was a good experience for me. And I thought the music in the background was a nice touch this time.

Ron—A touch of class. That piece has been repeated so often that I'm beginning to like it.

Ellen—And we've heard enough of it, too. You can shut that thing off now. That one part where they all leap in as loud as they can makes me jump every single time. Turn it off before they do it again.

Ron—But Schubert is Dad's favourite. And it is music while you work.

Ellen—Have you noticed your father is not here to listen to it, or to work to it either? If you want music to work to, get some march music or some Strauss polkas. [Miss Wray turns off the music.] Thank God. What a relief. And there! I've worked out the balance sheet. Thanks to Louis, we have brought in over $12,000. Didn't I tell you he knew how to get things done! Your father could never have organized such a successful showing, not even with a year's lead time.

Ron—But it sure cost us all a lot. I just hope Dad thinks it was worth it.

Ellen—Of course it was worth it whether he thinks so or not. What are you talking about? What cost? Yes, I know, I know. Louis upped his fee, but his 45% of $12,000 is still a lot better than our 100% of nothing. It certainly was worth it.

Ron—Dad was as mad as hell that nobody told him about the fee increase. The percentage ought to be in some kind of contract. Yes, don't tell me again, "Louis wants us to catch up with the paperless age, and Gentlemen's Agreement." What a load of crap.

Ellen—Do not use such language in an art gallery. Anyway, it worked out to everyone's benefit in the long run.

Ron—But there were other costs, and they're hard to put a dollar figure to.

Ellen—Just as there were other benefits hard to cost out, too. Like all the publicity—our pictures in the arts and fashion pages, the folks that now know we exist and what we sell besides paintings.

Ron—No, I mean the cost in terms of overtime. Just think of how many hours Miss Wray had to put in here for the last three weeks. Did she get any extra pay, or did I?

Millie—I didn't mind the overtime, Ron. Actually, I rather enjoyed it. Your father would point out that it's good experience.

Ron—But that cruise with your friends. You had to postpone it. That was a loss for you.

Ellen—Only postpone, Ron, not cancel.

Millie—You're the one who lost out on basketball.

Ellen—We gave him time off for every single game. He didn't miss one. Now you just tell her that yourself.

Ron—It wasn't because of the games, Mom. I've told you I had to miss too many practices.

Ellen—Then it's too bad you didn't ask Louis to rearrange your practice schedule. He has a way of getting little things like that done. Pick up a phone. Call the right people, and presto!

Ron—That's something you could have done.

Ellen—Now just what is that supposed to mean?

Ron—Well, it's just that you've been spending a lot of time planning and prioritizing in that office of his. If you thought he could have . . . Oh, forget it. It's over now.

Millie—Mrs. Thompson, I've taken out all the boxes and put the empty wine bottles out in the recycling bin.

Ellen—But have you collected all the glasses and washed them yet?

Millie—The rental company will do the washing, Mrs. Thompson. But I still have to box them. Oh, look. A visit by Red I suspect. The limo is pulling up in front.

Ellen—No, that will be Louis. He wants the final figures on the sales.

Ron—I thought you gave them to him yesterday.

Millie—They weren't complete, Ron. We had to be sure the money for the large seascape would come in.

Ellen—So, our final total is $12,500 profit. And 55% of it is ours! Hand these figures to Mr. Thompson when he comes in, Millicent. Pretty good for one weekend. Louis will be pleased.

Ron—Why don't you let me take him the good news? [Ellen hurries out the front door.] Or, better still, why don't you phone him? Or why not let Millicent get in his comfy mobile cocktail and T.V. lounge? Have you seen that mobile office of theirs? [Phone rings] I thought we were supposed to be closed.

Millie—Good evening, Thompson Galleries. Millicent . . . Oh, Red. Are you out there in the office? Doesn't Mrs. Thompson know? Just a minute. He left me a note on my desk somewhere. And while I think of it, I better warn you, though. Mr. Thompson is not at all happy about the surprise fee increase. Yes, here it is. 9:30. That's ten minutes ago. He should have been back by now. Certainly . . . it won't be a long wait, I can assure you. But not in here, if you please, Red. Mr. Thompson permits smoking only during artists' showings and at no other time. See you in . . . . [She glares, then slams down the phone.]

Ron—What?

Millie—You would think such a civilized man as Mr. Fondrake would give Red a few lessons on telephone etiquette.

Ron—What did he do this time, whisper something tantalizingly salacious in your little pink ear? [Alan enters side door]

Millie—No, worse than that. The man is simply a boor. He's unmannerly, uncouth, ignorant, and rude. Besides—

Alan—Not describing me, I hope. You have to be talking about Red. He's stepped on your toes, I gather. He has kicked me in the shins just once too often. If he's coming over to collect his percentage, he better wear some shin guards. I'm sticking with the 35%.

Millie—That was the gentlemen's agreement. Here are the figures for the showing. Your wife just completed the calculations.

Ron—Unfortunately, Dad, Red ain't no gennamin. Better get your kicker ready, he's already out in front, smoking.

Millie—Mr. Fondrake won't let him smoke in his limo—

Alan—And I will not let him smoke in here. Hmmm, $12,500 profit. Not bad anyway. Look, I've got two minutes grace. Maybe I can sneak out the side door. Tell him to come some other time for his cut. I want a word with Mr. Fondrake, not with his lackey.

Millie—Then he'd really be fighting mad at me. He'll know you've come in. He seems to fall over easels and rearrange displays when he can't get his way. If you are leaving, I'm clearing out too.

Alan—No, don't worry, Millicent. I'm staying. This is as good a time as any to have it out with him. Where's Ellen just when I need a back-up line of defence?

Ron—She may not give you much support on this one, Dad. She says 45% of profits for Louis is better than 100% of loss for you.

Alan—But where is she?

Ron—Out in front in the mobile office with "wonderful Louis."

Millie—Was out in front. The limo is just pulling away now and Mr. Fondrake is shouting something at Red. He's stubbing his cigarette out on his shoe. My, Mr. Fondrake must have taken a strip off him, he doesn't look at all happy.

Alan—That makes two of us.

Ron—I count four. Three of us here against one gives us a fighting chance. [Red enters.]

Millie—Good afternoon, Red.

Red—Five thousand, six hundred and twenty-five, cash only.

Alan—What !

Red—Don't act like you haven't figured it out yourself. Mr. Fondrake told you how I communicate. And you can communicate with the cash. Let your money do the talking, Al. You did it nicely after your first showing a few months ago.

Alan—Hold it right there, Red. Just hold it. My calculations come out at $4,375. That's according to our agreement.

Red—What agreement? Show me where there's anything written down about 35%. That might have been Mr. Fondrake's starting fee, but that was six months ago.

Ron—And next year it'll be 65%.

Red—If Mr. Fondrake wants it that way, that's the way it'll be. In the mean time, Junior, you can butt out. And my instructions are for you, Al, to pay out or—[he pulls some paintings onto the floor.] Oh, say, I'm sorry. "Clumsy Red," Mr. Fondrake calls me. Just a bull in a art shop, me.

Millie—Now get over here and away from those. They've not dried yet. You'll get yourself covered with oils.

Red—These? They're not wet. Look. Oh, yes they are. And this one too.

Alan / Millie / Ron—Look out what you're doing / Be careful with those / Hey, watch it. Those are valuable.

Red—OK. OK, OK. I knew you'd get the message.

Alan—Take that phone out of your pocket and get Mr. Fondrake. I want to talk to the boss right now.

Red—You are talking to him right now. I'm his deputy. Talk to Red and you're talking to Mr. Fondrake. Besides, his motto is, Pleasure before business, and you wouldn't want to interrupt him right now.

Alan—I don't care what he's doing. Get him on the phone and tell him to turn right around. He hasn't gone that far.

Red—Oh, you're making a big mistake, a great big mistake. If he comes in here, he'll want to see that I've—ah—done my best to convince you. But it's your funeral. [He pulls out cellphone, presses speed dial button] Presto! Mr. Fondrake? There seems to be a Code 13 here at the art store. Great! Sure, I'll get right on it. He'll be agreeable, I'm sure. [closes phone] The boss'll be right over.

Alan—Good, now we're getting somewhere.

Red—I was admiring these latest works of fart. [he punches one]

Ron—Airhead! Idiot! You couldn't make it in the boxing ring, could you, Red? Were you a poor loser or just a—

Red—I don't lose fights.

Alan—This is one you're going to lose, both you and your boss. Get out of here, now!

Red—OK, OK, OK, I'm getting out, and taking you with me, this way. [Red clutches Alan's arm and begins to drag him to the front door. Ron attempts to tackle Red, gets kicked and thrown down. He collapses, unconscious. Millicent runs for the phone. Red rips it from the wall. Alan stops Red from preventing Millicent from running out the side door, then attempts to run out after her.]

Red—I said this way! [Red grabs Alan, puts a quick hammer hold on him, pulls him to the front display window and hurls him through it. He calls out to Alan] You should be more careful when you're setting up your displays. [He puts on gloves, and moves the ladder to the window, pushes it through the broken window, then runs out the side door.]

[After a time of silence]

Ron—[Still on the floor] Ow! My head. Dad, I'm bleeding. There's blood all over me. Dad? [He sits up and holds his head] Dad? Millicent? [struggles to get to his feet] Good God! What the hell . . . ? [staggers to the window] Dad! [limps out the front door. Voices offstage] Mom! It's Dad. He's hurt.

Ellen—[offstage] Oh, Louis, bring him in where there's light.

Fond—[offstage] Grab his feet. Easy now.

Ron—[offstage] Wait—he's too heavy. OK, I've got him. [They enter centre upstage carrying Alan, followed by Ellen.]

Ellen—He's done it, Louis. Red has done it. There's blood all over him. He's killed him. Can you get any pulse? No, open his collar . . . his neck . . . Can you feel any? He's killed him.

Fond—We can't be sure.

Ellen—That there's a pulse?

Fond—No, that Red did this. Looks to me like he fell off the ladder, right through the window.

Ellen—Call an ambulance, somebody. God! So much blood! He's . . . he's . . . oh, Louis! CURTAIN

Chapter Five

Either Ellen or Lois:

Lois

Ellen stands at the kitchen window of her residence apartment. She is aimlessly looking out at the university students returning from classes and throwing snowballs. She turns her attention to the flurries swirling out of the streetlights and disappearing into the blackness. She can't help watching Alan's reflection as he sits pensive, hugging his mug of coffee.

As January of their final term drags its slow, cold length along, his impassioned fling with Ellen is losing its warmth. Simultaneously she becomes more and more conscious of and impatient with his inability to make decisions. "Why not move in with me? Give me one good reason," she pleads. "just one! My place is too big for me, and good God, you're still living with your mommy and daddy. There's even a vacant room down the hall that we could rent for you to paint in."

You had to hand it to Ellen. She had an impressive awareness of rhythm. She demonstrates this by tapping the kitchen table to emphasize the iambic force of her demand, "For heaven's sake, why won't you move in here! Oh, God, unrut yourself at least this once."

Alan's stage experience enables him to recognize the rhythm instinctively. Pentameter. She'd make a good Lady Macbeth.

As he doesn't respond immediately, she nails her argument with two heavy beats, knocking her knuckle on the table top and charging, "Why Not?" Alan hears echoes of Lady Macbeth's "We Fail."

"Well, why not?" she repeats.

Alan is cursed with the ability to see both sides of any argument with equal clarity. Her "why not?" unavoidably arouses his "why?" and the pendulum she flings in motion swings back and forth: "Why not? . . . Why? . . . Yes, why not? . . . Why? . . . Move in with her? . . . Stay where I am? . . . Now? . . . Later? . . ."

He can easily see merit in her proposition, but can't bring himself to agree. "Let's think about it?" is about as much as he can risk, all the while reflecting that such a move for so short a final term hardly makes sense. "Anyway, it's late, almost two a.m." Unthinking, he adds, "Besides, it shuts the door on other alternatives."

"Other alternatives? What other alternatives?"

Alan, not aware of which part of himself holds the answer, can't say. One submerged part of him is thinking of Lois, her wide-eyed shock the evening he told her not to wait any longer for him. He will ask his best friend, Roger, about moving in or not. He needs help to choose the better path.

Because of their daughter's ecstatic praise of Alan during the Christmas vacation, Ellen's parents, the Orgles, began the drive down from North Bay to meet him.

"Sounds like Ellen's really found her man this time," Mr. Orgle said expansively to his wife as he snapped his seat belt into place and they headed off to a new chapter in their family life.

"But he's an artist, Arne, an artist!" Mrs. Orgle hoped that the word might convey to her husband all of the impecuniousness and insignificance that she pictured. Images of an unheated garret and mittened hands clutching a cup of tepid tea flitted across her mind.

"He'll never have much money. Not much at all. After the way we brought up our daughter, do you think she'll be content with the kind of life a struggling artist might provide? Do you?"

Mrs. Orgle never tired of tagging onto the end of all her questions and accusations a final phrase that was intended to hammer her opinions home. "Well, do you, Arne?"

"We can help them with that, Ilse. We can set him up here in town, and besides, Ellen is determined to be a teacher. With their double income, things will work out. Don't you worry." He settled into the pre-heated leather seat of his luxury car and divided his attention between navigating the snow-covered highway and fantasizing about assisting a new son-in-law. "Anyway, we can always find something at the plant if his painting doesn't work out."

"And the sooner the better," she said to the frosted window beside her. "An artist!"

Since Mr. Orgle needed to concentrate fully on driving along the icy highway, he tuned out his wife who mumbled imprecations which only further steamed up the windows. Through the veil of fine sleet, a flashing blue light warned that an oncoming snowplough was spreading salt and sand. That meant sprays of brown sludge would be thrown onto the windshield by passing cars.

Whenever a slow vehicle loomed ahead, appearing to be backing up due to their own speed, Mrs. Orgle would thrust a protective hand onto the dashboard, let out a gasp and stab her right foot onto an imaginary break pedal.

"I see him, Ilse. I see him. Everything's under control," which was exactly where he, mistakenly, thought he kept everything.

"I don't know about you, dear, but I want to arrive in Toronto in one piece. We've got all day. They won't be expecting us till this evening. They've both got late afternoon classes. So what's the hurry?"

By the time they arrived at the International Hotel, set up court and greeted their daughter with hugs and kisses, Ellen was already beset by doubts. Her father, the personnel manager of a chemical plant, considered himself an expert in assessing potential employees—and potential sons-in-law. Alan was not the first.

In the heavily carpeted and draped lounge each of them sank into a luxurious leather armchair. The aspidistra that separated Arne from his wife and daughter drooped in despair from excessive draughts of rejected drinks, some "far too sweet. Don't they know how to make a decent Manhattan?" Others, "much too dry for my taste, gawd!"

Mr. Orgle drummed impatiently on the puffy leather. His wife arranged the pleats of her full dress for, after much deliberation, she finally decided to remain seated to greet the young artist. She folded her hands and dropped them into her lap hoping her comment would sound emphatic without revealing hostility. "You did say he was coming today," she asked in her favourite non-interrogative way.

Ellen raised her eyes and studied the chandelier that sparkled above them, then turned sharply towards her father who was extracting an aggressive looking cigar from his inside pocket and was preparing to bite off an end. "Not here!" she cried.

Her mother came to his rescue, "But he always looks so . . . so debonair when he smokes."

Her father smiled self-deprecatingly, "First impressions, my girl. First impressions."

Ellen's open mouth and dropping shoulders drew eloquent attention to her sigh. She turned and re-examined the chandelier and thought, This is going to be one bugger of a disaster.

Her fantasizing was interrupted by the sudden appearance of a crisply uniformed hotel serf who with great obsequiousness regretted to announce that Toronto's most unfortunate city bylaw rendered the innocent enjoyment of such a delectable cigar—of all things!—an illegal act. His apologies might have gone on much longer if Ellen and Mr. Orgle had not leapt to their feet on seeing her future fiancé cautiously allowing the doorman to welcome him into the lobby. The bellboy, having delivered the manager's ultimatum, backed away, fearing a confrontation.

The reluctant fiancé entered hesitantly, stopped, then headed towards the reception desk when he spotted Ellen and her parents in the cocktail lounge. Several competing scenarios immediately presented themselves: to greet the parents first, then turn to give Ellen what would be a self-conscious embrace, or to give her an enthusiastic kiss that demonstrated to everyone his intentions, and let her introduce him to Mom and Dad.

While he weighed alternatives (and even a few alternative alternatives), Ellen waved, called and ran excitedly towards him. Mr. Orgle strode across the foyer, his hand extended. My, but they are big people, Alan thought. He brushed melting snow out of his short, bristling hair, before he realized her father was about to shake his dripping hand.

"My daughter tells me you're an accomplished painter," he beamed as he felt for the firmness of Alan's handshake. Was Alan's denial evidence of humility or simply social awkwardness, he wondered. "My wife," he said leading him back to the woman enthroned in her inflated armchair. She lifted her hand graciously and almost sang, "How wonderful to meet a real artist. Well, go on, give Ellen a great big kiss. She's been impatient for your arrival. Haven't you just, my dear?"

After greeting her potential son-in-law, Mrs. Orgle opened her purse, ostentatiously extracted a folded handkerchief, fluttered it open, and frowning, wiped dry her moist right hand. Alan thought he read her downturned mouth saying "artist."

"I think we could set you up with a one-man show somewhere, certainly in North Bay, and probably in a prominent Toronto gallery," said Mr. Orgle, taking what he hoped would be control.

"Oh, I don't know, Mr. Orgle. Perhaps I should build up a larger portfolio," Alan countered. "The scope of my work is a little . . . a little limited at present."

Ellen's mother sensed a flaw either in her daughter's testimony about his "prolific productions" or in his own self assurance. Taking pains to make her action and its implications evident, Mrs. Orgle tucked her handkerchief in her spangled purse. "But my daughter has been telling us you have scores of first-rate paintings. Just dozens and dozens." Then she drove in the inevitable nail, "At least, so she says."

Alan was hoping her parents would not discover that it was their darling daughter who figured in most of them.

"A larger portfolio? Nonsense!" her father declared. In what sounded more like a command than an invitation, he boomed, "Sit down over here." He gestured towards a rectangle of leather armchairs designed to withstand just the kind of melting snow that was beginning to stream off the shoulders of Alan's long black coat. "If your other paintings are as good as the one you gave her for Christmas, you'll find a ready market. And price them high, my boy. Price them high."

Mrs. Orgle nodded knowingly as if her husband was repeating what she had instructed him to say. And to confirm that possibility, she added, "Let the people know what you're really worth," which, for Ellen's sake, she hoped would be a considerable amount.

Afraid of losing the mantle of authority, Mr. Orgle added, "A one-man show will win you the recognition you deserve."

Alan squirmed in his chair and struggled to find an out. It came to him ready made. He was good at fabricating reasons for not taking action. "Maybe by next year I'll be better known and can approach some of the smaller galleries along Mount Pleasant Avenue."

Moving forward on his chair and speaking quietly as if he had a hot tip for the races, Mr. Orgle said, "I've got a contact up Yonge Street, in the classier section. I'd like to move on this." He paused and assumed, corporate actor that he was, that his offer deserved an immediate response, or at least an acknowledgment, however tentative, that he had been heard. On receiving neither, he leaned forward, his eyes probing at first for signs of interest, then, after a moment, for signs of life. "Alan, I'm willing to move on this now."

It was the word "now" that assaulted Alan. Ellen, no longer able to conceal her anxieties about his indecisiveness, cast hurried looks of puzzlement from father to mother and back. Running his thumb along a leather seam on the cushion of his chair, the prospective son-in-law collected the courage to suggest, "Well, may I take a couple of weeks to think it over?"

Mrs. Orgle's eyes locked onto her husband's, and with a tone that suggested she was explaining something self-evident to an idiot, she turned and addressed the chandelier, "He would like a couple of weeks to apprehend the obvious. A couple of weeks."

Back in their hotel bedroom after a subdued dinner, the personnel manager catalogued what he regarded as significant defects in Alan's character. A few well placed criticisms of his apparent lack of gumption—or was it "his incompetence," Mrs. Orgle charged—further dimmed Ellen's admiration of him.

"No, Dad, it's just that he . . . just that . . ."

"It's just what, Ellen?" her mother wanted to know. "Was he nervous meeting potential in-laws? I think your artist friend has some serious weaknesses that would, in the end, sink your marriage. We're not telling you what or what not to do, it's your life. But you had better think about that." She pursed her lips, and with a squint and a nod of the head reiterated, "Serious weaknesses."

"No, Mom, it's just that, well, he's been carrying a heavy load lately, Christmas exams, several commissions to be done as birthday gifts. I heard a former girlfriend left him. And he's trying out for the university's spring play. Anyway, he'll go along with what I suggest about gallery showings." She sounded more positive than she actually was, hoping to convince herself that her parents were misreading Alan.

Her father's habitual way of indicating disapproval was to place a curved index finger over his upper lip and his thumb under his chin. This time he added a slow shaking of his head as he said, "No, Elle, I've met his type frequently before." His hand moved swiftly, palm down onto the table for emphasis, and leaning slightly forward he said, "He'll never go anywhere without being pushed, and I'm afraid you'll soon tire of pushing."

Her mother placed a firm hand over hers, gave it a squeeze and said, "Your father's right. From the very first moment, I sensed that Alan wouldn't be able to provide the kind of life we have brought you up to expect." In a gesture that implied insider knowledge, she patted Ellen's hand, "Not at all."

Ellen had observed that when he was working with the text of a play where the actions were explicitly scripted, he was confident and unhesitating. And he was swift, deliberate, decisive when he held a paint brush. But not even to be able to choose whether to order Chinese or Italian at their favourite restaurants, or to select this or that movie had eventually cooled "the Ellen and Alan Show" as Roger had dubbed it.

The less than enthusiastic opinions of father and the more than unfavourable assessment of mother resulted in their return home the very next day "because the weather bureau predicted a blizzard later this week. Tell him we just couldn't risk a snow-covered highway."

They had planned to regale their future son-in-law, introduce him at lunch to their member of legislature, visit some of the higher class art galleries, one owner of which had been in Arne's grade seven class in elementary school. Without the imprimatur of Mrs. Orgle, the Ellen and Alan show was cancelled before opening night.

Later that week, over their cooling cappuccinos at a Bloor Street coffee house, the decoupling pair sat glumly, neither one wishing to put the inevitable into words. Their mood contrasted dramatically with that of the other students who were pouring into the café, stomping brown snow off their boots, laughing and shivering as they wiped their steam-coated glasses. Loud music began to heat up the growing crowd rendering intimate confidences impossible.

Alan finally raised his eyes from the spoon that he had been twiddling, looked her in the eye and smiled wanly. He remembered how they had met at a dance less than two months ago when the band was almost as deafening. This time, with a voice barely loud enough to compete with the din of the music, he said, "Hi, I'm Alan." And she responded with an equally tired smile, "Yes, Ellen."

She knew he could not bring himself to say more, or to rise, give her a much needed kiss and say "goodbye;" so she gathered her gloves and scarf, rose, gave him a peck on the cheek and a wave over her shoulder as she walked out. He could at least bring himself to pay for the cappuccinos.

A slow drizzle warned of the coming annual mid-winter thaw. The worst would be for the droplets to freeze stealthily on branches, on power and telephone lines, transforming the mundane into a fairy land of glass trees and sparkling, drooping wires. If the drizzle continued, the black night would resound with the cracks of snapping branches which would strain or break heavily coated lines and poles. I know the feeling, he thought.

As Alan left the coffee house, he was so preoccupied with his turbulent interior world that he didn't notice that the weather, too, had changed direction. Heavy rain began flushing the slush of dirty snow towards blocked drains. Puddles exploded as cars sped by, spraying umbrella toting pedestrians who managed to remain dry from the waist up.

Soaked to the skin, Alan reached his room, undressed and thawed out under a hot shower. He wanted to sublimate his emotions onto canvas, but he also wanted to phone Roger concerning the split from Ellen. While waiting for the strength to decide, he collapsed onto his bed and turned on music that would mirror his mood. For consolation he scanned his collection of CDs for the one piece of music that would calm him down. He set his player on repeat at the second movement of Schubert's E^b major piano trio. Its slow, pulsing beat, and the mournful 'cello theme echoed by a pensive piano expressed his emptiness perfectly.

Sleep gradually eliminated the need to choose whether to paint or telephone. Two hours later, he was awakened by a combined piano, violin and 'cello fortissimo. He grabbed the remote control, released the repeat, and immediately the third movement waltzed, pirouetted, floated and finally shone about his room. He listened in amazement, his wide eyes roving to avoid looking at anything in particular. He was listening as much with his eyes as his ears. Instinctively he knew: there could be a whole different life, even without Ellen!

It was a matter of urgency that Roger move swiftly to reintroduce Lois into Alan's world. The urgency was compounded by Roger's scholarship to the London School of Journalism. He would be leaving as early as that summer.

Catalyst Roger was eloquent and persuasive. Even when he wasn't speaking he appeared convincing, with his frank penetrating gaze, his aquiline nose, high cheekbones and prominent chin. When he rested his elbow on a table, slowly lowered his pointing digit to aim directly at his target and tipped his head down as if to sight along his index finger, you knew his words would be as efficacious as his gesture.

"I have hinted, Alan, I have suggested, Alan, and now I urge you not to abandon Lois." He had not raised his voice; he did not need to. After his measured, understated admonition, he allowed the ensuing silence to confirm his charge. Slowly he permitted his finger to relax, and, elbow still on the table, eyes still fixed on target, he rested his chin on the back of his hand and gazed expectantly.

Alan was wishing his best friend would propound arguments, reasons for restoring Lois to her orbit. Those he might be able to rebuff, but this silence trapped him. How do you argue with a solemn, silent gaze, especially when you know the accuser is right?

Roger was equally successful when he addressed Lois, although his approach this time was marked by compassion rather than accusation. No targeting finger, no lowering of the eyes. After a pause she expressed her only objection in two words, "But Ellen?"

"He can't make up his mind, Lois. The reason for his indecisiveness about her is you. He told me that when he closes his eyes with Ellen it's you he sees, you he wants to be with."

Lois turned her head abruptly as she contemplated the scene. She really did not want to picture what Roger had mentioned, nor did Roger want her thoughts to be arrested, frozen on a mental snapshot. "It's you he wants to be near, to be talking with, but he doesn't know how to undo the awful damage of . . ." His voice trailed off as he realized there was no need to complete his sentence; he saw her comprehension leaping ahead.

By encouraging first Alan, then Lois, over several days, an early February encounter transformed both of them. Their reconciliation did more than restore them; it recreated them and set them on a path that could lead them into a wished-for future that they would want to claim finally as "theirs." For too many weeks both of them had been wandering aimlessly, their previous zest for life diminishing daily, Alan being swept along by Ellen's enthusiasms, Lois, overwhelmed by rejection. He had been missing her philosophical bent, her delight in debate, and she felt deprived of his creative skills on stage and on canvas. By the time catalyst Roger was preparing to leave for England, they were preparing for a life together whether they graduated or not.

Alan's initial chagrin at not being selected to play the leading role in the Hart House production of *Death of a Salesman* gave way to delight in being able to spend that much more time with Lois. They both had to remind each other not to slacken in their studies for their majors threatened to become intrusive. They would have preferred to major in Relationships 302 or, better, Passion 724.

How unfortunate that Roger was unable to harvest the gratitude they both felt for him. Email across the pond could not begin to convey to him their increasing delight in each other. Their only sorrow was his inability to extricate himself from his overseas university responsibilities to attend their September wedding.

As their wedding rehearsal party at the Century Hotel was winding down, his parents seemed eager to propose something to him. I'd like Lois to be in on this, Ray," Mrs. Thompson whispered to her husband. "You know what Alan is like when it comes to taking action on anything." She hoped her husband would not brush aside her suggestion as he had twice before. And since the time of the revelation was now minutes away, she was confident he would see reason.

"Of course Lois should be in on this. I thought we had already decided that."

That was typical of Raymond, Mrs. Thompson thought: reaching a decision and forgetting to tell anyone about it. Was that why their son was so unfamiliar with the decision making process?

The four of them sat down according to their various stages of fatigue, Lois flopping into the soft depths of the hotel lounge armchair, Alan straddling its leather arm, Mr. and Mrs. Thompson easing themselves onto the sofa across the low table from them.

"Your father has an idea, Alan. I think it's a wonderful idea, but of course you—you and Lois—will need time to think about it before you jump."

Alan had been anticipating this lecture. For the last two years, his parents had telegraphed the theme repeatedly via their incautious suggestions, "It's never too late to switch to computers, you know, son. Why don't you give that possibility some thought?" Then their thinly veiled anecdotes, "I hear that a classmate of yours is studying law at night school. If you're worried about course fees or text books, we'll be glad to help out." Their comments could only increase his anxiety about becoming a starving artist.

He slowly lifted his eyes toward the ceiling, then closed them, took a pained deep breath and wondered how he would react to yet another lecture, and this one on the very eve of his wedding!

The unfamiliar territory of weddings, the early morning dawn of fears that marriage may be unnecessarily formal and altogether too final, and news of the collapse of friends' marriages, all these contribute to pre-wedding stresses and jitters that can trigger arguments. The last wedding rehearsal he attended collapsed in just such an altercation. He was Best Man at a wedding the week after graduation. The bride and her mother strongly disagreed about how to walk down the aisle.

"This isn't a race, Moira. He'll wait till you get there."

"But Mom, if I walk slowly, my ankles turn because of these high heels."

"I told you they were stilts. But oh no, you had to have them."

"It's all right with me, Mrs. Watterly, if she hurries to get to me. As a matter of fact, I can't wait."

"This is her procession, Giles, not yours."

"And it's my wedding, not yours Mother. So butt out."

At the wedding the next day, Moira's slow walk down the aisle indicated that the mother had won that fight. Giles and Alan pondered the implications of an overbearing mother-in-law at the wedding banquet. Revellers unwittingly fuelled their fears by recounting other horror stories from other weddings. As more and more scotch and gin lubricated the storytellers' imaginations, the possibility of a debacle at Alan's own wedding became less remote.

He opened his eyes and gazed into the smiles of his parents. His father was looking extremely satisfied with himself, and his mother raised her eyebrows, smiled and nodded, inviting agreement from their son. What had they been saying? Had he missed the next instalment of "the lecture"?

"Well, son, what do you think about that?" his mother was asking.

In desperation he looked imploringly at Lois, then back to his father. "I . . . ah . . . I . . . could we think it over for a few days?"

Lois, perceptive soul that she was, realized what was happening, and to forestall any inappropriate response, she rephrased the offer. "It sounds very exciting that the Fire Department should be looking for an artist. What did you say the job could entail, Mr. Thompson?"

"Not just 'Mr', Lois. District Chief Thompson," his wife corrected, hoping the identification of her husband's rank indicated the job offer was a done deal.

"Well, to elaborate in a little more detail, Lois, they need an artist for a variety of jobs: to illustrate their P.R. publications, to prepare training cartoons for personnel, and, what will be right up your alley, son, to paint portraits of police and fire chiefs and assorted retiring municipal officials. You could probably talk them into using some cityscapes as gifts for visiting dignitaries."

The outcome of that welcome proposition was that within months of their graduation and within weeks of their marriage, he was one of the few lucky artists to earn a living that could support a family. The instant income enabled them to rent immediately a Toronto apartment large enough to include a room where he could paint.

It was with some trepidation that Alan undertook his first city commission, a portrait of John R. Glover, Toronto's retiring mayor. Over the last four years he had painted a significant number of portraits—several of his parents, many of Ellen, a few of university professors and of their friends. They were impressed by his firm, realistic style, his tonal harmonies and his balance. He had an innate ability to discern the subtle details that work together to make each depiction true and believable.

"So, what's the problem this time?" Lois asked. "Is it opening season jitters? You're good at portraiture. Heavens, you've had enough practice, and what you've picked up in your fine arts courses has helped you up to now. So what's the problem?"

"It's him, the mayor. Not because he's the mayor. I'd be willing to paint the queen. It's Glover, his arrogance, his . . . his desire to be in centre stage, his perpetual manipulation of photo ops."

"Just paint what you see!"

"If it were only that easy. I'm not sure what I see. Worse, I don't like what I see. How am I supposed to paint someone who's all show and glow and blow? And behind that impressive façade is a hollowness, a man who's paranoid about being upstaged by his advisors, his secretary, members of city council, and probably by God."

Lois pondered the predicament, "You've got to do something. How about painting the mayor's chair as if it were a throne, high and mighty?"

"Too obvious. It has to be less blatant. A throne would certainly make him happy, but everyone else would see it as preposterous, sheer ridicule." Alan was hoping that his characteristic vacillating wasn't going to invade his career as an artist.

"Were you listening to how you described him? Did you notice you said something about centre stage and his fear of being upstaged? Can you set him on a stage, maybe?"

Alan's eyes brightened, "Yes! Put him right where he wants to be. He'd love it. A hint of a spotlight on him, not quite a limelight. And in the background, not a real scene, but painted scenery to hint at his superficiality. O.K., that I can do. And it will make everyone happy, especially those who know how to read a portrait.

Three months later, the unveiling was well received. The mayor felt it showed him in his best light. His critics missed the irony and complained that it flattered him. The art critic of *The Toronto Star*, however, called it "a dramatic tribute, spotlighting a man of conviction who performed his duties with an egregiousness that Alan Thompson has captured admirably. As the artist has fittingly recorded, his Honor, Mayor Glover, has cast a long shadow." Lois and Alan concluded that the newspaper critic had caught and enjoyed the satirical overtones.

A year later, one portrait did trigger anger in everyone—newspaper columnists, city council members, a large proportion of Toronto's citizens—everyone except firefighters and the subject himself, a retiring chief of the Fire Department, Harold Brockbank. According to the chief, "The growth of Toronto's waterfront, its new marinas, its old fuel storage tanks, its burgeoning Ontario Place, the increasing traffic at the island airport, all require, no, demand a brand new state-of-the-art fireboat. Immediately. The expense of purchasing it will eventually be far exceeded by the cost of not buying it."

Budget conscious city counsellors and over-taxed citizens wanted Chief Brockbank to go away or at least to put another string in his harp. When the chief did announce his retirement from the force, Alan was instructed to provide city hall with his portrait.

"Don't sit me behind a desk," Chief Brockbank ordered. "Don't sit me anywhere. I spent enough years lugging hoses, climbing ladders, managing the attack on major blazes, enough to merit a setting with some action."

The result startled and angered most Torontonians. He planted the chief, not in his office, or at a fire station, but on a dock. He was holding his helmet beside him, the glow of flames illuminating his ruddy face, his right arm pointed to what was unmistakably the prow of an approaching fireboat, the rest of the boat lying beyond the picture's frame. The editor of one Toronto newspaper argued that the painting should be cropped to eliminate the boat. "And while we are at it, cut that spendthrift ex-chief down to size, too." The editor of a national newspaper called for the reassignment of the portrait to "an artist less politically and more fiscally minded."

It took another three years before a midnight warehouse fire which spread to ships moored alongside the slip justified Brockbank's plea for adequate marine fire fighting equipment. Alan's photo and the previously excoriated portrait of the chief dominated page one of most local newspapers. "Will we heed their call now?" trumpeted the *Star*. "Visionaries Revisited" announced *The Globe and Mail*.

In the eyes of the public, both the ex-chief and the artist were created anew. They were perceived differently, regarded more deferentially, and heeded more civilly. Alan was astonished at how thoroughly he was transformed by people who now saw him in a new light. A "visionary" now instead of an "ignorant spendthrift."

"What happened to the old me?" he asked his Fire Department boss, Joe Vittorio. "One neophyte reporter called me 'that pariah of the parchment'. What will they call me next?"

Joe had witnessed the fickleness of the public, especially when journalists felt hyper-righteous about a cause, (usually during a lack of truly significant news). "In the mind—if you can call it that—of the general public, the old Alan has died. And probably gone to hell. That's what happened. And don't you dare to convince them otherwise. People don't like the dead to come back. It only confuses them."

"But look, Joe. What if I'd put the chief behind his desk? Or what if I'd painted Mayor Glover looking out over Toronto from a city hall office? Then they too would have become different people."

Joe struggled to consider the implications. "Will the real Mayor please stand up?" he quipped. "Maybe if he did, we wouldn't recognize him."

"Well, the real Alan is going to stand up and go for a piss. See you later, Joe."

We hear of older couples who seem to know what each other is thinking. Incessant talk and verbal assents and reassurances become redundant, to be replaced not only by knowing glances and subtle body language, but, best of all, by silence. Often one partner can begin a thought, and pause midway, sensing the other's unspoken conclusion or corollary. So it was with Lois and Alan right from their first years together. Their silences, their musical rests, served to ensure a harmony that time would only enrich, or as the traditional wedding rubric expressed it, "Till death do us part."

One usually interprets that rubric to refer to the death of the husband or the wife. Not until the death of someone else bursts in upon the happy couple is the full devastating power of death understood—no, not understood, deeply experienced.

Only occasionally did Alan wonder what kind of life he would have enjoyed—or endured—if he had remained with Ellen. Where would we be? In North Bay? Would I be painting at home, in the Orgles' basement while Ellen taught kindergarten? But such ruminations occurred only occasionally, for with Lois, life was both full and fulfilling.

Although the Fire Department did provide a studio in one of the smaller, disused stations, he preferred to paint in their apartment. At least one long weekend a month, from Thursday evening till Sunday night, they visited nearby art galleries—Hamilton, Buffalo, Montreal, Ottawa, and some more distant cities, New York, Philadelphia, Cleveland, to help keep him in touch with the old masters and new techniques of painting and composition.

One of the works that inspired him was Jacob Jordaen's "Self portrait with parents, brothers and sisters." When he found it reproduced in poster form, he exulted, "I've been searching for this everywhere! Years ago I saw a postcard size reproduction of it in a catalogue of masterpieces from Russia's Hermitage. I knew this had to be my model for capturing the essence of a face. It'll hang in whatever future studio I paint. What a find!"

And then there were the many faces of and by Rembrandt, warts, crows feet, wrinkles and all, and the wonderful candlelit faces by LaTour, so smooth, pellucid, radiant. He was fascinated at how backgrounds could alter the spirit of a painting, the character of the person painted, and, yes, the attitude of the viewer. How easy to create and recreate, making the critic wonder where reality can be found, or if there is only one. Set a figure in a dark, brooding Rembrandt context, move him to the relentless clarity of a David, and the subject has changed, radically.

Although in painting, Alan was confronted with a multiplicity of styles and techniques, tints and tones, here his otherwise dormant intuition rendered him decisive and confidant. Such prompt certitude in the realm of art but absent from his daily life had annoyed Ellen and contributed to their separation. "If you can make up your mind without thinking," she would shout, "without calculating and recalculating when it comes to choosing colors or composition, why in heaven's name won't you make up your mind about other things!"

On the other hand, despite his hesitations about things practical, Lois had delighted in his quick and inerrant artistic judgments. They enabled her to see the artist behind the paintings, his moods, his fears, his longings.

Within a year and a half of their marriage, her obstetrician informed her that they would be the happy parents of twins. Immediately they began moving the apartment studio to the city's redundant fire station and started to transform the room into a nursery. During a regular check-up five months later, her obstetrician announced to her that both would be boys. Lois immediately opened her purse, extracted her cell phone, punched in the speed number for Alan and proclaimed, "Paint the entire nursery blue, and start thinking of names for—"

Alan interrupted and completed the sentence, "—for two boys! Yah-hoo!"

"Great idea," she bubbled, "call one 'Yah' and the other 'Hoo.'"

"Sure beats 'Whoo-Pee'" he answered. And two distant rooms erupted in laughter.

The cityscape he was working on later that memorable day had bluer skies and brighter colors than he had originally planned. And he put on the fourth movement of his favourite trio, turned up the volume and whistled along, almost mastering the stream of notes that cascaded and scattered down towards a triumphant resolution.

Suddenly borne up by the brightness of the music, its sweeping themes and variations, he moved aside the scene he had been labouring on and replaced it with a blank canvas. He allowed his hand to be guided by the jubilant flight of the three musical instruments and began his first abstract painting since his early student days. It would be entitled, "On hearing Good News."

When he arrived home, his first reaction was to lift Lois off her feet, spin her around, hug her hard, until he realized tight squeezes might not be welcomed by a wife expecting twins. As he grasped her hands and held her at arms' length, his face shone with pride and affection, and he reaffirmed, "Till death us do part! That long, that deep."

Charles and Mark arrived a few weeks after the second anniversary of their parents' marriage. Like most parents of twins, Lois and Alan's life became more planned, more organized, more serendipitous and, paradoxically, more chaotic. They looked for evidence of which of the fraternal twins would be likely be more dominant, which the better sleeper, which the livelier. Would there be creative or destructive competition between them? In their teen years, would they be friends? Would one be drawn to his mother and the other to his father? Or would both be closer to a mother who was constantly with them as contrasted to a father who was absent at least nine hours of most days? And then there was the obverse of that challenge: how can parents of twins minimize favouritism?

Four years flew by with astonishing speed. There was less travelling during that period. Holidays at a variety of summer cottages replaced the weekend art junkets. As the boys built sandcastles on beaches and dug holes below the waterline,

Alan painted. Sparkling lakes, red rowboats and multicolored sailboats featured in these works. And in the parlance of sales, they all "went." "'Cause people like to look at happy things where they live," was Charles' opinion. He was rarely short of opinions, and made certain that everyone within earshot heard them.

Beside the lake Mark bragged of the best collection ever of pretty stones. Charles insisted that his parents come and see the roads he was building. "Try not to throw sand around where your father is painting, boys. Come with me, let's collect some firewood so we can roast hotdogs for lunch."

They all managed to go camping at least once a month—all too infrequently for Charles the hunter, discoverer, runner, incessant talker; and for Mark, the collector, questioner, thinker.

The Fire Department was impressed with Alan's performance. His observations of the growing twins helped him prepare illustrations for an elementary school teaching unit on firefighters and safety in the home. He was able to capture the essence of several people on canvases so that their portraits proudly hung in the city hall to the acclaim of most relatives and the general public. Then, a few months into their fifth year of marriage, Lois suspected she was pregnant.

"This time, we don't need to know in advance whether it's a boy or a girl," Lois suggested. And so it was a happy surprise to all when Emily was born.

The boys vied with each other, earning praise and attention by playing with or holding their tiny sister. Neither competed for the privilege of changing her diaper.

"Was I ever this tiny, Mom?" Mark wanted to know.

"I was never that small," Charles insisted. They were both disappointed to hear that Emily weighed more and was longer than each of them.

"Then how come she can't talk?" Mark asked.

"Because she was born just six weeks ago," Lois replied.

"But me and Charles talked even before we came out of you, Mom."

In reply to their father's reproachful smile, Mark argued, "We did too, Dad. Me and Charles was talking even before we was borned."

"I'm not so sure about the talk. But I do know that you kicked each other an awful lot."

Mark scowled. "Only because he started it."

"Well, she'll start talking soon enough," Alan warned. "Now it's your turn, Charles, to get washed and ready for bed first. Come on, let's go."

In the morning, Mark was usually the first to squirm out from under the covers, skip down the hall and see if today was the day Emily decided to talk. Normally Emily was enjoying a soliloquy of gurgles and squeals, well lubricated with bubbles. But on this day, silence. Net even the usual arm flailings and fist clenchings.

"Can you talk with words today, Emily?" Mark whispered. "Say 'hi Mark.' Say 'I'm hungry.' Come on, it's easy. Say 'I'm hungry,' or say anything you want. OK, I'll come back later. I like it when you smile at me. Emily?"

On his way to the bathroom he looked into his parents' bedroom and complained, "She can't talk today. I tried to make her say 'Hi Mark,' but she wouldn't"

Alan groaned, "It's not five o'clock yet. Get back in bed, Mark." And he did, but not to fall asleep. About an hour later a shriek ripped apart the morning. "Alan! Emily!! Oh no. NO!" the boys crashed into each other and hurtled into their father who was standing, hand against mouth, holding onto the doorjamb. Lois was clutching Emily and swinging from side to side, wailing the baby's name, the dead baby's name.

After the funeral, neither Lois nor Alan had the courage to ask what Mark meant by saying "I tried to make her say something but she wouldn't. I tried to make her . . ."

In the ensuing weeks, their apartment became their prison. They were together, each of them in solitary confinement, each reliving that fateful morning many times over.

Did I hurt her when I poked her? Mark repeatedly asked himself. Was Mark trying to tell me in his childish way, to get up and see what was wrong? That was the central question of Alan's self-interrogation. Why did I choose that morning of all mornings to sleep in? She usually wakes me up—woke me—before five with her prattle. Why did I? was the tourniquet that Lois tightened in vain around her bleeding conscience. Charles wondered where Emily was. Will she ever come back? Will I go away just like her, fast, not even say "goodbye mom, 'bye dad, see ya later alligator"? Four separate inquisitions perpetually preoccupied the family.

Each one censured, denounced, condemned himself and herself. Worn down by guilt, would they eventually begin to accuse one another? "Why didn't you . . . ?" "If you had only . . ." "Didn't you realize that Emily . . . ?" The variations could be inexhaustible and exhausting. Then they could unite in condemning a common enemy, "Why did God let this happen? If he is really a God of love . . . ?

Alan tried the consolation of music but was angered by the skipping and the merriment in his favourite trio. What did Schubert ever know about death? he demanded.

Death did not part them from each other, but it succeeded in parting each person from himself and herself. After several months in their private prisons, and to prevent themselves from falling into the trap of blaming, Lois suggested that they reactivate their former travels, but this time, not simply to art galleries. "How about Paris, or London, or San Francisco? We need out of this apartment, together."

Response was unenthusiastic. "Or how about buying a summer cottage not too far away?" then trying to revive memories of camping, "We could go there on weekends and on holidays, put up our tents like we used to, go canoeing, fishing, build a treehouse . . ."

"Uh huh," replied Mark. "Maybe," answered Charles. "Whatever," whispered Alan. "But at least nobody is saying 'No'," Lois observed. Alan surprised himself by not saying, "Let's take some time to think about it."

The parents grasped to a much greater degree than the twins did that the choice they made, whether to travel or to buy a summer home, or to do neither, would direct the family in very different ways. It took several months to reach a decision and several more to begin acting on it. But act they finally did.

CHAPTER SIX

EITHER TRAVEL OR COTTAGE:

Travel

Every once in a while over the last two or three years I find myself motionless, staring at a cup of coffee or studying a photograph or simply looking into the middle distance. I put the cup down on the kitchen table, uncertain as to whether I have taken a sip or not. Time often seems to stand as still as I do.

When Charles observes my brief experiences of catatonia, he quizzes me. "What's wrong, Mom? Did you forget something?" How I wish I could! Then Alan, overhearing Charles's question, stops on his way to the coffee pot, turns towards me, and with casual unawareness, asks, "Something wrong? Lose something?"

To conceal the ache, I dissemble. "Yes, I had a pen here somewhere, at least I thought I did." Which sets off a hunt for some thing that can be brought back.

Once, I picked up a slice of toast, glanced at the clock—8:24 a.m., and then with no further movement, relived those minutes of horror, snatching her up, looking at her staring eyes, listening for a gasp, a whimper, anything, then clutching her, wailing, and hearing the howls of Alan and the twins. The vision was interrupted by the sensation of toast in my fingers. After that eternity of grief, the clock insisted that it was—8:24 a.m.

More than once last year, I became painfully aware of a rent in the fabric of reality. On one occasion, wearing my coat and holding my purse, I glanced out of the kitchen window and saw the sun shining. Now is a good time to get the shopping done, I remember thinking. I took the car keys off their hook, stared at them, saw and felt nothing for just the briefest flicker of time. Alan came into the room, saw me frozen there and brought me to my senses. "You're not going out now, in all that rain, surely."

"Rain?"

"Yes, it's been pouring for four or five minutes. And it looks like it'll freeze." For as long as it takes to sigh or to wipe away a tear, that quickly, I must have stepped into a black hole and emerged who knows how many minutes later?

I have so much in common with rain these days. Raindrops and my tears arrive unsummoned, uncalled for, unwanted, out of the blue. Or is it out of the black? But the most unsettling similarity between the rain and me is that we both can freeze, stopping in our tracks, brittle, perhaps even shatterable.

These mid-winter days when traffic on icy roads is slowed down to a snail's pace, Alan wants to change Emily's bedroom back into the studio, but for lack of my encouragement, he continues to work at the old fire station. Often, too often, I find myself standing in the doorway of her room, holding tightly to the twins. Not even they know how often or how long we are standing there looking for—what? Perhaps a black hole that can transport us back to carefree times, tears of laughter, summer rain.

Would it give me any relief if I could see through Alan's eyes for a few hours? Does he look for a different outcome, fantasize that Emily was suffering only from a brief encounter with apnoea? That on being lifted up, she inhales with a gasp and a splutter, making sounds that normally would alarm us, but on that morning, would cause us to sigh with relief? Is that what he dreams when he stares at the empty sketching paper?

What I see through my own eyes is burden enough without trying to bear the weight of his dreams, his fantasies, his regrets. But isn't that what women do—take the broken piece of pie, offer others the toast that didn't get burned, let the children have the last chocolates in the box? So maybe our traditional role is to collect the tattered hopes, patch them, and while we're at it, try to mend the broken hearts?

They say that the death of a child distresses a mother far more than it does a father, simply because the baby was flesh of her flesh. But how can they be sure of such a judgment, for men retreat behind walls of silence, concealing grief and rage until the unprecedented explosion when shrapnel lacerates loved ones, colleagues, neighbours. So out of the corner of my eye, I watch him for signs of pent up emotions, fists tightly clenched beside the dinner plate, lips pinched under squinting eyes. And above all, silence, long stretches of barren silence, as if nothing is worth commenting on or discussing.

I can't trust what I see any more, being uncertain that I'm finding only what I fear I might find. At times, it feels as if I am living not in an apartment, but in a chamber of mirrors with those glass partitions you bang into while trying to reach someone. There must be a way out, for all of us.

About a month ago we finally reached consensus. We opted for travel over buying a cottage. Either choice would open a door onto a new life for us, but finally, after vacillating and deciding and re-deciding, travel it would be. But what a chasm between decision and action!

Alan's parents hear of our intention to use three weeks of his holidays next summer overseas; so they make a gracious offer. "We don't get to see Charles and Mark as much as we'd like," Ray says. "Why don't you leave them with us and you two visit all the art galleries and museums and cathedrals you can squeeze into a twenty-one day holiday? Seven year-olds will get bored seeing such adult stuff. And the great paintings you'll find, son, will be an inspiration to you. What do you say?"

I know that Alan will say, "Yes, that's a thought. Give us a few days to talk this over." So I leap in with all guns blazing. "No! we're not leaving Charles and Mark with you."

Pat shrinks before the vehemence and suddenness of my response. "Well, I'm sorry. There's really no need to shout. If you don't want us to have the boys . . ."

Hoping to pacify his parents and to calm me, Alan says, "I'm sure Lois didn't mean it that way, Mom. What she is trying to say is that fate took away Emily and, well, maybe for a while at least, she finds it difficult to be, you know, separated from the boys."

I wince at this explanation, not because it isn't right, but because Alan and I agreed to call Charles and Mark "the twins." Calling them "the boys" only reminds us that there had been a girl. So in response to his explanation, all I can do is sob. Mark runs to me, puts his arms around me and holds on as hard as he can. "You too, Charles," is all the plea that I can muster.

"You're right, son," says Ray, observing the tight knot of mother and children. "The boys' actions and Lois's, too, speak louder than any words. Of course you all need to be together, even in art galleries. Just don't spend too many minutes in front of those voluptuous Rubens women."

All I can do is open up our little circle, wave Pat into it and hold on to them and to this minute which will too speedily pass by. Yes, we badly need to get away, but not away from each other. I just might need two children and a husband to pull me out of the next black hole.

It is not long in coming. The evening of our departure for Paris, Alan and the twins drive over to his parents' home to say goodbye to his mother and their grandma, since the five of us, along with our baggage, will more than fill Ray's car. They are to take some items from our refrigerator that won't keep till we return from Europe. They leave, promising to be back in an hour to pick me up. By then, I'll have finished the packing, organized the passports and tickets and closed off the apartment.

I swear it is for only a minute that I sit down to look at our passport pictures. But before I can examine them, the door bursts open and in run Charles and Mark. "Back so soon?" I ask. "What did you forget to take grandma and grandpa?"

"Nope, nothing. We're s'posed to help you carry down the . . . the . . . What did Dad call it, Marky?"

"Hand luggage. He said that's not too heavy for us. Where is it, Mom?"

"But your father said you'd be gone for an hour."

"Yeah, he says he's sorry it took so long. We got stuck in traffic."

Then it is that I realize an hour and a half has vanished from my life. Have I been day dreaming? The clock confirms the flight of time. I stand up, almost dizzy at the thought of what I should have been doing, and worse, at what I don't remember doing or thinking. Alan appears and is mystified that two bags are still to be packed, windows haven't been locked, and I still need to put on my travel clothes.

Al appears at the door and looks quizzically at me. "You're not having second thoughts about coming along with us, are you, dear?" he asks, half joking. "I'll give you a hand with the packing. Charles, you take this handbag down to your grandpa. He's double parked. Tell him we'll be a few minutes. Now hurry. He's waiting for us."

In the airport waiting room and later in the plane we have lots of time for me to wonder where I am when I'm not here. Recollections of being anaesthetized, once for a tonsillectomy, once for the extraction of wisdom teeth, remind me of how the theft of those two brief periods of consciousness disturbs me. They were unlived moments when one is neither dead nor alive, moments which can never be retrieved.

Not to have a memory of a brief period of time is an offence to consciousness. When I complain of these lacunae, Alan says, "You've just had a taste—not a foretaste, I hope—but a taste of Alzheimer's."

But no, it is not like that, for I know that I do not know what transpired. Not to be aware of what one does not know is a kind of death. On the other hand, for Goethe in his old age to say that he finally did know that he knew nothing opened the door for him to—what? To richer experience? To learning? Perhaps to life. For him and for me.

I shuddered to read in the *Toronto Star* a few months ago about a dentist who was charged with sexually assaulting several of his patients. Apparently the crime became known to one victim because she was not as totally anaesthetized as the dentist assumed. It's never enough to know. You have to know that you know.

In those occasional "black holes" of mine, have I tunnelled through to another time or place? Such thoughts lead only to madness. Or is all this a normal reaction to a traumatic loss? I don't know. I really don't. "Well, you know that for sure," says Alan when I talk about this to him.

It's no time before we are to board the 747. Mark has been sitting beside me playing his video game, occasionally looking up to observe crowds of colors and costumes ebbing and flowing along the corridor. "Are they coming from somewhere or are they going?" he asks. We scan the great variety of faces, trying to read this anthology of humanity, and I realize that never before has he or Charles witnessed such a mosaic. Does he see himself as part of it, I ask myself, part of this ever-changing kaleidoscope, seeds of tomorrow's history?

I realize that he has never seen so many different forms of headgear. It will take him years to learn their names: tams, turbans, fedoras, gold braided officers' caps, babushkas, headbands, bandanas, berets, sunbonnets, skull caps. Each of them proclaims that the wearer belongs—but to what, and where?

Mark thinks I've forgotten his question, so he asks again, "Mom, are they coming or going?"

I turn to him and perhaps all too cryptically lob the question back to him, "Are you?"

"Am I what?" he asks with a frown, perhaps—no, not annoyed, perhaps apprehensive that I may be playing a game whose rules he doesn't understand. Or maybe playing a trick that will make him look foolish for not seeing the obvious.

"Are you coming or going, Mark?"

"Going, Mom. Going to Paris. You know that. But . . ."

I let the pause hang there because he seems to be standing in front of a door wondering whether or not to shove it open. He could turn back and run towards what is certain, safe, foreseeable. But slowly he moves forward and looks into the dimness.

"But what?" I prod.

"Both, Mom. We are going to Paris, but we are coming from our apartment. And I'm coming from being little and . . ."

I don't push him any further. He'll be thinking a lot about not only where we are going, but where we've come from. He's the thinker. I may come to envy him for being able to know not only where he is coming from and where he is going to, but also, and most important, where he is.

Alan left his seat a few minutes ago in hot pursuit of Charles who considers every corridor to be a racetrack and farthest walls as finish lines. People raise their eyes over top of their newspapers and magazines as he gallops past, dashing headlong into the end wall which he slaps with both hands. Then he spins around, arms upraised in the victor's salute and awaits the crowd's applause. That it doesn't come this time is no deterrent, for there are other courses, other finish lines, and possibly more appreciative onlookers elsewhere. The waiting passengers who have not returned to their reading watch Charles elude his pursuing father. Some appear glad of the momentary entertainment, others must be exchanging harsh words about "this younger generation which needs a lesson or two on proper behaviour." I see an elderly couple lean towards each other, whisper and nod towards Charles. I bet they're saying "If he was our child, we'd teach him how to behave." But Charles will need all the activity he can get now, as it will be a long and claustrophobic sit till we reach our destination.

Aboard the plane, Charles demands and, perhaps regretfully gets, a window seat. Alan and I agree to follow the advice of the "Travel Tips" section of our guide book. "Separate your children to minimize name calling, territorial skirmishes, and food fights." Strategically, then, Alan and I sit between them. Across the aisle, busily drawing in the little sketch book we bought him, Mark is creating smiling airplanes in sunny skies. Every once in a while he shows his masterpieces to his neighbour, a man who, fortunately, seems to enjoy the privilege of a private showing.

"Don't bother the nice man, Mark. He may want to be by himself and have a rest."

He leans forward and replies, "No, he is no trouble at all. My wife and I have a boy back home. Chaucer is about Mark's age. Your son is going to be an artist."

Mark leaps out of his seat, crosses the aisle and informs me that he's learned that the man is a doctor, Dr. Liang, and he's going to Paris too. "He likes my drawings. Maybe we'll see him there."

"Not likely," I say. "Paris is a pretty big city, bigger than Toronto. Now put your drawings away because here comes our meal. I'll switch seats with you. Come and sit here, beside your father, so you don't spill anything on your new friend."

But Dr. Liang offers to help Mark with his meal. I think he has observed that our other son will be challenge enough for Alan without his having to referee both boys.

Before the in-flight movie, the TV news program warns us of a possible strike of air traffic controllers in Paris. That means the closing of both Orly and Charles de Gaulle airports. "Aren't we supposed to arrive at one of those?" Alan asks. "Maybe we'll land in London instead. Or since we're hardly out of Canada, they'll probably turn us back to Gander."

Our comments contribute to the rising tide of groans and sighs that spreads throughout the cabin. A few angry voices punctuate the general murmur of discontent.

The reactions of the twins are, as expected, poles apart. Mark wonders if we'll get lost, and Charles thinks it would be neat to drop onto Paris by parachute. He bounces up and down on his seat chanting "Neat to parachute, neat to parachute, neat to . . ." Mark solemnly cuts in with the charge that it isn't funny.

My contribution is, "If our trip is not meant to be, then it won't happen," to which Alan simply rolls his eyes and mutters "predictable." I suppose every one of us on this plane, in responding to the news, is playing a tape that has been in preparation since our birth.

I find it difficult to enjoy the movie, wondering if each tilt and bank of the plane implies a change of destination. Hmmm, "destination"—an interesting word. It presupposes a destiny. Can there ever be an amended destiny, a substitute destination? Despite what Roger argued a few years ago, I am all the more confirmed in my belief that "What is to be, sooner or later, will be." Yet, it was still tragic that for Emily, it happened so very much sooner. Would later be any easier for her? For us? I have run around this track a thousand times, alone and with Alan, the twins sitting on the sidelines, forlorn, and fighting their own dark and nameless memories of the past, and fears of the future.

I am jolted out of my ruminations by an authoritative announcement that interrupts the movie. "This is your captain speaking. I am pleased to inform you that the impending strike of air traffic controllers in France has been postponed. The new deadline for withdrawal of services will be midnight tomorrow. We will land as planned, at Charles de Gaulle airport at 7:50 a.m. Relax now and enjoy the rest of the flight."

Mark wakes up and looks anxiously at me. I move across the aisle and explain to him that we are not lost. He too had been jerked out of his slumber by the announcement and seemed convinced that only bad news is delivered in pre-dawn hours. Dr. Liang confided his relief to me, "They're expecting me to present a paper at an international conference of pediatricians in three days. I hope the strike is postponed again, otherwise I'll be quite alone and lost in Paris."

At the mention of "lost," Mark comes alive and says, "You won't be alone, we'll be in Paris too. You can come and stay with us."

"That's very thoughtful of you, my boy, but I already have a place to stay."

Then I add, "But he'd love to see you again, Dr. Liang, especially if you have time on your hands. We're staying at the Hotel de Suez for three weeks."

That was how Dr. Liang became a part of our life. By the time Charles and Mark had exhausted themselves and us at Disneyland Paris, we were ready to begin our visits to art galleries and museums. Dr. Liang first joined us a for a boat trip on the Seine. He told us that being with the twins and us was a wonderful consolation for the cancelled medical conference. He would nonetheless be able to submit his paper on his research work done at Sick Children's Hospital in Toronto. Alan told me back at our hotel how deeply disappointed the doctor confessed to being. "Our research team back in Canada has been cheated out of public and international recognition for their breakthrough analysis of infantile cancer. The report will still be published, but there will not be the audience, the newspaper or TV coverage."

I was greatly relieved that Dr. Liang, Victor, accompanied us to Versailles and Montmartre and to the Jeu de Paume art gallery, not only because he genuinely enjoyed Mark's intelligent questions and Charles' energy. He would also be near at hand in case I clocked out at some crucial moment, like waiting in the crosswalk to navigate across the wide and busy Paris streets. Alan noticed how tightly I gripped his arm and held onto one of the boys as motor scooters, bicycles, trucks, buses and cars threatened to terminate our trip in tragedy. When I found myself thinking, This is not where I want to be standing, I wondered if I was about to step back into a black hole again.

Quite unexpectedly, at supper one afternoon, Alan said, "Victor, we—Lois, the twins and I—would be honored to have you, your wife and son over to our Toronto apartment this fall for supper. I know you are extremely busy at the hospital, but . . ." he couldn't finish his invitation for the cheers that Mark and Charles raised.

Thanks to Victor, our Paris trip was a total success. He offered more than once—and we gladly accepted each time—to take the twins for a few hours while Alan and I went fine dining and wining. We longed for a restaurant which provided meals several notches up the scale from the usual french fries and hamburgers that the twins slathered with ketchup.

"Let's get an eatery where ketchup is banned," Alan entreated. And so began a gustatory quest that lasted for years. Successive vacations introduced us to marvellous exotic menus—chicken coated with delicious chocolaty mole in Oaxaca, fried eels and white bat (at least that's what the menu said, although it was probably white rat) in Nanjing. In Tunisia, we enjoyed wild boar meat with a sweet sauce, called marcassin, the only pork you could buy in the country. In the light of many such meals, is it any wonder the twins' eyes lit up whenever they saw a MacDonald's restaurant?

Not only to me, but to Alan's boss, Joe, at the Fire Department, it was evident that our travels enriched his painting. Torontonians, being part of such a multicultural city, appreciated the authentic representation of their cultures in some of his cityscapes and private commissions.

For several of our summer trips, Victor and his wife Zhi Yuan accompanied us. The three boys, their son Chaucer and our two, became fast friends over the years, even to the point of going together to horseback riding camps for a month in their early teen years. They had tired of museums and castles, and still clung to their preference for ketchup. Camps allowed them—even encouraged them—to pour America's favourite condiment on macaroni and, necessarily, on the reconstituted mashed potatoes. The boys were always exasperated at my refusal to include those combinations in my kitchen.

My experiences of catatonia or blackouts mercifully diminished, but occasionally resulted in publicly embarrassing moments. Once, standing in line at an automated teller machine in Lisbon, I failed to notice that the client ahead of me had retrieved and pocketed her money. Apparently other passers-by, not realizing there was a line up behind me, walked directly to the A.T.M. I was rudely awakened by taps on the shoulder and stern comments in Spanish that probably meant I should either defecate or get off the pot. How long I had held up the line I'm not sure, but judging by the anger of those behind me, it must have been an eternity. Why must civility be the first victim of our fast service society?

Our lives took a dramatic turn when we moved out of our apartment with its memories of prison, and into our first house, with its hopes for fewer nightmares and ghosts. Mark, being somewhat of a loner, had difficulty with his transition to a new school. We relocated in a different area of Toronto, North York to be precise. "Why the hell did we have to leave?" he asked repeatedly, as if each time of asking should reverse our decision. I told him to stop using that kind of language and that tone of voice. It was during those first months of dislocation that Alan and I began to notice Mark's anger, his sharp and often cutting comments, and even worse, his sullen silences. Charles, the socializer, however, made the switch easily, and was soon the centre of "the party boys" as they called themselves.

As for me, the challenge of creating a welcoming, gracious home sparked my imagination and fired up my energies. "What we need is a housewarming! Who will best share our excitement at our move here?"

Without hesitation, Alan identified Victor and Zhi Yuan, Pat and Ray "of course", even though Ray is looking more and more lost every month. "And how about the two women you go swimming with every week at the recreation centre?" he suggested, "and Joe Vittorio from the Department. Besides, a housewarming will give us a chance to show off some of the exotic recipes we've picked up on our travels."

"Very labour intensive," I note, "so you may have to lay down your paint brush and take up a pastry brush." I hesitated, not wanting to propose too much of a hiatus in his painting since his numerous recent commissions outside of the Fire Department were contributing opportunely to our mortgage payments.

When Mark and Charles were seventeen, our Christmas vacation trip to California was almost cancelled because of a backlog of paintings and illustrations which Alan had to complete before the new year. He simply could not manage to take the time off to accompany us. Pat, his mother, heard of our disappointment at the probable cancellation. "Surely, Lois, you and the twins are not thinking of giving up a chance to feel some warm sun in mid winter!"

"But I don't feel confident to look after these energetic teens all by myself," I replied.

"So why don't I come along to give you a hand?" she said. "Between the two of us, we should be able to wrestle those teens into line for eight days. I'm not so sure about the nights, but let's give it a try. And anyway, as reluctant as I am to confess it, both of us need a break. Leave hubby here to paint his way to fame and fortune."

It was true. We did need a break. Since her husband Ray had been slipping inexorably into the clutches of Alzheimer's disease, she had been visiting him daily at the nursing home. I had been driving her to visit him five days a week for months. Alan tried to fill in the other two days.

Now and then I would report to Alan and the boys, "She thought that grandpa recognized us for a brief moment today." They too had experienced his glazed incomprehension. Every visit dashed their hopes that maybe this time, he might make sense of their photographs that hung in his room. Mark, in his impatient, demanding way argued, "Why, if God is supposed to be so good and loving is my grandfather like this? If you can't trust God, then who can you trust?"

When Pat, out of guilt, demurred at the last minute, Charles gallantly offered to stay behind and help his grandfather with lunches and suppers. Besides, he was more drawn to some of his senior school chums than he was to San Francisco and Los Angeles. "It just might be good for you guys to enjoy separate vacations for a change," I said. "After all, one of these days you're going to be attending different universities." From where I was sitting, I couldn't tell for sure whether Mark's response was a smile or a smirk.

How welcome was the warmth of late December days in California compared to the chill of Toronto. Of course we missed the colored lights reflecting off the glittering snow, and the ice skating in front of the city hall. But there would be other weeks after our return when we could revel in those winter delights.

In San Francisco one of the essential tourist experiences is the cable car. What should have been a source of delight for Pat, Mark and myself turned into an afternoon of anguish.

We dutifully waited for the cable car to descend to its turnaround. Pat, being self-conscious at the age and energy difference between herself and Mark, bravely sought to compensate, saying, "Let's run and grab seats on the upper deck!"

They hastened up as fast as they could climb, and assumed, when I failed to appear, that I preferred to sit on the lower level. Their ascent was the last thing I remembered . . . until a uniformed guard led me aside and assured me there would be another car in about fifteen minutes.

"But where is the cable car?" I asked, rather foolishly as I soon realized.

"It left several minutes ago. We thought you had changed your mind about taking the trip. At the last minute a few people are afraid the car might somehow break loose and hurtle back down. But that's absolutely impossible, lady."

Two whole minutes had again been swallowed up by the black hole. Pat and Mark told me how frantic they were on discovering I was not on the cable car. Had I fallen off? Had I been kidnapped, abducted? Every fear was supported by dozens of TV murder mysteries that had entertained us down through the years.

I could very easily imagine the grizzly scenarios that would be assaulting them. Fortunately they were able to persuade the conductor that they should not have to line up to descend later. They found me waiting sheepishly at the turnaround. From then on, I noticed how I became the meat, and they the bread in our human sandwich.

On our return home, Mark bragged to his brother with anecdotes about the Santa Monica coast. He described the skateboarders, acrobats and weight lifters who showed off their muscles and their skills along the parkway. On hearing of the nearby Getty Center, Alan drooled, "Charles, let's you and me go there next Christmas!"

"Great idea, Dad. But I'll be off to university," Charles reminded him.

"Now, what about your time at home, Charles?" I asked. "What were the highlights of your nine days?"

"Just being with the guys, listening to music, watching TV together, and comparing complaints about school. That's about all," he said. "Oh, and Russell and I went skiing at Collingwood for three days. We found a motel in the town. His father lent him the car. We had a super time up there together, and thanks, Dad, for covering for me at Grandpa's nursing home."

He dispelled any fears we might have had that he felt martyred by being left behind. His only complaint—actually more of a lament—was, "Grandpa never once knew who I was. In fact, I'm sure he didn't realize I was the same person one day as I was the day before, or after."

Call it intuition if you will, something we women are supposed to excel at, but I sensed that there was something Charles wasn't telling us. Despite his being closer to the scene, Alan wasn't able to identify any unspoken issues. We would not allow ourselves to be drawn into the whirlpool of suspicion concerning Charles and any drugs, alcohol, or sex.

One of the priorities after our house purchase was to have two skylights installed on the second floor so that Alan could enjoy a well lit studio up there. He was eager to see that job completed since the trip to the old fire station where he had been painting was too time consuming, especially at rush hour. After establishing himself here at home, we were able to see much more of each other. That would be doubly important after the twins left for their universities in September.

Our next extended trip, over the Christmas and New Year's holidays—Florence and then Rome, this time leaving the twins behind at their universities,. Although we land in Rome, we tackle Florence first to satisfy our artistic and culinary appetites.

What tantalizing combinations: for a visual antipasto we have Fra Angelico, spiced with some luscious Botticelli, served with a touch of Cosimo, al fresco. A light lunch of bruschetta, some bean and garlic soup, and, not to offend the maitre d', a litre of house wine. Then, a rest at our hotel on the Borgo Pinti, followed by afternoon of delicious Michelangelo and various Fras before we collapse at a restaurant table and consume the *bistecca alla Fiorentina*, finishing off with the almond cookies, golden with egg yolks, which we dip in a rich raisin wine. And to think that this is just the appetizer for our five days here! It makes one wonder if there will be sensory overload in heaven, too.

For four more days we overdose on museums and art galleries. Even to stroll along the narrow lanes and the broad avenues window shopping is a thrill. But since all good things have to come to an end, we take one final morning walk past some galleries and antique stores.

"Alan, it's well past eleven. We mustn't wander too far from our hotel. Checkout time is in half an hour. We'll need to get a taxi to our two o'clock airplane."

Look at him! He's mesmerized by some artistic virtuosity that he sees in a window. "Look at this, Lois. The shading, the brush strokes, the . . ."

"We'd better get a move on," I say, revealing a hint of impatience, "and get our bags ready. We can't be late." Now he's stooping down to avoid a disturbing reflection I suppose. "Al . . . Alan! . . . Well, I'm going on ahead. See you in our room in fifteen minutes, no more." I know the way back, for as we have experienced when visiting an unfamiliar city, we find ourselves repeatedly—and even unintentionally—walking the same route.

The only challenge is the streets that break in at strange angles, and mopeds that roar and flutter before and behind. And taxis that cut off your escape, and police whistles and the shouts and the horns and the shouts and the shouts and the . . . No aachh . . . .

Chapter Seven

The Bottle or the Pulpit:

The Bottle

The unexpected change in the autumn weather caught everyone by surprise. Coat collars were turned up and heads hunched down. The few pedestrians still out at this dark hour leaned forward against the sudden wind or were prodded and hustled ahead with it. Cold gusts buffeted a thin young man who stood shivering as he waited to hand out leaflets outside the corner drugstore. Since few people passed by and fewer would slow down to accept the proffered sheets, he gave up and entered the store.

Discarded by passers-by, his leaflets swooped and swirled up past dingy second storey windows. Apart from the fluttering of the papers against telephone lines and the occasional whistle of the wind, the only other sound was the shuddering of a rusty sign that swung erratically above the entrance to an abandoned restaurant. In its recessed doorway, Steve, lightly clad, unshaven and unwashed clung to his most valuable possession, a large, half empty bottle of cheap sherry. "King's Choice—Double Rich" the label bragged.

Few shops along this commercial stretch of the street were open. Across from Steve was a coffee shop-cum-gathering place. Bibbi's was the only coffee shop in Toronto that kept a tab for its customers. And it possessed the only store windows for blocks that were regularly washed and decorated with white half-curtains. No wonder people found it a welcome oasis of warmth and quiet that drew them out of their stained plaster rooms. Halfway down the block was a convenience store, trapped behind its window bars, and further along, a tavern whose outdated sign boasted of exotic tabletop dancers. At the far end of the block, a pinball and video game emporium attracted the youths of this slum neighbourhood. Several stores had been "temporarily" boarded up years ago. Posters, faded and torn, advertised X-rated movies that had long been forgotten, and recommended names for the mayoralty race that had been run three years earlier. An occasional drapery made of a bed sheet was pulled aside when a tenant peered into the dark street or taped newsprint over a broken window pane.

The only evidence that time was passing was the change in the level of Steve's sherry and the eventual ritual smash of the empty bottle. That usually occurred around 10:15 p.m., just prior to his opening a mickey of gin. At 9:29 exactly, or so the police report indicated, a crash of glass that might have equalled an entire crate of broken bottles caused a half dozen window sheets to be swept aside. Bibbi, who was usually aware of what went on in the street, was in the back kitchen washing up after his last customers.

The first person to reach the body that lay surrounded by shards of glass was the bottle-clutching drunk, although it would be unfair to describe him as such yet. Ask any neighbours and they'll tell you that Steve doesn't begin singing in front of the restaurant till 10:30, and doesn't start to bully and stagger before 11:00. Consequently at this earlier hour, they had reason to believe his testimony about the blood-covered body.

Still holding his bottle, he bent down and stared at the splayed legs and twisted neck. Despite the absence of any street light at that exact location, Steve could recognize the man because a bulb from a second storey staircase shone unimpeded by its customary grimy window. The man had perhaps fallen down the stairs from the third floor, or was thrown, or jumped through the window onto the sidewalk.

It was Alan, unshaved, unwashed, and blood-stained.

In his haste to test for Al's pulse, Steve spilled some of his precious sherry over the broken man's shirt. "Al!" Steve cried, "Al, what the fuck happened?"

No one dared approach the two men, fearing, at first, that Steve had turned nasty ahead of schedule and might lunge at anyone who came within range of his bottle or his fists.

There was no pulse, or at least none that he could detect. "I've got to get you some help. Hang in there, buddy." Steve struggled creakily to his feet, and maintaining his grip on his empty bottle, hobbled to the drug store.

The curious onlookers peeking from second and third storey windows wondered who his next victim would be, and turned off their lights to see better into the dim street.

He burst into the drugstore, frightening the guard who leaped behind a counter shouting, "Down! Get down everybody!" which was unnecessarily dramatic since there were only two others in the store at the time. It was exactly 9:35, or so he reported to the officiating sergeant.

Out of breath, Steve panted, "It's Al! Dead. Outside on the sidewalk. Doc, call an ambulance." Three pairs of eyes belonging to the young leaflet distributor, to the guard, and to the pharmacist, slowly emerged from behind shelves of condoms, Coke, and vitamins respectively.

"Who?" the frail young leaflet distributor, Merv, called out. "Who's dead d'ya say?"

"It's Al," Steve shouted, an answer that still left the three uncertain as to whether it was Sally, "Sall," the local prostitute or Al the relatively unknown alcoholic. Last month he had moved into what used to be the third floor storage area of a shoe store. Sall's beat was from the drugstore to the all night pinball and video emporium.

Merv blurted out, "Oh, no! not Sall I hope. She was just in here ten minutes ago and picked up some gum," as if that ought to protect a girl from accident, murder, or suicide.

"No, it's Al, the new guy over the shoe store, Alan. Hey guard!" (Nobody ever got to know the names of these uniformed hulks, their location being regularly changed to minimize collusion with influential gangs.) "Guard! Get an ambulance on 911. He's on the sidewalk near the old restaurant." The guard grabbed his cellphone as Doc locked up his pharmacy area, clanged the grill shut behind him and quickly locked the cash register.

"Merv, you stay here and keep an eye on things." Hurrying out, the druggist shouted back, "Don't let anybody near the cigarettes or the till."

The guard dithered, beginning to run after Doc and Steve, hoping his first aid knowledge might finally come in handy, but then charged back to the store which, after all, he was paid to protect. The whole thing might be a scam, he thought, so he stationed himself outside and reported what he could see to Merv. The chill wind buffeted him as he described the scene. "They're bending over him. Looks like they're loosening his collar. Yep, now Doc is taking his pulse."

"Doc" was not really a doctor, but most of his neighbours regarded him as such. He was the first line of defence when a woman felt a lump in her breast, or dragged in a measled infant. It was Doc who identified and prescribed for D.T.s, venereal diseases, and more recently, AIDS. He knew of the ailments of teens long before their parents. Just last week, Al dropped by for some cough drops, but Doc knew from long experience with alcoholics what was needed to build up a degenerating body. A rare bonus for the pharmacist was finding an articulate person like Al whose mind hadn't been addled by drugs and/or excessive booze. Not yet anyway.

Only last week, Doc described to Al the new community he had moved into. "It doesn't look like it at first, but I'd call this part of town the discommunity of the fearful. Half the neighbourhood is afraid of neighbours and strangers, the other half, afraid of the police."

Al reflected on the idea, trying to imagine it, to image it as an artist might. He pictured an old woman glancing along the street before she hurried out from the convenience store clutching her canned goods and beer. He saw pale faces listening just inside locked and barred apartment doors. He could even fit in a terrified figure shouting from a third floor fire escape with the face of Edvard Munch's "Scream."

"Dyscommunity," Al repeated, half to himself. "I like that, so long as you spell it d-y-s. Yes, the dyscommunity of the fearful. But I see their fears differently, Doc. Of course I don't know this area as you do. My guess is that it's not neighbours or police they're scared of. Half are afraid of dying, and half, afraid of living."

"Well, you know what they say in the East, Al. We see things not as they are but as we are." He paused to let the implication sink in, then added, "Which is your fear? Of dying or living?"

"You're sharp, Doc. You scored a goal that time. This week? Well, this week I'm afraid of both. He hesitated, astonished at how rapidly and unequivocally he had responded. Not for a long time had he verbalized such intimate thoughts so succinctly. In the months after Lois was struck by a speeding motorcycle in Florence, Alan withdrew from the world. Alcohol became his sole consolation. It had been weeks, months maybe, since he found anyone willing to discuss what lay beneath the surface, behind the smiles or frowns. "Yes, I guess that's my fear." He wondered what Doc would do with such a confession, but the pharmacist looked at him, the tilt of his head seeming to invite more self revelations. Maybe it was time for Al to back away, to hide behind a laugh. "Yeah, afraid of living and afraid of dying. Imagine that. What have you got on your shelves to cure that, Doc?"

Doc scanned his cheerful displays. There were great promises portrayed on all the advertisements and labels: smiling faces, skimpily clad healthy young men and women admiring each other, even some athletic looking older folk these days. Promises, promises. Hope for a better tomorrow. Maybe that's the antidote for fears of living and fears of dying—hope. "Yes, I think I have something for you, Al, something that'll let you die rich or live happy. Here, take it."

He reached behind the counter. "It's on the house, a lottery ticket. This beats what's on the shelf in your room." He looked over the top of his glasses at Alan, and, realizing he might appear judgmental, he quickly remarked, "Just remember me when you claim your fortune—and your future. Hang on till you win."

But he didn't hang on, for that man was lying on the sidewalk, as scrambled physically now as he had been emotionally last week. Only once had Doc seen him since then, stumbling past the store, juggling an armload of liquor. If you're lucky, he remembered thinking, you'll drop the whole bundle. Too bad he didn't, might be alive today if he had.

Faint sounds of sirens echoed between the rows of shops. The pharmacist could not staunch the blood that ran from Al's forehead and his neck slashed by the broken window pane. Steve listened in vain for signs of breathing or moaning. Only the slightest hint of a pulse confirmed to Doc that Al no longer need fear either living or dying. Immediately as a patrol car arrived, the window spectators, the half that did not fear the police, reached for coats, locked their doors behind them, then hurried along their corridors and down flights of dingy stairs to be in on the excitement.

The small group huddled together to shelter themselves from the cold and to be as close as possible to Steve, Doc, the victim, and the police woman who was examining the alcohol on the shirt.

"Can't you do something about the bleeding, Doc?" one onlooker demanded, as if Doc's reputation for making people better depended on some action that only a druggist ought to know about. "Is he dead?" asked a boy. "Who is he?" At last a question several people could answer: "Al. His name's Al. He lives up there. Just moved in a couple'a months ago." All eyes followed Agnes's pointing finger and saw the light bulb swaying in the wind behind the window that the dead man fell through, or jumped through, or was pushed through.

Even though there was no traffic, the siren of the approaching ambulance screamed, warning that the growing crowd should make way. A camera flashed its lightning several times on the body, triggering a rumour that they were gazing at a murdered man. Doc got slowly to his feet, moved out of the path of the paramedics, and murmured, "Suicide. Couldn't hang on, could you?" The police officer swung around to look at Doc, hastily made some notes and collected his name and address.

By the time Alan was loaded into the ambulance, a police traffic motorcycle and a second squad car were on the scene. "Anybody see what happened?" asked a constable.

"He was pushed from that window," responded Agnes, whose winter coat strained to conceal her wine-stained bathrobe. The crowd leaned intently toward her, turning admiring glances to the one who could be counted on to know most of what goes on in the neighbourhood. Fearful that there may have been one or two in the growing crowd who had missed her declaration, she repeated, "He was pushed from that very window. I saw it happen." And as proof, she gave a quick nod and pointed toward the swinging light bulb.

"Where were you standing, ma'am?" enquired the constable.

"I was watching TV in my front room, right up there when I heard the crash."

"Thank you, ma'am."

"Don't you want my name?"

"No, but could you tell us what time you say you saw this happen?"

Agnes, attempting to sound as authoritative as possible, said, "The names of the actors was just coming on the screen. And that always happens just afore the last commercial. So, somewheres between 9:27 and 9:30." She gazed triumphantly at the crowd, then at the constable who was busy scribbling. He appeared merely interested when she thought he should look impressed. "Now do you want my name? It's Agnes. Agnes—" The woman officer stepped forward and led Agnes aside.

Before long, the investigating officers had a lengthy list of ear witnesses but no concrete facts beyond what everyone agreed was the time it happened. No who, or what, and least of all, why. Close inspection of the broken window and of the stairs that led to it revealed no secrets. The officers would return next day to repeat their examination. The building superintendent pointed out that since no one lived above the second floor any more, the stairway could be cordoned off without inconveniencing anyone. She had just come down from Al's room and reported that the large number of paintings up there might mean the dead man was a fence for stolen art work. The thrill of this news emboldened the superintendent. She added, "He couldn't have done all them paintings by himself. Either he was the guy who stole them or he was getting rid of that hot stuff for a ring of thieves."

The police followed her to Al's room, leaving behind a small crowd, each person shivering to keep warm, and struggling to convince everyone else of the reasonableness of their theory: "He fell when he was drunk. I've only seen him drunk." "I tell you, he was pushed." "Hold it, just hold it right there! You heard what Doc said. He committed suicide. He jumped." "Well, I think that . . ."

A voice caused them to pause in their gossiping. It was Bibbi, friendly, hospitable and generous Bibbi, holding the door to his coffee shop open for them. "C'mon in out of the cold. I want to be in on the gab too, you know." About fifteen locals shuffled quickly in and Bibbi called out, "Coffee's on the house tonight, folks."

Even though he felt insecure without a bottle in his hand, Steve led off the debate telling the opinion-hungry group that he knew Al best of anybody in the room. "Since he come here, I bet I spent ten or twelve nights down at the tavern with him. He stood me a whole pile of drinks. I'm real sorry he's gone. He was a good man, a kind man. And generous? Sometimes when there was three or four of us at his table, he'd buy us all round after round. He never said nothin' about paintin'. I know for a fact he was a musician, not a painter. He wouldn't know a paint brush from a tooth brush. But he knew his music like nobody I know. Told us about Shoobert and Bay Toven and Shoppin. Good music, none of the crap you hear on the juke box down there. I never been to his room, but I know for a fact he wasn't no artist. He would of told me if he was. But he liked his bottle. Even more than me." Glances of wide-eyed astonishment passed around the circle.

Since the drug store had closed for the night, Merv and the guard caught up with the evening's experience by sitting in on the debate. Merv who knew first hand of Steve's capacity for drink, and his incapacity too, stole the conclusion from Steve's lips, "Then he was so drunk, he fell down them stairs and crashed through the window."

Steve reclaimed his story somewhat by thumping the table with his fist and declaring, "It weren't right of Doc to say Al suicided himself. He wouldn't do that. I know that for a fact. He was drunk and he fell, and that's that."

"Or . . . Or!" commanded a familiar voice. It was Agnes, the local omniscient observer. "Or, if Tina—you know, the building super—if Tina is right, and there are a whole bunch of paintings up in his room, and if, like Steve says, he ain't no painter, then he must of had stolen stuff up there. He was s'posed to pay off the robbers and he didn't. He's sold some and kept the money for booze. They came to collect, there was a fight, and they pushed him down the stairs. Maybe they didn't mean to kill him, but they did." And as evidence for her argument, she glanced around the group with a mean look that defied argument. "Didn't I try to tell that cop out there that he was pushed? That man was murdered."

Agnes's authoritative voice and logical argument silenced everyone, even Steve who was licking his lips and thinking he needed a drink, bad."

"I don't believe a word of it." Here was a voice new to the community, from a man everyone had seen but no one had heard in the drug store, the voice of the guard, the uniformed hulk. "Al was a good man. Why would anybody want to kill him? He was the only man who called me Tom. That's my name, Tom."

Everyone could see that he wanted to say more, but all he could do was whisper with reverence, "He called me Tom."

During the ensuing silence, the group became aware of a woman sobbing in the corner. Bibbi stopped pouring coffee, hurried over to the woman, and with a soothing voice whispered, "Sall, what's wrong? Somebody do you dirt?" Sally slowly shook her head and wiped tears from her brightly rouged cheeks. "Somebody walk out on you without paying?"

She responded by inhaling a "No", then blew her nose genteelly. "It's Al. He's dead. I loved that man. Sure I used to go to his room a lot. He like to paint me, and always, just before he'd start, he'd put music on, always the same piece. 'Brings light into this dark room,' he'd say with a sigh. Or sometimes, 'Brings light into this dark world.' And at certain moments he'd look—not so much at me as into me, as if the music was saying things that he wanted to put into words but couldn't. I think he was looking to see if I could hear it. I felt, somehow, I don't know—alive? Happier?

"Sure, he asked me to take my clothes off. But he never hurt me, never even touched me, except at the end of each visit, he'd escort me down the stairway and hold my hand. Every time he'd give me the same warning, 'Step over the ripped carpet now. There. Thanks for coming.' Funny, though. Sometimes called me Lois. He painted my picture over and over again, sometimes my face, sometimes a hand, sometimes my whole body. He said I was beautiful. And now he's dead."

Eyes softened with sympathy rested on Sall, then slowly swing around to Agnes who was busy with a loose button, and finally to Steve who reached into his pocket for his mickey. It was 10:15. "Anybody wanna drink?"

CHAPTER EIGHT

THE BOTTLE OR THE PULPIT

The Pulpit

It was almost comical, how solicitous Mark and Charles were about their father's initial approach to a theological college. The twins recalled their own nervous first day at elementary school, the cruel laughter of the older boys and girls who watched them stepping cautiously and with excessive solemnity hand in hand across the playground. And now, twenty-five years later, their dad, at the ripe old age of forty-nine was seriously considering going back to school himself to begin a new career.

Since Lois's tragic death in the middle of a wildly busy street in Florence, he felt his muses deserting him. Beer did give him some relief, for a while. Relaxed him and helped him sleep. But the waking up was becoming increasingly painful. When the stock of good wine was exhausted, he settled for larger quantities of cheaper brands. They, too, enabled him to blot out the scene of Lois's mangled and bloodied body.

Dr. Liang, Victor, observed Alan's decline, listened to his ingenious justifications for stained suits, missed lunches and haggard appearance. "Look," Victor declared one day, "I want you to stop, look, and listen! You have a choice. What's it going to be: a dead-end or a new beginning? One is a single trail and it's downhill all the way, right to the grave. The other has many paths, all uphill, but I'll walk with you, and so will Mark and Charles."

"Are you speaking as doctor or friend?" Alan asked.

"Both. And not only your friend, but Lois's too. I'm a whole roster of Victors urging you not to give up on my friend Al."

Victor helped steer him through the myriad of choices that lay before him. "You may not know which path you want to take, but you'll know with certainty the paths you don't want."

One day, after eliminating another dozen possibilities, without warning, Alan made a watershed discovery. "I've been in denial, Vic. I've consistently refused to consider being—now don't laugh, please don't—being a pastor." Then he sounded the word several times, as if tasting it, "Pastor . . . a pastor, working in a church. Yes! that's it." He was mightily relieved that Victor didn't guffaw. "How do I begin? Would they even want a middle aged man with a degree in fine arts who paints pictures of fire trucks?"

Victor advised him to write a letter to a theological college of a denomination he'd feel comfortable with. "Tell them who you are, your past experiences, including the twins and the deaths of Emily and Lois. But most important, give reasons for choosing ministry. They'll be impressed that you felt in denial and that ministry seemed to choose you more than you chose it."

The letter was three weeks in the writing, and the rewriting. Late in February, without explaining to Mark his daily concentration on his composition, he finally mailed it. Charles had received a sports scholarship and was away at the University of Ottawa. On re-entering the house after dropping the letter with much hesitation into the mail box, Al exclaimed, "Damn, damn, damn! I never thought to keep a copy. Damn!"

Mark looked up from his textbooks. "A copy of what, Dad? You been applying for a promotion?"

"Well, sort of."

"Yeah, that is too bad. But if you set to it right now, you may be able to reconstruct the main points."

Alan was astonished at the speed of the college's reply. Early in March, the principal of the college invited him to meet with her next Tuesday at 10:00 a.m. When Mark returned home for supper, he found his father singing along with his favourite Schubert trio. It had been ages since his father sang anything.

"Did you get a raise, or something?"

"Better than that, a reply to that letter I sent to a theological college." Mark nodded sharply and blinked, and his jaw actually dropped. "You've got to be kidding! You, a priest or whatever?"

"Yes, you heard me, a theological college. I'm thinking of quitting the job of Fire Department illustrator, poster maker, portrait and cityscape painter." His son's head jerked forward and his eyes widened. Alan looked at his son quizzically and asked, "How'd you like to have a minister for a father?"

He gulped, then, "Wow! What a switch. How long have you been thinking about this?"

"Not long enough. And I have an interview with the college Principal next Tuesday. Suddenly I'm nervous."

"Well, I don't really know, Dad. Since Mom . . . since Mom left . . . you've become a different person. Maybe this new person is meant to be a minister. Let's phone Charles and shock the socks off him."

The new prospective college boy felt twenty years younger as he climbed the steps to the principal's office. Her secretary, Eileen Parvamantali introduced herself and suggested he call her Eileen. She looked distraught and frazzled, so much so that the "new boy" wondered what could disrupt his visions of the college as a peaceful oasis in a troubled world.

"I'm afraid there has been a horrible accident about a half an hour ago here at the college, Mr. Thompson, absolutely shocking. It may be that Principal Park may ask for a postponement of the interview. But she did ask that you wait to hear the decision from her if it is not too inconvenient."

"Not inconvenient at all. I have the entire morning. But I do hope that no one has been injured."

"Ah, it's worse that that, Mr. Thompson. But please excuse me, the phones have been ringing for hours—police, parents, reporters. Please forgive me if I run back to my desk." She fled, her heels clopping along the marble floor.

His image of a theological college as a quiet retreat where people spoke in unhurried and hushed tones was being shattered. Two men walked quickly past the doorway, one sobbing feebly, the other apparently attempting to comfort him. An office door clicked shut, and the murmur of their voices was swallowed by thick carpets and drapes.

After several minutes, very determined sounding footsteps echoed nearer and Principal Park walked swiftly into the waiting room. She wore an ankle length pleated maroon skirt, a matching jacket trimmed with navy piping, an amber necklace and no ear rings. "I'm so sorry the college is in such disarray on the first day of your visit, Mr. Thompson." He rose to accept her hand and was about to mutter something he hoped might sound appropriate when she turned and said, "Follow me into my cave here. It'll be quieter. I have told my secretary to block all phone calls but one, and that one may have to terminate our conversation. Please take a seat." She closed the door, paused with a hand on the brass doorknob, sighed, walked to her desk, reached across it for Alan's file, then collapsed into the armchair facing his. He was pleased that she did not hide behind her desk. "Thank you for your helpful letter of introduction."

And so began a fifteen minute conversation that relaxed both the interviewee and the interviewer. She noted his minimal contact with a local congregation, at least since his teen years. She explained that it would take at least six months to rectify that lack. "I shall give you the names of several ministers in several congregations, any one of whom will be happy to introduce you to the challenges of church life. The thought of ministry, Mr. Thompson, is often more appealing the act of ministry."

A telephone ring startled them both. Principal Park reached for the phone and heard Eileen say that Professor Arnold was calling from the hospital. He had been trying for ten minutes to get an open line. His news was as she had feared, "Margaret lost all vital signs during the ambulance ride. The poor young woman was dead on arrival. I'm so sorry," he whispered.

Alan heard the principal instruct Professor Arnold to telephone Margaret's parents, Mr. and Mrs. Hillary, in Scarboro. "It would be awful if our students were to call the family before we reached them. Then take a taxi and speak with them face to face. Offer to go with them to the hospital. I will visit Mr. and Mrs. Hillary there as soon as I can. Thanks, John. This is not easy for any of us . . . terrible." Tears brimmed in her eyes. "Terrible." She hung up and stared into the middle distance for a few seconds, considering options.

"Mr. Thompson, I'd like you to come with me to the quad. That's the site of this awful tragedy. I want you to see a spiritual community in action, particularly how people care for one another in crisis. The students and professors have lost one of our most promising candidates for ministry. We believe she leapt from her fourth floor window, but the police are investigating other explanations. Bring your coat. It will be cold out there."

She rose, exited, and glanced back at him in a way that indicated she was accustomed to lead. He followed her to the group that stood around a sheet which lay where Margaret had thudded onto the unforgiving ground less than an hour before.

To the assembled group, Principal Park expressed the grief and disbelief that was in the minds of everyone—professors, kitchen and caretaking staffs, students, librarians. She announced that all classes would be cancelled until the day after the funeral, that each student was to meet individually with the college chaplain, that reporters would pry to uncover every detail of Margaret's life. "I ask all professors and lecturers here today to meet with me and a police representative at 2:00 o'clock in the Board Room. I encourage you to love one another and to love your neighbour as yourself. Loving self will be harder since we will all feel we had not done or said all we could have for Margaret. We will try to blame ourselves because we could not live one hundred percent for everyone, an inhuman task. So be kind to yourself. And meditate on Romans, chapter twelve.

"My door may not be as open as I'd want in the next few days, but if you wish to speak with me about this tragic event, please persist. I am going to ask our Chaplain to lead us in prayer, remembering Margaret, her family, and us all here at the college."

Following the prayer, students and staff gathered in small groups, wept, and hugged. Alan stood alone, watching the sheet on the icy lawn. A young woman had lain on the hard grass, broken and lifeless.

He imagined himself back in Florence, kneeling beside Lois. And he, too, wept. He had been gazing into a store window and barely heard Lois pleading, "Come on, Alan. We've got to pack our bags and check out of the hotel before twelve. Then we have to get the bus to the airport. Come on, let's go." She'd watched him studying the brush strokes on a particularly striking painting. "Well, I'll go on ahead. I'll meet you in our room."

That was the last he saw of her alive. When horns honked and people shouted, he turned and saw her, frozen in the street, oblivious to the frenetic traffic about her as a truck swerved and struck her.

He knelt beside the sheet and reached out to it. A professor bent over and touched him lightly on the shoulder. "Did you know Margaret well?" Dr Feldon asked gently. "I guess your tears are answer enough. Yes, she was admired and loved by everyone here. We may never know what went wrong. You have my deepest sympathy." Not wanting to intrude further on the grief of this stranger to the college, Dr. Feldon patted him caringly on his back and walked away.

Alan was relieved that he did not attempt to explain his tears, or that, caught up with an image of Lois on the hard ground, he hadn't blurted out, "She was my wife," or some such lament that would sound foolish in this context.

Seeing Principal Park cross the dead lawn towards him, he rose and wiped away his tears. "Oh, I am so sorry," she said, "how thoughtless of me. Your late wife . . . and today, a woman who died just as inexplicably. Please forgive me."

"There is no forgiveness required, Dr. Park. I feel as if I belong here. I feel that death can be the start of . . . of something new."

The principal clenched her eyes and saw on the screen of her remembrance the several losses that had wounded her—a loving father, several dear friends. She inhaled deeply, stood erect, and looking with understanding, shook hands with Alan. "You are needed here," then nodding in the direction of the world outside the walls, "and out there too. Please pick up the names of the ministers and the congregations from Eileen. I would like you to make an appointment to see me in four or five weeks, Mr. Thompson."

After innumerable meetings with committees and subcommittees, with the Rev. Dr. Julian Barbour of St. James' Church, with Principal Park, and with a psychologist, Alan was accepted seven months later on probation as a candidate for the college.

As any student, whether of engineering, history, teaching, or whatever can testify, the years of study pass by at an incredible speed. Subjects of study whose names he had previously not understood, and indeed had misunderstood—like dogmatics, apologetics, eschatology, apocrypha, all such polysyllabic mindbenders, gradually made sense and helped him put pieces of reality together for him. But not fast enough for him to feel ready for his first congregation. His first year of field work in a prison he found fascinating, exhausting, and often frightening, like crossing the Niagara gorge on a tight rope he often thought. His second year working in a psychiatric hospital opened up new and unsettling worlds to him.

By his third year he began to comprehend some of the factors that might have conspired against Margaret, resulting in her suicide. The police had been satisfied that no second person was directly involved. The autopsy certified that she was not pregnant. But the psychological and spiritual issues were innumerable—perhaps a sense of unworthiness or of fear to undertake a task that she considered was far beyond her capabilities. Had she despaired at the awful gap between the good that is possible in the world and the evil that prevails in the lives of so many people, corporations and institutions?

What disturbed Alan was his own fear of not being able to express in words what he knew of a redeeming love. He wondered if, despite his studies and prayers, he might, after all, be better able to communicate through the paint brush. What had been in her mind, he wondered. Where would she be now if she had not leapt to her death? Futile thoughts, these, paralyzing and confounding.

He heard the faint echo of Lois's voice, "If it's meant to be, it will happen." He refused to believe that premature death could ever be "meant to be." Meant for what? Meant why? Did such puzzles drive Margaret to her death? He knew he would be dealing with people who were wrestling with just such mysteries and would expect answers from a man of faith.

All too quickly, the day of his ordination approached. He was thrilled when Charles drove back from Ottawa and Mark took time off from his studies at U. of T. to join Victor, his wife, and three former Fire Department friends. They all drove the two hundred kilometres north-east of Toronto to Trinity Church, Newerton. There Alan was to be ordained and received as the congregation's new minister. He even felt the presence of Lois, present *in absentia*.

During the final hour of their drive, they watched the blazing fall colors of the forest swing past. Canada geese argued among themselves as to whether late October was still too early to fly south, for after all, no frost had yet threatened them and skies were cloudless and deep blue. Home-made weather forecasters were keeping an eye out for flight patterns and whether or not caterpillars were putting on thick coats. "Looks like a mild winter," they agreed.

When the ordination ceremony was concluded, his Toronto friends gathered around him. "What do we call you now," Victor asked, "your Reverence, Alan T. Thompson? Or the Reverend A. Terrence Thompson? Or just Rev. or what?"

"Same as before. Just Al." he smiled, fingering his clerical collar which he'd discovered most ministers referred to as their dog collar.

The congregation was uncertain about how to handle a pastor who was not married. All were saddened to hear of how, four years earlier, his wife had died; some of the single women were hopeful that their charm might hasten a relationship with this very eligible and still young widower.

Trinity was a thriving church, about one hundred and fifty families, accommodated in a building that was in good repair. The staff consisted of four people beside himself. Tim Sullivan was the youth minister, a necessarily energetic young man who seemed to draw young people to him through his endless activities—summer and winter camps, week-end canoe trips, discussion groups, dances, Bible studies. It took a while for Alan to discover that Tim referred to him as "the Rave," a term which seemed to endear the new minister to the exuberant young people. "Sure we can have a youth event in the park. Just ask the Rave to help us make it happen," he overheard Tim say to the group.

"Oh, to be single and young again," said Renata Stearns, organist and choir director as she watched Tim playing basketball in the church gym. Her own energy was drained by her alcoholic husband, but restored by the quality of her musical skills and the dedication of her choir.

Bonnie Armour was the pastoral visitor, commissioned to welcome newcomers and to visit the elderly at home and in nursing homes. Fred Charters was the building superintendent, gardener and groundskeeper.

Alan and his staff met at the church monthly, and individually as planning or circumstances required. One of the new minister's first challenges was to meet and support Renata's husband, Oscar. Being unemployed at the time, he spent most afternoons and evenings at "The Hole in the Wall," a local tavern famous for its long and generous happy hours.

How to encounter Oscar in a nonthreatening way kept Alan alert and thoughtful for several months, long enough to realize that Oscar would never attend church, and did manage occasionally to land very brief jobs as a carpenter when builders found themselves shorthanded. He had erected some fencing for the town around the car dump on the outskirts of Newerton. Rumour had it that Oscar worked on and off for weeks at what others might have done in days, and even then, didn't finish the fence.

One wintry day when a delegation of young people met with "the Rave" and suggested an event in the park, Alan realized that here was a way to reach out to Oscar, the occasional carpenter. "We'll need a small stage for our band. We've got all the mics and loudspeakers and lighting we need. So what about it, Rave?—uh, I mean Reverend Al?" asked the president of the group.

The decision makers of the congregation approved the event to take place in the spring. The band started rehearsing after Christmas, and Alan headed over to talk to Oscar late one morning while Renata was practising at the organ and before Oscar left for his regular descent to The Hole in the Wall.

No dog collar for this visit, Alan said to himself as he dressed down for this long awaited encounter. The sidewalk leading to the Stearns' door was not shovelled, and Alan could tell by the one set of footprints that Renata was still out and her husband still in. Several knocks on the door brought no response, so he hammered with his fists until he heard a chair scrape on the floor.

"Jesus Christ almighty! I'm coming, I'm coming," boomed an angry voice. Oscar, holding a half empty beer bottle flung open the door. "Holy shit! If it ain't the Rev. Pardon my French, but I thought it was somebody. I mean, I thought it was somebody else. You've missed her. She said she was going to practise the organ. Ha! I'd rather she stayed here and practised with my organ . . . sorry. Bad joke. I'll tell her you came."

"No, I came to see you. There's a small carpentry job I'd like you to do for the church," Alan said, suppressing a smile at catching Oscar so completely off base. "Mind if I come in for a minute?"

"Sure, come on the hell in. You'll freeze your balls off out there if you don't. You'll be needin' a beer, I'd think."

"Thanks but I never drink before lunch."

"Ah, what the hell, it's twenty to twelve. I'll getcha one. Nobody needs to know you're twenty minutes ahead of schedule." With astonishing dexterity, he flipped the cap off a bottle and banged it onto the table. "There. Now, what's this job? And so's you don't get any crazy ideas, it's cash on the barrel head."

Alan explained the need for a small stage about five meters wide, four deep and one high, to be built by late April in the town park. He wondered how many details Oscar would recall the next day.

"Sure, just gimme the plans and for cost plus a hundred bucks you've got yourself a stage, Rev."

"No," Alan said, "I'll give you the dimensions and the number of people it should support. You draw it up and build it for the last Friday of April, and you've got yourself cost plus a two hundred."

As the weeks passed, Renata was surprised to see her husband sketching plans. He even visited Alan several afternoons at the church office to get approval for changes and improvements. By mid April, townsfolk were astonished to find him sawing and hammering in the park. He dismissed Fred Charters abruptly, "I can do this myself. I don't need your help or anybody's." The floor went down near the end of the month, giving enough time for the lighting crew to fix their spots and floods to the four-by-fours that stood at the corners of the platform.

The vitality and enthusiasm of the young people ensured a wide variety of talent, including four who had practised Irish dancing with the Youth Band. There would be a few solo singers, the local branch of the town's Barber Shop Quartet, and a skit that in not too heavy-handed a way, would tell the audience what Trinity church was all about.

Newerton, being your average small town community where everybody either knows or is related to everybody else, the event could not be anything but a roaring success. Apart from week-end DVDs for the couch potatoes, what else was there for Newertonians on Friday nights? This could be the first of a series of monthly events, all going well.

People carried their folding chairs and stools and blankets, and while settling down, complimented themselves on their typical fine spring weather. The previous dry weeks ensured a lack of mosquitoes and blackflies. Mercifully, the P.A. system was squawkless, with nary a hint of feedback, at least until the final moment. Tim welcomed everyone, especially the mayor and his wife, then introduced each item on the program. As the sun nestled down into the trees behind the stage, the spotlight turned on the Irish Dancing team.

That was the turning point of the evening. The skit never did get enacted, nor was any final benediction pronounced by the Reverend Alan Terrence Thompson. As later investigations revealed, Oscar felt that the amount of cross-bracing that had been proposed was excessive, too expensive, and in a word, unnecessary. Boards that were to have been screwed were held together with nails that were too short.

As the dancers started to leap and thump about in perfect unison, the platform began to quiver. The drummer was so engrossed in his pounding rhythms that he failed to notice the uprights swaying at the ends of the stage. It felt to him that the whole world was dancing! The electric guitar players incited the dancers to leap even higher and to stomp even louder, until the front supports collapsed and dancers, band and all slid onto the front row of the astonished crowd.

A foot of one of the wide-eyed dancers broke through a drumhead; a mother cut her hand on cymbals that slithered towards her child. A four-by-four upright supporting a spotlight crashed forward, barely missing his honor, the Mayor. And then a moment of utter silence that was terminated by the screech of microphone feed back.

The church staff members responded quickly to the screams of infants and the angry shouts of parents. Tim ordered the lighting crew to cut the power lest any bare wires or broken plugs should start a fire or electrocute anyone. Bonnie Armour was quick to comfort wailing children who had been suddenly plunged into darkness. Fred Charters warned people to stay clear of floorboards for fear of stepping on nails.

Behind the crowd, Oscar, who had stood with arms proudly crossed on his barrel chest, fled as speedily as possible to the one place church folk rarely visited, The Hole in the Wall. Renata avoided as many people as she could, walked home and dreaded a midnight encounter with a drunken husband.

Calls to "sue the bastard," (whoever the bastard might be), and questions like "Did the church have insurance for this?" were pitched back and forth among the dispersing spectators, leaving Alan speechless, anxious, and alone.

No one, certainly not band members, parents or church officials, slept at all Friday night. The next morning, at 8:30, the first of many phone calls drilled holes in Alan's consciousness. "Alan, it's Renata," came a tremulous voice. "I am bringing over my resignation as organist and choir director. Will you be home within the next half hour? Don't try to dissuade me, Alan. My mind is made up. I wrote out my resignation at three this morning, and it's final."

"Yes, I'll be at home, Renata. Come right over."

One of the many advantages of small town life is that no one lives far from anyone. There is no traffic gridlock, and in Newerton, only one stoplight. But smallness can also be a disadvantage since one cannot be anonymous, lost in a crowd, with secrets.

Her neighbours saw her lights on all night. "How can Oscar face anyone after the stunt he pulled? It's a wonder nobody got killed." Some held aside curtains and watched Renata hurriedly back the car down her driveway. "Where's she going so fast at this hour of the morning?" Ingredients for rumours were being picked over, selected, and distributed by telephone: "It would serve him right if she just up and left that alcoholic, no good husband of hers,"—which was transformed into—"Janey says Renata left her husband this morning after an all-night fight. Serves him right!" which morphed into "Somebody saw Renata drive her car away like a bat out of hell. Oscar was shouting after her and chased her, some people say, with an axe!"

Renata was oblivious to the specifics of the rumours but not unaware that stories would be spreading like clouds of toxic fumes. She was comforted that Alan did not live beside the church under the scrutiny of half the town. He had purchased a house just beyond the eastern outskirts of Newerton, on the crest of a hill from which in winter, when the trees shivered without their leaves, you could just see the spire of Trinity church silhouetted against the evening sky. The grounds around his house were a popular meeting place for church picnics and young people's volley ball games. The highway curved and climbed past his semi-circular driveway, then descended to rich farmland in the next valley.

Alan waited at the front door for Renata to pull into one of the two gates of the looping driveway. He watched her through the bushes and trees that celebrated their new spring clothes. After waiting for a car heading into town, she swung left onto his property. Whoever it was in the passing car would recognize hers, he thought, and add some fuel to the lethal fumes. The passer-by was already on his cellphone. "Bert, it's Jimmy. I just drove past the Reverend's hilltop house. Guess who just pulled into his driveway? And it's not even nine o'clock."

Apparently Mother Nature hadn't read the outpourings of poets, for she disregarded what ought to have been an appropriate response: swirling, threatening clouds and advancing thunder to echo the chaos in the lives of Alan, Renata, and so many Newertonians. Not even an admonitory flash of lightning. Instead of pathetic fallacy, there was only a mocking pathetic irony as goldfinches skipped and swooped through the new springtime foliage. Two hummingbirds were jealously monitoring the bird feeder that hung outside Alan's kitchen window. Splashes of sunshine danced on bright yellow forsythia bushes. Only the two human beings radiated gloom, the one sitting frozen in the front seat of her car, the other, slouching as he waited on the front steps of a small, neat brick house.

Renata closed the door of the car, without much conviction, Alan thought. She unfolded a piece of paper as she approached him. "Here it is. There's really nothing to talk about. People will not expect me to show my face at church tomorrow, although there'll be a very large turnout just in case. I don't envy you having to turn up yourself."

"I know. A lot of them are quite angry, not so much at what happened as at what could have. Or at what I should have foreseen. Come on in and let's at least have a cup of coffee." He held open the screen door and as she walked through, he asked, "You'll have to pardon me for enquiring, but how on earth did you get tangled up with Oscar?"

She walked into the kitchen, sat at the table and with obsessive precision arranged the letter squarely in front of her. She stared at it for a few seconds and exhaled deeply. "Yes, how did I? Alan, I'm thirty-eight years old. You met our son last Christmas on one of his rare trips east. Blaine is twenty-two years old. Most people around here think he's a mature eighteen year-old, and at times he acts like an immature one. But he is twenty-two. You don't have to be a wizard to see that I was only sixteen, and Oscar was just one year older. His parents and mine said marriage was our only choice. Besides, Oscar was the life of all the parties in town. Imagine, being married to the life of a life-long party. What a ball it should have been and it was, until he started drinking.

"Our parents propped us up as long as they could. I always played the piano, and filled in at the organ when the regular organist, George Flaherty, was away. He taught me. Now I teach piano and work at Trinity. That and Oscar's few carpentry jobs keep the home fires burning. And the booze flowing. Last evening when his stage collapsed, I finally realized the party's over.

"Five years ago, Blaine left home in search of a job on the west coast, almost as far away from his father as he could get. Vancouver. So I have an absent son and a husband who's as good as dead."

The long silence that ensued was intensified by the tinkling of two spoons stirring two cups. Alan lifted his mug to his lips, mused over it for a moment, "How strange. Here you are with a living husband who is dead for you. And here I am with a dead wife who is still very much alive for me. I'm hard pressed to agree that the universe is unfolding as it should. Don't repeat that to anybody as

I suspect it's heretical. Both you and I had very different universes in mind than what we see today."

They contemplated their roads behind and the many paths that lay ahead. Alan broke the silence. "What will you do?"

She placed her elbow on the table and rested her forehead in the palm of her hand.

"Will you leave him?" Her pained concentration caused him to pause, then whisper, "Leave Newerton?"

Through the mists of uncertainty, she tried to conceive of another life, perhaps lost and alone in an unwelcoming city. Or possibly feted as a notable choir director in a large, historic downtown church.

She folded her hands on the table, stared at them as if they held answers, and finally said, "You began again, Alan. You went back to college. You left Toronto and started afresh. I can too. There must be a need for organists and choir directors in Kingston or Toronto or some other larger centre, perhaps even Vancouver. Oscar doesn't know, but I've been stashing away small amounts of money for an emergency. And now it's come.

"Tomorrow is Sunday. I'll get a replacement organist. Then after I've scoured the want ads and sent out applications, I'll be gone. You don't need to tell me the congregation and the choir will miss me. I know they will."

Alan didn't argue, except to say, "And so will I." His ability to empathize prevented him from trying to change her mind. She slid the letter of resignation across the table, stood up, turned, and without looking back, left.

Awkward wasn't the word for the Sunday church service. She had not been able to find an organist on such short notice; so the tentative a capella singing was ground out with frowns in competing pitches. Following the worship, the choir met to work out their strategy.

Erna Offenbach, head of the math department at Memorial High called the meeting to order. "Lock the door, Elmo, we don't want our kids running in and out and carrying tales. And we don't need the pastor telling us what to do."

"Or what not to do," boomed Percy Coulter, the church's bass lead.

Although Erna seemed to be chairing the meeting, that role did not prevent her from doing all the talking. "Helen, pass this schedule around. We can take turns phoning Renata. Tell her she's not to blame for Oscar's incompetence. Tell her we can't get along without her. Tell her how much we . . . well, you get the point. Sign up if you want to give her a call. If she refuses to continue as our director, we won't have next week's choir practice here at Trinity. Instead we'll drive over to her place and hold it on her front veranda. But don't tell her that part of the plan. Agreed?

Heads nodded and several voices called out, "Agreed!"

"And," Percy roared, "and we can sing just a little off key. That usually gets her."

"He oughta know," sniggered one of the sopranos to her eye-rolling neighbour.

When he heard about the plan, Alan didn't interfere with holding the rehearsal at the Stearns' home. He realized that most of the choristers had known her years longer than he did. Pastors come and go, but choir members go on forever.

Their persistence and ingenuity paid off, partly because on hearing the first bars of four-part harmony on his front steps, Oscar made a dash for the back door, out the garden gate, and along the alley that led via several side streets to the back door of his favourite hideaway. Bass-booming Percy found that his pugilistic precautions were not required.

After the second verse of "Abide with me," Renata relented, opened the door, and with tears glistening in her eyes, knew she could not abandon her beloved, almost harmonious choir. All eighteen of them accepted her invitation to continue the rehearsal in the living room, an event that was climaxed by the unexpected delivery of six extra large pizzas and soft drinks. Alan timed that well.

Several days later, he telephoned Renata and asked her to return to his house on the hill Tuesday evening to retrieve her letter of resignation and to hear his suggestions for a more active choir program. From that time onward, Renata, occasionally accompanied by Bonnie or Tim, met at his home to discuss next Sunday's service, or the coming church season. When those meetings were discontinued for the summer, Alan became aware of just how important all his staff members were for his own personal life. Victor and his wife were disappointed that Alan preferred not to join them on their visit to Japan. "Thanks, Vic, but my world travelling days are over. Sightseeing without Lois has lost its appeal. Besides, I'm looking forward to the visits of Charles and Mark. They've managed to preserve two weeks between their summer employment and their return to university to be with me in tranquil, tree-sheltered Newerton."

Much to Renata's surprise, Oscar managed to hang onto a summer job. She suspected that their slightly more affluent condition would, as usual, come to an abrupt end. And so it did, precisely when she felt that their marriage just might be reviving. But she could never have imagined how brutal and catastrophic would be the final termination of their life together a few months later.

The second year for Alan at Trinity began on no less a positive note than did his first. He was known by a wider spectrum of townsfolk, most of whom, by now, pardoned him for what could have been a tragic spring event in the park. There were little jibes that he had to endure in good humour, like people calling him "Joshua", comparing the pastor to the biblical figure who engineered the downfall of the walls of Jericho. It was in his best interests to laugh goodheartedly on being greeted with "Well, look who's in the convenience store! If it isn't Josh himself!"

"No, that's Earthquake Thompson" came a quick reply from one of the customers.

The town's one arts and crafts shop was proud to display half a dozen of his paintings. Four of them were done locally, the most detailed being the view from his hilltop house down into the valley, needlessly entitled "Sunset over Newerton." He indulged in a little artistic licence by heightening the church spire so that it might project noticeably above the distant trees.

Renata was pleased when the weekly planning meetings resumed in September. "I am so glad the choir encouraged me to remain. The thought of starting all over at my age scared me half to death."

"But thirty-nine is not that far over the hill. In fact, it's not even up the hill. And besides, you know what they say begins at forty."

She grimaced. "I have no yearning to begin a new life with Oscar. That party's still over, although I don't think he's noticed."

Leaves began their slow turn to yellows and reds, and then their inexorable flutter and gyration earthward. The sun started on its trip south for the winter, despite the howls of protesting winds. One of the sources of light and warmth was the Tuesday visit of Renata.

"If you find the drive up the hill worrisome as winter approaches," Alan reluctantly said, "we can always meet at the church."

"No, the church folk will be happy not to have to heat your office, especially since you have a perfectly comfortable place here. And besides, it does me good to escape from town even for a few hours."

It was no secret that every Tuesday evening, the organist of Trinity Church climbed into her car, and regardless of snowfalls or high winds, backed down her lane and drove away. "Poor woman. Her husband won't even shovel out the driveway for her. There she is, having to do it all by herself," her neighbour said sympathetically over the phone.

"Well, I'm not surprised," replied Jimmy. "I hear that she spends every Tuesday evening up at the pastor's place.'

"But not by herself. She picks up some other staff members occasionally."

"Yes, Janey, but less and less occasionally, from what I hear."

"Oh, Jimmy! Who are you to talk?"

"Now just who has been gossiping about me?"

Early in December at ten p.m. on a Tuesday night, Oscar stood unsteadily, arms akimbo in the doorway of their home as Renata tried to get in out of the cold.

"On church business, were ya? Ha! You used to be able to finish your meetings with him in an hour when ya met at the church."

Shivering, and stamping the snow off her boots, she returned the volley, "How would you know? You're never back from your booze hall before two. Now get out of the way. You're cooling off the whole house, and it's me that gets to pay the fuel bill."

Not much of a push was required to move him out of the way, but enough that he lost what little balance he had. He stared up from the floor with a look that was somewhere between astonishment and fright. Something has changed, he thought. He watched her fling her boots into the boot basket and hang her coat in the closet. He cringed when she slammed the closet door.

She stopped in her tracks when she heard her husband call her by name. When was the last time I ever called her name, he asked himself. "Renata, we're into the snow season now."

How odd it was to hear something that sounded like pleading from him. From him, of all people. Years ago she had quit her pleading: please give up drinking, please drink less, do try to get a job and hold onto it. Never before this had he pleaded with her. He wrestled himself to his feet, held onto the wall, and repeated, "This is the snow season. What if you get snowed in up at the pastor's house?"

"Don't worry, Oscar. I can always borrow his skis and ski down the road. I won't spend the night with him if that's what's troubling you. But would it really matter to you if I did?" She waited for an answer, and when none was forthcoming, she turned, went into the bedroom and closed the door.

For all three of them, Alan, Renata, and Oscar, the next six days passed excruciatingly slowly. For the pastor, there were the usual predictable interminable committee meetings. For the organist, night after night in her living room, the regular music students showed that they had been practising their predictable errors. The choir practice on Thursday and the service on Sunday shed a glimmer of light on the bleak sunless days of December for both of them. As for the former "life of the parties," he suffered the usual burdens of guilt and anger: too much booze, too few good intentions carried to completion, and no effort to find work.

The next Tuesday, much longed for by all three, finally arrived. When Oscar failed to turn up at his usual early hour at The Hole, the card sharks, pool players and bar flies assumed he was ill. Although some of the regulars pointed out that he had been there in fine form just that afternoon, animated, talkative, agitated. All rumours were quelled when he finally arrived around 9:30 p.m.

"What? The wife make you do the dishes, Oscar?"

Camaraderie characterized the early hours of the tavern's habitués. It would not be until midnight that friends customarily transformed into antagonists and light-hearted back slapping mutated into heavy fisted punches. "We figured you were attending the Tuesday night church planning session." Loud prolonged guffaws celebrated that taunt. He turned a sour grimace towards the joker.

"Hey, Barrel-nose, that's Oscar's stool you're sitting on. Go find yourself a new perch. And Slugger, hurry up and give the man a pint. Can't you see he's ready to drop from thirst? Several of the poker players did comment later on how pale he looked. None had observed his rapid, shallow breathing.

The games of cards and pool resumed, punctuated by laughter that indicated it was still before midnight. Oscar sat smiling at his beer. He had lost his afternoon animation and talkativeness.

Back at the eastern edge of town, Alan and Renata stood at the front door of his house. "Thanks, Alan, for the new life that you've brought to our congregation, and . . . and to me, too. These Tuesdays are what I look forward to all week."

Their conversation had been free, open, and honest all evening. But now that the planning session was over, Alan was lost for words, a hazardous block for a pastor and preacher. She walked towards the coat rack. He assisted her to don her parka, reached towards the door handle, paused, then put his arm around her waist and drew her to him. There was total awkwardness, she in her heavy coat and winter boots, one arm clutching a briefcase of music. Despite the clumsiness of the situation, he kissed her on the mouth.

He's keeping his eyes close, she noticed. Is that because he's kissing Lois? It has been ages since a moment like this. Oh, don't let it end.

After stepping back, "Next Tuesday . . ." was all he could say. "Next Tuesday." She turned a melancholy smile towards the opening door and walked out into the lightly falling snow. He stood at the door and watched her drive away.

"Next Tuesday," he said aloud to himself. "Tuesday next." He had too much to think about before he began collecting the coffee mugs and the cake plates, too much to try absorbing the ten o'clock T.V. news of world turmoil. There would be nothing new on the news anyway, only more international atrocities, more business fraud, murders, rapes, robberies, corruption of officials, adultery of . . . . Adultery . . . "Next Tuesday?" he asked himself. He turned off the living room lights and sat pensive in the dark, staring out the window, ruminating on his personal—and hopefully private—turmoil. Outside, the full moon shone on the snow, casting shadows of branches on the icy ground. The world—even time—seemed frozen. With a shudder he recalled the black hole that Lois had feared.

The jangling of the telephone wrenched him out of the refuge he was constructing for himself. "Alan, sorry to be the bringer of bad news." It was the chairman of the church maintenance committee, Dr. Rolf Montroy, the one man whose sad task it was to report smashed stained glass windows or roof damage after storms. There was always something costly that was breaking down, the furnace, the water pipes.

Alan sighed, realizing that there never was a "good" time, least of all tonight, to hear damage reports that would drain the congregation's coffers.

"It's Rolf."

"Yes, I recognized your voice. What's the bad news this time, Doctor?"

"I'm afraid it's Renata."

Alan froze, knowing that sooner or later someone would counsel the pastor about what could be perceived—only by gossip mongers, mind you—as an inappropriate relationship with a staff member. Might this warning provide an escape from the dilemma of next Tuesday, he instinctively thought.

"I'm on duty tonight at the hospital. Renata was brought in by ambulance. She smashed her car coming from . . . coming down the east road. It doesn't look good. The police wondered if she even tried to stop. Can you come right away?"

"But I was just . . . she was here only . . . How bad is it?" and without waiting for an answer, he blurted, "I'll be right there."

He dashed for a coat. Forget the boots. There wasn't that much snow. "The keys, the keys! Oh where are the damn keys?" He found them on the third search in the coat pocket where he always kept them, ran out the front door without bothering to lock up, climbed into his car and drove off. He didn't take the time to examine or even observe the footprints that linked his car to Renata's.

At the same moment, the front door of The Hole exploded open, and for the second evening in a row, in ran Gerry. Yesterday he'd shouted proudly for all to hear over the braying juke box, "It's a boy—a seven pound boy. Drinks all 'round." But tonight he shouted, "Oscar! Where's Oscar?" There had been a few complications in the birth and he was visiting his wife in the hospital when the ambulance delivered a badly injured woman—Renata.

He glanced around the tavern and saw Oscar slouched at his usual table. "Oscar! It's your wife. She's had an accident. She's in the emergency room at the hospital."

Oscar contemplated the level of the beer in his bottle, slowly turned and gave a sneer to the panting Gerry.

"She's hurt real bad." Oscar turned his attention back to his bottle, took a swig and assessed how much remained. All eyes were on him. The hall would have been silent were it not for the passionate whining of a country and western singer who competed, unsuccessfully, with his band. Gerry put a gentle hand on Oscar's shoulder. "I'll go with you, Oscar, back to the hospital. Oscar . . . Oscar?"

The tippler placed both hands on the edge of the table, gave enough of a push to lean back, look over his shoulder at the messenger and mumble, "No point in goin', the state she's in. They won't let me in considerin' the state I'm in."

Looking confused at the others, Gerry said, "I'll let them know you're on your way. Better hurry though. There may not be much time." He backed away, gave his friends a shrug, then skipped around some tables and hurried out the door.

Between the trees down the road ahead, Alan could see the flashing red lights of police cars. By the time he was rounding the curve, he caught sight of a fire truck, a tow truck and several bright red flares. There was no need to stop there since Renata was already in the town hospital. But he did want to catch a glimpse of the wreck, to judge the possibility of her survival.

The brake pedal slammed to the floor, and before he could reach for the emergency brake or engage a lower gear, the car, increasing in speed, swerved to miss the crowd, plunged into the ditch and bashed headlong onto the massive rock through which the road had been cut. Glass showered about him, metal clattered over the face of the rock. Then a black silence.

Alan had not attached his seat belt. When the ambulance returned for him, there was but feeble indication of heart beat, and great loss of blood.

Rumours spread of a suicide pact. Those rumours ceased when the police reported that both sets of brake cables had been severed.

CHAPTER NINE

TRAVEL OR THE COTTAGE:

The Cottage—Part One

Mom and Dad and Charles and me finally decided that getting a cottage would be better than doing a whole lot of travelling. Mom heard about some property in the middle of nowhere that was up for sale. She tried awful hard to get Dad to go see it. She said, "Al, it will at least be worth looking at." She's reading from the ad. "It says: 'a well-built cottage, three bedrooms, kitchen, a handyman's delight, on a lake, boathouse, beach great view, 10 km. south of Norvale'."

Dad said it sounded pretty expensive to him, a lot more than we could pay.

"No, it shouldn't be that much. It's up for sale because of back taxes," whatever that meant. I was only eight so I didn't understand a lot of things then. Sometimes I wonder if I know much more now I'm fourteen—or even want to know."

"Where the hell is Norvale? Never heard of it. Is it even on a map, Lois?" Dad was awfully growly then. He said the Fire Department wasn't happy with his work and he just wasn't happy about anything. Of course none of us felt very good because my baby sister died in her crib. The only time Dad could even try to smile was to help Mom when she cried almost all day long. I guess he was trying to look strong. But even I could see it wasn't a real smile, just his mouth. His eyes still looked sad.

It seemed to me that Dad didn't want to go anywhere any more, or do anything. Before, he used to take me and my brother fishing. And before Emily all four of us would go camping for a weekend, or bicycling for a half a day. But not any more. He sort of scared me sometimes, the way he'd sit and stare. At nothing.

"Al, the ride up there to see the property will do us all good."

Mom packed a lunch and we took our bathing suits, just in case the lake wasn't a swamp.

"You don't need to put mine in. I won't be swimming," Dad said. But I threw it in anyway, and Dad told me in a tired kind of way, "Mark, I won't need that. Now put it back in my drawer where you found it."

When we travelled up there, it felt like our van was standing still, and trees and rocks were passing by us, but we weren't getting anywhere. And even if we were, I figured we might never know how to get back. Charles, he's my brother, my twin, my know-it-all twin, was leaping around in our van shouting, "Look at this! Look at that! Did you see those?" Couldn't he see I was more interested in my video game?

After hours and hours of smooth highway, the van began swerving and jolting and slowing down for deep puddles and racing down this narrow dirt lane. Charles would let out a whoop when we shot over some hills. At times it was like a roller coaster ride. I opened the window 'cause I thought I was going to be sick. Finally Mom shouted, "We're here!" and she looked at Dad as if she wanted to say, "I hope you like it." He was looking worried.

What we saw first was water, a lake that sparkled through the trees. Then after a last curve we pulled in behind a little house. They kept calling it a "cottage" as if that might stop us from seeing that it was a wreck, a wreck in the middle of nowhere. The screen door was off its hinges, some of the windows, all covered with cobwebs and dust was broken, and inside, I seen animal cages at the zoo that were cleaner. Father looked into the kitchen. He frowned and said, "Squirrels, porcupines, and a lot of their shit."

I was trying to rack up a best score on my game while Charles was running all over the place with his "Mark, come 'ere," his "Look at this." Then not a minute later, "Wow, an old dock. Maybe there's a boat." Anybody with half a brain could see it all added up to a whole lot of work, sweeping and cleaning and fixing.

"There isn't even any water," I mumbled. I remember how Dad glared at me, pointed to the lake and said, "There's your bathtub."

"I mean water to drink, and we're a long way from any stores that sell Coke or Pepsi." So Mom pointed to that great big bathtub and said, "You won't find cleaner water in the city." I was picturing water snakes and bloodsuckers and octopuses in my drinking water. "Yuk!"

Mom and Dad went off by themselves, talking serious as they been doing ever since little Emily died over three years ago. Charles was skipping stones on the lake, shouting, "Four!" and "Wow, six!" Then a minute later a crunch of an old tree falling over, helped a whole lot by Charles, and Mom yelling, "You boys be careful now!" How come when he does the damage, I always gotta share the blame?

We had to unpack the van, set up our three tents, one for Mom and Dad, one for cooking and eating, and one for me and Charles. Of course we had to fight about where it should go. He wanted it down by the shore. I wanted it up on a hill case it rained. Dad told us it should not be too far from our campfire. There was tons of firewood around, and before long, Dad had a big fire going and supper was ready. We hauled logs up near the fire and dug in.

It was right then while we were sitting there and everything was quiet that we could hear the wind hiss in the trees—white pine Dad said they were—and the birds, even some ducks quacking out on the lake. It was like watching a movie, a 3-D movie that's all around you. The clouds caught on fire and burned red and yellow and all of a sudden I knew I wanted to stay there forever. We could keep the fire going all through the night. It was even fun washing the pots and pans in the sand at the beach. Then Charles had to spoil it by flicking sand at me, and when I retreated into the water, he started splashing.

It would be a nice place except for him. Sometimes I really hated that guy, and then I started hating myself for thinking that way.

Mom and Dad walked around. They looked at the cottage and the boathouse, the dock and a little tiny shed that they said used to be a toilet, a "two-holer", whatever that is. Mom kept glancing at Dad. I guessed she was hoping he would say, "Yes, let's take it."

They came back to the tents where I was unrolling my sleeping bag. Dad looked right at me as if he saw me and asked, "Well, what do you think?"

All I could say was "I like it here. It's nice." What I really wanted to say was, Let's move here. Let's get away from our sad place in the city. I can't imagine Mom crying here, and maybe, Dad, you'll want to paint pictures of everything—the lake that looks like a mirror. You look down into it and you see the burning clouds and trees upside down. There's even a moon down there! Dad, all you have to do is copy what you see. I bet it's even more pretty when the leaves turn red. Let's live here.

That's what I wanted to say, 'cept it would have sounded stupid. He looked down at me and said, "Yes, Mark, I like it too. It really is very nice."

And then I knew. I never knew it before. Maybe he wanted to say more too, but he didn't know how to either. Maybe other people besides me can't say what's really inside them.

*   *   *

We bought the place. And for twelve years, mostly summers, we were happy there. Dad's painting really picked up. It took a while, but once the cottage was back in decent shape, he'd spend more and more time at his canvases. And Mom, too, came alive again. There would be days when she would stand looking at nothing, but then the flash of sunlight on the lake or the song of a bird would bring her back.

I was always aware, perhaps even subconsciously, that is, if one can be subconsciously aware, that life could take an abrupt turn, possibly disastrous. Probably I learned that lesson the day we found Emily lifeless in her crib. We hear of forest fires that devastate everything, of caterpillars that wipe out trees, leaving ugly, leafless trunks. Vandalism was a major fear, especially as the years passed and more and more townsfolk and tourists launched their boats at the far north end of "our" lake, or left snowmobile tracks near our cottage in winter.

I've learned, however, that what one imagines as least likely to take place can happen. I often wondered if Dad had these thoughts too.

Each of those twelve years brought new experiences, like the time Mom and Dad let Charles and me paddle across the lake for the first time by ourselves. It was a wonder we made it alive to the other side because of our anger. As usual, he insisted on steering. He always got to decide where we'd head the canoe. So I'd splash him with my paddle and he'd pretend to tip the canoe. Of course he chose the most impossible site to land at, and the most impassable slope to climb. We fought our way through brambles, poison ivy, thorn bushes, scrambled up the steep hill and found a ledge that looked down over the lake. The view below reminded me of that first night three years before when we sat around the fire as the setting sun put on its startling display of slow motion pyrotechnics.

Our pushing and shoving and insult hurling ceased as we stood beside each other, gazing at this wonderful view. What a great place for a secret lodge, our own private "Ledge Lodge," I thought to myself. Nothing or nobody to spoil it, except Charles maybe.

Then he says, "Hey! Why don't we build a secret hut on this ledge? Who'd ever find the way up here?"

"I thought of it first," I shouted.

"Did not. It was my idea. Anyway, I said it first. You're always thinking, but I said it."

"Yeah, you're always talking, Charlie. Talk, talk, talk. That's all you ever do." And I flung some pebbles at him.

He swerved around to dodge them, but he was too close to the lip of the ledge. Maybe the edge broke off or maybe he slipped. His arms went up like he wanted to grab at something. There was nothing to grab. Backwards he fell, his eyes staring wide and mouth screaming, "Maaarrk!"

I threw myself down on the ground as close to the edge as I could and saw him about four meters below, motionless on the white rocks. I remember the whiteness of the rocks so very clearly because blood oozed in a stream across a flat boulder, a bright red slash on a pure white background. I watched it writhe across the surface of the stone, the one as frail as life, the other as hard as death.

I stared down, paralyzed, just as years before I looked down at the white sheets of a crib and at Emily's lifeless body. The people closest to me always die. I touch them and they die. Who will be next? I was the one who found Emily's still body then, and now it is me again who finds Charles dead. Finds him dead? Or causes his death? I didn't really hate him. Not really, did I?

Tears blurred my vision making it appear that Charles moved. God, don't let him die. I know it was my fault. Was it my fault again? Let him live. I wiped the tears from my eyes and saw his arm slide up—not down, but up the inclined rock surface.

I scrambled to my feet, eyes darting this way and that in search of a path down to him. He was holding his ribs when I reached him. "What happened?" he rasped. "My arm. It's broke . . . I can't move my—my leg. And blood. I fell . . ."

I knew I should have been doing something to help but words tumbled from my mouth—"Charlie, I'm sorry. I didn't mean to hurt you. I didn't mean for you to die."

His eyes got awful big when I said "die," and he groaned, "Dead. Dead!" I couldn't breathe when he said that to me. Then I realized he was trying to say "Dad—get Dad."

I hardly remembered stumbling and jumping and falling down through the bushes, down the steep slope to the shore. I waded to the canoe, leaped in and paddled like crazy across the lake, screaming all the time, "Dad, Charlie's hurt. Mom! Dad! Help," over and over again.

I was almost to the shore when they met me in the row boat. Because I was crying so hard and screaming half sentences they had no idea of whether he had drowned or fallen or broken something or maybe was even dead.

It took a while to climb up through the bushes and trees and rocks to find him. But he was still breathing. Let him live, God, let him live, I kept praying in my mind. Don't let him die like Emily. I was scared that Mom or Dad would ask, "Did you poke him, too?" But they didn't.

They said not to move him, and again his eyes got big and frightened. "We'll air-lift you out of here and get you to a hospital as fast as we can, son," Dad said.

Mom stayed with him while Dad and I paddled fast back to get to the cottage and telephone for help. My head was in two places—up there with Charlie, wondering if he would pull through, picturing Mom holding back her tears, and at the same time down here in the tilting canoe, wondering what to say if Dad asked what happened. But he was too intent on digging his paddle into the waves. In times of crisis, he seemed to shut down.

When we beached the canoe, he ran to the cottage. Funny, he phoned the Toronto Fire Department to find out how to locate the nearest air ambulance.

It took over an hour to get there. They instructed us to wave sheets or light a smudge to guide the rescuers. The helicopter hovered over us back at the fatal ledge, then swooped away to a rocky clearing that we had never seen about fifty meters back of the dense brush.

The paramedics examined him, stopped the bleeding, and put on splints. He was looking at me all the time and groaning. I guess I wasn't much help, me sobbing and whining. They lifted him onto a stretcher and with Dad's help, carried him to the 'copter. Mom went in with him. The propellers slapped and thumped, the motor whined, and they all floated up over the treetops and drifted away.

Dad held me tight and said, "It's all right to cry. He'll be OK."

I have forgotten how many broken bones Charlie suffered, how many pins held him together and how often casts had to be changed. Everyone told him he was fortunate to be alive. The day he was released from hospital, as he was limping along on his crutches, Mom put her arm around my shoulder and said, "You're lucky to have a twin brother who lived through this ordeal." Then she gave me a little hug. I couldn't help wondering why she said that "I" was lucky. Why not "we" were lucky? Was she saying it's lucky for you this time? Did she think I pushed him? I tried not to think about what she might have meant, Or what I might have done.

Dad was as happy as if Charles had died and come back to life again. What a party awaited us when we got back home from the hospital. He told us that next spring, one of the first things we should do is return to the lake, climb up to the ledge and face our fear. "Begin again," he said, "yes, begin again," as if he were talking to himself.

For the first time since Emily died, Dad really did begin again, painting with enthusiasm, in colors, even before we returned months later to the cottage. Joe Vittorio, his boss at the Fire Department, was proud of his own role in connecting with the air ambulance. Nobody around here knew exactly how to get in touch with the flight rescue system; so Dad called Joe. He made the contact and fast.

Before Dad made his turnaround as the Department's revived "artist in residence," as the Chief called him, Joe had been worried about the backlog of unfinished portraits and illustrations. But when it was evident that Charles would live and not be too badly damaged, Dad slowly began to produce impressive work.

The next spring, we did return to the lake. Mom and Dad worked from the first morning bird chirp to the first cry of the loon at nightfall. We even cut a path up the steep slope across the lake, and over a few days, built a lean-to on the fateful ledge.

On our sixth summer, when Charles and I turned fourteen, Mom and Dad bought us a sleek new sailboard. That was when I learned the thrill of being—how shall I say—linked with nature, made one with the breeze and the waves and the gliding seagulls. A few years later, we began to bring friends up here to share what we loved so much, the sounds of the forest, the slower pace of life, the peace and the quiet.

When it came to inviting friends to our paradise, Dad was of two minds. He was pleased to see people enjoying nature, delighted to hear the echoes of their laughter across the water and through the trees. But he was never sad to watch them drive away. Once again he could appreciate the silence and the solitude.

June, my girl from high school, didn't care much for the place. "Not enough action, not enough pop music, no pizza restaurant, not even any fast-food delivery," she complained to my friend Jordan. I liked him. He showed me how to play some interactive computer games in Toronto. When he was dodging missiles and monsters and mountains, he was pumped up, really alive.

"Standing on a sailboard looks boring to me," he said. They left a day early to get back to the city "where there's at least some of the latest video games. Is three all the channels you can get up here? Why don't you get a disk? That'll bring in thirty or forty."

I was not sad to see them go, even though I liked June. We had to follow them constantly, stamping out their cigarette butts. They couldn't understand the significance of the forest fire alert during that exceptionally dry period.

We worked on insulating the cottage because each year we arrived earlier and left later. You could have some serious snowball fights even in April, long after the white stuff gave up and ran down the sewers in the city. And once, we got caught by a surprise snowstorm in late October.

On our tenth year, we rented snowmobiles and roared in for our first winter here. It was a test run since Dad had been told that as long as he dropped into the Fire Department office once a week, kept in touch by email and telephone, he could work at his painting and illustrating wherever he wanted. That was the year he discovered he could paint winter scenes. Later that season Mom and Dad let us borrow the car and bring up a few of the guys from school. Some brought snowshoes, some, cross-country skis, and we all brought beer and food.

As the years and the cottage progressed, until our twelfth year here, what was best of all was seeing Mom and Dad laugh, and his paintings really come alive. The colors rubbed off the skies, off the rain-polished trees, off everything, and onto his canvases. It was smart of the Department to let him work up here, undisturbed by the politics and the pressures of the office.

And Mom took up experimenting with leaves, berries, and bark, to dye yarns that she would use for her rug hooking. Mrs. Laplante, our neighbour—if you can call people seven kilometres away a neighbour—taught Mom the intricacies of this natural art. Both she and her husband would drop by every five or six days to bring some mail from town or some fruit they had just bottled.

In the spring of the eleventh year, the last of our happiness at the cottage, Mom was bitten by the antique bug. "Alan, don't you think it's about time we bought some interesting old furniture for the cottage?"

"Why?" he asked, not noticing that the creaky chair he was sitting on was one of the items we'd picked up from roadside garbage. And the kitchen table had porcupine teeth marks on two of its legs. "Why? What's the matter with the old furniture we've got?"

"Quit trying to prove that you're a man!"

"Now, what's that supposed to mean, Lois?"

Mom looked up from her boiling kettle of vile smelling bark. "For one thing, now that we're spending more time here, winter and summer, we need furniture that comforts our souls as much as our bodies. And we do need more beds since the twins are beginning to bring up their buddies."

Aware of all the guests who stayed with us, often sleeping in sleeping bags on the floor, we had already changed the name from "The Cottage" to "Lakeside Cottage."

So, occasionally Charles and I and our friends would enjoy having the place to ourselves while our parents visited antique barns. They began bringing home interesting chairs, a tall floor lamp, a glass-topped coffee table (to give it a little class), a second hand sofa bed, a brass bed, and assorted items like wall switches, towel racks, a fireplace screen and some carpets. Charles and I became experienced furniture movers and arrangers until Mom was satisfied with what she saw.

"Is your soul comfortable now?" Dad teased. "Shall we sell our Toronto house and move up here?" And I suddenly recalled my thoughts on the first of our visits here, Let's stay here forever.

That winter, Charles booked our cozy Lakeside Cottage—of course not the frigid Ledge Lodge—for five days between Christmas and New Year's Day. He wanted to bring up three of the guys he knew at university. They ended up spending their evenings at the tavern in Norvale, and their afternoons keeping warm in front of our reconstructed stone fireplace in the living room.

He didn't seem to want me up there with them, but that was OK with me because June's parents invited me to go with them to Florida. When I got back to Toronto he told me about the great time he and his friends had, and their hopes to return next summer.

T.S. Eliot was horribly right, April is the cruellest month. In that month of the twelfth year of our cottage, Mom was struck down with a debilitating fatigue. We feared the worst when she had no energy at all. Even talking took a great toll on her. We raced back to Toronto, our anxiety outpacing our car. At the hospital, the doctors told my father it was, as we feared, leukemia, a type of cancer that was very sudden, irreversible and incurable. Suddenness is one of the greatest horrors that attacks us, an emotional tornado that devastates.

With pale, lifeless hand and weary eye she bade us farewell. It was just as hard for her to whisper "goodbye" as it was for Emily to say "Hi Mark." And this time, there would be no coming back as Charles had come back to life after his fall.

We didn't return to the cottage that summer. It would have seemed too insensitive of the lake to sparkle, too pitiless of the birds to sing. The clouds could only hang too low and the rain drum too loud on the roof. We stayed at home that wintry summer, incarcerated once more in our solitary confinement. Charles and I feared for Dad as we headed out in September for our second year at university. But he said he wanted to be alone. Alone, to think and to try to do what they paid him to do: paint.

The Cottage—Part Two

That you might not want to come into our wilderness was for many years a source of anxiety for me. I admit, this lakeside cottage is not for people who prefer a busy social life. It's a painter's oasis that suits me supremely. You may find this a perverse idea, but I think that what defines us as human beings is an ability not simply to tolerate but to enjoy our aloneness.

People insulate themselves against themselves, allowing—no, inviting—noise and busyness and things to possess them. We are consummate consumers of data, wouldn't you say? gorging ourselves on words, the information explosion effecting a personality implosion until only our mutual reflections remain. But here, away from the relentless pursuit of "news" that is never new, each of us meets what is unique in us, our aloneness. Terrifying but glorious. It may be that you know much more about this than I can imagine, but then again, is it all foreign to you?

The world urges one to say, "I am busy," or "I am poor," "I am rich," or "I am lonely," "I am a housewife," a bricklayer or a retiree, a goalie, a genius, a slob—whatever. In the Gospel of John, a crowd is searching for a particular man to do him harm. The man asks, "Who are you looking for?" and they answer, "Jesus of Nazareth." His response overwhelms them and they fall back, for his reply is pared down to the essential oneness of the man: "I am."

Out here, alone, I am. It is not essential to be called a painter or an employee of the Toronto Fire Department. You have certainly observed that what one does doesn't define who one is. I crawl out from all other definitions and descriptions simply "to be—all by myself, just . . . just to be" Don't get me wrong, your coming here delights me, thrills me in fact. Total unrelieved solitude such as one can experience here at the lake can get to you after a while, if you let it. I guess that's one of life's many paradoxes. Ah, I'm heartened you agree.

As you probably noticed, my nearest neighbours are at least seven kilometres away. They're at the farm house high on the hill overlooking the turnoff where the secondary road meets our infamous roller-coaster route to the cottage. The Laplantes live out there, an elderly couple with a widowed son. He's a little strange, given to occasional bouts of sobbing and silence. They say his young wife disappeared on him. Some of the gossipers in town figure that she left him for someone with money. Others wonder if he didn't murder the girl and bury her body in the woods. He certainly doesn't seem to have the personality of a killer. Quite reliably he looks after the cottage in winter when I can't get up here. You know, ploughs the road, shovels snow off the flat-roofed porch and the boathouse, checks for vandalism by any snowmobilers, and none so far. With such isolation, thank goodness for telephones, and cell phones, even if I do have to drive or walk up the hill behind the house to get a signal. The information highway to the cottage is well paved, but the road we traverse on wheels needs constant care—deep snow drifts in winter, beaver dams flooding the low levels in spring, torrential washouts in summer, and in all seasons, winds toppling ancient pines across the one and only road. It's almost easier in winter by snowmobile as so many sports enthusiasts and the twins know.

Once you reach here, however, it's paradise. I notice your smile, just like so many others who wouldn't want to inhabit a paradise like this. If you had not come on such a grey day you would be seeing a glorious sunset out there a few minutes from now, those black spruce trees silhouetted against a red horizon, the entire sky one immense rainbow from red in the west to purple in the east. Years ago, when little Mark saw that sight for the very first time and reflected on the still lake, he stopped complaining about the cottage being "a wreck in the middle of nowhere." Strong words from an eight year old, wouldn't you say? But Charles! I wish you had been here to see him skipping and leaping about, shouting, "Hey Dad, there's a broken dock down here. But we can fix it easy. And when we pick up the rocks, this'll be a perfect beach," to which Mark muttered, "Work, yuk!"

That was seventeen years ago when we bought the place. How everything has changed . . . everything . . . absolutely everything. Nothing is as it was.

Oh, I'm sorry. My mind just saw the panorama from then to now at supersonic speed. I guess you often see things that way too.

No, I never thought of selling after leukemia killed Lois. The lake, the hills, the trees and clouds all conspired to put color back into my days as they had done once before. Remember how Emily Dickinson expressed it? "Tears have washed the colors from my life."

When Lois and I bought this place, I stood here on this dock and was totally incapable of perceiving the panoply of colors. All in black and white, or as it appeared then, black and grey. If the boys had not come up here with me that first time after the death, if I had been here alone, this silence might have called out and silenced me. "Dad, remember what you told us when we fell off our bikes and never wanted to ride again, or when we were afraid to climb back up to the ledge: 'Begin again.'" Both Charles and Mark reminded me.

How I longed for a visit from you then.

The words I uttered so convincingly at the Hart House rehearsals raced and raged back over the years, "To be or not to be." But when I saw Lois's hooked rugs in the kitchen, her vegetable garden beside the boathouse, and the old disused outhouse that she painted bright red and black to look like a British telephone booth, when I reflected on them, her silenced voice whispered soothingly, "I'm here, with you, as long as you want to stay." At first I feared madness, but still hoped to survive, somehow even so alone.

Look over there, beside the cottage, that pile of wood. How astonishingly therapeutic harvesting firewood can be: cutting down trees, sawing them into fireplace lengths, and a year later, chopping cords and cords of firewood. It's true what they say: chopped wood warms you twice.

Well, enough of that. Come on into the kitchen with me and let's have a good hot cup of something. But wait, first of all, I want to point out our secret lodge. Step down these rocks and follow me over there to the curve of the beach. We'll have a better view beyond these leaning cedars. Careful! Yes, right here.

See on the other side of the lake, that highest point of the hill? Just to the right of it you can barely make out a white dolomite cliff. It's actually quite high. At the foot of it on a solid ledge we built our Ledge Lodge. It's really an elaborate lean-to, open to this splendid view. Charles nearly died there when he fell. As the years passed, Lois added a simple kitchen with a propane stove and a cooler. Charles built a primitive table and a bed on a hinge that could be lowered by pulleys. We would all snuggle onto it with our heads at the open side. At dawn you could roll over on your stomach, watch the colors creep out from under the shadows, and follow the dark ripples that the breezes chased across the surface of the calm water. Then, sunrise.

I always regretted that my mother never lived to see this place. But father would often come up here with the boys after he retired. He'd clamber up there, stand on the ledge, shaking his head and murmuring, "Just look at all that—the beauty, the colors! An unforgettable sight."

He'd wax poetic every time as if each new visit were a first. Whenever I painted up there, I'd hear his exclamations, "You've got it! Perfect!" or, "No, that's not quite right. What's missing?" Looking at a midnight scene of the lake he'd ask, "Is it more flakes of silver you need on the path to the moon?" Or examining a sunset, "Should there be more gold over there on the clouds?"

Since he went into a nursing home, it should have been these views that he'd remember, each an unforgettable sight. How ironic. But at least he has three of my cottage landscapes on his wall. I take them down and hold them in front of him, hoping that maybe this time he'll exclaim, "I've been there. And there are the twins." But no. Well, as I said, everything changes, everything.

And besides all that, it's really too bad that you were never able to join us up there on the ledge. That's where I have been for the last four days, painting and reading and hiking. The tragedy was that as I was lifting the supplies from the canoe to our little dock, the cell phone slid into the lake, right out of sight. But who was going to call, anyway? Mark and his wife are holidaying in Europe. Charles and a friend signed up for a Caribbean cruise. I think they are really cruising for mates, but he won't say. And since this is the middle week of my summer vacation, the Department won't call.

I had planned to stay over at the Lodge five days or longer if supplies lasted. But yesterday morning just after 7:00, reflections from a moving car behind the boathouse caught my eye. Binoculars revealed it was the Laplantes' son, Michel. At first I took little notice for he or all of them have been known to drop in to say hello or to deliver a mail package they'd pick up at the town post office. But never so early in the morning. They probably think that when no one passes by their house to come here over a period of weeks, and when I don't go into town, that I would welcome some company. Michel knows how much I enjoy his mother's blueberry pies.

He seemed terribly intent on rousing me, pounding on all the doors, and calling too I suppose, but all I could hear on the ledge over there was the swish of wind through the tall black spruce trees and the occasional chatter of angry chipmunks. When he noticed the boat was gone, he figured I must be fishing. I could spot him standing on the end of the dock scanning the lake. Patches of white morning mist were trapped in a few of the bays; so I could have been anywhere out there, too intent on catching the big one to respond to his voice even if I did hear it. Then he marched up to the picnic table and apparently scribbled a note which he stuck in the screen door. They had never done that before.

I hated to stop painting. For some reason, the colors on the canvas shone—a bright blue sky with just the right gradations from horizon to horizon, golden sunshine on the rocks, an infinite variety of greens in the trees. It felt as if the brilliance of a Guatemalan or a Provencal scene was flowing from my brushes. My feelings cannot be distilled into words, only painted. Can you understand what I'm trying to put into words even now?

The intrusion of Michel, his frantic scampering about, and even his reluctant departure eroded my serenity. I should have packed up there and then and paddled over to read the note, but there were a few necessary touches to the painting at hand so that it would be, as Dad would say, perfect.

But it wasn't. The more I pondered and mixed and experimented, the more it eluded me. After lunch, perhaps, inspiration would return. Radiant moments such as I felt and could express earlier are precious, and besides, the painting was nearly complete—not finished, because a creation is never finished, only complete. Following a lunch of chili con carne, made over a wood fire rather than the too utterly civilized propane burner, plus camp coffee and an apple, an afternoon snooze came easily. Surely, rest restores creative energy?

But it didn't. When I awoke, the luminescence had faded, even on the painting, it seemed. So in the afternoon I switched to some sketches, maybe something to be worked up into a painting next winter. Evening fell ominously fast and gusts on the lake discouraged me from packing up and paddling back to the cottage. That was yesterday.

Have you ever had days when nothing seemed to go right? Well, this morning began this way until finally, after lunch, I decided to quit. The sky was clouding over, not yet threatening but hinting at rain. Anyway, curiosity about yesterday's Laplante note got the better of me and I packed up my paints, canvases, boxes of food, any garbage—those bears can smell it a mile away—and paddled back here. The frothing waves prevented me from seeing down where the cell phone dropped, but retrieving a waterlogged electronic device would be pointless anyway. The Laplantes had probably been trying to call me and wondered why they got no answer.

When I reached the cottage, yesterday's note was flapping on the porch door. "Come and see us as soon as you get back. Urgent!!! Michel." There was food to put into the refrigerator, garbage to dispose of—it's still over there by the incinerator, paint brushes to clean—they're stiff now, and the canoe to put on the rack. Maybe you can give me a hand with that later. It was the word "urgent" and even more so, the three exclamation marks that sounded the alarm.

Life is so leisurely around here that my sudden haste to get the keys and run to the car registered on my leg and back muscles. I'm not so young as I used to be, a lot older than when I first saw you. Driving fast over the roller-coaster route is dangerous, especially when an oncoming car might be just over the next drop or around a sharp curve. The sun was struggling to penetrate a layer of clouds, and my artist's eye noticed a gradual paleness of things, a loss of yesterday's lustre. Then suddenly, as I sped along, it dawned on me—or, in times of peril why don't we ever say, it sunset on me? The Laplante boy! Michel. Perhaps he had committed some drastic act, maybe even murderous. What had happened years ago to his wife? I wondered. And now, would some horrific scene await me in their old house on the hill? Or had I watched Alfred Hitchcock's "Psycho" once too often?

A little too fearful to catapult onto a bloody scene or confront a demented killer, I pulled the car over to the side of the road to think. After all, the note had said, "Come and see us" or was it "me"? No, I was almost certain it was "us." But why his pounding so frantically on all the cottage doors and his calling?

How thoughtless of me! I'm sorry. It's getting cool down here by the water. You're shivering. Let's go up to the kitchen, out of this chill. Come on in and sit in Lois's favourite chair. She designed the embroidery that she put on it. I let very few people sit in that chair, but you're special, especially to Lois. The rug is hers, her design, too. Even used natural dyed materials. It's amazing the variety of colors she extracted from leaves, barks, berries and flowers, all set in urine, of all things! When the boys and I would come back from a day of canoeing and fishing, we could smell the stink of a cauldron boiling down by the boathouse. Strange how such lovely hues could be extracted from such putrid messes. At least they seemed to smell bad to us who had been raised on deodorants and eaux de toilette and air fresheners.

Now, where were we? Yes, the terrifying roller-coaster ride to the Laplantes'. Go on, do sit down in the her chair.

At the very moment I pulled over and stopped, their car flew over the hill ahead, and in a cloud of dust, they skidded to a halt just behind me. They hesitated to get out, and now I know why. No one in their car knew who should deliver the news or how. I'm glad you're here, because it helps me tell the news to myself. My watch insists that a whole day has passed since their message wrecked my soul.

"Quite unexpectedly, your father died at the nursing home three days ago," they told me apologetically. They had tried in vain to contact me, and of course Mark and Charles were heaven knows where. By some clever detective work, the funeral parlour learned about the cottage from my boss, Joe Vittorio at the Fire Department. I guess the name Laplante had come up in conversation, and that is how they found me. Died three days ago. Alone, although he probably never knew he was alone. But I know.

I wanted to talk to you because you know what it's like. Your mother would never let me refer to Charles and Mark as "the boys", always "the twins." Any mention of "the boys" reminded her of you. Every so often we'd hold hands and say, "this would have been her first day in high school;" "this would have been graduation day for her"—for you. Our life would have been so different with you beside us. So I'm glad you came on this of all days, when there is little power in my words, "I am." It is much truer to say "I am sorry." There is another earlier version of the "I am." It is "I will be what I will be."

I need you to tell me. Tell me, will I be?—alone up here as my father was in his last days? Will you tell me? Can you?

CHAPTER TEN

ALONE OR WITH OTHERS:

With Others

The one-way conversation with the virtual visitor stunned Alan. Alone in the twilight he stood unmoving. His eyes, however, glanced back and forth among three objects in the cottage kitchen. Would they offer him some bearings? He shuddered as it occurred to him that Lois, in her black holes had penetrated some barriers, moved into timeless chambers. "Chambers of horrors" she had once called them. In just such a "place" she breathed the fumes of Florentine traffic before all breath was snuffed out amid the cacophony of braying horns and screeching brakes.

Am I, too, he wondered, being drawn into uncharted, perhaps unchartable territories? In years gone by, particularly in the forest not many meters beyond Ledge Lodge, several times I lost my way. That was remediable. To lose one's way is bad enough, but to lose one's very self! I must take arms to oppose this downward, darkward pull.

In his attempt to locate himself, to anchor himself in the here and now, first he focused on Lois's embroidered chair. A few seconds later he gazed more through a key on the table than at it. Then his eyes darted down to the floor where on the rug lay the Laplante note, crumpled where he had dropped it before dashing to the car.

Moths bunted against the screened window and a nighthawk thrummed, plummeting through the darkening sky. A mosquito sang of thirst and passed Alan's right ear. The chair with its pallid tones on the right, the cottage key barely visible on the left, and the note, ahead and below, fading into Lois's hooked carpet, each of them, though barely discernible, was here, a real presence, as motionless as he.

Wondering how long he had been transfixed, he turned his head slowly to read the clock, but it was not there, or rather, it had been consumed by the devouring darkness. On the floor, the fateful note that had precipitated him into a new level of sorrow was gradually vanishing. On the kitchen table the solid key that Lois had kept in her purse to open to cottage was melting into its background. But even in the deepening gloom, the chair was conspicuously empty.

Has my daughter been here? Really? What is real? he mused. Is there only one reality or could there be many? Can all those vibrating atoms and molecules that surround one be reassembled differently to disclose some other reality?

He recalled the laughably futile discussions with Mark about many worlds and observer-created reality. As he felt a tingle on his right temple, he mused on why any observer would want to create a mosquito. Alan was discovering how much of what we don't wish to know we filter out, how much we project what we yearn to believe, and how toilsome to live with all else.

For this cottage he was extravagantly grateful. Had it not been for this place, this salvific retreat, his spirit would have been extinguished first by Emily's tragic death and almost two decades later, by his wife's. The cottage had completely restored him but that restoration vanished when the Laplante note arrived to bear the news, "He died. Alone. Three days ago. The funeral parlour tried to contact you but could only manage to locate us." Limited only by her dialect,

Mrs. Laplante offered sincere words of solace beside the road earlier today, an event which he could hardly recollect in the blackness of the cottage. Grief at its darkest obliterated all but the memory of the lost loved one.

By reaching out and groping along the kitchen wall he located the light switch. When he flicked it on, everything changed. The chair flared into delicate hues, the cottage key shone like gold, and the note glowed white hot against the colorful carpet. Everything changed, he observed, absolutely everything. "I am here, with you, as long as you want to stay. We are here with you, as long as you want to stay."

"I?"—yes, Lois. But "we?" We!? Of course—those colors in the chair were encouraging him, living hues, even lively. And the key? A key that had the power to unlock, to open a future. Even the fateful note refused to condemn him, but reminded him of his father's words exclaimed over at Ledge Lodge, "You've got it! Perfect." No hint of condemnation, but instead an invitation to live, to celebrate life, to begin once again, to paint, if he chose to accept the invitation. How strange that light could come out of darkness, that life could come out of death.

*   *   *

Those were the steps that led Alan to make an uncharacteristically swift choice between remaining alone or transforming his lonely hideaway into a joyful gathering place, an oasis where anyone, everyone could delight in life and color, where recreation would truly re-create.

It will take planning, he thought, but with autumn almost here, I can send out invitations to Mark and his family, Charles and his circle of friends, his co-workers. How about several artists' weekends next summer? Let as many as want to come bring tents and barbeques and canoes and beer. Don't permit any of this magnificent scenery to go to waste. And why keep the secret Lodge a secret any more? Perhaps amid the laughter of infants, children, teens, young and older folk, I'll be able to hear echoes of Lois, of Emily, and now of father.

An elderly four-cylinder car interrupted his thoughts as it coughed its way into the gravel-covered yard behind the cottage. Three Laplantes emerged and in the dark felt their way slowly over the uneven flagstone path that led to the kitchen door.

"Now, don't be surprise Alan cry," Mrs. Laplante told her son in her persistently broken way. They had migrated from northern Quebec over twenty-five years ago. The tight little French-Canadian community limited their need to be fluent in English. "You not only one to lose wife. And now he lose father too." She turned to meet Alan who was coming out of the cottage. They had spoken with him that morning and wondered why he had not come out to drive to Toronto or at least to ask them to look after the property when he left. "Poor Alan. You our good old friend. I bring you soup. Who wants to cook after real bad news? We have only one father, no?"

Michel began to sob, his shoulders heaving as he gasped for air. "Enough, boy. Dere's enough tears here today without yours." The young man's stoic father had endured too much of his son's grief since the disappearance of the daughter-in-law.

Alan gave the ever mournful Michel a hug, took the father's strong and calloused hand, then followed Mrs. Laplante into the kitchen where she was placing the soup pot over a propane flame. "Thanks, Mrs. Laplante. Thanks for the soup. I haven't given a thought to eating and right now I could eat a horse. Would you put on some coffee for us, then let's all sit down. I want to tell you about a wonderful plan that has dropped into my mind in the last few minutes. Here, Mr. Laplante, sit in this chair."

The aging neighbour paused, "But this is Lois's."

"Yes, yes. It is Lois's. but so are these antiques, that floor lamp, the glass-topped coffee table, and this hooked rug. So are those flowers along the flagstone walk, this cottage—all Lois's and mine and everyone's. Everyone's. That's the idea. That's the plan."

Mrs. Laplante turned from the stove and eyed him suspiciously. If she had known the word "manic," she would have used it to describe his enthusiasm, his excitement which appeared not only to her but to all three neighbours as inappropriate. "Mais, ton pere . . ."

"That's right! My father. It's almost as if he gave me the idea."

"Poor Alan. Where you keep bowls? I give you soup. You feel better. You must be starve. Come, sit down." She poured a generous helping of her favourite cure-all potato and leek soup.

He didn't need a second invitation but sat down and peered into the steaming bowl. "I can't eat this, Mrs. Laplante."

"Why? What is wrong? You hungry, maybe too hungry for eat?"

Before she could look too offended, Alan laughed and said, "No, it's not that. I can't eat this soup because I don't have a spoon."

"Oh, you! No time for funny businesses," she said. "Ton pere, he . . ."

"That's right! His last days were pathetic, lonely. He's had enough sorrow, far, far too much loneliness. That's why I'm sure this plan of mine came from him. He doesn't want anyone excluded. This place can be for everyone. For everyone to play and sing and have bonfires and paint and fish and swim and eat and drink and be merry."

She frowned at him. "Prends ta soupe. That will make you better. Then you must think of other plans. Tell your boys, your beautiful boys we see grow up, tell them about the grandpere. And then the funeral."

"Tomorrow morning, I'll return to Toronto. When Mark and Charles return from wherever they are, yes, then we can have the funeral. Dad loved this place, loved the canoeing and the fishing. He helped Lois and the boys build Ledge Lodge across the lake, and got to know the folks in Norvale.

Michel surprised everyone, "Let us know when it will be and how to get there. I liked your father very much. I want, we all want to be at the funeral. And then maybe I can help you with your plan, your father's plan."

"Our son is right," his father said, "let us know about de funeral. But I doan see how Michel could help you wit' plans to make dis a . . . what do Americans say . . . a people-place?"

"I'll need a lot of help."

"Even Michel?"

"Even Michel."

Alan decided that his father's grave should be nearby in the Norvale community cemetery. Almost two weeks passed before all the people could be located and invited to the funeral service. It was a small event as so often is the case with elderly folk. Most of Mr. Thompson senior's friends had died, and Alzheimer's erased along with everything else the possibility of new friends. Mark and his family were there from Chicago, Charles and a co-worker from the office who shared in the driving to and from Ottawa, and the Laplantes. A couple of old timers from the Fire Department who had been hired at the same time as his father drove up with Joe Vittorio, and several townsfolk, mostly frequenters of "Karl's Hair Emporium", came along.

Alan couldn't seem to get the boys together long enough to discuss his plan. They both had to get back to their respective cities, in a little too much of a hurry, Alan thought. Have their childhood animosities and competitiveness re-ignited?

So began a series of letters and emails, extolling the beauty of "Lakeview Villa", its peaceful encircling forests and the lake that mirrors the moods of the sky while lifting the spirits of its observers. How's that for reality that created observers, Charles? He sent letters far and wide.

> Dear Roger and Roberta
>
> We have been drifting apart too long. And now with Mark and
> Charles settling into their busy worlds, with Lois and my father gone,
> I am beginning to understand the feelings of the last of the curlews. It
> is my hope you both can fly over and visit . . .
>
> Your old friend, Al

Capt. Joe Vittorio, Toronto Fire Department

Dear Joe

I have often spoken to you about how my lakeside property up at Norvale has kept me going after some pretty rough times in my life. Now that I am the sole person to inhabit this paradise, it has occurred to me that others might like to book a week or a weekend up here beginning next spring.

I'll be taking early retirement at the end of this year and hope to do a lot of painting and villa managing. But I do want to keep in touch with some of the old team at H.Q. My plan is . . .

Your colleague, Al

Email to Dr. Victor Liang and Zhi Yuan

I'd love to have you all up to my "new and improved" Villa here on the lake. Don't forget, I have only seen photos of your grandchildren. Is there any chance you both, Chaucer and his family can come and stay here next summer for a week, plus or minus? If you hit it right, either Mark or Charles will be here. What a reunion that would be!

I'm not sure you know that I'm retiring as artist in residence with the T.F.D. and will soon be living permanently near Norvale. How many years has it been since . . .

Your old friend—Alan

P.S. I'll let you knew when my retirement roast will take place. Hope you both can come.

The responses were not long in coming.

Hi Dad—got your email yesterday and talked over your proposition with Gwen and our daughter. Monica was excited about coming up, especially if she can bring a couple of her school friends along. Sounds like you want lots of people to enjoy what for so long we favoured few delighted in by ourselves. We're unanimous in hoping we can book a whole week at the end of June or early July. It will be OK if we have to share space with another small group or family. But I do have one request: that we not be there when Charles and his friends come up, if they're planning to.

I'm embarrassed to mention this but there has been a falling out between him and us—nothing fatal, but Gwen and Monica will, I think, be more comfortable if he's not at the—"villa", as you've renamed it—while we're there.

Before you get too embroiled in resort management, why not plan to spend a few weeks after retirement with us in Chicago? Regretfully, the cut-throat office I'm in charge of may require too much of my time, but we'll see as much of each other as I can possibly arrange.

Love from the three of us—Mark

Hello Al

An ocean of water has passed under the bridge since we last saw each other. News of Lois's death hit me very hard. I recall with much nostalgia the agony you experienced deciding between her and Ellen. I know you made the right choice. The pain of loss testifies eloquently to that. Deepest sympathy, too on the recent death of your father.

As to coming over to your summer place one of these years, I hope it can happen. Roberta, "Bertie", remembers you with great affection and often talks about your and Lois's trip over here to help us celebrate our wedding. My crushing responsibilities, however, in this world of journalism imprison me. But, as Lois would say, "If it's meant to be, it will happen." And within a few years I'm going to make it happen. Meanwhile, tell me . . .

Your old friend,—Roger

Great idea Dad!

Got your message you left on the answering machine last Thursday. Ten of us would like to go up to your paradise. Could we have the whole place to ourselves for two weeks at the end of August? One wants to bring his motor boat. Is that allowed on the lake, or are the only power boats permitted still only muscle power? Would you be there with us?

When is your retirement party? I want to drive over from Ottawa with my significant other and stay a few days with you. Will Mark be there too for the big farewell bash? I'll phone you on the weekend.

Tons of love—Charles

Dear Mr. Alan Thompson

Our "Gallery Gang of Eight" were thrilled to get your invitation to paint at your lakeside resort. We expect to do our own cooking, and can accommodate four or five families in tents. Would you give us some ideas about activities for children and not-too-artistic spouses? Any fishing, hiking, antique barns, etc? Also we're thinking of some weekends in the autumn for more advanced painters. Some hardy folk wonder if your place is open in winter for snow scene painting.

Yours gratefully

Freda Clompdale, President,

The Gallery Gang of Eight

The Toronto Fire Department did itself proud in honoring their retiring "painter-in-residence" who had distinguished himself by mastering not only portraiture but cityscapes. The surprise ingredient of his retirement party was a succession of former police and fire chiefs and even two ex-mayors whose portraits graced significant lobbies about the city. What some said in their testimonials was true: he showed people in their best light.

Mark couldn't get away from his hectic office to attend the roast, in fact had the unenviable job of firing several employees who weren't "measuring up." So only Charles came over from Ottawa, but only by himself to visit with his father for several days and be part of the roast. They both were heartened by the frequent reminiscences about Mr. Thompson senior, Alan's father. One former chief quipped, "Charles, your grandfather provided us with the most excusable example of nepotism the Department has ever had."

In the spirit of the festivities, Charles shot back, "And the only example, I'm sure." The repartee elicited howls and guffaws and a few blushes. Several junior officers frowned and nodded at each other as if to say The cat may not be out of the bag, but the meow sure is!

The M.C. for the event deadpanned an announcement, "I urge all the members of the crowd to book a week or three for everybody and their uncle at 'Al's Shangri-La.' Discounts are available for groups of thirty or more, provided," and here he lapsed into a grin, "provided Al doesn't kill me first!"

Al leapt from his seat and dove to the mic in mock rage. Only the M.C. and he knew the announcement was the signal for the guest of honor to come forward, respond to the many gibes and accolades, then bid farewell to his colleagues.

Following the roast, Joe Vittorio, his wife, Victor, Zhi Yuan and Charles came back with Al to the house for coffee and more private chatting. "I had hoped Mark would have come over from Chicago for tonight's event," Joe said. "It's been quite a few years since I've seen him." Charles turned away quickly for the coffee pot.

"I remember seeing you bring your boys over to the central station. They raced against each other to see who'd be the first to sit in the driver's seats of the trucks, and who would be first to get on your back as you slid down the pole. Are they still as competitive as ever, or are they getting along a little more evenly now they've grown up?"

"We're working on it," Charles said as he went into the kitchen for cream and sugar.

Al poured. "Mark couldn't come. Gwen, his wife, is quite ill. But I'll get to see them at Christmas. Then after I return, we'll sell—or rather, I'll sell the house and move full time up to our villa near Norvale. The town is at the north end of the lake, about ten kilometres from our place. I'm expecting you two up there, Joe, but you'll have to book early. As the M.C. said, everybody and their uncle has expressed interest in camping or staying at the Villa. Mark and family will be up for the last week of June. Why don't you try to make it then?"

After the Vittorios and the Liangs left, Alan felt it was time to clarify the disagreement between his sons. "What's Mark's problem, Charles? He told me Gwen and Monica don't want to be up at the villa while you're there." Charles took off his glasses, extracted his handkerchief and began polishing slowly, meditatively, as if he were searching for the easiest way to explain.

His father waited, then tried to prime the pump, "Is it money? I know you borrowed from me and I told you there's no rush to pay it back. Do you owe him a lot?" Charles stopped polishing and put his glasses back on.

"Look, son, I'll lend you the money so you can repay him. In fact, I'll give it to you. I wouldn't like to see you and him—"

"It's not that, Dad. It's just that, well, they don't approve of my life-style."

Alan took a slow, deep breath as if preparing to take a dive, "So what you're trying to tell me, or maybe not tell me, is that you're gay. Am I right?"

"Are you disappointed? Angry?"

Alan sat down on the sofa, "Only disappointed that you couldn't tell me sooner. And no, I'm not angry. Not really. No, not at all. Now that I think of it, I'm disappointed that Mark seems to have given up on you. He lives his way. Why won't he let you live yours?"

"So you don't disapprove?"

He leaned forward, bowed his head and looked at one hand which clutched the fingers of the other. "I can't say I approve, but I don't disapprove. It will take me a while to adjust my . . . well, just to adjust."

A painful silence eventually broke. "Would Mom have been disappointed?"

"No, definitely not. She loved you. And so do I." the conversation was a game of tennis played at dusk with barely enough light to discern the other player. Each heard the whap of the opponent's racquet. But to know where the ball was heading, at what speed and if it had been sliced made each lunge and swing doubtful. His father had just lobbed him an easy ball and he couldn't reply.

Fifteen love.

Alan tried another serve. "Just don't let this break up our family."

Silence. Thirty love.

Charles was too much of a novice, untaught, unpractised, unskilled at this game. But discuss economics with him or current events or films and you'd find him as agile as a basketball star on a brightly lit court.

His father served again. "I'll speak with Mark. I have a feeling that it was Gwen and their daughter who are having trouble with your homosexuality. They've probably never met a gay person. Will your friends that you bring up to the villa in August all be gay?"

"Yes, and you'll find that they're an OK lot. They're awfully proud of their physical shape, so give them some heavy work up there to do, like putting on a new roof or digging a well. You'll like them, Dad, I'm sure."

Thirty fifteen.

"Great idea! But don't forget, Norvale hasn't had much exposure to different life-styles. It's a pretty conservative community, although they won't be around to the Villa or on our property. I'm looking forward to meeting your friends. And yes, tell them to bring hammers and shovels."

Game called because of darkness. Not the darkness of a sunless sky, but of the uncharted, the unfamiliar.

Next morning, after Charles pulled out of the laneway to drive through autumn splendours to Ottawa, his father turned and studied the face of his house, knowing that soon he would be bidding it farewell. Perhaps a house becomes accustomed to these farewells as young people move away, as pets die, as tenants and owners leave for warmer climates or nursing homes. Although the dwelling itself is not touched by these generations of goodbyes, the people who depart feel the pain. Every severance marks the end of a dream and hopefully the beginning of another.

Each room was for Alan the site of a memorable experience—here his father sneezed his teeth into the toilet; of an awful secret—in the kitchen Lois learned that aunt Agatha's son was diagnosed with AIDS; of a special emotion—they all celebrated as they stood in the doorway listening to horns and church bells declaring the beginning of a new millennium. And now, as of last night—the living room, where he encountered a son he hadn't really known.

When it comes to saying goodbye to home, Shakespeare had it all wrong. There is no sweetness to it. Parting is just pure sorrow—unless the roof leaked and the floors creaked and the neighbours peeked and the sewers reeked.

He suddenly became aware of the emptiness of the dwelling despite all the familiar furniture and all the carpets which, if they could speak, would tell a thousand stories, and the old photos and portraits which, although silent, did speak: "Take us with you. We promise not to age, not to languish or weaken. We'll always be with you. Time has happily frozen for us on these celebratory moments. Let us release you from the heedless rush of time. We'll inspire your paintings up north. Take us with you."

If a camera had captured his forlorn posture, alone in front of their—of his soon-to-be abandoned house, the photo could be entitled, "An Empty Soul Waiting to be Filled." Had things gone differently, Emily might have been smiling at him through the living room window. Would she be holding his grandchild? Would her husband be beside her, or might there have been a painful separation leaving Emily a single mother? If the way things are was not the way they had to be, Lois would already have started the clean up of the house before their drive back to Norvale. If I had married Ellen . . .

The spattering of raindrops alerted him to the fact that like it or not, this was the world he was living in, a world of a deceased daughter, wife, and father, of widely separated sons, and of a father's plan to share a paradise with as many people as possible.

The first step in initiating the project was a quick trip to the villa before autumn frosts and early snow could postpone some necessary building. Toilets and showers for campers and a small cottage for less hardy folk needed to be constructed. The place to start hunting for reliable builders was the fount of small town wisdom, Karl, the barber.

"Karl's Haircut Emporium" nestled between the Norvale hardware outlet and the corner convenience store. This autumn it stood out from all the others along the main street because of its new paint job. A gaudy combination of sky blue and lime green set off the traditional red and white barber pole.

The bell hanging on the barbershop door clanked unmusically to proclaim Alan's entrance. Three regulars concealed by their newspapers peered over top and greeted the returnee from the metropolis. "Al, you're back in town!" Karl said. "What on earth have they done to your head? It looks awful." The boy who perched on the board across the arms of the barber's chair turned to look for evidence of a hideous head. Only the child was unaware that this was Karl's ritual greeting to anyone who had their hair cut in the big city.

"Never mind my head," Al replied, "What have you done to your shop? You could almost say it looks like it's been painted."

"You're pretty observant for a city fella. But you otta know by now it gets painted every twenty years whether it needs it or not."

The men always enjoyed laughing at the expense of any one individual, and for that reason they gathered most days, especially the older folk, for a haircut or just a sit. One of the men, Eric, a bald-headed customer who never ceased complaining that his cut cost as much as any Samson's, broke into laughter, "But Karl, it was eight years ago, not twenty that you painted it last."

Billy, the short man with the long beard, said, "Come on, Eric, it was probably fifteen. But you never could count past ten."

"Unless you take off a shoe," added another as he clapped the bald headed man on the back.

Eric felt his honor impugned and argued, "No, Billy, it was eight years 'cause I thought Karl had the place all done up to celebrate my grandson's birth. And that was eight years ago." He turned to the boy sitting high up on the board. "Tell the boys your age, Brian."

From his perch on the board, the youngster looked around for some "boys" to tell. Finding none, he announced to the aged men, "I'm gonna be eight nex month."

So why the sudden splurge with paint?" Alan asked.

The barber stopped in mid clip and stared in unbelief. "Well, you otta know. It's all because of you this whole town is gettin' gussied up. Or didn't you notice for a start that Lee decorated his restaurant, and Kay's Drug and News Store hung a fancy awning?"

"And the guys at the motor shop piled up their old tires and even swept up," added Eric the Bald.

The three men joined in a laughing chorus of "We're sending you the bills," and "All because of you," and "It's all your doing, Al." Karl continued trimming young Brian's hair and nodded agreement.

"Sure, sure. Go on, blame me. Blame the city slicker."

The scissors froze in mid air. "No, Al, it's not because you're a know-it-all rich boy from Bay Street. It's because you'll be bringing up carloads of tourists and campers and artists and who knows what-all next year."

"How'd you hear about that, Karl?"

Billy stroked his beard and winked at the others. "Don't you know? Haven't you heard? Barbers have got spies all over the place. If any one of us so much as smiles at another woman, it gets reported to information central here at the Emporium."

Karl looked preoccupied as he concentrated on combing Brian's locks. He managed to say with all seriousness to no one in particular but to everyone in general, "My Toronto sources are never wrong. And I never reveal who they are, neither."

"Toronto sources, my foot! It must have been Michel Laplante who passed on the news," Alan said, for he had noticed the young widower was sporting a recent haircut. "Anyway, I want to tap into that data bank of yours and find four or five good workers to put in some toilets and build a cabin for eight people. Besides that I'll need somebody to clear sites for a dozen tents."

The barber shop-cum-employment agency quickly provided enough names of handy men who could build all that Alan needed before the first carloads arrived in spring.

As the development of his father's plan came to fruition, the townsfolk welcomed the successive contingents of visitors, even if they were all city folk. Thanks to Toronto's burly firemen and their families, the beer store never had it so prosperous. The Norvalians gradually discovered varieties of wines and coolers they never dreamed existed. And they marvelled at a novelty for which they had no word: women "firemen."

Six members of the Liang family arrived: grandpa, grandma, Chaucer and their son, his wife and their two pre-teen children. The only days common to them all unfortunately fell the week after Mark and his family had left, and a month before Charles and his gay friends would arrive. The twins would not have the joy of reminiscing with Chaucer about horseback riding camp and their families' world excursions.

Victor and his wife were seated on the dock, nervously monitoring their son's family zigzagging across the bay in a frantic canoe race. Al joined the worried grandparents. "They'll be OK. The life jackets won't let them down. I remember how fearful Lois and I were that first time we let Mark and his brother cross to the other side of the lake. As it turned out, that was a day that changed Mark for life when his brother fell off the ledge."

Zhi Yuan signalled that she had something difficult to express, difficult not because of any linguistic impediments, but rather because of the personal nature of her comment. She leaned towards Al, looked directly into his eyes for a brief moment, then down at the dock. She placed the back of her hand against her mouth and sighed. "Please pardon me, Al, if I am butting in on your private life, but I can't help noticing that you often speak of Mark, his work in Chicago, his wife and daughter, his sadness about your being so far away from him. But you seldom talk about Charles."

Al pressed together the palms of his hands in front of his lips and nodded slowly but said nothing.

"This is not for us to enquire about!"

"But Victor, we don't know if Charles is well, if he is married. Does he have a job? Is he still living in Ottawa?"

Al extricated himself from his deck chair, took a few steps to the side of the dock, peered across the choppy water and saw in the distance the two canoes tacking erratically back towards them. How like me, he thought, uncertain how to steer through this situation. He turned, "Yes, you're right. Very perceptive of you Zhi Yuan. And very caring. I am annoyed at myself for not realizing that Charles is, well, that he's gay." He glanced sheepishly from Zhi Yuan to her husband and back. "Lois occasionally had some questions, but I always brushed them aside."

"So you are blaming yourself," Victor said. "Blaming yourself for forcing Charles into an unnecessary and painful silence."

"I'm only beginning to realize just how painful it must have been for him."

Zhi Yuan extended both hands up to Al and drew him towards her. "Just don't follow him through that very same painful and unnecessary silence."

Abruptly they all faced the lake, trying to discern whether the cries they heard across the waves were screams of terror or delight. Laughter affirmed the latter.

It wasn't until late August, three weeks after the Liangs' departure, that complaints began to emanate from information central. Some of Charles' gay friends were fascinated by small town life. "I don't mind all the business they bring to my store," Kay said, "and I mind my own business. But I don't like the way they parade up and down Main Street in their skimpy shorts and their tight T-shirts."

"And their bare feet," Karl said. "They come in here, two at a time, and expect me to shave their head. Why I've never had reason to cut all a man's hair off in my thirty-five years as a town barber."

"That's right," bearded Billy said, "and they know you won't do it. Then an hour later, another couple will come in smirking to beat the band and ask for a head shave. They seem to get a kick out of the way you say, 'Not on your life, mister!' I think they're trying to cause a disturbance."

"My Clara thinks most of them never had all their hair cut off and don't even want me to do it. Maybe I should give a head shave to the next bushy headed one of them that comes in. That would teach them not to play games with us."

The town's boys who congregated nightly at Rosie's Tavern soon got wind of the aliens that were visiting their turf—"Invading it," Clara said to her barber husband. "No, infecting it!" said Bart, the captain of the county hockey team. Three of the boys set out in a motor boat newly acquired after the boating regulations changed on the two lakes and the river within the town's jurisdiction. They were armed only with fishing rods so as not to advertise the purpose of their reconnaissance.

Bart, their leader, had laid the foundations for the latrines and the new cottage at the villa last autumn. "I'll tell Al the fish have nibbled off all our bait and we're willing to trade some of the fish we caught for the bait he gives us. And while we're there, I'll tell him my two pals here would like to see the work I did for him. Keep your eyes peeled to see if these guys are as gay as they act. If anybody asks, we're there to get some bait. You got that?"

Bart planned to report their findings at hockey practice next day. The secret of their success was that they practised ball hockey on roller blades throughout the summer when opposition teams of lesser commitment succumbed to the lures of fishing. A couple of times when the topic of gay bashings came up at post-game victory celebrations at the tavern, the unanimous opinion was that if guys want to be gay in private, that's their problem. But dragging their perversions onto the street is asking for a fight.

And sure enough, as the boaters passed the beach heading for the dock, what did they see but two young men, naked, lying on a blanket, getting a tan and reading.

"Look at them. Like lizards sunning themselves on a rock," said Ralph.

"Or snakes," Corky added with a sneer.

On their way up to the villa, they found two more returning along the nature trail, the taller one with his arm around the shoulders of a man whose arm was around the first man's waist.

Bart noticed his team mates tensing up. "You go right back to the boat. Now. No rough stuff, you hear me? I'll look for Al and ask how the buildings are holding up. Now get! I'll be back in five minutes."

"But the bait?" asked Ralph, "What about the bait?" Ralph wasn't too swift, except on skates.

"Forget the bait, Ralph. Get back in the boat."

Not one to back away, he shouted, "How can we fish without bait? What the hell good are the rods without any bait, Bart?"

Since Bart was by then out of hearing, Corky answered, "We've done with our fishing, man. We've found a whole school of suckers." He hooted, "and they all need to be taught a lesson." Ralph laughed only to follow Corky's example.

What Bart couldn't understand was why Alan allowed these men on his property in the first place. Maybe he'll tell me how frustrated or disappointed or maybe even enraged he is to have discovered the truth about these queers.

The proprietor of the villa was nowhere to be found. He and Michel were at Norvale's only general store buying food that the cook had ordered. The boaters roared off to town leaving a wake that spread like their machinations.

It wasn't much of a practice next day. Strategy was the "Norvale Shooters'" strength; so they were enlivened, energized by the prospect of a team plan to eradicate the blotch on their community. The tactics agreed on were to divide the aliens into smaller groups, if possible, and to overpower each group, tie them up and give them a good scare.

Karl had provided some key information: "There are nine homos plus Charles and his father. Before lunch and supper, there is also Deedee, a part-time cook." She had been embroidering some tall tales about what gay men do when they're off by themselves in the woods. Eric the Bald contributed his observations, "Judging by the way they behaved in the tackle and bait shop where they bought some paddles, two of them are apparently expert canoeists. From the tavern, reports came that two others had bragged about their 40 horse power motor boat." The hockey team tried not to look intimidated on hearing that at least three of them were heavily into pumping weights.

Bart instructed the team, "Bring lots of rope. If we can't locate all of these guys—some may be off hiking—go after their belongings, their cars, their clothes. When we leave, the message has gotta be clear, 'We want you freaks to clear out.' Now something else. Keep away from the owner, Alan. I don't want him hurt. You got that?"

"'ow will we know 'im when we see 'im?" asked Pierre, one of the half dozen county boys that lived in the mill town, 46 km. away in the woods.

"Why do you want us to go easy on him?" asked Corky. "Have you a soft spot for him?"

"Or maybe 'e's got a hard-on for you, heh?" Pierre said. The joke prompted only nervous sniggers, for those were fighting words.

Bart glared first at Ralph who was attempting less successfully than the others to smother his chuckles, then at Pierre. The goalie decided to ignore the dig. The team had to stick together to win a more important fight. "Is there any of you can't be at the south end if the lake tomorrow evening at 6:00?"

Three hands went up. "OK. So that leaves us with nine. Four in Corky's boat and five in mine. You decide who'll bring their fishing gear so nobody'll be suspicious."

Partly to express his sudden alarm, but more importantly to redeem himself, Pierre said, "So dere'll be ten huv dem to nine of huss?"

The responses were immediate, aggressive and unanimous: "Hey! We're a team, and they're not." "There won't be no penalties for high sticking in tomorrow's game." "If you're scared, Pete, we'll go without you and win with eight against ten." Pierre slouched on the bench, unredeemed.

The ball hockey practice broke up early so the team could celebrate a pre-fight victory at Rosie's.

The highlight of the next morning at the villa was a volleyball game with all ten men participating, followed by a swim and lunch. The two expert canoeists proposed an afternoon of fishing followed by a barbeque across the lake up at Ledge Lodge. At four o'clock, six headed off, two to a canoe. Alan stayed in the cottage, trying to iron out problems of a double booking in September. Under his son's supervision, three remained at the camp grounds to dig trenches to protect the water supply against cold weather. Charles explained, "These surface hoses may freeze up by late October. Dad wants to keep the place open until early December. Then we'll drain the lines that you bury. After that, smaller groups can stay in the Lake Lodge where Dad will be living. If you run into some rocks or huge roots, come and see me at the Lodge. I'll be helping my Dad with bookings and accounting. I may need to find you some heavier equipment."

Just after six p.m., three cars bumped over a seldom used logging road that led to the south end of the lake. There was a period in the early 1900s when logging trails crisscrossed the forests and led down to the water. Magnificent white pines were toppled, dragged by horses on roads like this, then floated north to Norvale. From there, the now disused railway transported them to the mill 46 kilometres away, where some of the team worked.

Most of the hockey players were familiar with the route that they bounced over. It led to a thoroughly secluded site popular with lovers. It would be to the team's advantage if none arrived this evening to testify that the team was in the vicinity, although judging by the villagers' views on gays, nearly everyone would applaud this attack.

A bright late afternoon sun shone approvingly on the men as they slid their two boats off the trailers and into the restless waves. Looking northward, Bart and Corky, the two boat owners, surveyed the whitecaps that rolled in slow motion towards them, and studied the swooping gulls. As expert hunters and woodsmen, they knew how to read the swaying of the trees and the patterns of the clouds. Their boats, when not overloaded, could easily navigate in these conditions.

Ralph, who couldn't perceive irony or implications, made up for that blindness by his phenomenal ability to spot a motionless deer in the bush or a partridge concealed behind a fallen log. He squinted across the curling waves and shouted, "Look, three canoes. They're heading for the shore across from the villa."

"Can you make out how many are in each canoe?" Bart asked.

"If they'd just hold still and stop bouncing around for half a minute I could. The way they're flailing their paddles from side to side, I'd say they're not very good at canoeing. It looks like . . . it looks like two to each canoe. Yes, I count six men."

"Men? Hah! Fairies you mean," Corky said.

Bart stood on a rock and spoke. "OK, here's our plan. Corky, you four go in your boat. When you're sure they've climbed up from the shore and are out of sight, I want you to tow their canoes to the swamp that's south of their landing place. Throw their paddles away so that even if they do walk around and find their canoes, they won't be able to use them."

"What, them pansies walk anywhere around here without getting lost?" said Clint, an experienced woodsman and guide. "They'd lose their way walking along a shore." Clint had earned the admiration of his county chums by orienting himself inerrantly through dense forests on cloudy days without benefit of compass. Hunters were advised to ask for Clint if they wanted a reliable guide.

Bart continued the plan, "The five of us in my boat will go directly to the Villa. Corky, when you and your boys have stashed their canoes, whip across the lake and join us. We should have the rest of them tied up by then. You can look after their clothes. I don't want any of those guys badly injured, just scared to hell outa here. For ever."

Corky and his crew were disgruntled that their task was so effortlessly accomplished—no skirmishes, no chases, no action, not even any re-action. The players who so relished rough play and body checks on the ice had looked forward to adding some high sticking on the slopes of the shore.

"Let's hope there's some excitement waiting for us on the other side," Daryl complained. Corky supervised the roping of the canoes in tandem. Whitecaps threatened the motorboat with its cargo of four men more than they did the canoes, each of which bobbed along, borne up by the swells.

At the Villa, a lone fisherman in bathing trunks sat on the dock, renewing bait on his hook. The boatload of five landed. Bart motioned three to go inland and nodded to his chief defenceman who carried a coil of rope to approach the fisherman. "Catch any?" he asked.

"Yep. Got two beauties in my net down here."

That was the last he could say for Bart's bandanna gagged him as his defenceman put a half nelson on the unsuspecting man. Within minutes he found himself tied to a tree.

Clint took out his hunting knife, slipped it under a leg of the victim's bathing suit. "You won't be swimming today," he said as he sliced the material and left the man naked.

The trembling man's wide eyes testified to his terror. He shook his head and struggled vainly to cry out. Bart turned approvingly to Clint, "You go find the others. They may need help. I'll check these knots."

Clint ran through the trees towards shouts of men and sounds of twigs snapping. A few hundred meters away up at Lake Lodge, faint echoes of hollering contended with the peaceful whoosh of wind in the trees.

"Sounds like your ditch diggers are having fun out there," Alan said as he flipped through pages of tax laws.

Charles, arranging letters that confirmed reservations, replied around a pencil that was in his clenched teeth, "Probably having a sand fight." He took the pencil from his mouth, "Want me to take some beer to them and shame them into working?"

"No, they need a little fun."

Bart stood in front of his naked and gagged victim and slapped the palm of his hand with a switch that he had stripped off an alder bush. The man closed his eyes and waited for the sting of a lash. Instead, he heard Bart say in a voice that sounded solicitous, "I see you had a can of ginger ale beside you on the dock. You did, didn't you?" It was difficult to determine whether he was shaking his head rapidly in denial, or simply quaking with fear. "Well, you may get thirsty, so I'll bring it over."

He swept aside heavy foliage, jumped down onto the dock, picked up the can, clambered back to the tree and snapped the can open. "Here, this otta keep you cool," he said as he poured half of the can on the man's head. "And that should keep the ants happy." Then he sloshed the remainder on the trembling man's genitals and turned towards the sudden silence where only minutes earlier, there were muffled shouts. "'Scuse me, I want to find out what my boys are up to. I'll be back in a few minutes, or hours."

Bart was pleased with what he saw although his cohorts were apologetic that one of the trench diggers had fled into the dense underbrush. His team had gagged two of the aliens and tied them face to face on either side of the same small tree. He complimented his boys for the innovative way they lashed the hands of each man behind the back of the other. "Looks like a passionate hug, except mother nature got in the way. OK, Clint, let's do some tracking, just you and me."

Turning to the onlookers, he said, "Do the same to the others, and when you're finished, clear their stuff out of the new cottage."

Clint was already busy examining the bushes for branches broken in the escapee's flight and for widely spaced footprints in the sand. "Just a matter of minutes, boss, before we score on this one."

Bent pine twigs pointed out the path of the alien who was beside himself with fright. He never imagined that such a peaceful scene could so suddenly erupt into a battle ground. He cursed himself for fleeing with such cowardly haste. How was I to know what legions of attackers were about to pounce on me and my friends? Scenes of gay bashing flooded over him as he bolted blindly through the woods. Stiff dead branches ripped his T-shirt and flesh in his mad dash. Little did it matter where he was running and limping to. He was running from what amounted to a matter of life and death.

While the stalking was proceeding, Corky and his crew were landing after hijacking the canoes. They were congratulating themselves on their easy victory. As they drew their boat up to the dock they were anticipating a more violent outlet for their adrenalin.

At first the naked man dared to hope that rescue was imminent. His shouts were transformed by the gag into muffled grunts. Then he realized that the coils of rope on their shoulders and their stealthy scurrying towards the Lodge identified them as a second wave of bashers. He craned his neck to peer through the dense bush, fearing the arrival of additional boatloads.

With Bart and Clint in unhurried, assured pursuit of their prey, the remaining seven met on the path leading to the Lodge. In the absence of their leader, Corky felt that his own captaincy of the only other boat entitled him to take charge. "Pierre, take Ralph, Zeke and Daryl with you over to the Lodge and look after anybody you find there. Two with me will be enough to handle whoever's in the new cottage. And their belongings. OK, let's go."

Pierre and his team of three moved swiftly towards the Lodge, crouching low as they approached a large window. Ralph peered cautiously over the sill and reported what he saw. Inside, Alan had risen from his chair, frustrated and annoyed at the complexities of tax regulations for people who run summer camps. He was now standing beside his son who was seated in front of rows of sheets of paper.

"Dad, I think there'll be no accommodation problem since half of this group says they're bringing tents."

Alan sat down beside his son, resting one elbow on the table and the other on Charles' shoulder. He smiled in relief that his son so promptly solved the first problem, gave him an affectionate cuff, and said, "I'm going to keep you on staff here."

That posture and that gesture were too much for Ralph. He knew the opening stages of sexual foreplay, for after all, he had practised it often enough with the young wife of Bearded Billy. He was swift to take over command: "Zeke, you and Daryl go to the back door. Pierre and me'll go to the front. When I whistle, we go in and tie those buggers up. If the door is locked, kick the bloody thing in."

Alan and his son were rearranging the rows of confirmation letters when they heard a shrill whistle. They leapt to their feet as four men burst into the room, shouting. Daryl flipped over the table, shattering mugs and scattering papers. Charles grabbed his chair and swung it into the face of one of the attackers. Alan was paralyzed with horror as he saw a rope encircle his son. Was this going to be a lynching party?

He picked up the glass topped coffee table, gripping it as a shield. Two of its short wooden legs cracked against Pierre's shins. Ralph lunged towards Alan, wrenched the table from his hands and crashed it over his head. The splinters and shards became projectiles, slashing Ralph's arms, slicing Alan's head and chest.

All the men froze as Alan collapsed onto the broken glass. Louie shot a glance of fear when Charles yelled, "Dad! Dad!" Daryl let go of the rope and Charles bounded over to his father, "Dad?"

With distant sounds of an aged four-cylinder car sputtering toward the lodge, the silence ended. Daryl shouted, "Get to the boat."

What Michel saw on entering the lodge was broken chairs, an overturned table, and amid spears and triangles of glass, two men on the floor. Charles yelled, "He's hurt. Bad. Help me stop the bleeding—a towel. Get some towels."

They lugged Alan to the car and while Charles staunched blood from his father's chest and neck, Michel drove dangerously fast to Norvale's doctor. "He'll need more help than I can give him around here," the doctor said. "I'll call an ambulance. They may even have to take him to Toronto. There's glass embedded in his chest. It's too near the heart for me."

CHAPTER ELEVEN

EITHER ALONE OR WITH OTHERS:

Alone

Night's sombre cloak was settling over Lois's chair in the kitchen of the Lodge. Alan, peering at the waning colors of the empty seat heard himself plead, " ... will I be?—alone up here, as my father was in his last days? Will you tell me? Can you?"

With a quick jerk of the head and a blink of the eyes he inhaled in surprise. "What's happening to me," he asked aloud, "talking to myself? Or was I? Am I?"

He had been totally unaware of the dark roiling grief that lay interred in his past, buried deep in his mind, a reality he had been rejecting for over twenty-seven years. During that lengthy Dead Sea voyage, his ability to console Lois over the loss of their infant daughter enabled him to think of himself as the one necessary stabilizing force in their marriage. He would not allow himself to mourn in a way that might jeopardize what appeared to him to be his wife's all too fragile hold on life. At times he felt as if he were swimming and pulling a lifeboat towards a shore that had to lie just over the horizon. From time to time, when the waves ran high or the stars hid their fires he would clamber aboard their tiny boat, and together he and Lois would drift. Weary with dragging their devastating past into a hopeless future, he was not entirely surprised that his painting failed him. His art should have been a source of creativity, of beauty and renewal, but after Emily's death, for the first time in his life, color ceased to nourish his spirit. Instead, infinite shades of grey clothed his cityscapes, even shrouded an attempted carnival scene until finally he feared his painting days might be over. His career as illustrator, and graphic designer for the Fire Department, and official portrait painter for the city would soon terminate.

The officer in charge of public relations had to advise him repeatedly, "Brighten up your latest posters, will you? Let the red of the fire trucks, or even the lime-yellow, shout to people, 'Help is on the way!' Don't forget, some of these will be submitted to the calendar design people. Nobody wants to look at lifeless colors and static images for a whole month."

Rousing himself day after day over two years to face increasing frustration at the office, and at home witnessing another period of Lois's tears, he was tempted daily to remain in bed. He forced himself to go to work, and there, had to strive to make his time productive. Then on returning home, he struggled to make his hours cheerful. Little did he realize how much it was he who was being sustained—by Lois. Eventually she suggested buying a cottage in hopes that pastoral scenery, blazing scarlets and golds of autumn, dramatic sunrises and sunsets might restore the whole family. "The twins," as she preferred to call them, never the boys, "need an infusion of splendour and peace in their lives just as much as you and I do," she had pleaded.

Over the first several months at the cottage, the magic of nature gradually revived him and enabled him to begin once again.

He reflected on the twelve wonderful years at the cottage with Lois, and the months that led up to that day, the day he heard of his father's death, the day of Emily's visit.

The darkness was beginning to dissolve everything. A key on the table and Michel's crumpled note on the floor were fading into nothingness. His hand moved hesitantly in search of a light switch. He addressed the empty chair, "No. No light. Not yet. A candle perhaps, but not a brutal, unforgiving, insensitive uncompromising, heartless hundred watt bulb. This dark is almost light enough for me. Was I? talking to myself?"

The open window above the sink beside him framed a pale luminescence. He turned and gazed at the ghostly trees barely moving in response to the breath of a chill autumn breeze. He expected a young woman's voice to ask, "What are you looking at?" but no. No such luck. He glanced back at the embroidered chair, just to be sure. Then with an effort, he turned away and stepped towards the door that led outside.

He stopped and watched the sliver of a new moon tussle with scudding clouds and jostle with pine branches. Wearily he shuffled down the worn path that carried him to his painting shed, his studio. On entering, he breathed in the smells, a comforting component of his painterly refuge—oils, thinners, cleansers, rags, old floor boards. No smell of death in here these days. Behind him, the door creaked shut as it had done for over half a century, long before Charles as an eight year-old explorer first peered into the ram shackled board and batten shed.

"Is it ever spooky in there!" little Charles told Mark so many years ago. "Come on. Maybe we can find a treasure." The two children walked completely around the shed, noting the cobwebs and grime that rendered the three windows almost opaque.

"It'll be dark in there," Mark whispered.

"Yeah, won't it!" Charles said enthusiastically, for to him the unknown, the unfamiliar was a challenge, whereas to his twin, it was a warning. Charles, with arms akimbo and a pout of disapproval said, "Oh, all right. Go and get Dad's flashlight, scaredy-cat."

While Mark was scurrying up the slope to their tent site, his brother surveyed the setting of the shed, halfway between the cottage and the beach. One of the windows, when cleaned, would look out onto cedars that bowed to the lake and pointed to the far shore.

"I got it. I got it," Mark called from afar. They entered warily and sniffed the fetid air. "There's dead things in here. Charlie, I don't like this place."

"Prob'ly mice. But lookit all the funny stuff."

Being city boys, they couldn't name half of what they found: wooden horses, pulleys, burlap bags, a twisted whipsaw, pitch forks, a butter churn, a cast iron pot-bellied stove, chopping blocks, a rusted adze, wooden planes, a half repaired bee hive. The tailor's dummy startled and intrigued them. Everything testified to another world, an alternate reality, fossils of an alien culture. No wonder, they called it "the Ghost Hut." It retained that name long after Lois and Alan cleaned it up, scooped out the mouse and bat dirt, nailed plywood on the walls over top of insulation, enlarged the window which gave onto the lake, and brought to the shack electricity and water. When they tore up some rotted floor boards they found several animal skeletons. "Porcupines, by the looks of things," Alan said, "killed by fishers, weasel-like critters. No wonder the place smells of death."

It remained "the Ghost Hut," even as Alan stood alone in the dark on the night of his daughter's visitation. He didn't feel alone, for familiar voices of the past played in his mind. On second thought, not all were familiar. Emily's was not a voice from the past. Couldn't have been. Nevertheless he had heard it, heard her.

The jumble of memories and speculations drowned out the faint sounds of the Laplantes' ancient Ford that was labouring away from the Lodge. "Nobody in the old shed," Michel had reported from the back door of the cottage. "There's no lights on down there."

"Or anywhere," his father noted.

"I leave de soupe for 'im, hennyway," Mrs. Laplante said. "'e can warm it hup when 'e come back."

"He looked broken up this morning when we gave him the news," Mr. Laplante said. "He's probably out in his rowboat, thinking and mourning. So much loss—his baby, his wife, and now his father. Let's leave him to himself."

The thin rind of the moon was the sole source of light inside the shed and inside Alan's soul, a glimmer he felt must slowly wax into a fullness. How that glimmer would grow and how long it would take did not occupy his conscious mind in the least. He simply wanted "to be", not even to be aware of being.

So many hours, yes years, had been spent in the Ghost Hut that if blindfolded, he could put his hand on the hooks that held his palettes, the cups that cradled his brushes, the shelves that displayed his art books. With little difficulty he located the candle stub and the small box of matches on the ledge beside the door. "You never know when the lights will go out around here," he had taught his sons. It just needs a branch to fall on our power line along our winding road. Whenever you come up here, be sure you know where to find flashlights and candles. And be sure to bring batteries and matches from the city." Despite the availability of electricity in the shed, he usually preferred the warm glow of an oil lamp unless he was painting.

The match flared, causing his pupils to contract momentarily then dilate when it became evident that no greater light would assault them. He lifted the chimney of the kerosene lamp, lit the wick, turned it low, and set the lamp on his work bench. Feeling the cold breath of winter's herald, he swung the window closed, sat down and gazed into the yellow flame.

His many selves debated. I know that important life-changing decisions should not be made immediately after the loss of a loved one. I know that. After her death by leukemia, Lois seemed to be saying that she would be with me. Here. Here and now. So perhaps, just perhaps, I should continue to stay at Lakeside Cottage with her memory, with their memories. Alone. But alone with them.

Let their absence become a presence through my painting. Let them live in and through my art work . . . laugh, embroider once more, cook up her dyes, stand at Ledge Lodge saying in father's old raspy voice, "You've captured it. Perfect!" The boys can canoe forever on my canvases, and carry Emily on their back and run races and swim with her. In a painted air ambulance, and with no fear of dying this time, both boys can fly over our lake.

Through Alan's mind, the ideas began to course—fast moving streams of consciousness, bounding rapids of prescience. The clarity of successive scenes thrilled him. He was in a theatre audience watching himself play out on stage the role of his life. The scenery consisted of large blow-ups of his future paintings. At least they would never die, would long survive him.

He carried the lamp to his photo collection pinned to the studio wall, each of them enlargements of family settings that captured significant moments in their life: Lois holding Emily on her lap on the infant's first Christmas, the boys toasting marshmallows at the first campfire on these grounds, his father sitting in a wheelchair in the nursing home staring blankly at the photo of his late wife, Roger and Alan together gripping their frothing bottle of champagne while waving their B.A. degrees aloft. He moved the lamp again so that its golden flicker could bring to life his favourite Jordaens print.

Yes, he thought, Lois, Emily, father and I can live together on my canvases, hug and dance, laugh and cry, all in deathless exuberance. And others too.

The next day, he phoned the Fire Department and told them to expect his resignation in writing on Tuesday, to be effective at the earliest. And what need was there for a house in Toronto? For the last five years, Lakeside Cottage had been as much of a beloved home as their city house was, and with fewer tragic memories for Mark and Charles, and for Alan.

He extinguished the lamp and said, "Time for you all to go to sleep. Me too, if I can. A special good night to you, Dad."

Next day, he drove south to Toronto, composing sample letters of resignation as he sped forward in time, in space, and in determination. How very unlike me, he thought, to decide so promptly, so effortlessly. What I am doing must be right. I can see the headlines now, "Noted Procrastinator Takes Quick Action," with a sub-heading, "Toronto's Painter Laureate Makes Daring New Beginning." And the article would read: "Alan Thompson, best remembered for his controversial portrait of ex-chief Harold Brockbank handed in his resignation yesterday. Captain Joe Vittorio, Mr. Thompson's supervisor, spoke highly of his ability to work in a variety of styles—portraits, fire safety cartoons, and cityscapes. We wish him well as he continues his career in northern Ontario. He is the son of retired District Chief Ray Thompson who passed away last week and whose ashes will be spread at the Thompsons' camp near Norvale, Ontario."

Three months, spent mostly in Toronto, rushed by but not so speedily as Alan wanted. His imagination drew him persistently to the planning of sketches, scenes, portraits that could generate a new community for him. Although he was unconscious of the drift, they would regenerate him as will.

In a phone call from his home in Chicago, Mark expressed bafflement at his father's desire to leave Toronto. "For heaven's sake, Dad, how will you survive in winter, all alone up there? You'll have to buy a snowmobile and drive along the lake!"

"Great idea!" his father said. "I hadn't thought of that. Yes, by road it would be about ten kilometres into town. But over the lake, only three. I'm glad you suggested that."

"I am not suggesting it. It's not what I want you to be doing all by yourself. And what if the water pipes freeze? When there's no water to flush the toilets, don't tell me you'll use the old two-holer that Mom painted to look like a British telephone booth."

"Another great idea. But don't forget, you and Gwen traipsed off to Chicago to join the frantic rat race there. You're not blaming me now for wanting join the much more peaceful muskrat race out in the bush, far from traffic gridlock and overcrowded elevators, and ubiquitous, domineering, insomniac cell phones. Anyway, I'll be only a phone call away and can keep in touch by email."

"But that's not the point! There'll be nobody around to talk to, or to keep an eye on you when you go swimming. Besides, the nearest neighbour is God knows how many kilometres away."

"Seven, Mark. Or in winter, only three. Meanwhile, I want you, Gwen and Monica to drive up to the Toronto house on the next long weekend and claim whatever old high school and university texts and furniture you want before I move out. Charles has already taken his stuff to Ottawa."

Adopting his office style tough talk, he objected, "But the whole thing smells pretty stupid to me, Dad. For God's sake, at least don't sell the house until you discover, pretty damn soon I hope, that a move to live alone, miles from civilization is, well, it's just plain stupid!"

But the memory of Lois's promise never to abandon him won the argument for Al. Perhaps the greatest longing after all his loss of loved ones was to be by himself, to be left alone with a virtual family that would always be there for him on canvas, cheerful, eager and healthy, there where the best of the past and reveries of the future could become present.

He was not discovering in himself a misanthropic streak, rather, a tendency that is disanthropic. Whenever he began to doubt that distinction as he settled into his hermitage, he would stay longer in the village after his regular and punctual Wednesday shopping trip. He would drop in at the tavern to chat with the usual clientele who divided their time between gossip swapping at Karl's Hair Emporium and games of cribbage with rounds of beer at The Wild Ones.

The habitués, mostly retired or unemployed, hardly lived up to that daredevil name, with the exception of Bart, a tall, lanky fellow, captain of the Norvale Shooters hockey team. A covey of girls in the Norvale region regularly flocked around the pheromone-enhanced wild bird. They strutted around his table at the tavern and outside the dressing room door at the arena, hoping to be Bart's mate of the evening. Another fixture at The Wild Ones, one who distinguished himself by his irrepressible humour, especially after his third drink, was Billy, the shortest man in the tavern—in the region, in fact. "I'm Billy. But just call me 'B-for-short'" was his predictable introduction to any newcomer at the bar. "Now don't you look down on short people," he said as he dangled his feet over a barstool. "Why, I mop the floor with folks taller than you."

"Or with that long beard of yours," Eric the bald always felt obliged to retaliate every time, without fail.

"So," said Alan, "You're B-for-short. You mind if I call you 'Beefer.'? That's even shorter."

In winter, particularly, with leaves gone, and the lake frozen over, Lake Lodge was a lonely place. An occasional moose glared at him before it bounded away in its graceful springing motion. On windless days when the sun shone, heavily laden branches would punctuate the stillness with sudden plops of snow. Then a deeper hush would envelope him. Miles above, solitary airplanes whispered across the clear blue sky leaving their crisscrossing of graffiti. Everything intensified his sense of isolation.

One escape from aloneness was the physical and emotional satisfaction of chopping wood, a task which also provided a break from hours of reading and painting. For an additional diversion, he decided to attempt ice fishing, having heard so many locals boast of their catches. Karl provided the basic tools of the sport and explained how and when to use them.

On his first attempt, Al skidded out over the ice to plant his very first ice hole, chopped through what seemed like half an arm length of uncooperative ice and dropped his line, lure and hooks into the slush, sat down on a little stool and began a long and lonely wait. After an hour of stillness, the silence was shattered by what sounded like a rifle shot. He turned to scan the shore line in search of hunters or vandals. Images of the bullet-pocked "Keep Out—Private Property" signs flashed to his mind, and he recalled seeing punctured beer cans skewered on long poles beside the road to his lodge. Was he to be the next target, he wondered.

He crouched low on the ice surface, and suddenly felt like a sitting duck. What had been peace and quiet now was transmuted into fright and uncertainty. From his cowering position, the forest along the shore seemed to assume a menacing aspect, each ever deepening shadow a possible source of alarm and every movement a possible threat. Where only minutes before, the tall pines and cedars had testified to all that was noble, peaceable and carefree in nature now a malignant aspect glared at him. How could he go back into those shadows? Yet for how long must he remain transfixed on this cold, exposed shooting range?

And then, another crack, louder and nearer than the first, in fact, beneath his feet, right in the ice. Then he realized: of course—this was no rifle shot but the sound of ice expanding under enormous pressure. However, the carefree joy of fishing eluded him that day. He would try again, perhaps.

And indeed he did, emerging from those very shadows where terror had briefly lurked, and slithering into the blinding blaze of sunlight. But when the wind whistled down the lake, and the ice thickened and required repeated hacking to reach the water, the dedication that was needed to sit, shivering beside an ice hole or to build a shed and drag it out from shore chilled, in fact, froze to death his interest in the sport. Besides, all loneliness had been abating as he brought friends and loved ones to life on canvas.

Why does the creation of my virtual community offer me so much contentment, week after week, he wondered. Is it because I have the power to control them so absolutely? Is it because they are powerless to impose choices on me, choices that could reroute my life into unwanted directions?

He began to look forward to Wednesdays. At the general store, Audrey, cashier, shelf stacker and bag carrier for the elderly, greeting him as one of the long-time Norvale family. Ever since her husband was shot in a hunting accident three years before, all the townsfolk pitched in to keep her afloat. Surprise loads of chopped firewood would suddenly appear in her front yard, baskets of fruit or eggs at her side door. She looked for ways to return the favours to her community. Fortunately, her son earned a huge post-graduate scholarship at an American university.

"Anything special you want me to order for next week from the depot, Alan?" This was her usual request to all customers. It was a service motivated by rural neighbourliness, not by self-serving competitiveness.

"Sure, how about some Bosc pears?"

Audrey stopped packing his purchases into a carton. With a puzzled frown she asked, "Bosc? Never sold any such thing around here. Pears, you say?"

"Yes, cut up on breakfast cereal, they're my favourite. Bought them all the time in the big city. You can slice them thin on crackers, spread with Stilton cheese and walnuts, and wash it all down with a shot of Chambord. Now that's living."

"Sounds pretty fancy for Norvale. But I'll see if they stock them. And believe me, they won't have Stilton cheese. 'Bosc,' I better write that down. Got a mind like a cylinder."

"A what?"

"You know. What you drain veggies in."

"Ah."

Al, the sole customer in the store at the moment, was about to leave when heartthrob Bart made his trademark entrance. As was his custom whether at the barber shop, the tavern, Audrey's grocery store or wherever, he flung open the door, stood stock still in the doorway and awaited the shouts of recognition, the hoots of acclaim that would greet him. His favourite welcome at the arena involved a bevy of lasses who gleefully grabbed his arms and pulled him into the building. But at the store, without even glancing at the open door, Audrey called instead to Al, "Don't forget, you offered to bring those bags of potatoes in off the back stoop for me."

Mystified, he followed her into the back storage room. "Just stick around, please, until Bart's gone," she whispered. "I don't want to be alone with that guy."

Bart was not pleased with such total lack of reception. After all, Audrey was attractive. Her bosom must have been aching to be caressed. He collected his case of mixers, selected his usual dozen packages of frozen dinners, then squinted a sneer at her, paid and left.

"I usually smell him coming in here before I see him."

"Smell?"

She looked in wide-eyed astonishment. "You mean you haven't noticed? The guy must bathe in aftershave. Some of the girls around town call him 'stereo.' They say he uses two different underarm deodorants. 'Country Moss' in one armpit and 'Wild Musk' in the other."

Al picked up his box of purchases, shook his head in disbelief, muttered, "Stereo Bart," and elbowed his way out the door.

After a few days, she phoned Lake Lodge. "Alan? Audrey. I've asked about those pears, the Bosc ones. They don't usually carry them, but they can order if we take an entire crate."

He couldn't imagine consuming an entire crate of pears.

"Thanks for enquiring, Audrey, but maybe we should just forget it. There's always bananas."

"No, if you take half a crate, I'm sure folks in town will buy some. That'll be the most exciting event of the week around here."

Several weeks later, as Alan was treating himself to Bosc pears sliced onto his bran flakes, he wondered about adding Audrey to his portrait gallery. He could imagine the others down in the shed whispering, "Who let her in? She doesn't belong here."

With the exception of Mrs. Laplante, Alan decided not to add any Norvale acquaintances to his growing canvas community. They were worlds apart. The townsfolk were vulnerable to aging, disease, and death—to say nothing of possible duplicity, obsequiousness, egotism. Besides. they would be victims of decay. He recalled reading of Cezanne's revulsion on finding the apples shrivelling and rotting that he was attempting to paint. Alan's creations would last forever, permanently enshrined in whatever attitude or setting brought him most delight. They would eventually become a precious legacy for his sons and grandchildren.

On entering the shed after a trip into town, he surprised himself by saying, "I'm back." He flipped on the lights and noticed what to him appeared to be looks of pleasure, of relief almost, on the faces of his paintings.

"Glad to see me, are you, Roger?" he said as he took down the painting of his old friend and placed it on the easel. "I hoped you could have taken a break from your editorial work and flown over to my private paradise here. But until that happens, you'll just have to make do with your framed view of my studio."

One of his most restorative treasures was his CD player. He pressed the power button. "I guess you know my musical preferences by now, Roger." He selected one of his favourite CDs, the nocturnes of Chopin, performed by Toronto pianist, William Aide.

"Sorry, old friend, I need the space on this easel. Now where did I put . . . ? zounds! I still haven't given him a name." He turned and addressed a portrait on the end wall, his precious depiction of Emily as she might have been in her mid twenties. "What name shall we give your fiancé?" Can't keep calling him your No-Name boyfriend. How about Pol, short for Apollo. No? well, we'd better find some name for him and soon. Mark would complain indignantly that your fiancé must not be "Untitled', and I'd have to agree." He glanced from portrait to portrait as if seeking their approval, or perhaps their suggestions.

He replaced Roger on the wall, stopped to add some kindling to the fire in the old pot-bellied stove, washed his hands and took down the no-name portrait from the rack above the door. Holding the painting at arm's length, he examined it critically. Over two weeks had passed since last he worked on it.

Was it the absence of reflected light from the snow, or perhaps a burnt-out light bulb that gave the young man a certain lifelessness? The eyes, the mouth were not right, not what he wanted, not what he had painted. Alan knew full well that the portrait of the imaginary man was far from completed, but there was something about the expression that needed altering, a look of disapproval, a scowl of impatience. Alan remembered Dorian Grey and laughed to himself.

No, not anything metamorphic here, he thought, nothing Kafkaesque. "Perhaps I was tired or in a hurry when I was painting you." He wondered what on earth made him think of Kafka? Was this some kind of synchronicity? It had been only the previous day that he was studying some lush Dutch still lifes. Their varieties of flowers and insects never ceased to fascinate him. Painters of bygone days often included butterflies, spiders, grasshoppers, dragonflies, even worms and slugs in their still lifes. He wondered why most modern artists, he too, excluded them. They don't seem to belong in a sanitized, fumigated world. Dogs, birds, cats, yes. Horses, decidedly. He smiled broadly at the thought of Rigaud's painting of Louis XIV, standing gartered, imperious in brocade, but with a snail on his silver shoe or a beetle camouflaged by the ermine draped over his shoulder.

That very morning when he had the stove roaring and the chimney pipe radiating heat, a wood bug emerged from its cool slumber between ancient planks. It laboured across his work bench, the undeviating path indicating that it knew where it was going. It reached the curved underside of a piece of canvas that Alan had just unrolled. Abruptly it stopped, calculated angles, the pull of gravity and the strength of its many legs. Then, as only insects know how, it clambered upside down onto the canvas, pulled itself over the edge, and hurried onto the flat surface. The micro-armadillo stopped to look for—what?—a Dutch garden with marigolds, peonies, roses and scrumptious decaying underbrush? Finding nothing to satisfy its appetite, its curiosity, its desire for a mate, the bug rotated one hundred and eighty degrees and returned on the same path by which it had arrived.

Synchronicities imply metaphors, meanings. Omens? Alan tried sedulously not to put interpretations on the event. The attempt reminded him of a challenge Mark gave him as a little boy, "Dad, try not to think of pink elephants for the next two minutes." Now it was pink wood bugs and beetles and Kafka.

Gawd, he thought, my first winter half over and I'm going strange. Perhaps I should try to keep in touch with the world out there, that aging, decaying, perishing other world I can find in Norvale. Thank goodness it won't have to be a choice of either this world or that, one or the other. For a change, it can be both and.

He reflected on the one-or-another decisions he had made: studies in art instead of law as his father had preferred; going to U. of T. rather than McGill in Montreal; marrying Lois instead of Ellen; accepting a position with the Fire Department instead of perhaps opening an art gallery; buying the property up north. Each choice opened a new door. And shut others. But this time, two doors were beckoning: his community in the studio, and the one in town. Sounded like a win-win situation.

The road into town was still passable. He knew it was only Friday, but maybe a surprise visit to the barber shop was in order, or, if nobody was there, over to The Wild Ones. That was the beauty of a life lived alone. Nobody to say, "I wouldn't if I were you. What if it snows heavily?" or "What if the winds pile up drifts? What if you get stuck, or have a flat, or the fuel line freezes on you, or you have a heart attack, or . . . or . . . or?"

He recollected his mother's urgent, panic stricken voice when he was a child, "Now you climb right down from there this very instant. You're going to fall and break your neck." Or was that his own sharp command to Charles?

He knew there was risk involved in nonessential winter drives in that sparsely populated part of the world, but would life without risk be worth living? After all, the view through the branches of the tall, swaying maple tree, ten or fifteen meters up was glorious. "I'm the king of the castle, and . . ."

"You heard me, you get down right now!"

Why not, like so many timorous souls, just go to bed and wait it out? He scrutinized the portraits on the walls for signs of encouragement. Standing or sitting in various poses, they all waited to be asked for their advice: Emily, Lois, Ellen, Charles and Mark, Roger, Victor Liang, and others.

"Joe, lets start with you. Did I ever tell you why I brought you into this community? As long as I worked under you, there was never a time when you didn't support me. I guess I know what you'd say about this winter drive into town. You'd want to come along.

"Now, how about you, Mrs. Laplante. You still look *bouleversee* at being in this company of friends. If I know you, you'll drop off some pork chops or a marvellous home-baked pie some time this week, despite the ice and snow. You'd tell me that if the weather prevents me from driving back from town along the seven kilometres of my roller coaster road, you and your husband would put me up for the night. I won't refuse your pies or your hospitality.

"Mark! I know, I know—a tree could come crashing down across the road, or I'd miscalculate on the gas tank and run out of fuel and freeze to death. But I understand. You always seemed to blame yourself for what happened both to your baby sister in the crib and to Charles across the lake at the ledge. Then the suddenness of Lois's fatal leukemia drained away so much of your zest for living. You were far away when grandpa died in the nursing home. And now you're far away from me. But don't worry, I'll be careful."

Among the many paintings was one photograph, an 8 x 10 of the portrait that had aroused such controversy. Harry Brockbank, the Fire Chief, stood confident, ardently pointing the way to the future. "Yes, Harry, that's sign enough for me. I'll risk it."

That trip, he felt, was a deviation from his plan. His paradise by itself was to have provided all he needed, its breath-taking beauty in winter and summer, its even more inspiring glories in autumn when tamaracks turned gold, and maples red. His dependable, reliable, painted community had been offering endless joy both in the act of creating and of communing. The drive into town could be considered more unnecessary than improper. Yet there was about it a certain frisson of the forbidden, not unlike climbing a tall, swaying tree in order to peer beyond the usual, the expected, the permitted.

The dirt road was by now very familiar to him—each hill and curve, the narrow shuddering wooden bridge, the high outcroppings of rock, the occasional moose or bear lumbering out of the dense forest. What caught his eye as a possible painting was the succession of hills that succeeded one another in a straight line. The boys used to whoop when they flew over them, weightless as the car catapulted over crest after crest. Gotta capture this on canvas, he thought. And give it to Mark or Charles. Maybe paint it twice, but not in this freezing season.

In town, he parked diagonally, the nose of his Buick pointing towards the snow banks left by the highway plough. In front of the barber shop he paused to wave at Karl and noticed Stereo-Bart getting a trim, and several team mates from the next village waiting their turn. What were they doing in town? he wondered. They weren't dressed for a hockey game. He wouldn't go in and have a coffee with them. In passing, he cast a glance at the blistered and chipped paint around the grungy window, and muttered to himself, "Change and decay in all around I see." Then, thinking of his portrait gallery, he added, "All you who change not, abide with me."

"Alan! Hey, Al! Are you in town for the dance tonight?"

The scene of multi-scented Bart and his team mates at the barber shop suddenly made sense. He turned and saw Kay, the proprietor of the town's drug and news store. She waved frantically and hurried through ankle deep snow towards him.

"Hi Kay. Who's minding the store?"

"I put up a sign on the door, 'Back in 20 minutes.' Nobody'll know when the 20 minutes began. I was just talking to Michel on the phone. He mentioned he saw you drive past, probably heading for town."

"Where else?"

"So I threw on my coat and hoped to catch you. Let's go into Lee's for a coffee if you're not in a hurry."

Lee was watering his collection of rubber plants. "Hi Kay, Alan. Have I got my dates wrong? This isn't Wednesday, is it?"

"No, you haven't, Lee, but I couldn't put off till next week having a cup of your delicious coffee and a slice of my favourite lemon pie."

"Freshly baked, as always," Lee boasted.

"A coffee for me, too. You know how I like it."

They sat at the table nearest the oil burning heater. On the wall beside them, the photo of a slim, coquettish Chinese girl in a brilliant red sheath decorated a calendar. It was last year's. Christmas decorations, early for that year—or, more likely, late from last—festooned the dusty chandeliers.

"You don't mind if I smoke," Kay said. It wasn't a question. "I've been dying for one all afternoon, but people don't like to see me smoking in the drug store part of my shop."

Lee arrived with the coffee and two generous slices of pie. She smiled and looked over her glasses, "Freshly baked when, Lee?"

"You want some ice cream with that?" She shook her head and waved a no at him.

"We've got to stop meeting this way," Alan jested.

"Oh, come on! Our first date and already you want out? Well let me tell you, Audrey and Michel and I, and two or three others want to have a date with you every Sunday afternoon."

"Only if it ends in group sex," he replied with a leer.

"Very funny, Al. But no, a gaggle of us in town want you to give weekly painting lessons. Some of us are tempted to go a little stir crazy in this hole. We thought you could put some color in our lives, something to do, something worth doing. What do you say?"

Al studied his pie, then reached across the table, plucked the cigarette from her hand and took a long draw on it.

Her eyebrows were still far up on her forehead as she said, "I didn't know you smoked!"

"I don't," he said, returning the cigarette. Choking on the smoke, he struggled to add, "And I don't give painting lessons either."

"You don't, or you haven't tried?"

He wiped his eyes between spasms of coughing, "I haven't tried."

"Good," she cried, clapping her hands. "We all want you to try, beginning after Christmas. We've got a room in the old school house. We'll pay for supplies and a meal after each class. Besides, we're planning a regional art show in June to include our masterpieces and, if you'll go along with the idea, some of your paintings too. What d'you say?"

His coughing subsided. A voice from the back of the restaurant announced, "And I'll provide the lemon pie for his meals."

Al downed his coffee, plunked the cup on the table, glanced around the dining room as if looking for some excuse to say no. It would provide an opportunity to live in both worlds, that of the community in his studio and that in town. "OK, let's go for it. But I'll be at my son's place in Chicago for three weeks around Christmas, then another two weeks with Charles in Ottawa. I can buy enough supplies in either city. So let's begin the first Sunday in February."

"Great," she said, glancing at her watch. "Only fifteen minutes, not bad." She turned to pick up her scarf and began to wrap it around her neck. "The coffee's on me."

He noticed the entirely different kind of attractiveness of a northern small town woman, the naturalness, the ruggedness that contrasted with the studied elegance of a Toronto crowd. He observed the happy ad hoc-ery of jeans, casual sweater and boots.

"I better get back to the store. By the way, you haven't answered my question."

"Which was?"

"Are you in town for the dance?"

He chuckled at the absurdity of the thought. "Sure, and I brought along one of my portraits as a partner."

"Audrey will be jealous," she said with a knowing nod. She waved to Lee, pointed to her generous pile of coins on a nearby table, and hurried out. The rubber plants shivered at the gusts of icy wind rushing into the restaurant.

On returning to the Lodge, he did not go into the studio. The wood fire would have burned itself out long ago, but his electric heater would have automatically switched on, providing enough warmth to keep paints from freezing. And besides, he didn't have the heart to tell them of this new project of teaching art. They'd understand though, he thought.

Time goes supersonic when you're enjoying yourself, as indeed it did while he was visiting Mark, Gwen and Monica in Chicago and Charles in Ottawa. They excused him for the long hours he spent at museums and art galleries, knowing that such institutions are galaxies removed from Norvale.

When he returned to the northern village he discovered that eight people from the town and from a neighbouring community had signed up for his Sunday classes.

As months passed, and snows melted, and blackflies proliferated, his students were rapturous about their new interest. They borrowed his art books, they demanded extra attention, they begged for private lessons, until he found he was sacrificing time that he ought to have been spending with his own virtual family. A certain trace of guilt accompanied him whenever he left his studio early to attend to his Norvale friends. Despite the connectedness he enjoyed with his art students, with Karl and the boys at the barber shop, with the ever solicitous Laplantes and all the others, he sensed an indefinable discontent, the apprehension of possible future deprivations when those people would inevitably move away, or worse, pass away. An anticipated grief.

On his way back from town, he recited the succession of features he would navigate along the road: that dangerous "S" curve, then the dip down towards the stream, along the low slippery section by the bog, up, up towards the granite outcrop. Next those roller coaster hills that follow one another, the ones he would some day paint. Hey! Why not start today? he asked himself. I've got my stuff from the class. And the spring foliage allowed light to penetrate the forest floor spotlighting the flowering mandrakes.

As he approached the crest of the first hill, he gradually slowed to a stop and admired the familiar vista of hills that narrowed to a vanishing point beneath mountains of white cumulous clouds. Better park on the top of this hillock in case some driver lost in these backwoods should speed along the road, he thought. From the trunk he carried out his small collapsible table, his easel, the box of paints, brushes and a palette.

To make a preliminary sketch or not, he wondered. No, first a series of photos for future reference. He removed the camera from the glove compartment. The sound of the car door slamming suddenly caused him to be aware of the silence of the forest and his absolute aloneness. When he stood still, he felt as if he were in someone else's painting, an image never to move from his frozen posture. Not a leaf stirred. Time seemed to stop for him as so often and so unpredictably it had for Lois after Emily's death.

He shook himself out of his paralysis and raised the camera in search of the best frame for the scene. As he peered through the view finder, he detected something moving in the distance—a porcupine? No, too lively. A faun? No, too small, as it stumbled and wove from side to side. Through the telescopic lens he discerned the glad animal movements of a bear cub as it gambolled towards him. Do I want to include him in my painting? Well, take a photo anyway and decide later.

How unusual for a cub to run towards a human being, he thought. Surely, it has been taught by its mother to remain motionless or to flee as fast . . . Its mother! At that Alan turned around and saw scampering toward him one very large black beast. No time to pack up. He let go of the camera, lunged towards the car, snatched open the door, climbed in and struggled to find keys to active the power windows. The bear slashed at the door and thrust a powerful paw through the open window. Al slid to the passenger seat, and opened the door. If he could stand up, he'd more easily rummage through his pockets for the keys. The bear clambered onto the engine hood and with a thump, slithered off the shiny finish, and just as quickly clawed back up. Al re-entered, key in hand, and using both hands to stop the trembling, managed to insert it. No time to close windows, even as the bear reached in and tore his shirt. Gravel shot back from the spinning tires leaving a stunned and furious mother bear in the dust.

Maybe tomorrow he'd return for his art supplies and camera. Or maybe next week. But not to paint that scene on site. He'd stick with portraiture. Lonely forest scenes can be injurious to your health. What if I'd dropped the keys or if momma bear had managed to reach in a little further. When would anybody find me. Better not tell Mark about this or he'd have me certified as mad and put me away for my own safety.

The next day, in the light of his encounter with death, he felt an urgency to complete yet another painting of Lois. This time she stood on the dock, facing the lake and the distant Ledge Lodge, with her back to him. He contemplated his work for several minutes until a couplet from a sonnet sprang to mind,

But if the while I think on thee, dear friend,

All losses are restored and sorrows end.

When summer arrived, his boys with family and friends came back and compared notes on how things had changed. Charles lamented that the cedar tree that used to lean over the lake had tumbled into the water and lost its leaves, its bark, its life. "I used to sit on a branch far out over the lake, and fish," he told his friend. "You could see the trout below, snubbing the bait. I did finally catch one there. But not any more from that tree."

Mark was disappointed to see how overgrown the path up to Ledge Lodge had become. "Don't go anywhere near the edge," he cautioned Monica and her girlfriend.

"I won't fall," his daughter pronounced, scornfully protracting the final word. "I won't faawl! I just want to see how far down it is."

He turned away from them, cupped his hands over his eyes and shouted, "Not there. Please. Don't!"

Monica glanced at her friend, smirked, and in a voice barbed with ridicule said, "Fathers!"

Time that Al spent with his family, as enjoyable as it was, meant time away from his virtual community. Love is not supposed to be a zero sum engagement, he thought.

Contrary to his original stand, he relented and allowed his art students to visit his property just once. Ostensibly they wanted scenery to paint, as if there were not plenty of other lakes and rivers and sunsets all around Norvale. In reality, they were curious to see how he could live alone. Perhaps they would be granted the privilege of encountering the characters who were said to people his studio.

On one occasion, unannounced, Audrey arrived with her son during his summer university vacation. "I thought you might enjoy a picnic for a change," she said. By this time, she knew his food preferences from his weekly purchases at the store and what his wish list might include. At some considerable inconvenience she brought avocados, farfalla pasta with some rather wilted cilantro, sliced lamb, a fresh pineapple, Stilton cheese, a vintage South African wine, and a small bottle of Chambord. She was absolutely certain that since over the preceding years he had mentioned each one of these separately, together they must, somehow, combine to create the utmost in culinary art.

It was evident even to Alan that this combination of disparate elements was a metaphor for a possible combination of Audrey and himself.

Hesitantly, almost guiltily, he found himself more and more attracted to her as the autumn painting classes resumed. Not until a sudden early snowstorm marooned him in Norvale did an opportunity present itself for them to be alone together.

All of the out-of-town students were wise enough not to attempt the drive through the blizzard. Since the town's power went off in the middle of the lesson, everyone but Audrey went home. Alan accepted Audrey's invitation to dine with her since Lee's restaurant would not be open in this storm.

"I'm quite used to cooking on the old wood stove by lamplight," she said. "Anyway, you're not driving home after supper through this weather."

He had to agree. "I'd never make it past the Laplantes'. My road is always the last to be ploughed."

The car fishtailed its way through deepening snow drifts to her house. She had to struggle to open the front door against a pile of snow. They entered, shook the melting flakes off their coats and out of their hair.

"Sorry I don't have any lemon pie," she said.

"Or Chambord, either, I bet."

"No, but there's half a chicken. Look in the vegetable bins and see if you can find a turnip, some potatoes, maybe some onions. Let's make a stew. Tomatoes are too expensive up here at this season. There's kindling for the stove in the woodbox by the back door. How about getting a good fire going."

"Two fires," he said. "The stove and the fireplace."

As he headed towards the woodbox she flashed a risqué smile, "Maybe three . . . ?" She wasn't positive that he heard. He returned with some old newspapers and an armload of wood. "Have you ever been out west?"

She frowned at this unwelcome intrusion into her past. She took the chicken out of the fridge and began to unwrap it. "To Duluth for the wedding of my sister."

"No, I mean really west, to B.C. or Washington, or Alberta?"

Audrey was annoyed at his mention of British Columbia. Was he going to stir up what she had been struggling to forget? Did he already know that she and Paul had flown to Seattle and Vancouver for their honeymoon? "Yes, to the west coast, but just for a week or so." I hope he doesn't go on to ask me why or who with or when, she said to herself. Not tonight.

"Did you get up into the mountains? I mean really high up?"

She stopped carving the chicken off the bones and wondered, What's this "out west" business? Do I want to spend the night with a nice man who isn't really here? "Did you find the turnip and the other vegetables?"

"Maybe you were at the Great divide," he said, half to himself. His look of intense, almost passionate concentration unnerved her.

"No, Vancouver. And Seattle, too, for three days. Here, I'll cut up the veggies. You get the stove going. This stew will take an hour." He didn't move. His eyes were fixed on the fireplace as if he were watching a TV screen. "I've always wanted to go there." She swung around and stared at the unlit fireplace, then at him.

In hushed, almost reverential tones he said, "I've always wanted to go the Great Divide." He turned and looked at her excitedly. "It's amazing." He hoped she understood. He wanted her to know what he knew about it. "It's truly amazing."

"I'm sure it is, Alan." She nodded slowly, and without enthusiasm. "The onions? There should be some in the fridge. And don't take out the Spanish onion. Two cooking onions ought to be enough. Here, let me put a match to the newspaper."

He handed her the box of matches. She doesn't understand, he thought. She doesn't seem to be interested. He had to make her comprehend. He explained, "What is so astonishing is that at that north-south dividing line along the mountain ridge, water on the west side of it ends up in the Pacific, and water just a centimetre to the east, less than a centimetre even, ends up in Hudson's Bay or the Gulf of Mexico."

She pondered this information. "Well now, that is astonishing," she said flatly as she poured water into the stew pot. "You never know, do you?"

"That's right," he said with a smile and a look of relief. "You're right. You never do know at least not in advance."

He held up his hand showing a tiny gap between thumb and index finger. "Water this far away at the beginning ends up thousands and thousands of kilometres away. It's as close as yes is to no." He could not bring himself to add that it is as close as Lois is to Ellen. That, she wouldn't understand.

And then, suddenly he understood. I am talking not to Audrey but to myself. About Audrey. Tonight may be a great divide that will eventually re-shape me. I'm straddling it right here in this kitchen.

The thrum of an engine outside interrupted his meditation. As he walked to the window and peered through the sheets of snow to investigate, the sound became a whine and then a growl. The frame house vibrated as a monstrous highway snowplough roared past her front yard, flinging a wave that completely blocked her driveway. His first thought was that now there was no possible way to reach the Laplantes'. Perhaps the decision concerning tonight was being made for him.

"Looks like nobody's going to be able to get in here tonight," she said with a Mona Lisa smile.

"Or out," he said as he walked to the back door for some larger pieces of wood. He grinned as he began to appreciate that, as satisfying as his virtual community was, it had its limitations.

When the stew began its slow simmer, they slid the sofa bed closer to the roaring fire and peeled off their sweaters. Thoughts and acts were becoming acceptable, natural, justifiable, desirable, given this new setting, and none of it seemed to require the perplexities of choice or the burden of decision.

What would have been unwelcome in the studio shed was possible here. What would have been unthinkable in the classroom of the old schoolhouse after the departure of his students now became excusable. Perhaps even necessary?

They took turns unbuttoning, unzipping, unfastening articles of each other's clothing. The flaming glow felt like the sun's warmth of a summer day on their naked winter bodies. Little did it matter to him whether the rivulet was flowing east or west, but it was fast transforming into a creek, a stream, a river, cascading over rapids one way or the other.

Their entire thrilling adventure was an answer to prayer, unoffered at least by Alan. There were the unavoidable hiatuses—the restocking of the fireplace, the condom she provided, the moving of the stew pot to the side of the stove. Mercifully, the telephone went unanswered. It would probably be Kay asking if she had got safely home through the snow, or Michel wondering if Alan had got stuck between Norvale and his parents' house. He was not able to get through to Alan's by phone.

Since the electrically driven fan on Audrey's furnace was inoperable, there was no question about where they would sleep. In front of the fireplace they ate the overcooked stew, drank the room-temperature (chilled, that is) wine, and hugged each other closer as the embers dimmed.

Of sexual intimacies, Audrey and Alan agreed with Haliburton's dictum (though on another subject) that "too much is just enough." Late next morning they benefited from breakfast in bed and observed that the snow had not diminished.

After lunch, he enquired about the possibility of renting a snowmobile in town. The machine and motor repair shop that kept several in stock would not be open, although the proprietor might be reachable by telephone.

"No, wait," she said. "Paul's is at the back of the garage. I used it last winter. It should run OK. But we'll have to dig out a space to open the doors and back out the car."

It took him two hours to free the snowmobile, have a final coffee and linger over several farewell kisses before he set out on the three kilometre ride over the snow blanketed lake. It occurred to him that, without power, his emergency heating unit would have ceased functioning almost eighteen hours ago. Relighting the stoves in both the shed and the Lodge became a priority to prevent freezing of paints and water pipes. In fact, it might already be too late.

The vivid blue sky and the bright sunlight that created myriads of diamonds on the pristine snow made his trip down the lake seem like a dream, were it not for the rattle and roar of the antique snowmobile. On arriving at the Lodge, he waded through snowdrifts to find a shovel then speedily dug a path to the shed and called to his virtual family inside, "Sorry, everybody. But I will have the heat up as fast as possible—if not faster."

When the stove was vibrating with its fire, he decided to telephone Audrey to let her know he had arrived safely and to thank her for the "electrifying" time together. He was particularly pleased with the suitability of his adjective, for at last he was aware that his bright world of painting left some very dark corners, even when the power was on. But the telephone was dead. A branch, overloaded with snow, had snapped, startling a moose or a deer, and silencing his telephone, probably for four or five days. He had heard tales of how often the animals had a habit of entangling their antlers in downed power lines.

He found the experience of this isolation exhilarating. The challenge of keeping the fires stoked and of preparing hot meals on a wood stove animated him. The Hair Emporium would be closed, the tavern empty; his larder was adequately stocked, his supply of firewood abundant. He returned to his studio, rearranged groupings of his family and friends and undertook a new series of portraits in winter settings.

On his second afternoon of splendid and productive seclusion, his concentration was disturbed by the growl of an engine. It was much nearer than his road and more thunderous than a snowmobile. He looked out onto the lake in time to see a ski plane descend over Ledge Lodge, touch down and glide speedily towards the line of nearby trees along the shoreline. It taxied nearer and swung parallel to the beach. The engine and propellers slowed but not to a stop, and a winter-clad figure wearing snowshoes slid clumsily out of the door. A hand lowered a backpack to the visitor, waved goodbye and pulled the door closed. Alan could not hear the shout, "Tomorrow, same time, same place unless there's another blizzard."

The mystery man waded unsteadily away from the plane and tried unsuccessfully to turn to wave as the engines revved. A man-made blizzard obliterated the staggering visitor until the ski plane picked up speed and slid beyond the tree-lined shore. The visitor remained immobile until the airborne plane returned, swooped low, dipped its wings and rose high in the cloudless sky, leaving a silence that became audible because of the sudden contrast.

Alan put on his coat, forced the door open against a snow drift, and pushed his way around the side of the shed to greet this *homo ex machina*. Judging by the man's inexpert use of snowshoes, Alan could see that this was no northerner.

The soft snow muffled the shout of the arm waving intruder until finally, as he approached, Alan could discern the cry, "Dad . . . !"

It was Mark—domesticated, city-slicker, unadventurous Chicagoan Mark. Alan could not believe what he saw. Was this a vision of what his subconscious was urging him to paint?

After several ineffectual attempts to climb up the slope from the lake, Mark stooped, unstrapped the snowshoes and promptly sank up to his knees. They both laughed heartily.

"Am, I glad to see you," Mark called out.

"I guess you are. Otherwise you'd freeze to death if I wasn't here to rescue you." He took his son's backpack and, using a snowshoe, pulled him up the rise. "What on earth are you doing here?"

"Oh, I just happened to be in the neighbourhood and I thought I'd drop by for a cup of tea," Mark said with a serious look that failed to mask the humour. On the shovelled pathway from the shed to the Lodge, Alan gave his son a bear hug, "It's great to see you. You look a little pale. Your indoor sedentary life needs this kind of kick start."

Despite the smiles and humour, Mark made it abundantly clear that he, his wife and daughter, regarded this isolation unacceptable. "We've tried to email and telephone you for days and got no answer. We were worried sick. And winter has hardly begun. We know you survived last year all by yourself, but have you any idea how much we've been suffering, worrying about you night and day? And your cell phone. What's the use of having a cell phone if you keep it turned off all the time?"

His father endured about forty minutes of this vehement diatribe until he rose and invited his son to follow him. Without stopping to don a winter coat, he led his son out the back door into the blinding glare of sparkling snow, and down the path to the studio. The old shed had been familiar territory to Mark. His flashback brought to mind the smell of bat dung, the sight of the scary tailor's dummy in "the ghost hut," the way Charles shone the flashlight through cobwebs and under his face to make a terrifying mask of death.

"You are about to see what I've shown no other mortal. This is my joy, my pride, my very life." He left unsaid that he would not—could not—abandon this beloved family.

It took a moment for Mark's eyes to adjust to the gentler indoor light. He looked with awe at his mother, sitting in her favourite wicker armchair, reading. The closest parallel he could envisage was that of a shrine. Beside her, he and his brother were toasting marshmallows as young boys, not twenty meters from this very shed. On another wall, he and Charles were paddling a familiar looking canoe with a child, a girl, sitting cross-legged between them.

"And there you are, Dad, holding up what must be a university degree. Who's the man with you?" Mark had never met Roger. "And who's the pretty young lady on that wall facing Mom?"

"That's your sister, Emily." Alan heard his son gasp. "Your sister as she might have been if she had lived."

Mark gave a shudder and walked slowly forward to the painting that seemed to float in a carefully aimed halo of light. He closed his eyes and murmured, "Emily, it's me. Say 'Hi Mark.'" Without turning to face his father, he said, "She would never say 'Hi Mark.'" He gazed at her and sighed deeply, "Not until now."

Alan cleared aside a clutter of brushes, notebooks, pencils and sketches on his work table. He moved the unlit kerosene lamp from the high stool to the cleared space, carried the stool to the centre of the floor and gestured that Mark should sit there and survey the paintings.

His son perched on the elevated seat, turned slowly in a circle and perused the faces that surrounded him, faces that seemed to welcome him. He could imagine them saying, "You're one of us. We know you. Better than you think. We've watched you grow up."

"Who's the guy in the fancy Elizabethan get up? And the very attractive girl lying on what looks like a table?"

"That's one of my few self-portraits. I wanted only one of that period when I acted at U. of T. and had a hard time deciding whether it should be in my role as Hamlet or Romeo. But since the flu cancelled my appearance as Hamlet, in fact, cancelled the whole play, I opted for Romeo. Fate decreed that Hamlet was not to be."

"So the girl has to be Mom when you knew her there." When he completed his silent scrutiny, he returned with moist eyes to the scene that revised what was etched on his memory. It depicted him and Charles not as children, but as young men, standing at Ledge Lodge, an arm around each other's waist, their backs to the artist, looking down at the lake and across to the very shed in which he was standing. It was difficult to know whether they were looking at their lake below, or their lives ahead.

"Yes," he said in response to a question he put to himself. "Yes, Dad, you must stay here. As for me, I've got to visit Charles." The reference to his brother was as ambiguous as the painting. And as unequivocal. With a little hop down from the stool, he approached his father and embraced him. They walked out into the blazing sunlight.

"The plane will come for me tomorrow afternoon. Between now and then we have a lot of catching up to do. Gwen and Monica want to know if you're lonely. That and a dozen other questions. I've brought photos of your granddaughter. You wouldn't believe how she's grown since last you saw her."

"No, not lonely, especially with my community in the painting shed. And then there are my four footed friends—the deer who drop by for lunch. You'd hardly believe that in summer, a beaver often circles around me when I'm swimming in the lake. As well, there's all the folk in town"

"Monica bought you a birthday gift and was going to mail it to you next Spring, but when she heard of my sudden flight up here, she wrapped it and asked me to give it to you." He delved into his backpack and brought out a small package. "It looks like a watch but it's state of the art technology."

His father unwrapped the object, stared at it, then strapped it onto his wrist. "It certainly look like a watch."

"Yep, but more than that. It's got GSP, like many new cars. You can locate yourself by satellite positioning so you don't get lost in the bush. It works the same way as a cell phone. Which reminds me. Why couldn't we get you by cell phone. That's why I had to come up here. Lately no telephone connection, no email contact, and your cell phone must always be turned off. We wondered if you got burned out or were frozen to death or—"

"Or trampled by a mad moose, or fell through the ice, or—

"OK, OK, I get the picture. But think of us. Please. So what if you wear out a few batteries? But do keep your cell phone on, at least during certain hours we can agree on."

"Sorry, Mark, but down here by the lake, we can't be reached by satellite connections. Up at the ledge lodge, yes, but not down here. I will wear this GSP watch when I go walking in the hills. Tell Monica thanks for the gift."

"But surely, Dad, there must be a whole lot of things you do need, for warmth or entertainment, maybe something you need for boating or hiking or whatever."

"Need, need, need. You sound like a big city person where sales people sell needs, then invent something to satisfy those so-called needs. Like at the cosmetic counter where the sign advertises, 'For your beauty *needs*.' Commerce and industry have metastasized those needs. But right now I think we do need some hot chocolate and a good sleep."

The son talked about possible terrors in the wilds, the father, about terrorism in the big city. Neither was going to persuade the other, and gradually the pauses lengthened and sleep tranquilized their fears. Mark slept well despite the chill of the cottage and the periodic crackles of logs flaming in the fireplace.

He was able to take home some unforgettable memories. The chief was encountering the community in the studio. He would regale family and friends, proudly telling and retelling about the lessons in snowshoeing his father gave him, and their hike through the forest, soundless but for the occasional whoosh of snow sliding from overburdened pine branches. Then, of course, there was the elation of skimming over the snow, rising into the sky, banking and flying homeward.

Alan didn't tell his son about Audrey. It's too soon, he thought. This rivulet, whether flowing east or west, may dry up. But I think I'll see that a little water gets poured into this incipient stream. That's what I'll do, prime the river.

He made the trip to Norvale by snowmobile, filled its little tank at the gas station which had just opened, and found Audrey at the general store.

"People need candles, lamp chimneys, perishable food items," she said, "and I'm feeding this hungry old wood stove."

Once the electricity was restored, Alan transported Audrey to his Lakeside Lodge several times. There were, that winter, a few snow storms and the usual number of power outages. The art classes were cancelled until early spring. That year, there would be no exhibition of students' works, but Alan laboured to prepare a private showing for Audrey that would help him decide about their future together.

She was beginning to tease him about his studio. "I think you've got an extremely compliant mistress in there, you spend so much of your time hived away!"

"You'll have a chance to see soon enough. I want my community to be ready to receive you."

"What a strange remark. You're always putting me off. Every time I go to the cottage you tell me 'soon' or 'soon enough' or 'pretty soon.'"

He aimed the palms of both hands at her and patted the air, "All right. I'll give you a date then. If I can finish your painting by—"

"My painting?" she cried.

"And if I can get three others framed, I will introduce you to everyone in the gallery on Saturday. That's a promise."

"But," she drawled it out laden with doubt, "but you said 'If. If I can finish your painting.' Is that an yet another escape from committing yourself that I hear?"

"No, not at all. No ifs, ands or buts. This Saturday for sure, ready or not. Double promise. It still gives me four days. I'll come for you on Paul's machine around six. We'll have supper at the cottage, then your introduction to the community."

"You make it sound like an initiation."

"It is, in a way."

"Are these paintings of real people? People who are alive?" With a slight shudder she added, "People who have died?"

"Wait and see. Then, if you like what you see, perhaps you'd spend the night with me?" The promise was sealed with a kiss.

By Friday night, Audrey on canvas still eluded him. "Your eyes are not quite right yet," he said. "Sad, somehow. They have a sort of pleading look about them." He backed away from the easel and glanced up at Emily. She was not looking.

The wooden shed creaked as the wind rose outside. He thought about the night-before nerves that had troubled him on the eve of showing mayors and the fire chief their portraits for the first time. "I'll put some wood on the fire, then come back and study your face. I've been looking so long at your eyes, I can't see them any more."

Gusts of wind hurled sharp crystals of snow at the window. Oh! he thought, let's not have another blizzard. Not tonight. As he slid some pieces of wood through the stove door, the lights went out.

"Not again! Not this, of all nights," he said into the gloom. The glow flooding from the stove sent shadows dancing around the studio. He found two candles and two kerosene lamps, lit them, and placed one lamp on the stool in the centre of the floor. Holding the second lamp aloft he addressed the assembly, "Now what do I do? For God's sake, tell me!"

Silence but for the clawing of the wind against the walls.

With supreme indifference to mere human bewilderment, the gale caused the shed to quake. The building had endured decades of storms—wind, hail, rain, snow. It would survive all of nature's attacks except age and rot and decay. Those three were the enemy and the motivation for his painting. Each of his portraits was a declaration of his war against the ravages of time, its silent invasion of rot and decay and death.

To the accompaniment of a moaning wind, he raised a lamp under the affectionate face of Emily and recited to her from one of Shakespeare's sonnets:

So long as men can breathe, or eyes can see,

So long lives this, and this gives life to thee.

He raised the lamp in salute. The changing angles of illumination altered the light in her eyes. He backed away slowly. Her face, brighter than the background, seemed to emerge from the frame. From left to right and back again he swayed the lamp, marvelling at the three dimensional effect.

He took another step backward and stumbled against the stool. The second lamp slid off the seat and crashed to the floor. He regained his balance, set the lamp he was holding on the work table and watched in terror the wave of blue flame. The line of fire spread its circumference following the fuel that burst from the smashed globe. In a futile frenzy, he stomped on the flames spreading around cans and open jars. An empty pail sat in the sink under a tap. He turned the tap on, but for lack of an electrical pump, water dribbled into the container. In disbelief, he cranked the faucet and stared at the lethargic trickle. Yellow flames began licking a wall beneath the portraits of Joe and Ellen and Mrs. Laplante. Not to them, for it was too late, but to Lois and Emily and the twins he called out, "You'll be all right. We'll go into the snow." He yanked frames from hooks and stacked them against the door. Flames flared into swirling smoke.

He wanted to rescue more of his community. There were so many on walls and shelves that must be saved, but now, must be left behind. In the flickering light, he saw Audrey looking at him. He understood her eyes.

Choking, he stooped low to escape the toxic fumes, and pushed at the door. Snow, banked against the wall, blocked the exit. Bracing himself, he forced the door open far enough to slide some paintings through the gap. It slammed shut as if on a spring. He was gasping for air.

The window! He lurched into the flames, headed towards the window, and collapsed on the burning floor boards.

By morning, nothing remained but a smouldering pile of wood, fragments of blackened insulation and a cracked cast iron stove.

By eleven o'clock Saturday evening, an impatient Audrey muttered, "Promises, promises," and prepared for bed.

CHAPTER TWELVE

VOICES

" . . . any significant changes recorded here. We may be needing his bed. But we'll notify you if we move him to . . ."

Gabble, gabble, gabble. Must you, must you do it beside my bed as if I weren't in it? Put on some music why don't you, for God's sake—for my sake. You know what I want to hear. Someone brought in my favourite CDs and used to play them for me. But no, you have to talk, talk, talk, while I lie here and think, think, think.

"That's it. Put your hands right under. Don't lift, roll him. A little more. Good, now the folded sheet. Then . . ."

This doing nothing exhausts me. Fewer friends drop by these days. Or is it these months? Can't blame them, though. Must be like conversing with a brick wall, or a cadaver. I mustn't lose touch with reality. That would be a kind of death. A kind of? Are there kinds of death: dead to the world, stone cold, as good as dead, the sleep of the dead? That there are degrees I am dead certain and I'm dead tired.

"Excuse me Mark. Sorry to wake you up. It is Mark, isn't it? I get you and your brother mixed up. I always forget which of you has the business length hair cut. Your brother is in the lounge and he's wondering if you are expecting your wife to drop by to see Mr. Thompson."

"He's here in Toronto, nurse? At the hospital now? Why is he wondering about my wife? No, I get it. There's some tension between the two of them. Tell him to come right in. Gwen didn't come over from Chicago with me. Better still, I'll go out and bring him in."

Well, this is a first. Both of them here at the same time. Ottawa meets Chicago in Toronto. How I wish I could grunt or smile or even burp or fart to let them know that I'm alive inside this black cocoon. I feel the approach of bodies. You don't have to tiptoe into the room like that as if I'm sleeping. Go on, clatter and bang and stomp. Do whatever it takes to rouse me from this fourth floor grave.

"God, Charles, he looks awful. So pale and wrinkled and thin."

"Shush. They say people in comas can hear. But I don't know. Come on, Dad. Remember when you said we had to climb back up to our Ledge Lodge as soon as we could, and start all over in spite of our fears and bad memories. Up an' at'em, Pops"

"Yeah, Mark, that was one big bad memory all right."

"I've never had the courage to ask why you fell. Did I just throw stones, or did I . . . did I—"

"Nah, I slipped because stupid me, I was standing too close to the edge. It wasn't your fault."

How kind of you, Charles, to lie to your brother. That's not what you told me as you were being moved from the helicopter into the hospital. Tried to punch you on the face as you stood teetering on the lip of that overhang.

"Because if I thought I had done something to make you fall, then I would know for sure that, somehow, I must have done something . . . maybe somehow I did . . . I did something to little Emily that last morning of her life."

What! You're saying maybe you killed her? Shook her? You? Frightened her to death? What did you do? No, no, no, no.

"Look, Mark, his little finger. It's moving I can see it twitching."

Killed her? To hear that, Mark, I'm not sure I want out of this black hole. How can I face you if you did cause Emily's death or even if you suspect you did?

> Don't be absurd! Of course you want out. He'll need you more than ever. I certainly want another chance at life. Ron is no less dear to me than Emily was to you, and my son Ron is alive. And so is Marianne. Those roses she has been delivering each week are a great comfort. I want to see them again, and her too. She is not only alive herself but able to enliven me, to revive the artist in me thanks to the painting she brought me back to in the theatre.

> Me too. I want out. Newerton wasn't heaven, but it offered more hope than this non-existence. What I would give to be able to jump-start my ministry there even without Renata. Do you think that what is happening right now happens to most people? That there's still a kind of choice to be made? Maybe not for the likes of that tragic theological student who leapt to her death, but for victims of—

> Shut up, all of you. Just shut up. I got trapped by booze and sad friends like Steve. Do you think I'd go back to the bottle and that hell after this hell that I'm in now? Three hells and you're out forever. Surely I've learned my lesson.

Silence, at last. Nothing but the horrible thought of what Mark may have done. Nothing but silence, at long last. And darkness, uninterrupted, continuous, empty blackness. Too much darkness is bad for the eyes of the soul. Infinite blackness?

What's this? The room sounds different. Have they moved me? These are the acoustics of a vast, reverberant hall, not the amplified echoes that rebound from hard plaster walls, from a low ceiling, polished terrazzo floors and shiny tile. A distant cough, muffled by space that could be as huge as an amphitheatre, unnerves me. Voices . . . ?

> *Your choices are completed now*
> *Save one remaining to be made*
> *Before the course of life is done.*
> *You are no stranger to this choice,*
> *One you have chosen thrice before.*

What the hell . . . ? Who are you? A heavenly choir or a hellish? I can't turn to face you faceless heralds. Who's there? Why this charge and all this ceremony? Roger . . . Victor? are you in that group? Ron? Audrey? Can't you hear me? Are you deaf? Or am I dumb? Doc . . . Steve? Is that you, Kay? I don't recognise the voices. Do I know any of you? Who then?

> *Enough for you to know is this:*
> *That each divide, a Great Divide*
> *Became; and now the hour has struck*
> *When you must make your final choice,*
> *The paramount decision—now!*

Hey! Can't you hear me either, or do you assume I've nothing to say that's worth listening to? Are you tricks my own mind is playing on me or are you external voices? This is some comedy routine. Let's call it, what? How about "Al's Pals' Chorales." No, better not. They sound more tragedic than comic. Maybe "The Fall of Al," or "Al's Ultimate Decision." Too bathetic, that one.

Ouch! Must you plunge that ear thermometer so firmly. I do have feelings, nurse. Or did you know that? Apparently you aren't hearing these declaiming voices. I've memorized this twice daily ritual, or is it weekly: remove the thermometer, pause, rustle a few papers, scribble some numbers I guess, and maybe a few observations on appropriate lines. Next, adjust the covers under my chin, check the drip bag—that's when you talk to yourself. "Almost empty, hmmm." Then you leave for a day, a week, or a month.

You chant about a paramount decision. What do you mean? Who are you? And who are you to tell me what the greatest decision in my life must be?

No response.

Are you still there? Or, come to think of it, am I still here?

Oh, that swirling darkness again, black on black. Once again the crash of glass, followed by the crunch of shards breaking under foot. "My God, there's blood everywhere. Be careful, he may have a broken spine. Can you get a pulse? I think he must have . . .," the words fade into nothingness. Silence, but somehow, neither peaceful or tranquil. Rather the noiselessness of a too tightly wound spring.

> *You know full well one final choice remains,*
> *The greatest of them all to be confirmed.*

You're back. But this time your chanting sounds impatient. And you've upped the ante to pentameter. Sounds seriouser and seriouser. Is that final one a choice of life or death? That, surely, is the ultimate choice.

> *Suspend these fruitless silly chants*
> *And do what must be done to him*
> *For no decision will he make.*
> *He's useless to the world and to himself.*

Another group of choristers. But you, you sound vehement, angry, accusatory. Your measured, rhythmic words penetrate my soul. These threats are shattering what little hope . . .

Is't not enough this man has made
His final choices oft before?
Why yet again must he decide?
Would you have him start again
Nor ever die as mortals must?
'Tis time for you to rest, to sleep,
and all your dreaming days conclude.
Forgo, forsake life's burdens now;
Consider "not to be" your goal.
Delay no more to cut the thread.
Come, sing his praise about his bier.

What lies before me now? An end to all? Your sudden silence frightens me.
Why this pause, this lengthy pause. And how long—a minute? An eternity?

This pitiable mortal thinks as do they all
That life or death is all that's left to choose.

Thank you, gentler, kinder whispering voices. But why a tone that suggests
you are instructing a dim-witted child?

To live or die is not the choice most paramount;
Results alone are they, decisions prior made.
But greatest of them all is one beyond your ken,
Too obvious to be observed. Do fish perceive
The water round about them as they blithely swim?
Do birds see air? Your final choice surrounds you—
Choose!

You're speaking riddles. I could die while I'm trying to solve your puzzle. Then what would the coroner's report say? "Died of an acute case of enigma." If that ever leaked out, Rodger would stand beside the casket and say, "Poor guy, he never could make up his minds."

Hmmm, you don't seem to have much of a sense of humour. And you other, harsher voices—I almost recognize some of you. You remind me of Mrs. Orgle. Or is it that failed carpenter, Oscar? Surely not Ellen. Far too . . . too theatrical. Did you know me from my days on the Hart House stage? Tell me your names, who, or what you are. I'm lost here, lost in the dark.

A silence that lasts a day, or days. Time to think. Time to take stock of . . . what? of knowledge? as if knowledge were power. If knowledge is power, why do so many doctors become addicted to drugs, or so many police become ensnared in fraud and corruption? With so much more to know every passing week a revised maxim is becoming increasingly incontrovertible: "Know the truth and the truth will make you mad." No, there is no power in knowledge. The power lies in the right response to knowledge, the will to act on what I know. Is that what these phantoms are exhorting me to do, to act?

Ellen must be among them. I can imagine her at the group's rehearsal breaking in upon their measured, dignified deliberations and angrily saying, "Oh, for heaven's sake, let's just tell him to make up his mind." Lois, though, in more conciliatory terms would counsel the Voices to "give him time. Don't rush him." I can hear her favourite dictum, "If it's to be, it will happen."

I want Steve, chief of sherry drinkers, to state his laissez-faire opinion, so often expressed against that raucous jukebox music, "What's the hurry? We've got all evening. Another round. What d'ya say, Al? you payin'?" Put all these together along with Roger and that enforcer, Red, and maybe even Emily. And what admonition, charge, pronouncement will you get? People say and do in groups what they would never say or do alone.

Obviously you choristers will not be interrogated as to your identity. Nevertheless, I will persist in calling silently to you, pleading. You say that I have one final decision to make. What if I refuse to decide? Ha! I've got you, whoever or whatever you are! I think I've figured it out: if I don't choose, then I will not be opting for either life or death. Unless . . . unless there is something other than them—a third alternative. What could that be? Tell me, Voices, is there a state between living and dying? Is there? Purgatory, perhaps, or sheol, limbo? The living dead? Not—oh please—not an interminable coma. I don't want that.

Is that the choice I must make—coma or death? But no, for you say I must "confirm" my choice. That means a decision I have made before.

> *Yes, more than once you opted for that choice,*
> *And slowly you began to live again*
> *Though death constrained you not so firmly then*
> *As now in this decisive final hour.*

Relief at last! How glad I am to hear the clatter of a pail on rollers and the swish of a mop.

"Hi, me again. Eugene. Time to give this ward its morning bath. Just like outside where all the streets and trees and buildings are getting showered down. Don't you worry, my man. You'll be up and around, able to see it all for yourself soon."

I love the way you hum as you mop under my bed. How strange that I know you best of all now. Your daily visits, your singing while you work provide a landmark, a timemark on my churning starless midnight landscapes. I've got this puzzle, see, a choice I have to make. It's not as if I can't make up my mind between this or that. There is no "this" or "that." Is life one unending lottery, a continuous crapshoot, where with a lucky roll of the dice you live, snake eyes and you die? What number should I choose if I'm to win another chance at life's table?

And yet they tell me I did make the right choice before, more than once and began to live again. What was it the loveliest organist of Newerton, Renata, said as she stared into her coffee cup at the kitchen table? Something about her beginning again just as I had done. Something about my having started afresh. Is that it? Is that the choice: to begin again?

> *Many are the tragic mortals who*
> *Would rather die than once again begin.*
> *Beware that you consider not this choice*
> *An easy, painless step for you to take.*

I recall standing for the first time at the lip of a high diving board, unsure of the depth of the water far below. And now, this time I am staring not down into space, but ahead into time. I wonder if the unfledged chick has these fears as the mother bird nudges it out of its comfortable roost. But it knows nothing yet of height or depth or distance, only that on this day, at this hour, now, it is time. As we know from the chrysalis and the human foetus there is nothing more natural—not easy, so the Voices warn me—than to begin again. I've known this to be true most resolutely since my role as Brutus in our high school production.

"Catch you tomorrow, same time, same station, my man. Same old mop but fresh new dust balls."

In feeble tones I try to recite aloud—ALOUD—" . . . a tide in the affairs of men which taken at . . ."

That has to be Eugene, startled to hear my faint sounds, clutching my shoulder, "What's that you're . . . Are you speaking? Your lips—move them again."

" . . . leads on . . . to fortune . . ."

"Wow! The nurses won't believe me!" The handle of the mop slaps the floor as Eugene runs out to the nurses' station. Footsteps and voices, human this time, echo along the hallway. Scuffling feet stop by my bed.

"What did he say, Eugene? Were they actual words or nonsense syllables?" inquires a nurse—not she of the double chin and the auburn hair and the impossibly short skirt.

"I'm not sure. His lips moved, and there were sounds. I never seen no movement for the last eight months, until today. Look! They're moving now."

And indeed they are. Maybe they need a lip reader to decipher my two words, as I repeat them over and over, "Begin again. Begin again . . ."

> *This mortal's choice is bold.*
> *His decision is confirmed.*
> *He's opting to—*

"Begin again." I can say them though in a barely audible voice. "Begin again. I will, I will begin again. To be or not to be? I will be once again."

"Check for pupil dilation, Marcy! Here's my pen light." Easy, Marcy, easy on my eyelid. It's not a can of Pepsi you're opening. I can hear all you nurses congregating and clapping and making little leaps of joy. "Call the resident—"

Ah, I recognise your voice. Head Nurse they call you, at least to your face—"and call Dr. Liang. His number is in Alan's file. The monitor, it's . . ."

Now what? A shrill buzzer and a sudden silence of nurses.

"Al, Al!" it's me, Eugene. Damn, damn, damn. He's going on us."

"Call the emergency response team. The line. It's flattening."

Ah yes, the line. Another Great Divide. I can barely whisper, "Begin again."